W9-AVR-011

Praise for Eric Jerome Dickey

Thieves' Paradise

"Dickey exposes L.A.'s gritty underworld in this smartly paced novel." —*Publishers Weekly*

"Provocative . . . another gem from one of America's most popular authors." —*The Seattle Scanner*

"Passionate, sensual, rhythmic, comical. . . . If Eric's previous novels are food for the soul, *Thieves' Paradise* is the nectar and ambrosia of life." —*Chicago Defender*

"A street-savvy cruise . . . with page after page of punchy dialogue and gritty writing."
—*The Boulder Sunday Camera*

Between Lovers

"Lust and confusion collide in this supple novel about a woman who wants it all." —*People*

"Dickey's done it again. A provocative, realistic love story with real characters that we root for."
—*The Cincinnati Enquirer*

"A witty, sexy romp." —*The Sunday Denver Post*

"A hip, funny, and realistically bittersweet love story of our times." —*The Sun* (Bremmerton, WA)

"Provocative and complex." —*Ebony*

"*Between Lovers* will hook audiences and draw them into a world where characters are multilayered, language is street-smart, and emotions are intense."
—*Style Magazine*

continued . . .

Liar's Game

"Steamy romance, betrayal, and redemption. Dickey at his best."
——*USA Today*

"Dickey hits the mark with *Liar's Game.*"
——*The Detroit News and Free Press*

"Fast-paced . . . sexy, sassy . . . a high-spirited roller-coaster ride of a novel."   ——*Florida Star* (Jacksonville)

"It's almost scary how well Eric Jerome Dickey knows women."   ——*The Cincinnati Enquirer*

"Masterful . . . humorous and convincing . . . avoids all the usual clichés."   ——BookPage

"Dickey hits his stride . . . with wit, energy, and deft sensitivity."   ——*Heart & Soul*

"Skillful . . . scandalous . . . a rich gumbo of narrative twists."   ——*Minneapolis Star Tribune*

"Steamy romance, stinging betrayal, sweet redemption, and well-placed humor."   ——*Miami Times*

Cheaters

"A deftly crafted tale about the games people play and the lies they tell on their search for love."   ——*Ebony*

"Wonderfully written . . . smooth, unique, and genuine."
——*The Washington Post Book World*

"You can't read *Cheaters* without becoming an active participant."   ——*Los Angeles Times*

"What gives the book a compelling edge is the characters' self-discovery. . . . Thankfully, Dickey often goes beyond the 'men are dogs and women are victims' stereotype."   ——*USA Today*

"Hot, sexy, and funny."   ——*Library Journal*

Friends and Lovers

"Crackles with wit and all the rhythm of an intoxicatingly funky rap. A fun read." —*The Cincinnati Enquirer*

"The language sings . . . fluid as a rap song. Dickey can stand alone among modern novelists in capturing the flavor, rhythm, and pace of African-American speak."
—*Fort Lauderdale Sun-Sentinel*

"Dickey uses humor, poignancy, and a fresh, creative writing style." —*USA Today*

"A colorful, sexy tale." —*Marie Claire*

Milk in My Coffee

"Rich *Coffee* steams away clichés of interracial romance . . . a true-to-life, complex story of relationships." —*USA Today*

"Heartwarming and hilarious." —*The Cincinnati Enquirer*

"Frothy and fun. . . . Dickey scores with characters who come to feel like old friends." —*Essence*

"Controversial and sensitive." —*Today's Black Woman*

Sister, Sister

"Dickey imagines [his characters] with affection and sympathy. . . . genuine emotional depth." —*The Boston Globe*

"Vibrant . . . marks the debut of a true talent." —*The Atlanta Journal-Constitution*

"Bold and sassy . . . brims with humor, outrageousness, and the generosity of affection." —*Publishers Weekly*

ALSO BY ERIC JEROME DICKEY

The Other Woman
Between Lovers
Liar's Game
Cheaters
Milk in My Coffee
Friends and Lovers
Sister, Sister

ANTHOLOGIES

Got to Be Real
Mothers and Sons
River Crossings: Voices of the Diaspora
Griots Beneath the Baobab
Black Silk: A Collection of African American Erotica

ERIC JEROME DICKEY

THIEVES'
PARADISE

A SIGNET BOOK

SIGNET
Published by New American Library, a division of
Penguin Putnam Inc., 375 Hudson Street,
New York, New York 10014, U.S.A.
Penguin Books Ltd, 80 Strand,
London WC2R 0RL, England
Penguin Books Australia Ltd, 250 Camberwell Road,
Camberwell, Victoria 3124, Australia
Penguin Books Canada Ltd, 10 Alcorn Avenue,
Toronto, Ontario, Canada M4V 3B2
Penguin Books (N.Z.) Ltd, Cnr Rosedale and Airborne Roads,
Albany, Auckland 1310, New Zealand

Penguin Books Ltd, Registered Offices:
Harmondsworth, Middlesex, England

Published by Signet, an imprint of New American Library, a division of
Penguin Putnam Inc. Previously published in a Dutton edition.

First Signet Printing, May 2003
10 9 8 7 6 5 4 3

For Richard Jones

U of M
Memphis, TN
Thanks for looking out for me
the moment I got off that bus
and walked across the yard at the U of M.

Prologue

Momma shrieked.

The walls echoed her cries for Daddy to get his hands off her, brought her pleas up the stairs to my room. I jumped and my algebra book dropped from my chestnut desk onto the floor.

My father cursed.

By the time I made it to the railing and looked down into the living room, Momma was in front of my father, begging for forgiveness. Her petite frame was balled up on our Aztec-patterned sofa. She was holding her lip to keep the blood from flowing onto the fabric. I watched her rub away the pain on her cinnamon skin, then run her fingers through her wavy coal-black hair.

My old man looked up at me and grimaced. "Go back to your room, boy."

I was fifteen and a half. Less than half of my old man's age.

He stomped toward Momma.

She screamed and moved away from him like she was trying to run away from the madness that lived here every day.

My chest heaved as I stumbled past the grandfather clock and rushed down the stairs. My heart was pounding. I tightened my hands and hurried to my momma's side.

"Momma," I moaned as I kneeled next to her. "You okay?"

"I'm alright, baby. It's nothing. Nothing."

I looked back at my liquored-up old man. He bobbed

his head and pointed back at the kitchen. "I work hard all day and come home to no dinner?"

He was slurring and sneering down on us.

I said, "Nobody knew you were coming home tonight."

Momma tried to get up. "I overslept. My pills made me—"

"Carmen," he shouted. "Get up off that sofa and cook. *Now. Planet of the Apes* comes on in an hour and I want my food on the table by the time Charlton Heston—"

"Don't ever touch Momma again."

"What you say?"

"He didn't say anything." Momma touched my arm. "I'm okay, baby. Go back and finish studying for your test."

Daddy's back straightened, his bushy mustache crooked as his lips curved down, his eyes widened. "What you say to me, nigger?"

"I'm not a nigger. My name is Dante."

"So, the nigger speaking up for himself."

"You heard me the first time. And I ain't a nigger."

"You challenging me? What, you think because you got a little hair over your dick you're a grown man now? Ain't but one man in this house."

Momma spoke carefully to Daddy. "Don't get upset."

I frowned at the shiny badge on the chest of his tan uniform, then at the gun in his leather holster.

He sucked his teeth, nodded, and jerked the badge off. He threw the gun holster on the love seat. He stepped away from the glass coffee table, opened his arms, and snapped out, "You want to be a man? Come on. I'll give you the first shot. Nigger, I'll knock your black ass into the middle of next week."

Momma gripped my arm tight enough for her nails to break my skin. I glanced at the golden cross she had on her chest, the one she had got from her mother just a few weeks before Grandmamma died. I looked into my momma's light brown eyes, eyes that looked like mine. "Let me go, Momma."

"No." She put her nose against mine and whispered, "Momma's okay. It's just a little scratch."

My knees shook when I stood and faced my old man. When his eyes met mine, his anger held so much power that I forgot how to breathe. Heart went into overdrive. He balled up his right fist, slammed it into the palm of his left hand; it echoed like thunder. "What are you gonna do, nigger?"

I trembled, backed away, and said, "Nothing."

"Nothing, what?"

"Nothing, sir."

I kicked my bare feet into the rust carpet, then slumped my shoulders, wiped my sweaty hands on my jean shorts, and turned around to go back to my room.

Then that motherfucker chuckled.

A simple laugh that stoked up the rage inside of me.

I charged at him as fast and as hard as I could.

Momma screamed.

Daddy's eyes widened with surprise.

Pain. Anger. Fear.

Three screams from three people.

From the backseat of the police car, I stared through the wire cage at the colorful rotating lights that were brightening Scottsdale's earth-tone stucco houses. I was hostage under a calm sky. The spinning glow from twelve squad cars looked like rainbows chasing rainbows. Colors raced over all the sweet gum trees and windmill palms, moved like a strobe light over the vanhoutte spirea in the front of the three-car garage. The reek of cordite was on my flesh. Couldn't really smell it over the stench of my stress sweating. I concentrated on the colors to make the pain from the tight handcuffs go away. Watched the rainbows come and go.

The door opened. A dry May breeze mixed with the sweltering car air. A police officer stuck his sweaty head inside. His face was hard, his voice angry and anxious. "Your mother wants to say something to you before we lock your ass up. We shouldn't let her say a damn word to you after what you did. Do you mind?"

I stared straight ahead. "No."

He raised his voice. "No, what?"

"No," I repeated in a way that let him know I thought that all of them were assholes for making me out to be the bad guy. "I don't mind."

He gripped the back of my neck. "You're pretty belligerent."

I was a knob-kneed reed of a boy. Hadn't lifted anything heavier than an algebra book and could barely run a mile in P.E. without passing out. That was before I started pumping weights, before squats, before doing two hundred push-ups in the morning to start my day, doing sprints, before the hooks and jabs and side kicks and roundhouse kicks and spinning back kicks became my trademark.

I said, "Fuck you."

With his other hand he grabbed the front of my throat and squeezed, made me gag and look into his blue eyes. He growled, "Say, 'No, sir. I don't mind, sir.' You insolent bastard."

He let me go when another officer passed by. I gagged and caught my breath while perspiration tingled down my forehead into my eyes. I tilted my head and looked at him.

He smirked. "Now, what you have to say?"

I spat in his face.

His cheeks turned crimson. He stared at me while my saliva rolled down his scarred face into his ill-trimmed wheat-colored mustache.

"That's your ass, boy."

Veins popped up in his neck while he stood there, handkerchief in hand, clenching his teeth and wiping my juices from his eye. He kept watching me, wanted me to break down and show my fear. It was there, but I refused to let it be seen. Another officer passed by and scarface told him what I'd done. It looked like they were about to double-team me, but the second officer said

they had to report the assault and they both stormed
away.

A second later the door opened again and my mother
eased her bruised face inside.

She said, "Don't hate me."

"Love you, Momma." I smiled. "Get away from here."

She fondled her wedding ring. Tears formed in her
eyes. She dropped the police blanket from her shoulders, took her cross off, and put it around my neck.

She used her soft fingers to wipe the sweat from my
eyes.

"Somebody'll come get you out. Maybe Uncle Ray.
You might be able to go back to Philly and stay with
him for a while."

"Uncle Ray don't like us. We're Catholic; Jehovah's
Witnesses don't like nobody but Jehovah's Witnesses."

"Stop saying that."

"It's true."

"I'll call him anyway. I'll tell him you made honor roll,
so he'll know you're still doing good in school. Let him
know you might get a scholarship. You could help him
around his grocery store in the evenings."

I shook my head. "Don't worry about me. Get away
before he hurts you. All he's gonna do is beat you up,
then go out to Fort McDowell and spend the night with
that Indian woman. He ain't been home in two days,
then walks in complaining about some stupid dinner.
Tomorrow he'll be mad about his shirts. The next day
his shoes."

My old man was standing in a crowd of badges, guns,
and whispers. The ambulance crew had bandaged his
head and he was back on his feet. I'd beat him with
everything I could get my hands on.

He made a single-finger gesture for Momma to come.

My beautiful momma looked tired of the life she was
living, and that made me sad. She wiped her eyes and
kissed the side of my face. "You understand, don't you?
You're a big boy now. Almost a man. You can take care
of yourself. You understand."

I kissed the side of her face as my answer.

"Don't be angry." She twisted her lips. "Don't be like him."

"I won't." I smiled for her. "Go back inside before you get in trouble. Stop taking so much of that medication."

She rubbed her eyes, then dragged her fingers down across her lips. "It calms my nerves."

"Why you wanna sleep so much?"

"Sometimes," she patted my legs with her thin fingers, "sometimes I have nice dreams."

She was distant, reciting and not living the words.

I said, "Dreams ain't real, Momma."

"Sometimes—" she started, then stopped and kissed my forehead. Her voice became as melodic as the poetry she always read. "Sometimes they're better than what's real."

I fought the dryness in my throat that always came before my tears. I was scared. Fifteen and a half and living in fear.

She wandered away, wringing her hands and looking back at me every other step. We blew each other dysfunctional kisses.

I'd be in juvenile hall, then a boys' home until I was old enough to register for the draft and vote.

Living with criminals would be like going to a different kinda school. Nigerians, Mexicans, Whites, no matter what nationality, they were all caught up in the same game. And didn't hesitate to lend to the schooling on everything from Three Card Monte to Rocks in a Box to Pigeon Drops, even broke down how to pass bad checks. A few were bold enough to run telephone scams from the inside.

That was different from the education I was after.

I had dreams of getting into Howard, to a frat life and a world filled with sorority girls. Always wanted to stomp in a Greek Show. Make enough money to get a small place, get Momma to move in with me. I was working on our escape.

But that night, guess I had had all I could stand and

couldn't stand no more. I wanted to be like a superhero and rescue my momma. That was my mission in life. What motivated me.

Hard to save anybody when you're locked up, when you're too busy trying to fight to save yourself. When you've made yourself a prisoner.

I did want to save her. That gave my life a lot of purpose.

But there would be no Howard. No sorority girl at my side. And the closest thing to a frat I would see would be a bunch of young hardheads lining up for roll call, all wearing prison blues, most with tattoos. Our Greek Show was marching in sync to go get our meals.

Momma would find her own way to freedom.

My momma would take too many pills and become an angel.

My daddy would be found dead behind the wheel of his Thunderbird at Fort McDowell. Ambushed and shot outside of a married Indian woman's place.

On that night of changes, I sat in the back of that squad car staring at the colorful lights that were dancing in the night to make my pain go away. Watched the rainbows chasing the rainbows.

1

The phone rang.

Jarred me from my sleep and severed me from my past.

Time to time, I had nightmares, felt the pain from the fights and heard the screams from the midnight rapes in juvenile hall. But I learned to kick ass before I got my ass kicked.

The phone rang again.

I opened my eyes. Focused on the red digits across the room.

3:32 a.m.

Not quite yesterday; not quite today.

Traffic in NoHo—that stands for North Hollywood—was breezing by outside my window on Chandler. Somewhere down by North Hollywood High a car alarm was singing a song of distress.

I snatched the phone up and answered, "Yeah?"

"Where've you been, Dante?"

I knew who it was. Hearing his voice jarred me all over again. I sat up in my queen-size bed. The room had a chill and I kept the covers wrapped around me.

He chuckled, then said, "I was beginning to think you were dead or something."

"A'ight, how you get my number, Scamz?"

"There isn't a number I can't get."

"Just got it changed last week."

He laughed his irksome, sneaky laugh. "Happy birthday. You made it to the big two-five."

"On a hot wing and a prayer."

"A black man's not supposed to live past twenty-five."

"Then that makes me a senior citizen. I should be eligible for Social Security and a ten-percent discount at Denny's."

"You crack me up." He laughed. "That's why I like talking to you."

I yawned, then checked my caller ID. No number was on the box. Last time he jingled, the ID box told me he was in New York, lounging at Fifth and Fifty-sixth at the Trump Tower. That was two weeks back. He didn't leave a message, he never did, but I knew that was my homie. Doubt if Donald Trump would be ringing me up to talk shop about the market. Nobody but Scamz. Time before that he told me he was down in South Beach. Time before that Montreal. Before then it was the W down in New Orleans during the Essence Festival. Before that Playa del Carmen.

I set another yawn free before I asked, "You back out in La La Land?"

"For a hot sec. Wrapping up some business before I go on vacation. You should've accepted my offer and left with me last time. Aspen had great skiing."

"Whatcha been into?"

He boasted that over the last few weeks he'd been running scam after scam after scam. All nonviolent. Most of his dealings were in credit and green cards. Since he had women who worked everywhere from the DMV to the IRS, I already knew there wasn't any information he couldn't get, so his criminally gifted butt getting my number didn't cause me to raise a brow. Not right then.

"Up until a few days ago, nobody around the pool hall had seen you for months," Scamz said.

"My job was keeping me busy."

"Thought One Time might've shackled you down and had you on the gray goose heading out to Chino."

"I don't do prisons." One Time was a nickname for the police. I yawned. "Like I said, I was working."

"Was?"

"Got laid off. Everything came to a screeching halt when the commercial side of the company stopped producing and the aerospace side picked up. Been out looking for another j-o-b."

Sounded like he took a draw from his cigarette, then blew the smoke out before he spoke again. "Why do you keep wasting your talents on a nine-to-five?"

"Makes me content, that's all that matters. Don't need to be rich to be happy."

"What's the word, any luck?"

I told him I had called my old gig to check my status. Over twenty technicians with more time than I had were waiting to get called back. No one had gotten called back in six months and a few thousand more were getting kicked to the curb. The unemployment office told me to check back in a week or two, which was the same robotic line they ran on the twenty people in front of me.

I'd been hitting a lot of career fairs. Hit one down at the Bonaventure and put in apps with everybody from Aerospace Corporation to Sears. Never seen that many borderline-bankrupt people coming in from all over California and Nevada and Seattle looking for a job. After that I'd flown up to Oakland, hit the Alameda County Conference and Training Center, but five thousand out-of-work people beat me there. Most were in a line that circled the block by sunrise.

I told Scamz, "North or south, ain't nobody hiring."

"There's a synchronous world recession, especially in the high-tech world."

"Translate."

"No jobs out there. Jobs were already scarce, and those terrorists exacerbated the situation."

I said, "I got an interview next week."

"Another widget factory?"

"Labor gig. Slinging boxes on a truck from dusk to dawn."

"You're overqualified for that kind of work."

"A man with no job ain't overqualified for any kinda work."

"Spoken like a true member of the unemployed."

"You got jokes."

"Seems like a lot of people have been humbled."

I cleared my throat. "They're offering twelve an hour, but I know they have a stack of apps thicker than your little black book."

He laughed at that. "What're your ends looking like until that comes through?"

"They ain't looking. Almost as blind as Helen Keller."

"Your economic recession is in full effect."

"Yep. Seems like the world is fucked up."

We said a few words about the war that was going on, on how it had done a number on people both emotionally and financially.

Scamz said, " 'Ours is essentially a tragic age, so we refuse to take it tragically.' "

"Shakespeare?"

"D. H. Lawrence. The opening lines of *Lady Chatterley's Lover*."

I yawned. "A regular Nostradamus."

"Come see me today. I got a few things lined up."

"Can't. I'm a legit man."

Scamz asked, "You heard from Jackson?"

I met Jackson a few years back through Scamz. They were the best of friends when I came along. But Jackson had been off the grift for almost two years. A good woman and a steady job had him on the straight and narrow.

I said, "Yeah. I've been hanging with him almost every day."

"What you two got going on?"

"We've been teaming up and looking for jobs together."

"So, he's getting back on the hustle?"

I debated telling Jackson's business, but Scamz wasn't the type to spread the word about someone else's misfortunes. And nine times out of ten, he already knew what was going on.

I said, "His ex is suing him for back child support."

"Sabrina slapped Jackson with a lawsuit?"

"Yep. She filed papers and claimed Jackson never gave her a dime."

"I don't believe that. He cared about his kids if nothing else."

"He showed me the papers from the district attorney."

We said a few more things about that.

In the end Scamz told me, "Be careful where you stick your dick."

I laughed at those sage words. He laughed too. They were laughs of disbelief.

We chitchatted about a few other people from our little clandestine world. A few were on lockdown, a few were about to get out. A couple had died along the way.

"Big Slim told me you were down at Eight Ball gambling with Nazario," Scamz said.

Eight Ball was a place people went when they were desperate for cash. Trouble and money was always down there. You just had to outrun the trouble to get the money.

"Yeah," I said. "That psycho was so mad he lost his mind."

"Then he didn't lose much."

"He wanted to pay me on the spot."

"People say he made a scene."

"Big time. He made his wife give me her wedding ring to cover his debt."

Scamz said, "He hates to lose, especially in front of a crowd."

"I pawned the ring. Got five hundred."

"You know he's looking for you. He wants a rematch so he can get that ring back. Heard he's been down at the pool hall at least three times a day trying to find you."

"Kinda figured that. That's why I ain't been back down to the pool hall."

"If you sweating over chump change, you must need some economic relief."

My eyes went to my pine dresser. My bills were over there, piled up next to a stack of job rejection postcards. Frustration was bringing out the wolf in me.

I told Scamz, "Just need something to hold me over until one of these jobs come through."

He said, "Come see me. You're a good worker. I could use your help."

I paused. The jury in my mind went out to make a decision. "I'll pass. I have a few job interviews around the corner."

"Then come make some ends so you can take your woman out and have a good time."

"Me no got no woman. Got my eye on this waitress at Ed Debevic's."

"You ever stepped to her yet?"

"Not yet. She has an L.A. face and an Oakland booty that won't quit. Pretty much out of my league."

"How can a waitress be out of anybody's league?"

"True."

"Be a man at all times. Never let a woman scare you. Never."

Scamz was working my disposition in his direction word by word, phrase by phrase.

"Either way," he said, "it's hard to get a woman being broke."

Scamz wasn't lying. L.A. had its own mentality and it cost to be the boss out here. Whenever I hit Atlas Bar and Grill it was five bucks to park, twenty to get in, and close to ten bucks for one drink. If I met a honey, triple that drinking budget. Breakfast at Roscoe's would add another twenty. If I got lucky, a box of condoms would cost another five. Trojans were the cheapest thing on the list. Not using one was the most expensive thing on the list.

Scamz said, "Pussy and money, Dante. Got money, you can get pussy. Got pussy—"

"You can get money."

We chuckled at his phrase.

My eyes closed when I thought about that waitress,

saw her dimples, heard her mature voice, even could see her hips when she did her sensual stroll, and wondered what she was doing right now.

A second later I exhaled. "Is this hot or cold?"

Hot meant difficult. Cold meant smooth, minimal problems.

I could hear Scamz smile when I asked that. His easy words had worked me toward his team.

He replied, "Easy rent money."

"Let's be up front. I'm not down for nothing long-term."

"What do I have to do to get you to reconsider?"

"You can't."

He didn't say anything for a few seconds. He did that when his mind was in overdrive. Sometimes I thought he had so many thoughts he had to shut down to keep from overloading.

Scamz said, "You know how to find me."

We left it at that. He wasn't going to give the specifics, not over the wire.

I hung up.

3:41 a.m.

I dialed another number. Jackson answered on the first ring.

I said, "You're up?"

"Yeah. What's up, Cool Hand?"

"Scamz called. He's back and it sounds like he has a few things going on."

Jackson hesitated. "Yeah, Dante. We can check on those interviews after I leave court."

I understood why he was talking in code. I said, "Robin must be over."

"Right."

"See you in a few hours."

We hung up. No matter what time of night I called, he was awake. I didn't think much about that because I wasn't sleeping on a regular schedule my-damn-self. Not having a job stole away the importance of an alarm clock. It also made it easy to lose track of my days.

When a man didn't have a job, didn't have a Monday, a hump day, and a payday, all days started to blend and lose value. All were just today. All he wanted was a better tomorrow.

I was on edge, a little hungry. I walked over my two-shades-of-brown carpet, went to the kitchen sink, washed my face, dried it with a paper towel, then opened the fridge, let that light fall on the off-white walls. Don't know why I opened the fridge. Not like the food fairy had come while I was sleeping. Not much was in there except leftover salmon and rice and a frozen Healthy Choice meal.

Restless. Scamz had left me agitated.

I did two hundred sit-ups, crunches, worked on my obliques. Did half as many push-ups. Stretched my legs into a split on the left side, did the same on the right, then went down into a Chinese-style split. Shadow-boxed against my old memories until a layer of sweat glistened on my skin.

I looked at that stack of job rejection postcards.

Anxiety was all over me, clinging to my skin like a thousand ticks.

More push-ups until my arms burned. More sit-ups until my abs were on fire.

Dealing with Scamz meant I needed to be in shape. Ready to rumble, ready to run.

I rested in my sweat. Put on my Levi Chen *Liquid Gardens* CD. Meditated a few minutes.

Then with that music calming me, I stood in my window and looked out at the palm trees.

I was lonely. Broke and lonely.

L.A. was an expensive bitch. A whore who sucked your dick and swallowed all of your money, then left you sleeping on the concrete.

A man stayed broke and hungry long enough, his value system was bound to change. And when it did, Scamz was waiting.

2

By eight in the morning I had met Jackson on the out-
skirts of downtown L.A., on Commonwealth, in a shiny
black building that had the words SUPERIOR COURT
etched across the top. We copped a squat in room 2G, an
Alaska-cold courtroom that had wooden benches about
as comfortable as a slab of concrete. People were shifting, frowning, checking their watches.

Some woman said, "It's cold in here; really cold."

"Cold makes you mean," the female sheriff said.

"Not as mean as marrying the wrong man."

Every woman in the room laughed.

I was sitting next to Jackson. My homie had deep
brown skin, stood tall and thin like a Sioux Indian from
the Dakotas. His hair was long and wavy; sometimes he
wore it in cornrows, but today, since we were in court, it
was parted down the middle and pulled back.

I was down here with him for moral support.

He rocked a bit and said, "So Scamz is back."

I said, "Never heard of anybody named Scamz."

"Me either."

Both of us laughed.

Jackson was a good guy. Part black, part Sioux. Two
different kind of warriors, both who were mistreated by
the white man in this land. He loved his family. Had a
soft hand and a strong heart. But when needed he
could have a strong hand and a hard heart. And the
mood was never misdirected at a woman. The kind of
man I wished my old man had been. Jackson drinks no
more than he can handle, and I've seen him gamble

from time to time, but he never placed bets with his rent money.

When it came to the women, from what I'd seen and heard, the relationship part of his life was no different from any other man I'd ever met who dealt with those wonderful creatures. Jackson was forty and some change, closer to fifty, and I would think that by now he'd have mastered the art of womanology, but it seemed like he was always swimming upstream.

He asked, "What you think Scamz got going on?"

"Knowing him, he's dibbling and dabbling in everything."

The double doors opened and Jackson's fiancée came in. Robin had come down for moral support as well. Since Jackson was her man, she had personal interest in his situation. And he wanted her involved in all aspects of his life, good and bad. He hid nothing from her. That was how he lived his life. Robin was prettier than a motherfucker: a dark-skinned woman with an Ashley Stewart figure, solid with all the curves in the right places, the alpha and omega of true beauty.

We chilled with the conversation about Scamz. Jackson used to be a bouncer at a few clubs and has done a little scheming in his day. Nothing major on the grift tip, but still more than the average hustler. His specialty used to be going into the DMV to sneak tests with all the right answers to people. He'd come in and pretend he was taking a test to get a driver's license, then switch test papers with his customer, and make somewhere between two and five hundred tax-free dollars for a good ten minutes of work. That was how he met Robin. Back then she wanted to drive a bus for RTD, a shitty job with good benefits, but had flunked that test too many times to mention. He did other schemes, but those were Jackson's old ways. He'd moved on and used that money to get a degree at DeVry and landed a gig with the dot-commers, until the bottom fell out of that world.

Robin made her way down our row and sat on the other side of Jackson. She smelled good. She had her flight attendant uniform on, a dark blue outfit that made her come across more military than a coffee-tea-or-pillow kinda girl. She'd been on that gig for the last year. With those benefits, she could travel around the country for next to nothing. No more dealing with crackheads and gang-bangers on the city buses; she'd graduated to serving alcoholics and cocaine connoisseurs at thirty thousand feet. She crossed her legs and bounced her left foot. Every time the door opened, we tensed up the way a person did when they expected bad news to swagger in at any moment.

I said, "Jackson, you a'ight?"

"Just hoping the judge got laid last night and is in a damn good mood."

A man on the other side of us said, "You and me both, brother. You and me both."

A few people within earshot chuckled.

The room was about as drab as the set to a Judge Judy show. A red, white, and blue USA flag and a California state flag with a bear hung behind the judge's empty chair. A jury booth with fourteen comfortable chairs was to our right.

Every other second the door swung open and somebody came in. Most of those people were either suing or being sued, not a smile in sight. This was a room filled with people who used to make love every night, now couldn't stand to be in the same room with each other for five minutes.

Somebody else asked, "Why are these benches so damn hard?"

The female sheriff overheard the comment and replied, "They were donated by the people at Preparation H."

More people laughed at the wannabe comedienne.

An Afrocentric woman with beautiful black and gray locks came in. Her locks were pulled back, showing off the sweetest face this side of heaven.

Robin said, "The militant poet is here."

Sabrina was a little over thirty, looked like a young

woman with old hair. She didn't wear makeup, just wore a silver earring in her nose and another in her left eyebrow. She had her wool coat in her arms, was wearing a dark red sweatshirt that had the phrase EACH ONE TEACH ONE laying across her breasts. No doubt she had the kind of breasts that made a man scream *Got milk?* I tried not to look at her like that because she was the mother of Jackson's kids, but some things couldn't be ignored.

Sabrina saw Jackson sitting with Robin. She frowned. Then she turned her anger into a sweet smile, one that showed no traces of animosity or fear as it warmed up the courtroom.

Sabrina pulled off her black leather gloves. Not a slim woman, and not heavy. She was right at five feet tall, most of that height distributed in her legs, dressed in Levi's that held on to her butt with a grip of life. Jackson had met her when he slipped into the DMV and took her C Class test for her. Guess my buddy has a thing for women who don't know the rules of the road.

She was surprised to see me. She spoke to me with a simple nod of her head.

I did the same.

At least fifteen people were with her, more than half of them women. All of them dressed in earthy fashions, strutting like they all came to front the man and challenge the system. Her crowd sported everything from bald heads and fades to dreads and twisted naps and Afros left over from the seventies. All of them were short with oval heads and similar features, reminded me of the munchkins coming out to greet Dorothy.

Jackson muttered, "She brought her whole damn family."

The sheriffs looked our way.

Robin patted Jackson's leg, whispered for him to lower his voice.

Robin looked back. Sabrina gave Robin a stern look; that kind of thing that goes on between women was going on once again. Robin took a breath, shook her head, and then nodded at whatever Jackson whispered to her. Sabrina went to the sheriff's desk to get checked in, then followed the militant munchkins and sat right behind us.

Robin closed her eyes; her leg bounced faster with each second.

Jackson's lips moved but no words came out.

I didn't say anything. This was way out of my realm of understanding.

Robin spoke right above a whisper. "You take your pill?"

Jackson snapped a little. "I don't need to take any pills."

"Sweetie, you have to take the pills. It's for your own good."

I asked, "What kinda pills?"

A look came over both of their faces. I'd stumbled into part of a conversation that I wasn't supposed to hear, but it was too late for me to backtrack.

Robin hesitated. "Migraines. He's been having headaches."

She became defensive and made direct eye contact when she told me that. She was lying. His body language co-signed her lie.

I let their business be their business.

"Are we ready to rumble?" A voice rang out and got the room's attention. "Come to order."

The judge strutted in like a cocky performer at the rise of a curtain. Short. Stubby. His mouth was too big for his oversize face. Forehead so tanned it looked like old leather. Hair in a Moe from the Three Stooges hairstyle. His robe hung like Dracula's cape.

He spoke in a God-like tone. "We know why we are here. They want people off welfare. If mothers were paying their child support, fathers wouldn't be on welfare. Right, men?"

There was a pause, and when people realized it was a joke, kiss-ass laughter came from all around.

"It's a nice morning out there. Could hardly taste the smog on my way in."

More kiss-ass laughter.

"So let's see if we can clear the air in here as well. Maybe a few of you can get out in time for nine holes on the golf course. I have eighty cases today and I plan to cover them all."

A Latino man and his European lawyer were the opening act. A dark-haired twenty-something D.A. in a Kmart seersucker suit reading loud enough for people in the hallway to hear: "Our records show that $6,523.48 is owed in back child support by Mr. Hernandez. Plus interest."

I muttered, "Damn."

"Dante," Jackson said. "Make sure you pay attention. This is your schooling for today."

Jackson was rubbing his hand up and down his leg hard enough to take the blue out of his jeans. Robin reached for his fingers, patted his skin, stopped him from moving so much.

"Your Honor, my client has four children and makes ten thousand a year as a self-employed gardener."

That meant he was making all of his money under the table; untraceable income.

When all was said and done, Judge waved his hand like a sorcerer and cast his spell. "The court orders you to pay fifty dollars a month. Subject to intercept clause, franchise tax, acceleration clause . . ." His voice trailed off, became smaller, sort of like the verbal fine print a used-car salesman spewed out at the close of a deal.

The next case was against a dude from the Pacific Islands.

"Our records show that $36,523.48 is owed, plus interest," the judge said in a dark tone. "How did you happen to miss ten years of support payments?"

"It slipped my mind."

The judge went at him, no Vaseline, ripped him a new asshole and filled it with a lecture on responsibility, remorse, repair, and repeat. The room was silent, unmoving. The judge made the man look at him while he talked; treated that fifty-year-old man like he was a six-year-old. His ex-woman was on the other side, crying, wiping her eyes, the whole dramatic nine.

"The court orders you to pay two hundred dollars a month. Subject to intercept clause, franchise tax, acceleration clause . . ."

Ten cases later, it was my friend's turn. They called his name and I felt him jump. Robin patted his leg twice, gave him a supportive smile. He stood up and got ready to face the judge, Robin and me at his back, but in reality he was on his own. Sabrina and her crew became restless, started mumbling until the sheriff told them to settle down or get kicked out.

I looked over at Robin. She looked worn. She saw me checking her out, and changed her whole demeanor, acted like she was down for the struggle. Her battle with Jackson's ex had gone on for a while. Robin had met Jackson while he was still with Sabrina. Robin was married back then. They had kept in touch, become good friends. Then a little while after Jackson and Sabrina split two years ago, Robin got divorced, somebody called somebody, and they hooked up. It's been a rough one, because of that baby-momma drama. It moved from a battle to a war when Jackson and Robin got engaged.

"Our records show that $16,199.52 is owed, plus interest," the judge said.

Jackson said, "I don't owe any money."

"Could you explain to the court?"

Jackson cleared his throat and said that he had been paying all along, most of it in cash, but his ex had lost her job a while back, and while she was in between gigs she applied for assistance, even though he was footing most of her bills. He ran down the welfare scam his ex was running, told him that she got busted, that The Man came after him. He refused to pay a debt he didn't owe, so they garnished his check, took his driver's license, intercepted his tax refund.

The room had fallen silent.

The judge nodded at Jackson. "Do you have any receipts to prove your claim?"

"No. I trusted her. Why would I keep receipts?"

"Well, without receipts you have no case."

"What can I do?"

Judge asked him, "Do you have any income?"

"Had picked up another job out by LAX at Direct TV in the sales department, was going through probation, but I lost my job after I missed ten days."

"Were you under a doctor's care?"

"Unfortunately, the court kept letting my ex call me to court whenever she felt like it."

Sheriffs, clerks, and strangers laughed. Even the judge smiled long enough to look human.

Robin looked like she had the headache of her life. She was leaning forward rubbing her temples. I looked behind me. Sabrina was back there. She looked cool and confident, as if the truth were her pillow and justice the covers that kept her warm every night.

Judge asked Jackson, "You have stock?"

"My stocks fell from one-sixty-two a share to around a dollar a share."

Judge asked, "Sounds like you were a dot-commer."

"For three years."

Jackson was in that group that had been talked into quitting the job they already had to go to a techno company that promised megabucks through company options, then realized that they were really working at a shit-on-a-stick company that had been called out at fuckedcompany.com.

Jackson said, "So much for being a millionaire before fifty."

A few people laughed.

The judge asked, "How are you supporting yourself?"

"My fiancée helps me out." Jackson motioned back toward Robin. "She's a blessing."

Sabrina made a loathsome sound.

Judge read over a few papers. "Your driver's license was suspended six months ago?"

"About," Jackson replied. "Taking my license won't put food on anybody's table. All that will do is make my auto insurance go up. More bills I can't afford to pay right now."

"For nonpayment."

"Because I don't owe."

"But you don't have your receipts."

"No."

"Canceled checks?"

"I always gave her cash. She said that made it easier for her."

"No receipts," the judge said to himself. He was checking out some documents. "Well, this is interesting."

My buddy stood there and begged for his license. Told the judge if he had his license he could try to get a gig as a limo driver, and if he couldn't, since L.A. was so spread out, he'd need to be able to drive from place to place so he could find a job.

"Well, Mr. Jackson," the judge said his name like he took offense, "consider public transportation until you can fulfill your parental obligations. Those are the breaks. That's how you get people to listen. You treat them like a child. You take something they value."

Jackson slumped. His character had been slaughtered, and in front of his woman. He had no dignity to lean on. He glanced back at Robin. Her eyes were closed.

Jackson said, "Judge . . ."

My friend struggled with his words, and I thought that whatever he was about to say would be a series of curses that could get him locked up for the next two hundred years.

"Yes, Mr. Jackson?"

He took a hard breath. "I would like to request paternity testing."

Mumbles came from Sabrina's crew. Sabrina was having a fit, bad-mouthing Jackson to everybody in her family, saying that he was doing that to get back at her and was gonna end up making his kids hate him. That was more than enough to make the judge slam down his gavel.

Silence covered the cold room.

He asked Jackson if he'd ever been given DNA testing for his two kids. Jackson said no. The judge asked Jackson if he and Sabrina had ever lived together. Again he said no. The judge asked if there was any doubt. Jackson told him that Robin had paid for him to see a lawyer, and the attorney told him he should get tested, just to be sure.

The judge said, "Let's not waste the court's time. You have doubts."

"The first one, my oldest daughter, Cree, she's six and she looks like me. I've always had doubts about the youngest one, Lisa. She's three. Me and the child's mother, we'd been so off and on, and she was seeing other people, so anything is possible."

"After all this time you want to establish paternity."

"Don't want to do it, but my lawyer said that . . . that I should be sure. That the DNA thing was all about fairness, not meanness, and the kid should know, that I should be sure. Your Honor, I'm not sure about anything anymore."

"At this late of a date, a request for DNA testing is always turned down." The judge looked over the paperwork and then stared at Jackson as if he were evaluating him. Maybe trying to find a way to balance out those receipts that Jackson didn't have. The judge said, "But for this case, I will make an exception. Request granted."

"Thank you, Your Honor."

"Since this is your first, the court will treat you to the testing. Consider it a present from the courts. And since you are available and both of the children are here in Los Angeles, I will order that the process be expedited. We would like to get the ball rolling today, if possible."

"Yes, sir."

"However, if you fail to participate in blood testing, that will result in judgment of paternity."

After he went on about arrears and lump sums, the judge said, "Since the children still have to eat—until

DNA is settled—the court is ordering you to pay fifty dollars a month. Half on the first, half on the fifteenth. Subject to . . ."

Robin's breathing was uneven; she'd gone off in a deep non-blinking trance.

Sabrina had unhappiness written all over her body.

One of the munchkins asked Sabrina, "Why is he doing that?"

"To disrespect me. To drag our children through the legal system."

"To make you hate him."

Sabrina and her crew of militant munchkins glowered at Jackson like they were ready to run him out of town with torches. They marched out of the room.

When all was said and done, Jackson took Robin's hand and walked out at a snail's pace. So many stress lines were in Jackson's forehead. Twice as many were in Robin's.

I followed them through a crowd of people who were waiting for their turn to pay the piper.

"I hate her," Robin growled out. "How could she screw over somebody who was paying child support in the first place?"

Jackson stopped right there and put his arms around his woman. I stood to the side. He rocked her in front of all those stressed-out people until she said she was okay.

We took the elevator down to the ground floor and filed by the metal detector, headed outside.

Robin told Jackson, "I have to get to work."

"You're off to North Carolina?"

"New York on a two-day trip, home long enough to change clothes, then right back out to North Carolina. I have to take a class on using an automated external defibrillator. The FAA would hate for somebody to have a heart attack at thirty thousand feet and all I was able to do was pass out peanuts."

I asked, "Ain't you afraid to be up there, especially on the coast-to-coast trips?"

"Scared as hell. Security is still a joke."

I said, "No shit. First there was the Middle Eastern guy who got by security with seven knives and a damn stun gun, then there was the fool with the bomb in his shoes, then a man with a loaded .38 got past security at both Tampa International and Hartsfield. Baggage screeners don't even have to have a high school diploma."

As soon as I rambled that, I wished that I hadn't jumped in on their conversation.

Jackson said, "Just for the record, since we're putting it out there, I don't like you flying, especially on the coast-to-coast flights. If security is still a joke, it ain't ever gonna be safe up there."

"I can't live my life in fear." That was Robin. "My God is on my side. When it's my time to go, it's my time."

Jackson gave in with a hard breath. "Same hotels?"

"Not sure which one they're putting us in this time, but it'll be one of the usual spots."

"Call me as soon as you touch ground."

"My family from Haiti wants to get together." She looked away from Jackson, stared at her feet for a moment. "All that death and destruction last year is making us appreciate each other. I'll be mobile most of the time. Let me call you; don't run your bill up."

"I can call you."

"We might catch a Broadway play, so I might not be able to hit you right back."

Her car was meter parked right outside the door. Robin kissed her man with no shame, gave him some deep tongue action and rubbed his back, waved at me, got in her silver car, then she was gone.

Jackson said, "She's a strong woman. Ain't nobody like her."

We stood under gray skies that promised rain, coats on, hands in pockets, absorbing as much sun as we could, and watched people racing in and out of the court building, some in coats, some in sweaters, some with briefcases, others with summons. Golden leaves blew from the trees and stuck to the curb and fences. It was the season of brown grass, seventy-degree days, and forty-degree nights. You could swim in the ocean during the day and ride two hours away to Big Bear and ski at night.

One of the women dropped a piece of paper, and when she bent to pick it up, that move made her backside apple up. Any other time Jackson would've stood next to me with a wide grin and eye-fucked her fine brown frame, but when she looked back at us and smiled, he turned the other way.

He said, "That's how trouble gets started. Just like that. Sabrina dropped something when I met her down at the DMV, I glanced at her ass, the next thing I know I'm sixteen thousand in the hole."

I took my eyes off that woman and said, "Sixteen motherfucking thousand."

He said, "Ain't that a bitch?"

He looked up and his frown deepened. I checked out what he was peeping at. A huge billboard for *Divorce Court* was right across the street, the words HIS and HERS on opposite sides of Judge Ephriam as she peered down over the top of her glasses at us. Wilshire Boulevard was filled with billboards for Judge Judy, Judge Joe Brown, and a few others who pimped people's misery for entertainment.

Jackson shook his head. "She straight-up lied."

"That's cold-blooded."

"Woman is the most fiendish device ever created. Robin is the exception."

I couldn't agree; I didn't disagree. Women were probably out there saying the same about men.

He told me, "Robin wants to have a kid."

"You wanna have another one?"

"She's thirty-three. She wants her own before she gets too old."

"You down?"

"Right now, that's like offering a drowning man a glass of water."

"I hear ya."

"I'm trying not to get in any deeper. Think that's creating some tension between us."

There was a look in his eye that said he wondered what he would have to do to get back on his feet. From what I've seen, what I've heard, once you get in that deep, you never get out.

He asked, "What did you learn up in there, Cool Hand Dante?"

"Never trust a big butt and a smile."

He chuckled. "Now all of a sudden I'm the bad guy. Remember that as a man, you will always be the bad guy."

"I don't believe that."

"You better ask somebody."

I said, "I thought everything would work out. Thought Sabrina was gonna be cool. Thought you and Robin would be married by now, riding off in the sunset toward a happy ending."

"Ask anybody walking through those doors. You want happy endings, get the Disney Channel."

"Disney's laying off too."

"I heard."

"The Seven Dwarfs are down to two dwarfs and a part-time midget."

"That damn mouse probably down off I-5 at an on-ramp with a WILL WORK FOR CHEESE sign."

We laughed at that. Laughter lightened the heaviest of loads.

With a smile he said, "Man, if I knew what I know now back then, I would've jacked off in a cup, stored enough to make three or four kids, gotten a vasectomy, then I could've had kids when I wanted to. No surprises. No trusting a woman when she says she's on the pill. None of that shit."

I stood and listened to what he was trying to teach me. Some days his advice was the best. Some days, when he was riled at the world, he sounded like Scamz: biased and cold. Both of them had me by at least fifteen years. I wondered if that was what time did to men.

He went on, "All because of my dick. If it weren't for

my dick, I'd be in a much better situation. Some days I think I should just cut it off. Every man in there was in trouble because of his dick."

"No, thank you. I'll keep mine. Don't use it as much as I'd like to, but I've grown attached to it."

"Should cut mine off and give it to the bitch."

That chilled me and killed my laughter.

His words softened but stayed just as intense. "All because of my motherfucking dick."

My problems didn't run as deep as his. I didn't have but one mouth to feed. And if my mouth didn't get fed, nobody tripped out. Still, I had to eat. When a man couldn't get a gig pulling down a solid forty so he could have enough cabbage to cover food, clothing, and shelter, he had to exercise his other options before the missed-meal cramps kicked in.

He said, "Tell Scamz I need help."

"Robin wouldn't like that. She told you to keep away from Scamz."

"Sabrina put me deep inside a trick bag." Again he chuckled hard and took another deep breath. "This is karma making its rounds. Yessir, I must've done something real bad in my last life, must've done a whole lot of wrong, because karma is coming at me like a hurricane."

"You know I got your back."

"Tell Scamz I need help. Anything he got, hot or cold, I'll take."

"I don't know, man."

"How many kids you gotta feed, Dante?"

"Calm down." I waited for some of the aggravation in Jackson's expression to disappear. I reminded him, "We're on the same team."

"Sorry about snapping on you like that."

I checked my watch. It was right at eleven o'clock. My stomach was growling. I asked Jackson if he wanted me to drive him back home or drop him off somewhere. He shook his head, said he had it covered, that he was going to go take care of a few things, spend some quality time alone.

I said, "Well, at least let me take you down to Ed Debevic's for some lunch."

"That's where that waitress you got the hots for work
at, ain't it?"

"Yeah. But that's not why I'm swinging down that
way. It's my birthday and—"

"Damn, why didn't you remind me?"

"No big deal."

"It is a big deal. Now I feel bad for asking you to
come down here. Happy birthday, Cool Hand."

"Thanks. It's cool."

"I should be taking you out to lunch, but my money
is funnier than Steve Harvey."

"I can treat you to some eats."

"When Robin gets back, maybe all of us can hook up
and do a belated celebration. Go have some fun today.
Go have your lunch."

"I got some change. Roll with me."

He shook his head. "I've got to pick up my little girls
later, but right now I need to be by myself so I can think
on some things. Need to consider my options."

"What are your options?"

"Let me catch up with you later."

He walked away. The way he blew me off bothered
me. He sounded hollowed out and that made me feel
hollow.

I headed across the street to a parking lot and my
buddy walked the opposite way.

I turned around just in time to see Jackson pulling out
a pack of Marlboros. He waved at me; I returned the
one-handed good-bye as I headed toward my car. He
thumped out a Marlboro, then ripped the filter off before he fired it up. He inhaled, twisted his lips, and blew
smoke out sideways. Did that a few times. Smoke
plumed around his head. Looked like he was trying to
get cancer in the express lane.

It had been close to three years since I'd seen him
smoke. We'd both stopped around the same time. Wondered when he started back.

I headed over to where Oscar was waiting underneath a palm tree. Oscar is my twenty-year-old
hoopty's name. I named him after that old grouch on
Sesame Street. My bucket looks like that raggedy mup-
pet. Pretty much the same color. Everyone has a personal relationship with their ride in a car town like L.A.
Out here you are what you drive, and you have to drive
everywhere.

Oscar coughed and spat a few times before he
cranked up. I headed up Wilshire Boulevard, tried to
blend in with six lanes of lunacy. My radio was on 105.9
and they were running a commercial advertising a product called Latitude, something guaranteed to give your
penis more length and girth in thirty days. I changed to
97.1 and they were running a commercial for the Boston
Medical Group aimed at men with pre-ejaculation
problems. Tried to signal to get over, some asshole sped
up and cut me off. I pulled up next to him to get some
eye contact, but the bastard wouldn't look my way. Typical chickenshit behavior, and since defensive driving
was bullshit, a brother had to drive like Emmitt Smith
during the Super Bowl, find an opening, cut a few people off, and take it before it closed up.

Robin's silver Passat was pulled to the side down at
Wilshire at Mariposa, across from the Equitable Building.
She was easy to spot because her vanity plates read EYE
FLY 4 U. She was in the right lane, emergency blinkers on.
Looked like her ride had stalled out. People walked by;
drivers sped by; nobody stopped to help. In this part of the
world, if a woman's car broke down, she'd better have a
cellular phone and a triple-A card. People were riding my
ass, but I slowed, tooted my horn, and got her attention.
Now we were blocking two of the three lanes.

Robin was leaning forward, face on the steering
wheel, rubbing her temples. A little at a time, she raised
her head. She jumped when she saw me. Surprise and
shame in its purest form. She looked so different, like
another person who resembled Robin, but not the real
Robin that I'd known for so long. She adjusted her uni-

form as if that would erase her angst before she let down her window. Her eyes were filled with enough tears to let me know she'd been sitting there having an emotional breakdown for as long as I'd been out in front of the court talking to Jackson about his woes.

That shook me up.

I asked that impulsive, stupid question that people always asked, "You a'ight?"

She wiped her eyes, cleared her throat, blew her nose, and tried to smile at me. "I'll. Be. Fine."

Horns blared.

I told her, "Follow me and we can pull over up the street somewhere."

She nodded.

A city bus rolled up on Oscar, bullied us into moving. I tried to find a place to pull over. Robin hadn't moved an inch. I didn't have the extra cash to risk a parking ticket, so I swooped around the block. By the time I made it back to Wilshire and Mariposa, her car was gone.

3

"We have seats available in other sections," the hostess said.

It was close to noon and I was on La Cienega's restaurant row, at Ed Debevic's. That hostess reminded me of the Asian girl in *Charlie's Angels*.

"Nah, that's a'ight," I told her, and then motioned toward a waitress, one who had a Debbi Morgan smile, an Angela Bassett disposition, and the body Jayne Kennedy had back in her day. A lot of territory on that frame. She was taller than me by at least an inch, maybe closer to two. Stood next to her once when I was paying my check, and she had on flat shoes that day. That height puts her at about six feet. To go with that smile she had an ass that could send Jennifer Lopez into early retirement.

"You want to sit in Pam's section?"

"Yeah. Pam's section."

I gazed toward Pamela. She was a fine lady with a shady, sensual walk. No wedding ring on her finger. Nice hair, thick and bushy, one of those straw Afro things a lot of sisters wore these days. Every week her hair had been different: ponytail, braids, twists, sometimes wrapped in a funky scarf decorated with rhinestones. Pam went from looking African-American to Puerto Rican in the blink of an eye.

The hostess said, "It'll be about a twenty-minute wait."

"I'll chill with the newspaper. Nowhere to go."

I'd seen a lot of drama this morning. The kind that

should make men and women avoid each other. The thing that got me the most was seeing Robin all messed up like that. I'd circled the block hunting for her, then gone back up Wilshire to look for Jackson to tell him that his woman had broken down like I did at my momma's funeral, but he had vanished.

A Tom Cruise–looking guy stormed in and rolled up on me like this was his world and I was in the way. I didn't back down. He was flipping through a *Variety* while he barked into his cellular phone.

He snapped his fingers at the hostess. "Hurry up. I have an important meeting after lunch."

Snap Snap Snap

She gave a plastic smile that masked her being pissed off, and she was good at that act—guess she was taught the customer was always right—then checked the seating chart.

Tommy Boy kept on rambling, "How did he get the fucking part? That was my part, goddammit. Look, you either get me an audition or I will fire you—hold on, got another call. Yeah? What? I'm on the line with somebody more important, so call me later. *What?* Wait. Hold on. Hey, more important call. Gotta go. Well, you *were* the more important call until this call came. Okay, I'm back. How did he get the fucking part? That was my god— Hold on, got another call."

I shook my head at that bastard. He acted like he was entitled to the world. But I guess that arrogance was the norm up this way. This was Beverly Hills, the land of images and illusions. All around people were reading scripts, *Dramalogue,* running lines. Others were having old-fashioned power lunches.

Everybody up in here wanted the world, or at least twenty million a picture.

I just wanted a damn job that paid at least twelve bucks an hour. Eight hours a day to keep me occupied, out of trouble, and just above the poverty line until I could regroup and get a master plan. But I might as well be asking to star in a fucking sitcom.

Pam passed by. Her long legs made her black skirt wave like a flag. She was the kind of woman a man looked at, got tingly, then went home and got mad at his wife for not looking like her.

No doubt that after hanging out in superior court all morning and watching men get sued for enough money to feed a million of Sally Struthers's starving kids, looking at a woman was the last thing I needed to do. Like Jackson said, one smile, next thing you know you're sixteen thousand in the hole. But still, California had 160,000 square miles, thirty-two million people; that comes out to two hundred people per square mile and over half of them women. Pam was the one woman I kept thinking about.

I smiled at Pam. She didn't reciprocate. That was cool. Rejection could save me a lot of cash.

I used that wait to chill out, get Jackson's problems out of my head, and read the front page of the *Los Angeles Times.* Scamz always told me to keep up, to get a worldview and not just a Hollywood review. *L.A. Times* wasn't a happy paper. Outside of war talk, pink slips were flying like pterodactyls at Lucent Technologies, Alcatel, and a few other places I had sent résumés.

"Sir, your table is ready."

"Thanks."

I was put in Pam's section. Three minutes went by before she came to my table. She gave me that identical picture-perfect, twenty-percent-gratuity smile that she'd given the white couple before me.

She asked, "What would you like to drink?"

"Lemonade."

"Same as usual."

"Yep."

"I'll be back in a moment to take your order."

She walked away. I watched her backside like it was the NBA finals.

I'm a man. I appreciate beauty.

I'm a black man. I appreciate booty.

I'd had a few dreams about her. In one we were sitting by the lake in Kenneth Hahn Park reading to each other. Think we had children and I was away from the crazy life I'd been living.

Tommy Boy was brought in and put two tables down. He snapped his fingers at Pam.

"Can I get some service here, for chrissakes?"

She lowered her pen, raised a brow, her tongue pushed out the right side of her jaw. She stayed cool as she went over to his table. While she was writing down Tommy Boy's order, she saw I was watching her. She paused, then she went back to taking that order. She finished over there, cranked that smile back up, and moved to another table. I was still watching.

Then she came to me. "You always sit in my section."

"Glad you noticed."

"Any particular reason?"

"Nice section, if you ask me."

She paused and gave me eye contact, the kind that said she was trying to decide how to respond to that, eyes that asked me if I was a stalker.

She asked, "Ready to order?"

"Not yet."

Chatter was loud enough to keep our words from carrying.

I asked what I already knew. "Actress?"

"Yup. Triple threat."

"What that mean?"

"Actress. Singer. Dancer."

"Oh."

"What did you think it meant?"

"On my side of town: gun, knife, and baseball bat."

She laughed. "Cute. Take that act up the hill to the Comedy Store."

"Show me some of your skills, Miss Triple Threat."

Just like that she broke into dance and song. I'd seen her do a number before, and that was part of what attracted me to her. She moved her hips and I tingled. Her energy made her magnetic. Her maturity made her stand out from the young girls. She had some quick wit about her too. I liked that in a woman. So far as singing, she wasn't the next Alicia Keys, but she had a strong voice; didn't move like Aaliyah, but she had some nice hip-rolling motions that made her real estate shake like a house in an earthquake. People around us applauded. I gave her a short grin.

She asked, "Impressed?"

"If I had a dollar, I'd put it in your . . . pocket."

She laughed. "I bet you would."

I asked, "What was that?"

"Aw, man. You never saw the musical *Grease*?"

I shook my head. "Not a musical kinda guy. I like real-life movies."

"Guess I should've done Smokey's lines from *Friday.*"

That made me laugh.

I said, "Why don't you give me your number?"

"For what?"

I've fought a lot of fights, but asking a woman for her number was still one of the hardest things I've ever done. A woman has a way of looking at a man and making him feel like a vacuum cleaner salesman.

I answered, "Maybe we can meet somewhere and you can do Smokey's lines."

Pam turned me down, chuckled a little, but didn't walk away. In my book, that was a good sign.

Tommy Boy snapped his fingers toward Pam once again. Snapped them eight or nine times the way a man summoned a pet. His food had been dropped off by another waitress, and he was still on his cell phone, still flipping through the *Variety* and barking at somebody. He didn't look Pam's way, just snapped his fingers in her direction.

She didn't lower her voice. "The things a sister has to do to get a two-dollar tip."

Pam didn't respond to the snaps. She stayed at my table, looked over my chrome dome, took in my cinnamon complexion, checked out the few scars that were on my arms.

More finger snaps.

Pam looked at me and twisted her lips. "How old are you?"

"Twenty-five. Today's my birthday."

She made a sweet sound. "We're the same sign."

"We should hook up and talk astrology."

Snap Snap Snap

"You're barely older than MTV," Pam said. "Thought you were older."

"You older?"

"Too old for you, sweetie. Happy birthday."

"Thanks. How much older is too old?"

"You remember when Michael Jackson was black?"

"Get the fuck outta here. Michael Jackson was black?"

"Kunta Kinte black with a Mr. Potato Head nose. You know who shot J.R.?"

"Was it O.J.?"

"Ever own a record player?"

"Never owned a record."

"Got you by at least one generation. Sorry."

"What makes you think I can't hang with an old woman?"

"Old? Thanks. I hadn't been insulted all morning."

"My bad. My thesaurus is off-line. I meant mature."

"Whatever. I already have a kid, don't need another."

"Now who's slinging insults?"

"I'm a tit-for-tat kinda gal."

"What you do, besides this?"

She said, "I do whatever it takes."

Snap Snap Snap

She went to deal with Tommy Boy. Frustration lines in her forehead every step of the way.

When she came back to check on me, I went for it, full speed. "Let's hook up."

"Persistent, ain't ya? I see you in here reading the un-employment section, circling jobs, so I know you're in search of. What do you do?"

"In between gigs. Right now I do whatever it takes."

She raised a brow. "A hustler."

"Just like you."

She smiled. Those dimples lit up the room.

I asked, "You got a man?"

"Ain't no ring on my finger, so I haven't been drafted."

Snap Snap Snap

She muttered, "Working my nerves; working my nerves."

She went to Tommy Boy, refilled his orange juice, took a few orders, then came back to me. Her body language was anxious. There was a new look in her eyes. She wanted something from me.

Pam asked, "This hustling thing you got going on, drugs?"

"No street pharmaceuticals. Never."

"I don't deal in genocide."

"Me either."

"Illegal?"

"Every job has its occupational hazards."

Either she was unmoved, or she was good at hiding emotions.

Again she left. Her eyes came to me as she dropped off food. Saw me watching her the way a man watches a woman. I think she was either amused or flattered, maybe both.

She passed by and said, "What you staring at?"

"Nothing. Just like looking at you."

"My face is up here. Face. Booty. Face. Booty."

"Was working my way up. Gimme a minute."

She moved on to another table, a big smile on her face. Most women love attention. This guy I listened to on 97.1, Tom Leykis, said that all women were attention whores. He wasn't my role model, but he ain't always wrong. I never met a woman who wanted to be ignored, not on this side of town, not unless she was in a witness relocation program.

She came back and we talked some more, felt each other out.

I asked, "What kinda ends you need to make?"

"Well, I need to come up with between six and ten grand."

"Damn."

"I can get by with six."

"You and me both," I said. "Mister Ed ain't kicking you down enough?"

"Please. I'm a waitress, not a shareholder."

"That's a grip. IRS on your ass or something?"

She hesitated and contemplated her answer. "Acting stuff."

"Never thought that acting stuff was so expensive."

"Ain't nothing free but dreams, and when you wake up those are gone."

"I hear ya."

"So far as reality, what can you do for me?"

"I'll contact my contact and see what he got going on."

"Face. Tits. Face. Tits."

"I ain't a doctor, but I understand anatomy."

She chuckled.

I laughed cool and easy. I never laughed too hard. Never too often.

She asked, "Ready for your order?"

I told her what I wanted.

"Ain't you the freak daddy." She laughed. "Stick with what's on the menu."

"Guess I'll have the usual."

"All that to get the same as usual."

"Guess I'm a creature of habit."

"You should try something different every now and then."

"I could tell you the same."

She smiled. "You're trying too hard, sweetie. Take it down a notch. Less is more."

Tommy Boy snapped his fingers. "Can I get some service over here, please?"

Pam's eyes tightened and I heard her suck wind between her teeth as she took short steps that way, as if she were counting backward from one hundred to calm her nerves and keep her job.

Tommy Boy was on a Dennis Miller–size rant: "I shouldn't have to pay for the hamburger."

"Why not?"

"It ... it ... it was cold."

"Well, you ate most of it."

"Obviously you don't know who I am."

"What does that have to do with the hamburger you gobbled down?"

"Get me your manager."

"With pleasure."

As Pam walked away, Tommy Boy grunted out, "Bitch."

Pam's stride broke. She stalled like she was thinking of what to do. Then she shook her head like she didn't get paid enough to deal with this madness, picked up her pace, and went to get the manager.

Tommy Boy told whoever he was talking to on the phone, "Not you, asshole. You're not the bitch. Just some old chick ... at least thirty ... right ... over-the-hill-looking bitch still working at a job that requires her to wear a name tag and she tried to get an attitude with me. Yep, put her ass in check. Yeah, she was black. How'd you know? Ain't that the truth. All of 'em."

Two minutes later, Tommy Boy was arguing with the manager. Pam came back to my table.

I asked, "Everything a'ight?"

She made an irritated sound. "Don't sweat it."

"Say the word and I'll meet him outside and treat him to a beat down."

"Calm down, Rambo. Tell me what you can do for me."

"Point blank. It's illegal."

"Duh. Just when I thought you was the Pope."

I was busy reading her, her body language, searching for contradictions. You have to read people in this business. From the ministers who con their poor sheep into donating an extra thousand dollars, to the real estate agent who tricks you into a loan with a too high interest rate and too many points, to the man who fucks your wife—we're all thieves. We're all trying to get over. Just

some of us get beat down; some get a trip to the free
hotel; others go to an early grave.

The manager shied down from a battle in front of the
rest of the room. He told Tommy Boy, "We'll deduct the
burger. The soda, the fries, you pay for those items."

"I should lodge a complaint with the owner. That
waitress was racist and rude. She should invest in a class
in racial sensitivity. Either that or get a job at one of
those chicken and waffle places over in Compton where
that behavior is appropriate."

As Tommy Boy got up to leave, he tossed a penny back
on the table as a tip. Pam saw that. She was two tables
down by then, being nice and friendly to an older Jewish
couple. Tommy Boy put on his leather jacket, took his
wallet out, pulled out some cash to pay at the register.

He crammed his wallet into his jacket pocket then
marched down the aisle, still on his cell phone. Pam was
heading back my way. Tommy Boy rammed into her.

He said, "What? You're blind too? For chrissakes."

Pam didn't back down. "Hope you drive better than
you walk."

I started to get up and follow him, but Pam had this
strange expression, this one-sided smirk. I backed
down, told myself to think first, ask myself if it was
worth it. Rainbows flashed in front of my eyes. Tingles
made my hands become fists. I swallowed, took a
breath, and opened my hands. I'd had enough trouble.

Tommy Boy got outside and started patting his pockets like he was looking for his keys. Then hurried back
this way, searching the ground, still screaming in that
phone.

Pam passed by me and tossed something in my lap.

I put it in my pocket.

Tommy Boy came back in staring at the ground,
rushed back to his table.

He asked everybody, "Anybody see a black wallet?
Can't find my wallet."

Pam and me kept our gazes fixed on each other, smiling and talking.

I asked, "No chance on seeing you away from here?"

"No chance. Keep it on the biz tip." She winked. "A handsome face with a cute smile is why I have a kid and no man around. Where you are right now, been there done that."

Tommy Boy ran back outside looking for his wallet. My eyes went back to Pam. She had a dark side, one that was hidden behind soft dimples and a Debbi Morgan smile.

Me and Pam stared at each other. She had plain brown eyes, but they were pretty. Her deep-brown lipstick made her lips look wet. A new hunger made me lick my lips, make them as wet as hers.

She said, "I might look like an angel, but don't expect me to spread my wings if you do me a favor."

"Every angel needs to fly sometimes."

"I'm fine sitting on a cloud with my legs crossed."

"Was just joking. No expectations of any horizontal recreation."

"What, you think you're dropping down lyrics for Jay-Z now?"

"Nah," I said. "Just letting you know where I'm coming from."

Her smile was gone. She let me study the seriousness in her face. Underneath that, if you scraped away the false Hollywood routine, she had the eyes of a woman who had been through a lot and wouldn't hesitate to cut you twelve ways to heaven or one hundred ways to hell if you fucked her over.

I let her study my face. Let her know that I had a résumé harder than hers.

She said, "I think we have an understanding."

"I think we do."

She gave me her pager number. I wrote down my digits, but she wouldn't touch it.

She said, "If you got a hook-up, hit me on the hip. No bull."

A pause. I saw her in a new way. A more fascinating way. I said, "Michael Jackson was black up until the Victory Tour. There are rumors that when he caught fire during a Pepsi commercial, the fire activated some chemicals in his Jheri-Kurl, some sort of anti-Negro gene that caused his melanin to fade. No one really knows. People have asked Bubbles, but Bubbles issued no comment. It has baffled the best of the best."

"I see." She fought but gave up some chuckle. "And who shot J.R.?"

"Puff Daddy. Then he changed his name to P. Diddy to throw us off."

That made her laugh real hard. Her breasts bounced like they were happier than they had been in a long time. She said, "That was . . . that was creative."

"I have my moments."

"Catch you later, shorty."

I watched everything from her bouncing hair to the sway in her ass as she moved across the room. She lit a thousand candles in my belly. I liked that, and I didn't like that at the same time.

I ate my food, left a ten-dollar tip, larger than what I could afford to give, walked out the door. Tommy Boy was still in the area, retracing his steps, panicking because of his lost wallet.

"I had it at the damn table," he ranted into his cellular phone. "It couldn't've vanished."

I looked back at Pam and she was putting that sweet smile on another customer. She didn't glance my way for final eye contact. I moved on to a pay phone and dialed the number she had just given me. The outgoing message said her name was Pamela Quinones, asked whoever was calling to leave a number, did that first in English, then repeated it all in Spanish, and if it was regarding an audition, to put in 9-1-1. Emphasized that 9-1-1 was for auditions only.

I headed up La Cienega and crossed over to the side that had the Stinking Rose. When I was away from all the eyes at Ed Debevic's, I dug in my pocket and took out what Pam had tossed in my lap.

Tommy Boy's wallet.

I understood Pam. People like us understand each other. Misfits have a special place in this world, next to each other, holding hands singing their own version of "We Shall Overcome."

Since I had gotten out of juvenile hall, I'd always tried to get ahead without asking anybody for a hand because I realized all I could depend on was me. I don't owe or burden anybody for anything.

No matter how small you are, it's a simple equation: if you got money, you got power. If you ain't got money, you can't even buy tissue to wipe the smell away from your butt. So, I gotta do what I gotta do to get what I gotta get done done.

Wasn't but three bucks in the wallet, but there was plenty of plastic. Looked like he was cash-poor and living large on credit. I went from having nothing to do to having an agenda.

Time was on my side, at least for an hour, no more than two, so my next destination became a gas station. Where everything was faceless and automated. The first one was a Mobil and they wanted the zip code, so I moved my operation to a 76 and found a pump that didn't ask for a zip code or a PIN number. I slid Tommy Boy's MasterCard over the reader, and treated Oscar to some ninety-one-octane breakfast. For Oscar that was like savoring a five-star meal.

Then I got my hustle on, offered a few people a chance to buy gas at half price. I didn't offer it to everybody, had to read them, pick and choose. When the machine stopped accepting Tommy Boy's MasterCard, I whipped out his Visa, and when Visa was declined, I moved on to his AmEx card.

Inside an hour, I'd made over three hundred. My opportunistic customers had pumped over six hundred in gas. Charge card peeps let you slide with the first fifty on a stolen card, so Tommy Boy would be paying a nice piece of change for his class in racial sensitivity.

One Time pulled up in the lot, radio squawking. I tensed and kept my eyes on him. One of the charge card places could've noticed a lot of activity at this one spot and phoned it in. Or Tommy Boy could've called in his card already and they were trying to catch me with the goods in hand.

Then another member of One Time pulled up into the lot.

My palms started sweating. Heart thumped in my chest.

Corners of my past came back and tapped me on my shoulders, eyes became clouded by images of me in uniform blue, not even sixteen years old and marching in single file, being told when to get up and when to go to sleep. And the fights, felt the pain from all the fights, too many battles to count.

I knew when to quit.

I fired up Oscar and drove away.

Then I heard the screams again. The scream from the midnight rapes in jail, when men would throw blankets over other men and violate them. Shook those yells out of my head.

Then I heard my mother's screams.

I had to pull over and park. Felt like I was hyperventilating. That hadn't happened in months.

Those were the screams that bothered me. Sometimes they were so loud. Sometimes they were low. They were always there. Always reminding me that I didn't save her.

4

I took the narrow and winding road known as Laurel Canyon over the hill into Sherman Oaks. Left Hollywood in my rearview and landed in the terrain of valley girls and surfer dudes; a melting pot for both the old money and the new rich. Blond and brunette trust-fund babies were cruising around in high-end drop-top rides, wearing dark shades, thick sweaters, khaki shorts, socks and sandals, holding smoothies from Jamba Juice in hands that were tanned to the bone. These were people who thought being homeless meant being in escrow.

I hid Oscar in the residential area near the Martin Pollard Public Library, a quiet area lined with two-story apartments and single-family homes. I didn't want any of those shysters to know what I drove. They could get the info on my tags, run it through the DMV, and know where I lived.

Eight Ball Corner Pocket was five walking minutes away over on Ventura Boulevard, next door to a tattoo and body-piercing joint and across from a strip mall that housed Jinky's Café. That strip was lined with miles of first-rate shops and eateries. It reminded me of a bourgeois version of the dilapidated and pothole-lined Crenshaw Strip, where my people went to cruise on chrome.

My leather coat was open, hands in pockets, sun on my head. I stood out in front of the pool hall. Looked around to see if anybody from the One Time crew was watching this place. Not an eye came this way. It was a discreet watering hole. There wasn't any advertising to tell the world it was here.

I stepped out of a cool breeze, went through those plain double doors, and landed in another world. Took a second to adjust to the dimness and the cigarette smoke. California had no-smoking laws for all buildings, but this was an old-fashioned joint that followed nobody's rules. Political correctness was left outside the door. Down here men were only any good if they could intimidate and women were summed up by how good they looked.

First thing everybody saw when they came in was a wall-size poster of movie legend Dorothy Dandridge in an expensive cherry-wood frame. The prettiest poster of a black woman that I'd ever seen was on the ugliest lime-green wall in the universe. Dorothy was surrounded by pictures of people who died long before their celebrity ever would: Robert Johnson, Bessie Smith, Billie Holiday, Casey Brown, Nat Love, John Gillespie, Joe Turner, John Lee Hooker, and others were all over the place. Near the small stage were three large white signs, the house rules, scribbled in bold red letters:

NO DAMN GAMBLIN' UNLESS I GETS MY CUT

NO CUSSIN' THE WIMMEN

NO FIGHTIN' WITHOUT PERMISSION

Four twenty-six-inch Sony TVs were on, two on sports, one on a talk show, the other on a court show, and on CD Bobby "Blue" Bland was singing a deep song about Memphis on a Monday morning.

I fanned away cigarette and cigar fumes thicker than the smog glued to the San Gabriel mountains. Damn near every purple-top table in the room was filled with the afternoon crowd getting their games of nine ball, eight ball, and snooker on. The sounds of balls clacked all around the room. Quite a few sisters were in the house; most of them younger than me, a couple twice my age. At least three of them used to be Scamz's partners in horizontal recreation. They knew he was back and were looking for Mr. Goodbar.

I nodded at a few people. They nodded back.

My eyes went to the heavyset man roosting behind the circular booth in the middle of the room. He had been watching me the whole time. Everybody called him Big Slim. On the front of his booth was another sign: FORGET ABOUT THE DOG—BEWARE OF OWNER.

I made my way to the booth, looked up at Big Slim's ancient face and asked, "Scamz around?"

"Never heard of nobody go by that name."

Big Slim's voice was bulldog mean. His coldhearted expression was cast in cement.

My voice had already changed as well, thickened to match the harshness of this world.

Big Slim was a robust man, lots of razor bumps under his jowls because no one ever taught him that a black man should shave down and never go against the natural curl in the hair that grows on his chinny-chin-chin. He always wore dark slacks and a colorful shirt and had an immaculate, pencil-thin gray mustache. He was as old as they came, had lived beyond the number of years promised in the Bible. He was always here. From what I understood, he lived here, and if he did have a nest somewhere else he hardly ever left this spot. I was younger and faster, but I'd put on a blindfold and fuck with Suge Knight before I came at Big Slim.

I told him, "Scamz called me."

His frowned deepened. "Young man like you can't find no honest work?"

"Easier for a man to find a job when he got a job."

"Try standing out in front of Home Base and asking for some day work."

"You know everybody would rather hire Mexicans. They've cornered those jobs."

"Ask black people when they show. See if they can give you some work doing this or that."

"You know black people don't hire black people. They want Mexicans to do everything but date their daughter."

He shifted his false teeth like he wanted to disagree, but he couldn't. He said, "Devil's a dog."

His hand came up and rubbed the crop of razor bumps under his chin. I'd seen Big Slim countless times, but my insides still jumped whenever I laid eyes on his hands. They were FUBAR to the max. Big Slim had three fingers on his right hand and was missing the ring finger and parts of two of the others on his left. It was an unwritten rule down here not to ask Big Slim shit about his past. But people talked. Rumor had it that the cause of his missing digits was why he left Memphis back in the late fifties and fled out here. However they were taken off, the ends are rugged, so the amputation wasn't pretty.

He said, "Watch the do'. Gonna go pass some water."

He struggled to get up, stepped off his three-foot-high platform, then limped past the small stage that had a disco ball hanging from the ceiling, and went down the dark and narrow hallway. He had a rugged walk, like a man who wanted to walk faster, but one leg was holding his pace back. The kind of walk that scared you and made you have empathy at the same time. He looked like a man who could've been powerful, but one bad move, or one bad decision, had taken him off his path and cut off his chance at greatness. I imagine that about most people. I imagine that about me as well.

He came out of the water closet, pulled that blue door up, took out his keys, and unlocked the green door to the room on the right side of the hallway. That green door was the room next to the Money Room, and no one ever went in but Big Slim. Rumor around this joint was that's where he kept his missing fingers. Some said he collected fingers from people who had done him wrong.

He came out of that room, locked the green door, shook the handle to make sure it was secure, then limped his way back into his booth, his keys jingling with his hard stroll.

He said, "I see you still here."

I nodded. "Still waiting on Scamz."

"Don't know nobody go by that name."

I should've left, but I waited. Wondered how much schooling Big Slim had had. Doubt if he made it to the seventh grade. He was probably too busy working in some cotton field down south.

He slid me some pool balls. "Get comfortable at table nine."

I did like he told me, took off my jacket, racked the balls, and broke. Then I looked around. One man nodded at me. He held up one finger. That meant ten bucks a game. I nodded. Four games later, I was forty dollars closer to being a millionaire and my opponent's pockets were as empty as the inside of George W. Bush's head. He ran out of chump change, then left broke and angry. Not his day.

After that I was feeling pretty good. Lady Luck was on my side. So I looked around again. Everybody shook his or her head. No one had money to gamble, not this crew. All were here waiting for Scamz to toss them a few crumbs.

Time crept by with me listening to Keb' Mo', Memphis Slim, Jonny Lang, Etta James, Ray Charles, and a host of others from the world of blues. Big Slim got out his harmonica and jammed when Popa Chubby came on singing "Since I Lost My Leg." That was his favorite. I'd been coming down here enough that I knew a lot of the songs, had actually started to like the music the way a man likes a woman he used to find not that attractive, the way he starts to like her after he gets to know her, after he has listened to what she has to say and understands her heart.

Made a few dollars as the afternoon passed. Lost a few, but managed to stay a few dollars ahead. Gamblers came and went, moods changed with the customer rotation, moments of frustration bloomed like a rose, an argument or two broke out, and Big Slim didn't hesitate to jump up and squash that ruckus before it became a fight.

The sun went down and blue shadows started falling over the city. A couple of times I went to the pay phone and dialed Pam's pager number, did that so I could listen to her voice. That's the kind of silly thing infatuation makes a grown man do. By then I was getting to the left of being hungry, feeling tired, ready to call it a night and take my ass home.

Then an engine roared outside the front door. Tupac was blasting from speakers that cost as much as a small house. It was loud enough to rattle the windows and make it feel like the start of an earthquake.

Everybody knew who that was. Everybody knew that hard bass line came from a tricked-out Trans Am sporting an eagle on its hood. A ghetto-red ride with sparkly paint that had a plastic Jesus on the dashboard, that kind of false idol that bobbed back and forth and went into convulsions whenever he hit a speed bump. To show how deep he was into his religion, that shyster had the Son of God resting underneath two furry black-and-white dice. The car's engine revved twice before it was cut off. Tupac shut up mid-rant, right between the *mutha* and the *fucka*.

Big Slim gritted his dentures, looked damned uneasy.

The sensor sang like a storm warning and trouble walked in with its chest stuck out.

Trouble had a name and its name was Nazario.

Nazario was an Ecuadorian, six feet tall and just as wide. About as loco as they came. He looked like a man who had been in one drive-by too many. He had just left the care of that wonderful all-male resort named Folsom two years ago, right before I met him. He'd been arrested by LAPD, but when that Rampart police corruption thing went down, Officer Friendly had to admit to wrongdoings and open the cage and set that vulture free. He owned a gangsta reputation, but he was a scab; a renegade who wasn't a card-carrying member to any of the local gangland franchises. That meant he flew solo and always had something to prove with someone else's blood.

A big-boned, big-breasted woman with long blond hair was hanging on to Nazario's right arm. She wore a red, white, and blue pleather Budweiser dress that was shaped like a short can of beer with a plunging neckline, the kind that pimped out her mammary glands to the max. Even with no ass, her shape was decent, but her speckled complexion said that she needed to lay off greasy foods.

All I knew was that the short woman in six-inch heels, she wasn't his wife.

Big Slim stood up and growled.

Nazario flipped the old man off.

Big Slim barked, "Don't keep coming round here disrespect'n my place of biddness."

When Nazario saw me, he nodded. He had a ravenous look in his good eye. His left eye had been thumbed out during a fight at an overcrowded prison in Lancaster, a racial brawl between over a hundred white and Hispanic inmates. He never wore a patch. People said the guy that damaged his eye now gets handicapped parking for life. The fringe benefits of challenging Nazario.

In that raspy voice he said, "D-d-dante."

I hated the way he stuttered my name. Made my flesh crawl every time.

"You st-st-still have my wife's r-r-ring, no?"

I nodded. That was a lie. That ring was resting at a pawnshop in the heart of downtown L.A.

I should've left right then, but I stayed. Nazario had a lot of larceny in his heart for me.

He said, "My w-w-wife, she want her r-r-ring back."

"Sounds like you ready to lose that Trans Am too."

A few people chuckled. Nazario didn't like that. Not at all.

"You think you f-funny, huh? Y-y-you think you the B-B-Billy B-B-Bad Ass?"

"One day we're gonna see eye to eye on things."

More chuckles.

"One day I will g-g-get tired of your eye j-j-jokes."

He clenched his jaw and flexed the muscles in his neck. Then he pulled out a wad of bills that was thick enough to choke a horse. Seeing him flash his cash brought out the wolf in me. I needed to double my money. If I did that, then I could pass on whatever Scamz had to offer, if only for a while.

I patted my right pocket. That let him know I had some cash. He nodded and held up one finger. For Nazario that meant a C-note a game. A hundred dollars is big money for a little man like me. But I had the gas money I had earned from Tommy Boy's charge card. Half of that was in my right pocket; the other half in my left. Never keep all of your cash next to the same hand.

I nodded at Nazario and held up one finger.

We played nine ball. I won the coin flip. On the break, I dropped the eight. The nine hung in the right corner; the one ball was staring it in the face. Nazario cursed, then his woman massaged his shoulder and rubbed those double-Ds up and down his arm. She tightened her eyes at me. I smirked and got ready to start packing my summer clothes. One smooth stroke, the one rolled and the nine dropped.

I was living a hundred in the black. I felt the sun coming out to make my night.

A few people gave up their hustle to watch us play. They loved seeing Nazario lose. Some were bold enough to cheer when he did, mad enough to curse when he won.

Two hours later, my right pocket was emptier than a bucket of condoms at a Death Row after-party. Twenty minutes after that, after having my debt go up and down like NASDAQ, I decided Lady Luck had abandoned me and I stopped when I owed Nazario two bills.

Flat out I said, "I'm done."

"You no d-d-done."

I told Nazario to give me two days to get his ends.

"I ain't n-n-no credit m-m-man." Nazario stood close. "You p-p-pay me now."

"Two days. Standard payoff time. You know the rules up here."

"N-n-no. When I lose to you, when I n-no have m-money, I find a way and I pay you the same day. I take my wife's ring. I p-p-pay you with me own wife's wedding ring, no?"

"You lost way more than two bills. You lucky I took that ring off your hands in the first place."

"I almost have to break her pretty little finger to get it off her hand. She c-c-cry a river when I t-take it from her. I pay you when I lose. You p-pay me with the same ring and we'll be even."

Took him a week to stammer out that thought. In the end I told him, "I don't owe you but two hundred. Stop using devil's arithmetic. You know that damn ring is worth more—"

"Then we shoot more p-p-p-pool until you l-lose that much."

He pushed me, did that like I was a bitch. I didn't like that. Refused to get punked by a bully.

My tone was so hard I didn't recognize my own voice. "Raise the fuck up off me."

"Your d-d-debt d-d-due now. Get me that r-r-ring."

"Don't bogart me, man."

He got all up in my space and bumped me. I growled and popped his chest with the flat of my hands, pushed him off me and got ready to counter whatever his ass was getting ready to throw.

People moved out the way quick, fast, and in a hurry.

He swung at me wide and hard. Air whooshed by like a 747, damn near took my head off.

My heart took residence in my throat. I was back in juvenile hall, in my prison blues, having to prove myself to a lesser man by getting ready to kick ass before I got mine kicked.

I weaved to the side of his vacant eye socket, fell into Sugar Shane mode. My deft moves didn't intimidate Nazario. He was about to jump at me, but Big Slim hobbled over as fast as he could. Sounded like an old freight train on a rusty track. That old man grabbed Nazario's shoulder and yanked his attitude back. Nazario jerked away from his grip, then snarled at Big Slim like he'd been betrayed.

Nazario balled his fist and drew back at Big Slim.

Big Slim didn't flinch; he made a grrrr sound, then said, "Ain't gonna say it no more. Take that ruckus outside. This a 'spectable place of biddness."

Nazario grabbed his crotch and yelled, "Suck my d-d-dick, you fat cr-cripple *pendejo*."

"Wha'chu say to me, boy?"

Silence and glares between Big Slim and Nazario; an aging buffalo staring down a one-eyed ox.

Nazario reminded Big Slim that every television in this place, the computers, even the security cameras, all of that electronic gear had been bought from him using his five-finger discount.

That five-finger thing was Nazario's idea of a joke.

Big Slim told Nazario, "That's your last time disrespectin' me, boy."

Nazario repeated his insult, said it loud enough for everyone on Ventura to hear.

Big Slim snapped, "Get your ugly woman and stutter your way out my place of biddness."

Nazario wrenched his shirt back. A pearl handle was sticking out of his belt. My heart tried to hide behind a rib, and when it couldn't go south, it moved north up to my throat.

Big Slim said, "Don't pull out nothing you cain't eat."

"Eat this." Nazario grabbed his crotch and offered Big Slim another shot at bent-knee intimacy. Big Slim stared, breathing sped up. Sweat flowered on his chapped lips; saliva edged from the corner of his mouth. Nazario headed for the door, bragging about his roughness, hand on crotch, massaging his sacs of brains and screaming for Big Slim to suck him dry.

His voluptuous Budweiser adjusted her double-Ds and followed with no words.

At the door Nazario paused, then sang, "D-d-dante."

I snapped out in my hardest tone, "What?"

"You n-n-no have my wife ring," he smiled, "you Alfalfa."

He was talking about Alfalfa from the Little Rascals. That was the ultimate threat.

The sensor beeped as the door opened and closed.

I looked around the room. All eyes were on me.

The engine to his ride fired up. Tupac came back to life and vibrated the windows, shook the building like we were having an aftershock. Nazario's car screeched away from the curb in front of the rest of traffic.

My palms were too damp. So was my neck. Heart thumped like a warrior's drum.

Big Slim was still near me. He gritted his false teeth together. He was staring up at that picture of Dorothy Dandridge, and sadness masked his face. His lips moved like he was talking to that dead star, then the sadness vanished. He grimaced around the room, at the women who were standing in puddles of fear. Then the old man glanced down at his mangled hands.

"Bastard stood underneath my picture and told me to put my mouth on his damn johnson. That mammy's boy told me to suck his nature. Gutter talked me right in front of three colored women."

Big Slim trudged away. His uneven steps echoed like an explosion. He took a seat back in his circular booth, his eyes locked in the direction Nazario had gone. Big Slim was mumbling, shifting and shaking his head. Without warning, he reached underneath the counter and pulled out a twelve-gauge shotgun. He slammed the death-maker on the counter. Every eye in the place enlarged and went to him.

He barked, "Everybody get the hell outta my place of biddness."

Everyone stopped shooting pool. I grabbed my leather jacket and turned to leave with the crowd.

Big Slim called out, "Dante. Lock the do' to my place of biddness and c'mere, boy."

His overpowering voice chilled me. I turned and came back to him, but his eyes were glazed over. He was in his own world, talking to himself. "Yessir, that boy come up in my place of biddness and told me to put my mouth on his private parts. Pink boys down in Big Foot Country didn't even talk to plantation niggers like that. That mammy's boy talked to me like I was a fool."

His lips kept moving, his southern accent so thick I couldn't decipher his words. At some point the words faded. He rocked a moment, then stopped.

He blinked and focused his eyes on me. "Scamz wanna see you before he leave for the night."

"How long ago he tell you?"

"Back when I came out of the shit house."

"That was damn near four hours back. You waited four—" I choked on my anger. "I could've still had some damn money in my pocket, and that whole thing with that loco mofo Nazario could've—"

His wrath rained down on me and he snapped, " 'Member who you talking to, boy."

I raised both palms and agreed with a nod. "Why you just now telling me?"

"Because I just now felt like it, nigger."

I said, "Dante."

"What you say?"

"Said my name's Dante. You can call me a boy, but I ain't never been a nigga."

"Then, boy, you worse kinda nigger. One who is and thank he ain't."

He told me where to go to meet Scamz, then sat back down and scowled at the front door, veins rising and falling in his thick neck, massaging his razor bumps and palming that shotgun like he was wishing for Nazario to come back to battle. He was an old man thinking the thoughts of the suicidal.

He said, "If anybody ask you where Scamz at, disremember what I done told you."

I nodded and headed for the double doors.

Then an engine roared out on Ventura Boulevard. Windows vibrated like a T-rex was outside. Tupac came back on. My anxious stride evolved into slow steps.

Big Slim commanded, "Lock my damn do' 'fo that bastard come back in here."

I sped up and locked the front doors. I was scared, but didn't want it to show. I didn't have any kind of a weapon and he could have anything.

"Alfalfa!" That cry came from the other side of the front door. "G-get my wife ring, Alfalfa!"

The doors shook; Nazario tried to rip them off their hinges. The dead bolts earned their keep.

Big Slim told me, "Hightail it the back way, come out down by Handy J's car wash."

The front doors shook again, and then there were other rumbles. Other voices speaking in the original language of this part of the world. Sounded like Nazario had run and got his whole country.

I did an about-face at a kick-ass pace and headed toward the back, but paused when I passed by that faded green door that was always locked. The one people said Big Slim kept his missing fingers in.

I took the door club off the back, creaked the reinforced door open, and stepped out into the alley. Listened before I let that heavy door close behind me. Outside of a barking dog and trash bins, the alley was clear. There was enough noise to hide my footsteps. Looked around for a weapon, anything that could double as a club. A few loose bricks were scattered on the ground. Had to settle for one of those.

I kept a greyhound stride over pissed-on and oil-stained pavement all the way down to Calhoun. There was nothing back here but businesses. I cut over a lot and went to Moorpark and clung to Lady Darkness like she was the woman of my dreams, made it to Oscar without them seeing me.

I dumped the brick, popped the trunk, and pulled out my Louisville Slugger. Then I tried to wake up Oscar. He let out the kind of cough that let me know that no matter how much supreme gasoline I fed him, he no longer wanted to put on his best Goodyear and race the autobahn. Cruising between forty and sixty suited him just fine.

Right now I needed him to go faster.

I pulled out into traffic and Oscar stalled. People blew horns, flashed high beams, and zipped by while he chug-a-lugged and let out a series of late-night hiccups. Fuel wasn't circulating the way it should. Then he growled like he was giving it his best, and everything evened out and let me know he was wide awake, ready to roll into the night. I patted the cracked dash, thanked Oscar for being here for me when I needed him. Morning, noon, or midnight, not once had he failed me.

I put that Louisville Slugger in reaching distance, kept my eyes on my rearview as much as I could all the way up Moorpark and cut over to Laurel Canyon. The road became narrow and a lot of headlights were coming my way at high speeds, so I had to stay focused to avoid a head-on collision. I took that winding route carved through the mountains for about ten miles and it dumped me out at the Sunset Strip, a boulevard that had as much foot traffic as Times Square and was lined with just as many larger-than-life billboards advertising everything from CK cologne to the latest whacked movies of the month.

It was nighttime and hard to tell, but it looked like a ghetto-red car was following me. I sped up and went straight instead of making my turn, zoomed by the Virgin megastore, made a few quick turns, and sped back out on Sunset down by the Guitar Store. Every time I saw a red car in my rearview, my heart double-timed and I turned and raced through the side streets like a mouse in a maze.

He had called me Alfalfa.

Alfalfa had been killed over a fifty-dollar debt.

5

"About time you showed up, Dante." Scamz put his glass of wine on the edge of the rose-colored tub. The jets were massaging his skin. Air smelled like jasmine. "I called you two weeks ago."

"Just a few hours ago. It's still my birthday."

"Seems like weeks ago."

"That's because you're an impatient brother."

Scamz was lying in a round bathtub filled with bubbly Calgon, relaxing while he slowly smoked a slender Djarum cigarette, a cancer stick that made the air smell like cloves. Chopin was coming out of the ceiling speakers.

He said, "Big Slim called me up ten minutes ago."

"Kinda figured he would. Shit got crazy down there for a minute."

"What did Nazario say to Slim?"

"Get it from Big Slim."

On the counter was a pullout section of the *L.A. Times*, the real estate part for homes in Hancock Park, Hollywood, and Hollywood Hills, where we were now. A few were circled in red ink, homes on Laurelmont, Nichols Canyon, Yucca Trail, Sycamore Avenue, North Hudson, and a few others.

I motioned toward the paper. "Rent scam?"

He nodded, picked up his Movado, checked the time, then put the timepiece back down. "You need to be self-employed. As long as you working for somebody else, you will be subject to getting laid off. A brother should map his own destiny instead of waiting for crumbs from any man's table."

Scamz hummed, waved his left hand like he was orchestrating each chord. A petite, bowlegged sister with exotic eyes and a face that reminded me of the Egyptian queen Nefertiti slid by wearing a denim vest and long floral skirt. She floated in and handed Scamz a fresh glass of Chablis. Her enchanting fragrance arrested my thoughts for a moment, had to struggle to look away. I'd guess that she was no more than twenty. Half of Scamz's age. That was the way he liked 'em.

"Dante," Scamz said without looking up, "meet Sierra."

Her face was as stern as it was beautiful. Small narrow nose, full lips, the extraordinary look of an African woman integrated with the striking looks of a Pacific Islander.

With a slight bob of the head, I tendered my tone, said, "How you doing?"

She dropped her head and swayed away, a supreme walk with a subtle side-to-side, I-am-woman rhythm. As she was about to turn the corner, she stopped and stared, caught my eyes that were following her silent rhythm. A chill ran from my toes to the base of my skull.

In between blinks it seemed like she vanished. Seconds later, pots and pans rattled. The kitchen was a good distance away, so she had to be slamming them damn hard.

Scamz chuckled. He said, "What you looking for?"

"What she mad about?"

"Wants me to stop seeing Arizona."

"She looks like Arizona."

"Think so?"

"Nicer ass. Lighter complexion. What happened to Arizona, anyway?"

"Tripping." He blew smoke. "So I shipped her out to Mo Val."

Mo Val was Moreno Valley, two hours deeper into the desert. That was where he sent his concubines when he'd had enough of them.

"Sierra looks kinda young."

"Older than she looks, but not as old as Arizona."

"What does she do?"

"She works at Wells Fargo."

That meant Scamz had access to credit card numbers, checking account information. In this business a teller who made seven dollars an hour was worth a million bucks.

I nodded. "What's Arizona, about twenty-five?"

"Twenty-two."

"Ancient. She'll be ready for Geritol and trading her thongs in for Depends pretty soon."

"Somebody got jokes. I don't want nothing old but money."

I laughed the kind of laugh that's shared between men.

He said, "Sisters over twenty-two or -three have too much baggage. And they blame it all on the black man."

I slid my tongue across my top teeth.

The pots and pans were still clanging.

He went on, "Lover, brother, or father, you have to carry the burden of every man who did them wrong before you."

More clanging.

He motioned toward the noise. "Let 'em stick around too long, they get emotional."

After a few minutes of conversation, I was standing there beating around the bush and hoping Scamz would tell me what he had in mind. He asked, "What made you modify your state of mind?"

"Who said I changed my mind?"

Scamz dried off, put a white cotton housecoat on, and didn't say much while he used Dermalogica products to cleanse his face. When he was done grooming, he boasted about a few other ventures he'd invested in. He and some associates—probably his stable of women—had run another credit card scam by calling people and telling them they had won some expensive prizes, but they would need to give their card numbers for verification before the prizes could be shipped out.

He said all of it was done without his name or image ever being associated. I don't know his real name. On top of the dresser, next to all of his bottles of cologne, he had five driver's licenses in five different names. I don't think *he* knew who he was.

I asked, "What did you need me for?"

"When are you going to sign on with me full-time and stop job shopping?"

"You're sounding like a headhunter."

"I recognize talent. How many schemes do you know off the top of your head?"

"Twenty, maybe thirty ways to rob a man without a gun."

Scamz moisturized his short hair, made it Creole wavy, then put on a dark four-button suit, dark blue shirt, golden tie. He looked like a financial planner from Dean Witter.

He said, "But you don't use your skills."

"You told me to come up here to talk about some work."

I followed him into the white-walled living room filled with impressionist pictures and European-theme knickknacks. We stood next to a pearl-white baby grand piano in front of the bay windows and looked down on the city.

He said, "The view of all views."

I nodded.

"When I was a kid back in Alabama, we didn't have hot water. No money for a decent hot water heater. Had to boil water to take baths. Would boil it in big pots, carry it to the bathroom."

I said, "You've come a long way."

"Everybody down on catfish row was always fighting for one bathroom. Hitting trains just to steal cans of soup. Not eating three, four days in a row."

"How many of you?"

"Twelve to fourteen, depends on the day of the week. My sister had six kids by six men." His voice was just above a whisper. "Momma had to take care of them all until the day she died. Most of us had to do what we had to do to get food on the table. Lie, cheat, and steal for every meal."

"Scamz?"

"Yeah?"

"I liked that story better when you said you were from Mississippi."

He laughed. The only part of that story that stayed the same was the part about having no hot water, no amenities, and his momma raising everybody's children. Always twelve to fourteen of them in a two-bedroom, one-bath house. There was never a man in his tales, never a father figure to keep him on the straight and narrow. So, if you asked me what I thought, those were the parts I thought were true. It just moved from state to state. That makes me think he's always lived the life of a grifter. Tells so many lies he has to believe them to make them ring true. He has to fool himself before he can fool other people.

Trails of cars were rushing up and down the Sunset Strip below, everybody looking for something. The windows were open just enough for a cool breeze to wash into the dimly lit place. I glanced around at this museum of a house. There wasn't a single picture of people anywhere in sight. This place was one square foot short of being a mansion. I wondered whose multimillion-dollar crib this was, because I knew it wasn't Scamz's long-term hideaway. That meant the doors could bust open with bad news at any moment. Before I could ask, the smell of fresh marijuana crept up on me.

Sierra was behind us on the red leather sofa with her legs folded up under her yoga-style, inhaling a badly rolled joint. A bowl of reefer and Zig-Zags were on the wood floor, right up under her. I hadn't heard her come into the room. Until then I hadn't even seen her reflection in the window.

She had a bottle of Alizé to go with her cannabis.

Scamz stared down at Hollywood like he owned the damn thing. Sierra was watching me. I glanced at her.

She inhaled the smoke, held it, then blew the fumes toward me. She sipped her Alizé, did that slow and easy, put the joint back up to her face, then switched her routine and let the fumes rise up into her nostrils.

Scamz said, "You can hit it."

I jumped out of my trance. "I don't get high no more."

"The way you looking at that joint, I couldn't tell." Scamz chuckled at me the way a man did when he was amused by a little boy. "You were looking at the joint, right?"

"That joint has more meat on it than your women."

He laughed a little harder. I was being serious.

He said, "Sierra, come here, sweetie."

She came to him.

He said, "Kiss Dante."

That caught me off guard. She cut her eyes at me. Then she kissed Scamz. After that she walked away.

Scamz drew his smoke and smiled like he owned the world.

That disturbed me. I asked, "What the fuck was that all about?"

"Loyalty."

6

I followed Scamz out through the kitchen door to a midnight-blue Benz—a CL600 with GPS navigation hardware, Bose sound package, and a device that lets the driver tell the car to stay a specific distance away from the car in front. A ride that cost at least a hundred fifty thousand. He pushed a button on the remote, and the car unlocked and started like it was the Batmobile. To Scamz all of that was no big deal.

I asked, "How much this set you back?"

"Not much. About as much as a used Miata."

I believed him. Scamz got all of his rides from chop shops. That meant the VIN on the doors and the engine never matched. Down at the local chop shop they had to take out the front window and remove the rear quarter panel because it had the VIN on it too. He could pay eight thousand and walk away with a sixty-thousand-dollar ride. The title would be clear, and even if he was pulled over, One Time never checked the VIN numbers, just ran the tags.

He said, "You come aboard and I can set you up with a ride. Get you into a nice place."

"No, thanks. Oscar is doing just fine."

"We could make a lot of money."

"Just let me know what you got right now, then I'm out."

We hopped in that ride and floated down the narrow, snaking hill. No turbulence on this flight. Made me want to forget about my grumpy old Oscar. Scamz played classical music, tunes with pianos and harps and people humming like angels. He played those kinda tunes all the way. Neither of us said a word. He was always quiet when his thoughts were brewing with schemes; I was silent because my thoughts were on Pam. Wondering how to get her that hook-up I had promised.

I asked, "So, is Sierra taking Arizona's place on the other runs?"

"Nah. The information she's bringing me from Wells Fargo will suffice."

I made a curious sound. "Can you use another employee on the runs you got coming up?"

"You still trying to get me to give Jackson some work?"

"That too. But was thinking you might need another woman worker."

"Who you got in mind?"

I told him about Pam. Told him how she had played old Tommy Boy up at her job, how she stayed cool and calm in the face of pandemonium. Asked him if he could use somebody like her. Told him she was mature, and I could tell she wasn't about no bull.

He asked, "She white?"

"A sister."

"Hmmm."

To most people that would've sounded like he was coming down with a case of negrophobia. It was all business and I knew what he meant. What he did was easier to do with white people. Black and brown skin labels you as a suspect from birth. And the whiter the better. Older the better. An old wrinkled-up white woman can take a bogus charge card, walk into a computer store with no ID, and walk out with ten thousand dollars in merchandise, NQA. A sister or a black man walks in with ten thousand in cash to buy the same state-of-the-art equipment, and they get stalled out at the cash register; LAPD gets summoned like a mofo.

He asked me what I had in mind for Pam, in the big scheme of things.

I said, "She just need to make some cheddar to knock out a big bill."

"Casual workers need to apply at the post office."

I did more to sell him on using Pam. Not pushing too hard. Just told him how she changed her hair and that gave her a brand-new flavor, anything from J Lo with braids to Foxy Brown with an Afro. A look that was hard to track. My verbal flow stayed easy, very matter-of-fact. I never pushed too hard, not with men. Not with a brother like Scamz. I wasn't one for begging. He just listened. This was business more than anything, so I kept my tone like he kept his, smooth and professional.

His phone rang. Scamz asked me to excuse him for a moment, then pushed a button on the hands-free, and Arizona's voice came in, her Filipino accent loud and clear.

Scamz said, "When did you get back in town?"

"My plane just landed. I'm leaving Ontario airport."

"What's up?"

She said something in her mother's native tongue. It was all gibberish to me.

"In English or Spanish," Scamz said as he changed lanes. "I can't speak Tagalog that well."

"Why are you acting so shady?" she asked in a tone that sounded like she was pulling her own hair out. "I'm starting to feel . . . I feel invisible. We need to talk."

"I'm busy."

"You weren't too busy when I was flying from Seattle to South Beach for you."

"I'm busy right now."

"Where are you?"

"I'm mobile."

She paused. "Well, can I drive out and see you tonight?"

"Not tonight."

There was a pause. She asked, "That manipulative bitch with you?"

"Talk like a lady, not a whore."

"I call her what she acts like. Is that bitch—"

Scamz introduced her to the click. He paused for a second; a stress line came and went in his forehead, then it vanished. He bottled his irritation and told me, "Tell me about your lady friend."

Before we could pick up our conversation where we left off, the phone rang again.

"What the fuck, are you a manic-fucking-depressive or something?"

Scamz hung up again.

The phone rang again. He clicked it on. Kelis's played-out mantra "I hate you so much right now" was being blasted on the other end.

Again, Scamz hung up.

He asked me, "How old is your friend?"

"Thirty-something. Dunno."

"I hope you're not doing this to impress her."

The phone rang again and saved me from having to lie. Again he answered using the hands-free. Arizona came on the line yelling in Tagalog. Scamz turned the phone off in the middle of her tirade.

He said, "That's the kind of shit you have to deal with with a twenty-year-old."

"That's why I go older."

"Mature doesn't mean sane. Thirty-year-olds get the same way."

Not if you treat 'em right was my thought. But Jackson had treated his women right. Had treated all of his women right as far as I knew. And even when a woman treated her man like a king there were no guarantees at emotional reciprocation.

I let that sentiment go and replied, "Spoken like a pro."

We ended that conversation. He parked across the street from the House of Blues and we went into the Comedy Emporium. The joint was a block-long, two-floor, three-stage, rambunctious comedy house. We got a table near the back, a spot where we could see who came in before they saw us.

I rubbed my palms together and asked, "Who we waiting for?"

"A friend."

"Male or female?"

"Female."

I relaxed a bit.

Laughter surrounded us while a waitress came over and whispered in Scamz's ear; he peeped over his shoulder. A slender white woman was standing in the doorway that separated the smaller rinky-dink stage with amateur performers from the larger comedy room with the paid professionals. She was pushing fifty but it didn't show, wearing a red business suit and a stylish black felt hat big enough to tint her face. Like most of the eclectic Hollywood set, she had on designer shades after sunset.

I knew her. She used to be one of Scamz's partners both in crime and carnal sin.

Scamz said, "Sit tight."

She disappeared. Scamz followed. I listened to the comedienne.

". . . damn anthrax got me so scared, I ain't opening my bills. Hell, bills look mighty suspicious to me. Especially the ones with the red writing across the front. I know the sign of a threat when I see one. Anytime somebody want my damn money, hell, that's suspicious."

Some time went by. Enough for me to get concerned. I went the way Scamz had gone. Didn't see him in the crowded hallway. I bumped by comics and groupies. I passed by the john and my bladder asked to make a quick pit stop. The john was like a train station at rush hour, people coming in and out, some drunk as hell. One guy still had traces of white medicinal powder on his thin nose.

In a serious Eminem tone he asked me, "Know where I can score some Ecstasy up in this motherfucker?"

"Ask anybody in the hallway. They should be able to hook ya up."

I heard jingling and grunts coming from the stall behind me. Thought maybe somebody had got some food poisoning or something. Then I saw a man's shoes, his pants around his ankles. Not Scamz's shoes, not his pants. But this guy wasn't alone. A pair of red pumps with three-inch spiked heels were on either side of his legs, facing the wall. The way his change was jingling, she was giving the man a serious ride.

I flushed, washed my hands, left the john, went back to the table. Stayed pretty nervous as I half-watched a tall, dark, and bald brother hit the stage and do his act.

"One of the big problems with sex is miscommunication . . . ," he said.

Chuckles were all around me and I jumped when I felt a soft pat on my shoulder. I looked up into the face of pale skin, blond hair with purple streaks, and jet-black lipstick. She pointed toward the exit. Scamz was waiting under the sign. My stress level went down ten notches.

Scamz made a head gesture, then vanished. I followed-the-leader once again.

". . . most men make love like a union worker. Clock in for fifteen minutes, then wanna take an eight-hour break."

Scamz had an envelope in his hand and slid it into his pocket. We bumped through the stench of funnier-than-thou attitudes and groupies in the crowded hall and walked out the back way.

He patted my shoulder. "Thanks for watching my back."

"Didn't know I did. I see the Bad Witch is back in town."

"Yep."

"Heard she was playing golf and eating quiche out at Club Fed."

"Nope. She's back."

We passed the Hyatt, rounded the corner, and headed up the steep hill toward the car. A green Mustang 5.0 screeched next to us. A thick, young Hawaiian-looking guy with a ponytail and goatee hopped out and slammed the door like he was doing a General Motors stress test on the car. If his headlights had been off, I would've hit the ground because I'd've thought it was a typical West Coast drive-by. But the driver in a drive-by never got out the car. Think that was rule one in Drive-by-ology.

He cut us off, glared directly at Scamz. "Where's Sierra?"

He sounded like an angry, jilted lover.

My body tensed and I sized homie up: about five-ten, wearing baggy Levi's and a sleeveless FUBU shirt. His hands were empty; that meant his threat was too.

"Hey, asshole!" Spit flew off the tip of his tongue. "I know you hear me."

I stalled and rolled my fingers into fearful fists. Scamz didn't flinch or slow his uphill stride. The guy tried to block his path. Scamz sidestepped him without a word. He grabbed Scamz's shoulder.

Big mistake.

I cringed.

Scamz elbowed him square in his face. I heard a cracking sound. Scamz mule-kicked the guy's nuts. His knees buckled and he dropped in so much pain he couldn't mutter a sound.

The violence jarred me because it came out of nowhere, had started and ended just like that. The boy was wiggling, oinking, and rolling around between parked cars. I was about to reach down and tell him to stay down if he wanted Scamz's agitation to end right there, but I stepped away. Like in juvenile hall, you have to know when it's your battle and when it's someone else's. Plus it was under control. Scamz was moving on. I stepped over the boy's moans and let it be.

Scamz wiped down his coat and strutted on.

I took a last look back at the man on the concrete. Never run up on trouble unprepared. He'd learned a lesson in Street Confrontation 101. Always know who you're fucking with.

Scamz said, "Pussy and money, Dante."

I nodded. "I hear you."

"I wonder if more people been killed over pussy or money."

He sounded like a cross between Tupac and Plato, and he was damn serious.

I asked, "You kill over money?"

He laughed that sneaky laugh.
I asked, "Pussy?"
He laughed again.

Scamz didn't mention the reason for the beat down
he'd just served that dude. I didn't ask. We hopped back
in his chariot and Scamz rode the boulevard with ten
thousand other vehicles that were cruising the strip. It
was bumper-to-bumper for a few miles until we made it
down by the Pantages Theater. They had the brightest
lights down that way, advertising *The Lion King*.

We didn't share a word as we passed people in top-of-
the-line threads, remained silent as we cruised by homeless teenagers, runaways and disposable kids who
squatted in abandoned buildings. I found myself staring
at a woman. She was leaning on a shopping cart out on
dead stars' names on the Walk of Fame, Styrofoam cup
in her callused hand, begging strangers for handouts.

I'm afraid I'll end up in that club. Sometimes I see my
face on them, and that keeps me up some nights, tossing
and turning from that nightmare back toward the
screams that live inside my head.

I blinked back to the here and now. "You taking the
long way."

"You in a hurry?"

"Nope, no job to go to in the morning." I yawned. "No
woman with a glorious ass to go to tonight. Ain't got
nowhere to go. Nowhere at all."

His phone beeped and let him know somebody had
called while we were out of the car. He got on the
hands-free. Started checking his messages. That "I hate
you so much right now" song was on the first eight. Arizona had called quite a few times, each message more
intense than the one before.

". . . you don't deserve to be with somebody as great
as me and as beautiful as I am and as loving as I am. You
need to be with a back-stabbing, lowlife bitch like
Sierra. Bitch used me to get to you. So you don't fucking have to worry about me calling you and wishing you

a good day or any of that stupid-ass shit I've been doing. When you end up in jail, don't expect me to send you books. Asshole."

She hung up.

Then there was the last message. Arizona was crying. All she said was, "I love you."

That was more powerful than all the other messages combined.

Scamz replayed that one twice, didn't erase it like he'd done all the others. If I didn't know any better, I'd say that one got to him a little, that Arizona was under his skin and he was resisting her by running to another woman. If we talked on the level I communicated with Jackson, I would've asked what was on his mind, but we never talk about emotional stuff, and that was cool by me. Made me wish I had a woman who felt that strongly about me. If I did have her, I probably wouldn't know what to do with her, outside of a few nights at Motel Dante. In my financial condition, I couldn't do much for her.

Scamz lit up another Djarum and turned his music up a notch. The CD player emancipated the sounds of Mozart while Scamz conducted his imaginary orchestra. His vibes were as relaxed as when he was laid out in the bath with Sierra serving him like he was Zeus in a hot tub.

"Not too crazy about using that many black people in a crew," he said, answering some question inside his mind before he addressed me: "So, you think your waitress friend can be trusted?"

"I'll vouch. Pay her out of my cut."

"You need the money. I'll pay her at a woman's rate."

"That don't bother me."

"Might need her. Can't trust Arizona."

"Whassup wit dat rampage?"

"She wants me to be what I can never be."

"A one-woman man."

"I recognize my carnal weaknesses, my love of making love, and I embrace who I am."

"Spoken like a true player."

* * *

By the time we made it back to the house on the hill, Sierra's clothes were in the living room, on the sofa, and she was walking through the place naked. We stepped in just as she was heading through the sliding glass doors, a towel over her shoulder, glass of Alizé in one hand, a fresh joint in the other.

A rectangular pool was out there on the edge, framed by white metal rails, a one-hundred-foot drop to the nearest neighbor. She dove in one end, swam to the other, the lights at the bottom of the pool highlighting her every stroke. She did the same, underwater.

Scamz asked, "What you thinking?"

"She could use a bikini wax."

"You crack me up."

We disengaged from dialogue and fell into conversational hiatus as Sierra provided the entertainment. I stood next to Scamz and watched her without shame. I could see why that dude ran up on Scamz when we left the comedy club. A woman who looked like that would be hard to let go.

He said, "Tell your woman friend I'll give her a shot."

"Thanks. I'll hit her when I leave here."

"And I'll get in contact with Jackson."

"Okay. He'll appreciate it. He's in a bind."

"Read the paper; the whole world is in a bind."

"C'mon, Scamz. Help the brother out. He's sixteen G in the hole."

"That's not my problem."

"You know how he got played."

"Learn that lesson. Long line of men with the same regrets. Clocks never run backward, not even for the best of men."

"All that to say . . . ?"

"Be careful where you stick your dick. Do wrong and the devil will come to collect his due."

I nodded. Once again he was my father. My brother. My mentor.

I said, "Jackson'll be glad to get his hands on some cabbage."

"Under one condition."

"Depends on the condition."

"Tell me what Nazario said to Big Slim."

I felt like a snitch, and a snitch was two rungs lower than a bitch, but I reminded myself who was my friend and who wasn't, and repainted that picture. Told him about the game that I had lost, then told how Nazario tried to jump bad in front of his mud duck with big breasts, then how Big Slim hobbled in and squashed that ruckus in the making.

Lines grew in Scamz's forehead. He cursed, called Nazario a few not so nice names. Scamz doesn't curse much, hardly at all. When he swore, it let you know that the other side of him—that side no one wanted to reckon with—was on the rise.

Scamz got on his phone, started talking to somebody in Spanish. I had no idea what he said.

Nazario's name was spoken. The tone became very intense and the words sounded final.

Scamz hung up.

Then silence. He was in an abyss of thoughts. Making hard, twelfth-hour decisions.

I asked, "Who was that?"

"Nazario's contact. Had to cut Nazario loose."

Scamz did that like he had more power than the judge I'd seen at Superior Court.

I got a little nervous but I didn't let it show.

"Nazario was supposed to do a couple of runs on the brown side of town. Racist people down there pimp those immigrants in the sweatshops. I was hooking them up with some documentation."

"Nothing like a man with a soft heart."

"Shoot me for being non-racist and liberal. So to keep my schedule on track I'll have to handle those runs myself. I made some promises, and I'm a man of my word."

"You don't usually do that kinda risky shit."

"Business is business. I made promises."

"You cutting Nazario out of the profits? You know that's not gonna sit well with him."

"I don't disrespect his people. Racist people can't work for me. Won't tolerate it."

"I hear ya. So, you gonna get somebody else to do that run or what?"

"Too late in the game."

"Sure you can handle it?"

"We can do it. In and out in fifteen minutes."

I rubbed my palms together. "Man, that's Nazario's side of town."

"Some good people are living down there in the middle of a bad reputation. Not all of those people are bad." He took a draw from his smoke and looked at me. "You look uncomfortable."

"You should too."

I told Scamz that I'd read in the paper, maybe seen on the news, that there were at least thirty-three gangs in Boyle Heights. That they had some sort of Operation Cease Fire going on.

"Every now and then a boss has to take on the role of an employee to keep the company going."

I said, "Every now and then a manager has to get on fries."

That got some laughter out of him, eased the tension.

"C'mon, now," I said. "What else you got that's not so hot? Show me the cool, easy work."

"Like I said earlier, renting out some property. Been running that for a week or so. Now we're in the final stages of that operation."

"That's why the Bad Witch is in town."

"Yep."

Sierra came in butt naked with a smile on her face, using a towel to fluff dry her back-length hair, Alizé in hand, water dripping from her skin, raining from her vagina. She looked like forbidden fruit ready to be dipped in warm honey, more erotic than the art in the Rondu collection.

I said, "Arizona made it sound like they know each other."

He nodded.

My thoughts went back to my old man and that Indian woman he was seeing. For a moment Sierra was that woman, and it seemed like my old man was standing next to me. I blinked away those rainbows and came back with a jolt.

Sierra headed for the bedroom and turned on some romantic music. I took that as my cue to grab my keys and head for the door. Hated to leave the warmth in this place, but it was time to go.

He said, "Hold up."

"Whassup?"

Scamz reached into his inside suit pocket and pulled out the envelope he had when we left the comedy club. He counted off twenty crisp Jeffersons that smelled like economic relief. The few ends he pulled out didn't even put a dent in the rest he had left. What he counted off didn't even faze him.

I asked, "What's this for?"

"Watching my back. Your birthday. You decide."

I didn't argue. Starving men never turn down a hot meal.

I thought about another hot meal I wanted to savor.

I asked, "You got a hook-up at 360?"

"When?"

"Tonight."

"I'll get you in. Get your party on, young buck."

"One more thing," I said. "Pass on two hundred to Nazario for me so I can get that fool off my back."

"I'm washing my hands of him."

His glare told me that a war was about to break out. I was afraid. Very afraid. Hoped I could get paid and get out before bombs started falling.

I said, "Don't let me down on Jackson. He got kids and shit."

Scamz rubbed his brow like he was fed up with me asking for that favor, but he pushed his lips up into a political smile and said, "I'm a man of my word."

He walked me across the marble floors to the front door.

We shook hands. That was the same as me signing on the dotted line using my blood.

I headed outside, strutted by the line of Mexican palms and evergreen trees. Oscar was glad to see me. Think he got kinda jealous when he saw me riding off in that Benz. I climbed inside and patted him on the dash. He was a little cold, but he started right up without coughing too much. He was ready to go burn off some of that high-priced gas in his belly.

I drove around Hollywood before I took the 101 South. Got on for about two exits, got off, then got right back on the 101 heading north.

Call me paranoid, color me cautious, but I did that to make sure nobody was following me. Scamz has a lot of enemies. A man in his field makes a foe with every sunrise, has an enemy in search of him every sunset. And I didn't need any foes by association, no more than I already had.

7

I paged Pam as soon as I got home. She called back within five minutes.

"Somebody beep me from this number?"

She sounded somewhere between anxious and irritated; had a very serious tone.

I said, "It's Dante."

"Don who?"

I reminded her who I was, told I her I had met her at her job. There was a lot of noise in the background, a lot of laughter. I had to talk loud and she had to yell.

She said, "Be specific. I have three jobs."

"How many wallets do you lift in a day?"

"Oh. It's you." She paused. Her tone became reluctant. "Didn't think I'd hear from you."

"I'm a man of my word."

"Thought this was a callback for an audition."

"The way you worked that wallet thing, you could say that."

"I see." Again she paused. More reluctance. "So, what's the word?"

"My friend said he can use you, if you're down."

"Okay. What do I do now?"

"Not over the phone."

"Why not? You just busted me out over the phone for lifting a wallet."

"Not over the phone."

"Well, I'm out on a date."

"With your boyfriend?"

She gave me a sigh of impatience. "Can we talk in the morning?"

"Tonight. If you want this gig, we talk face-to-face tonight."

There was a pause.

"What kinda money we talking?"

"Between six hundred and a thousand for an easy day of work."

Another pause.

She said, "Meet you where?"

I told her where I'd be.

She said, "After Melanie Comacho does her act, I'll see what I can do. No promises."

Club 360 was down at Sunset and Vine. I stood in the cold while people valet-parked and stepped toward the velvet rope. A bouncer who looked like Mike Tyson getting a root canal guarded that plush barrier. He was second to a sister in an auburn super weave. She had the guest list so she had the power to veto all who approached her domain. She guarded it as if it were the secret recipe to KFC.

Bundled up in my black leather coat, black wool pants, turtleneck, I waited about an hour. A stretch Humvee pulled up followed by cars with vanity plates that read 1 U HAF 2 C and 1 FINE AZ and BLK MN 4 U and CKLT STR and 2 TALL 4 U, and some with frames that read DESTINED FOR FAME and ACTORS ALLEY and BLACK ACTOR IS FRENCH FOR 'I BE UNEMPLOYED.'

Just about when I figured Pam had left me hanging, she pulled up in a green Nissan. Her ride was about six years old. She got out, put on her long leather coat, handed her keys to the valet, then looked around like she couldn't remember what I looked like. I waved. She tightened her coat and came to me.

She said, "You look different in your gear."

"So do you."

We did the handshake thing, no smiles, then she followed my quick stroll toward the velvet rope.

I told the guardian of that kingdom, "My name is on the list."

Pam shifted like she was having second thoughts. Or maybe she was just cold. She had on black pants, the tight kind that clung to her shape, but not made for thermal purposes. A black top that wasn't thick enough to hide the outline of her dark bra. Mocha lipstick. Her bushy hair looking pretty funky.

The guardian said, "I don't see your name, Don Trey."

"No, Dante. Like Dante's Inferno."

"Your name is Inferno?"

"No. Last name Black. First name D-a-n-t-e."

That woman had on all black, a boob shirt, glitter all over her skin. She eyed me up and down and in less than a second came to the conclusion that she'd never sleep with me. That's the litmus test for lots of peeps. Either you're doable or undoable. She was also in the latter category. Too much makeup on her face, the kind of mud that messed up a man's sheets, and not enough meat on her bones.

After the sister worked out that alphabetical thing and found my name, she nodded at big dude and he eased up the velvet rope with so much gentleness that I almost laughed.

Pam walked behind me, not too close.

Inside the lobby, two more women with perfect makeup stopped me for round two, a more thorough inspection. They checked out my spit-shined shoes. Gave Pam the once-over two times. Had to have a certain look, both cosmetically and wardrobe-wise—or recognizable fame—to be invited across that boundary and blend with a crowd of wish-they-weres and never-will-bes. A few used-to-bes stopped by too, but when you were played out like Urkel, or reduced to doing roach commercials like Gary Coleman, no one cared to remember your name.

One of the women raised a brow and asked, "Whose list are you on?"

"Roscoe Duvall."

"Roscoe Duvall?" She looked like Sierra, only about

eight years older. She knew that Roscoe Duvall was the name of a legendary con man, more password than anything. She got close to me, lowered her voice, and asked, "Scamz back?"

"I don't know anybody named Scamz."

"Tell him I said hi." She told me her name, slid me her card. "And call a sister sometime."

"A'ight. I'll tell 'im."

We were let by another rope. Another brother with an Emmitt Smith frame smiled at Pam like he didn't give a shit what I thought, then loaded us on the elevator. We were sandwiched in a corner, Pam's butt up against my crotch. The brother pushed the button labeled PH. Penthouse lit up. Homie did that as if that was his job assignment and nobody was going to take his job from him. Had to be a former aerospace or dotcom worker.

Pam asked, "What was that all about?"

"She knows a friend of mine."

"Please don't get me up in the middle of no mess."

People were packed on the vertical carriage. The women were dressed like grand marshals at a cleavage convention. Two girls, with hair in two blazing shades of red, hurried on last and kept gossiping.

"Yeah, girl." Her silver tongue ring caught my eye. "The nigga let me use his charge card."

"You musta finally broke him off some."

The first one giggled and took her lipstick out of her oversize Winnie the Pooh bag. "He's all that. He's kicking me down big time. Peep this ring I bought."

"Bling, bling."

"Keep it on the down low, 'cause if my man find out, he'll be all up in my grill."

"He getting you free tickets to all of his home games?"

"Nobody wants to see the Clippers."

"Feel the vibrations? Music is bumping."

"They jamming. Time to get crunk."

The bass line so tight it almost pushed us back on

the elevator. Hip-hop was bumping, room thumping before we could get off the elevator and squeeze our way into a crowd of tight clothes, short dresses, and small tops that showed off colorful tattoos on stomachs and arms, all in their classiest freak-momma gear, a few in their own too-skanky-to-be-classy J.Lo and I-can-out-slut-you Toni Braxton wardrobes. Brothers were primping around, drinks in hand, Cary Grant facades in full effect, ass watching, tit inspecting with blatant stares, all geared up in everything from Italian suits to Sean Jean. The brothers were twice as broke as the sisters. Out here brothers fronted in luxury cars, but were still living in one-bedroom apartments with their mommas. Everybody perpetrates in this neck of the woods.

I asked Pam, "Ever been up here?"

"Not my kinda crowd."

"Where you usually go?"

"To bed by ten."

"When you go out, where you go?"

"Little J's. Bistro 880. Townhouse—I mean Ladera."

"Never heard of those joints."

"Grown people clubs."

"Old people clubs. Bet y'all be doing the bump and line dancing."

"Whatever. What about you?"

"Sunset Room. The Gate. Garden of Eden."

"Never heard of those places. Must be where the teeny-boppers congregate."

Another guy, this one not as big, with soft tones and feminine gestures motioned us his way, gave an ear-to-ear faux smile as he checked to make sure our arms were stamped, then welcomed us to the club and asked if anyone had reservations for dinner.

I was the only one who did. Everybody else headed for the music.

She asked, "How many people at this meeting?"

"Just me and you."

"Oh. I see."

While we strolled, we checked out the view. From pretty much three hundred and sixty degrees you could see it all: the lights in the mountains, Church of Scientology, Knickerbocker Hotel, the old circular Capitol Records building, the Hollywood Freeway, a thousand houses carved in the hills.

She asked, "Are you a police officer or working with law enforcement?"

"No." I asked, "What're you afraid of?"

"Entrapment." Nervousness was all over her. "For all I know, you could be part of *21 Jump Street*."

"What's that?"

"Never mind." She took a breath. "So, Dante, tell me, where are your people from?"

"Why?"

"I need to know who I'm working with. Humor me."

"My daddy played guitar and my momma was a disco queen."

"Cute. Can you be serious for a moment? It would make me feel better."

That made me uncomfortable. I didn't like talking about my family. Too much negative history. The kind that made a woman want to back away from the table and tell you to have a nice life.

I said, "My mom was from Philly. Dad was from Arizona. Now relax."

"You from L.A.?"

"Born in Philly."

"You don't sound East Coast."

"Lived there until I was about two, moved to Arizona. Was there awhile."

Her eyes were on the dance floor. The rhythm encouraged her to shake a bit. "Really?"

"Dad was ex-military, got discharged after Vietnam, think the war did something to him. He lost his job back in Philly, went west to get some work; I've been out west ever since."

"You're mixed with something."

I chuckled. "My mother's grandmother was Seminole."

"You have a lot of red in your skin. Figured you had mixed roots. What about your dad?"

"His mom had a light complexion and gray eyes. Could pass if she wanted. So I guess that meant she had bicultural roots. My old man's dad was regular black, as far as I know. Why?"

"It's called a conversation. You do have those, don't you?"

"Time to time."

"So, some of your peeps are from the swamps in Florida."

"That's what I heard. Some of my ancestors lived on the Rio Grande."

"Interesting."

I asked her, "Okay, so where are you from?"

"Born in Puerto Rico, moved to Miami when my mother married my daddy, then to North Carolina when she divorced him. All that before I was two, so all I can remember is North Carolina."

The maître d' interrupted us then, told us our table was ready. When we got our seat at a table for two, one next to the window, Pam made an impressed face before she asked, "Why all of this?"

"Thought you might like to get out."

"Sweetie?"

"What?"

"You're a good-looking man."

"But?"

"You're shorter, under thirty, and unemployed."

"Is that three strikes?"

"Glad you can count."

"I'm between jobs."

"Between jobs is when you quit a job on Friday and have one to go to on Monday. You are unemployed."

"Comedian in the house."

"I'm not done."

"And?"

She held on to that smile. "Keep it strictly business."

"This is business." That's when I pulled out the hundred fifty I'd saved from this morning, her half of my profits, and gave it to her. I was tempted to hold out that cabbage—lack of money makes liars and cheats out of the best of us—but I didn't. I slid the cash across the table. Told her it was her cut.

She asked, "How much cash did he have?"

"Three dollars."

"And half of three is one-fifty?"

I told her about the gas game I'd run. Told her I'd made three hundred. She stared at me while I talked, stayed eye to eye, looking for any telling signs, checking for a lie. Which was why I was glad it was the truth. She didn't trust me. Rightfully so. If I were on the other side of that table, I'd think that if she were sliding me one-fifty, maybe I was coming up two, maybe three hundred short. That gleam of mistrust glazed her pretty brown eyes the way morning dew frosts a windowpane. My guess was that she'd been fucked over too many times to mention.

She said, without hiding her skepticism, "So you made three hundred?"

"Right."

"And there were three dollars in the wallet?"

"Right."

Bit by bit, her divine lips evolved into a smirk. "That means you still owe me a buck fifty."

"Geesh." I laughed out my own disbelief. "Are you serious?"

"Biz is biz." She gave me that Debbi Morgan smile and held out her hand. "Pay up."

I reached to touch her hand. She pulled it away.

I said, "Can't blame a man for trying."

"Lot of eye candy floating around this joint. About four women to one guy. Why don't you run out to the dance floor and get a twenty-one-year-old?"

"Because they're twenty-one and looking for an eighteen-year contract."

She laughed a real laugh and I saw her wall had come down a bit.

I told her, "You know, you're pretty when you smile like that."

"The way you look at me . . . what's up with that?"

"The way a man looks at a woman."

She didn't have a snappy comeback that time. Guess I'd pushed an inch too far, made her back off a mile. I always said the wrong shit at the wrong time with women.

A serious chant was going on out on the dance floor, sounded like female bonding was on hit.

Pam said, "That always messes me up."

"What you mean?"

"Song comes on about a brother having hos in every area code and, I dunno, seems like every woman who had any self-esteem, or sense of sisterhood, or black pride, would walk away from the insults, but instead we tune out the misogynistic words and embrace the beat."

"Guess times have changed."

"Not much. When I was hanging tough it was 'Bitch Better Have My Money.' "

"That classic hit played at weddings and bar mitzvahs all over America."

"You're funny. Anyway, sisters were screaming 'Bitch Better Have My Money' louder than the brothers do. Dunno. Guess we'll always be bitches and hos."

"And if you're basing it on the music, we're always gonna be niggas too."

"I'm over here sounding stuck-up, crazy, and older than T-rex."

"You have your head on straight."

The music segued over a few songs before it settled on Lil' Kim and Ray J yelling for the world to wait a minute. She had stopped smiling, no laughter from that side of the table, and she'd stopped bouncing to the beat a while ago. Looked like she had slipped into another space and time.

I raised my voice and asked, "So, this place a'ight with you?"

Pam nodded her answer, then asked me, "What kind of games have you run, Dante?"

She called them games. We all did. Some people called them crimes. We watered down the truth.

I shifted, cleared my throat. "Lots of stuff, I guess. Used to do the bicycle trick."

"What's that?"

"I'd roll through on a dented bike and let somebody in a nice ride accidentally hit me and make them think they messed up my ten-speed, tell them to give me seventy or eighty bucks on the spot and I'd forget about calling the police."

"Sounds dangerous."

"I have the scars to show it. You?"

"Mostly, I gamble."

"A Vegas kinda gal."

"Get me to Vegas and I'll stay on the blackjack table forty-eight hours without a nap. I don't do slots. I like to have some control over the outcome."

"I do blackjack time to time, but I go for the craps table."

"That wallet thing I did today," she said, her voice swimming in mixed emotions, "I was pissed, then I felt a little bad about it afterwards. A lot bad, actually."

"He pissed you off."

"I know. Think I did that to impress you."

"Bullshit. You were too smooth. You've done that before."

"A time or two."

Her eyes came to mine. Then she shifted, cleared her throat like she wanted to drop that issue before I started asking too many questions about her skills, about her past. She picked up the menu.

I said, "Order what you want."

"Okay, Sir Galahad." Her tone had changed, became a forced perky. She held on to her lighthearted grin as she browsed the menu. "I only eat chicken and fish. No fried stuff. Any recommendations?"

"I've only been here once. The breaded chicken was pretty good."

She looked around the room for a moment, watched

brothers lust after a few asses, saw others touching every pretty woman that passed by, doing all kinds of things to get a woman's attention.

Pam asked, "Do you think the physical plays a big part?"

"In what?"

"Never mind. I'm just rambling out my thoughts over here."

"It's cool. We're just talking. What you mean about physical playing a big part?"

She took a breath, stalled like she was choosing her wording. "Most guys I meet always make a comment about my shape, always something about my body. What I mean is, I meet men who are so into the body and women not getting fat, having a gut, yada, yada. Look at all the sisters up in here with their stomachs out, rings in their belly buttons. Hard to be perfect like them."

"That's typical. Women like men with bodies too."

"Like, the way you look at me."

"Okay . . . ?"

"I didn't know what to make of it." She took a little time to get her words right. "What I mean, when you first see someone, do you think their physical appearance makes them more approachable?"

"This a test?"

"Just a conversation. Humor me."

"Hard to play it down when you look so good."

"You're making me blush."

I felt pretty good about myself. Like Scamz had said, the money in my pockets was burning. Something about having on nice threads, a little cash in his pockets, a nice-looking woman on his arm, something about all of that made a man's personal value go up.

"Okay." Pam said that after our soups and salads had arrived, after we'd had a glass of wine and some conversation about nothing in particular, the kind of struggling conversation a man has when he's trying to ask all the right questions and give all the right answers. She blessed the table then smiled at me. "Start telling me what I need to know to pull down these ends."

"You sound a little nervous."

"It'll pass. Just tell me how this works. What do I have to do?"

I did just that, told her about the thing Scamz had going on. I ran it down to her. A lot of music and rumbles were in the background, so I had to repeat a couple of things. I expected her to back down, but she was all ears, didn't shy away from crossing the line into the land of crime. Her eyes told me that this wasn't new to her.

She digested all I had said. Her face told me that she was at a crossroads with Robert Johnson.

She whispered, "I can handle that."

"Sounds like you've done worse than lifting a few wallets."

"Maybe. Maybe not. That's not your business."

After soup and salad, she had breaded chicken and mashed potatoes; I had a shrimp-dinner thing. Dinner and drinks put me back close to a hundred dollars.

The wine had Pam jiggling to the groove. It didn't take but a word to talk her into hitting the dance floor. We squeezed in and danced for about three mixes, felt each other's groove, then when it got too crowded to throw them bows, we took a break, grabbed a drink.

I'd looked around while we were chilling out near the back. There was a cigar room back there. Women and men were inhaling stogies. And I could smell cannabis mixed up in that smoke. Down at the far end, in the thick of the crowd, I thought I saw somebody I knew. Only saw her from the back for a hot sec. She had a magnificent shape like Robin, but it couldn't be her because Jackson's woman was supposed to be chilling in Manhattan by now.

Pam asked, "See one of your women up in here?"

Then that magnificent shape was gone deeper into the crowd.

"Yeah. And she's walking with one of your men."

We headed that way. The crowd was thick. It took a minute to get to the other end of the club. A Ludacris song gave way to a Mack 10 jam.

Pam said, "All the sisters up in here dance like they're strippers at Peanuts."

I asked, "Wanna go back out there?"

Pam said her mules weren't made for any long dancing, but after another glass of wine she got into a groove. At one point she turned around and I touched her hips. She glanced back at me with a stare that asked me what the hell I was doing in her personal zone. I thought she was going to slap my hands away from her sexy sway, but she raised one brow and backed that soft and round mound of real estate up into me. I didn't shy away, pressed up against her.

That was when I saw Robin again. Jackson's loyal woman was passing by, dressed to the nines and looking like a movie queen. She saw me. I nodded and she waved. She had her coat and was rushing for the elevator. Her expression told me that she'd seen me chilling in the back and was trying to get out of here before she got busted. A guy was leading her through the crowd. Her hand was in his. He was dark-skinned, bald with a goatee and enough baggy gear on to mask his build. Was hard to size him up. Didn't matter. He wasn't a threat to me.

Pam asked, "Your woman?"

I forced a smile. "Friend of mine's woman."

"Whatever. You've got a lot of women friends up in here."

"Probably not half as many as you have men friends down at Little J's."

Robin was gone, had a head start on me. One phone call to Jackson would take care of that.

Me and Pam rubbed against each other, freak-grooved like that for a moment, not long, but long enough to make me want more from her. The spirits and music had loosened Pam up. She was smiling like a queen and dancing her ass off, moving like an exotic dancer and throwing them bows until the lights came on at one-thirty for last call. L.A. wasn't a late-night city like New York or Vegas, so that was when the crowd started becoming thinner than Burt Reynolds' hairline.

We blended with the rush and got on a packed vertical carriage. People still had sweat drying on their faces.

Three sisters rushed on. One was rambling, ". . . and I heard Beyoncé had a rib taken out. I'm thinking about doing that."

"I saw the two girls who got kicked out the group when I was in New York."

"Heard they was starting a new group called Angel or something."

"She with one of the brothers in Jagged Edge. Driving a Jaguar. Well, half-driving 'cause she had dented the thing up already. Brother she with has a bad Escalade."

"The way they spending, they ass'll be broke this time next year."

"When our group jumps off, we ain't gonna be all controversial and backstabbing and crap like that. We should get Mary J. Blige's personal trainer. She is looking phat."

Pam asked me, "How many play haters does it take to fill up an elevator?"

I laughed. Pam started laughing.

The women looked at us like we were the crazy ones. When we left the building, we were still holding back laughter.

Pam said, "Those were some *sad, sad, sad, sad* sisters up in there."

"I know."

"Great character study. Hope you don't think we're all like that."

"Nah. Judge you on a case-by-case basis."

I looked at those other young girls and had a better understanding of why I was attracted to older women. Pam was feminine without being girly. Not pretentious. All that was from what I'd seen so far. How much of that was true, too soon to tell. But that was the face she'd shown me.

Underneath the palm trees and bright lights, we shared easygoing words while Pam and I waited for her ride to be brought up from down below. A few high-end rides that rolled on serious chrome were driven out and put on display before her simple green Nissan was parked to the side.

I paid the valet guy, gave him a two-dollar tip. He pocketed the tip without counting it, raced to get the next car without a good-bye or thank you.

Pam said, "Thanks for the night."

We stared. Cool night air blowing on our faces, rattling leaves in the palm trees, my jacket on but not buttoned, my Denzel charisma and James Dean kinda cool in full effect.

She said, "You party like a Q, pretty enough to be a Kappa, as real as a Sigma, and as determined as an Alpha. I like all of those qualities in a man."

I moved up closer. She put her hand out and kept me away.

I said, "Business meeting."

"You're catching on."

We shook hands. I held on to her hand for a while. She didn't rush to take her hand back. She looked at me and didn't shy away. Read my face the way people read tea leaves. It was a moment before she finally took her hand away from mine, did that in no hurry, her fingers dragging over my palm, and my fingers doing the same to hers.

I knew when to let silence talk for me, so that was what I did.

That was how we stayed. That cool air all over us. Chatter all around us. People walking by, driving by, us not paying attention to any of that. We were focused right here, on each other.

She said, "You're coming at me pretty strong."

"I know."

Right above a whisper she asked, "Why me, Dante?"

Why me? That question a woman asked a million times, a question a man heard in so many variations. Women asked us what we wanted with them when we didn't know what we wanted for ourselves. A man had to have the right answer to be allowed to pass Go and collect two hundred dollars.

I responded, "Why not you?"

Then I waited to see if that was the right answer.

She pulled her lips in. Guess she was at a loss for words.

I said, "Sorry to yank you away from your date tonight."

"I lied. No date. I'm a waitress at this comedy club called Ha Ha's too."

"I know that joint. Down on Lankershim. Why'd you lie?"

"I never lie, shorty; I improvise."

Cars maneuvered around us. We were still in the same spot.

I asked, "Wanna do something else?"

She asked, "So, where's your woman?"

"Me no got no woman."

"I know you got some hottie waiting on you some-where."

"Well, Halle was busy, Bassett didn't return my calls, and Rosie O'Donnell don't like me."

"Cute." Her serious expression melted. "You're look-ing at me like that again."

"You look at me the same way, so let's cut the bull."

"Sounds like you got some fire under your ass."

I didn't back down. "Wanna or no?"

"It's almost two in the morning. On a weekday."

"Last hours of my birthday. Can we do something else?"

"We've already had dinner. We've danced for two good hours. We've talked both business and pleasure. We've had a few drinks. Full moon. Cold night. What else could you have in mind?"

My mouth opened but no words came out.

She said, "Know when to be a Q, and when to be an Alpha."

I nodded.

"Peace be with you, my brother. And happy birthday."

"Yeah. Later."

She closed her door. Put her seat belt on. I watched

that piece of sturdy material separate her breasts, made each stand out like mountains made of kissable, touchable flesh.

She turned her headlights on, shot me a good-bye grin, and pulled away, blended with traffic and vanished into the lights covering the buildings and billboards cluttering the boulevard.

I waited until she was gone and headed around the corner. That's where my grumpy old Oscar was waiting for me, in a crowd of Berthas and Ednas and Charlies. Yep, I'd save a few bucks by parking on the side streets where people with shitty rides camped out. A stream of brothers and sisters were all marching in the same direction. The girls we'd seen on the elevator dissing Beyoncé were around there. Seems like their four-door Bertha had a dead battery and they were in search of a man with either jumper cables or triple-A to jump-start that Diehard heart.

A car came up behind me. The lights clicked from high to low. The horn blew soft and friendly. I looked back and saw the plates on that silver Volkswagen. EYE FLY 4 U. I stopped where I was. Robin let her window down when she got up beside me. That beautiful woman had her hair done like she was ready to be on the cover of *Essence*, was dressed in shiny black, was wearing a clinging top that gave up a bit too much cleavage, had some of that glitter makeup on her dark brown skin. Smelled super sweet.

My frown was back. "How's New York?"

She sucked on her bottom lip and sighed. Her expression, the way she shook her head, said that there were a million clubs in Hollywood, that this was a land where you could party for two years and never run into the same people, and we had landed in the same spot.

"Dante, it's not what you think."

"Glad you read minds. Saves me a lot of talking. But since I can't read yours, tell me whassup."

"I'm just trying to get some time to myself. A sister just needed some space to think about things."

"Nice thinking clothes. And I guess that dude was your thinking partner."

We stared. She knew what I was looking for: the truth.

I asked, "You're going by Jackson's crib now, right?"

"Dante, don't do this."

I said, "You know I'm heading to a phone and tell Jackson I saw you."

"Dante, wait."

"Whassup?"

"Look, he's been through a lot."

"What's your point?"

"You think he needs one more thing? And you saw how I was today. I had a huge emotional crash in the middle of traffic. When you saw me, I'd almost had an accident because I was so stressed. I ran a red light, swerved to miss a car, could've run off the road and hit a pole, or I could've run down somebody's kid, or run up into a crowd of people. You think I need one more thing? I'm stressed."

That shut me down.

She said, "I can't go on like this."

"What do you mean?"

"I wanna be happy. That's all I want. I wanna be happy with Jackson. I don't care if he's laid off. We can bounce back together. But Sabrina. Damn. That ... she's doing her best to make our lives miserable. And she's doing a damn good job."

"Don't worry about Sabrina."

"How can I not worry about Sabrina? I hear her name fifty times a day. She's just getting warmed up. She's a woman scorned."

"Why would she be scorned? Jackson has been straight up about everything."

"You don't understand women, do you?"

I sighed. "You got me on that one. Break it down for me?"

"I love Jackson."

Her voice strained when she said that. Strained enough to make me feel like I was evil.

"I have to make some hard choices," Robin said. "I needed some space, needed to get out and get a drink, and have some conversation about nothing, wanted to talk and be normal without hearing about drama, drama, drama. Without my head hurting. I just need a few 'me' days and I'll be cool."

She reached for my hand. I moved near her window and gave it to her.

"It's not what you think, Dante."

"Who was the dude?"

"Just a friend. Nobody. He was just showing me a good time. He walked me to my car."

"Last time asking: Whassup with the dude?"

"We go to the same church. He's in the choir."

"You're trying to tell me he's gay or something?"

"He's not the director." She took another hard breath. "I needed to hear it from another male's perspective. I needed to talk to somebody."

I took my hands back, rubbed the bridge of my nose.

"Please?" She said that again. "Let this be between us."

Her voice was seasoned with fear and confusion. Walls were closing in; my head was trying to ache. I thought about Jackson, and I thought about how I'd seen Robin after court today.

I walked away from Robin, headed back toward Oscar. I didn't say good-bye, didn't make any promises, just left her sitting in her silver Volkswagen. She called my name over and over. I didn't answer. All of this shit had made me deaf.

She drove away. EYE FLY 4 U faded into nothing.

I asked Oscar what he would do. I was on my own. He knew less about women than I did.

I had to keep moving. Since I was out, before my cash got too low, I grabbed my coupon box from the dashboard, then talked Oscar into stopping down at Laurel Canyon and Riverside, at this ritzy supermarket named Gelson's. A nice marketplace that didn't lock up the liquor, and always had fresh fruit, clean floors, and smiling cashiers with European faces who wanted a brother to "have a nice day." I liked this joint. People would help you without throwing an attitude. The baskets weren't raggedy like the ones at Ralph's in the hood down on Crenshaw; the wheels didn't squeal like a dying mouse and the carts rolled in the direction you pushed them.

I parked Oscar next to a Double-R. Let him get his flirt on while I cruised the aisles.

I had been having a decent night, and running into Robin had wrecked my cooltivity to the nth degree.

An hour later I had five plastic bags of groceries. If I still had that money I'd spent at 360, I'd have five more bags. But I wouldn't have the memory of a damn good night. A damn good birthday.

I stopped at a pay phone and called Jackson. He didn't answer.

I listened to the radio as I drove home, tuned into people with urban attitudes talking out their relationship problems with a down-to-earth sister. Most of the women who called said their roughneck lovers were on taxpayer-furnished vacations at state prisons, Wayside or Folsom. Places men used cigarettes for cash and soap on a rope as family planning. One twenty-five-year-old sister said that she had killed her ex and his buddy, shot them both point-blank with a nine-millimeter over ten dollars and some change they owed. She did a few quick years out east at Chino, and wondered why she couldn't get a date with a nice guy when she told him the truth about her past. She was dead serious.

I laughed so hard I almost had to pull over.

Then I remembered that I owed Nazario more than ten bucks.

My laughter died.

It was close to 3 a.m. Blue shadows had covered the whole city.

I was still restless.

I wanted to see Pam. This fever was coming over me, and I wanted to call her and talk awhile. Ride out this insomnia and late-night loneliness with her words tickling my right ear.

Back home, I put away all the fruit and vegetables and packed the TV dinners and other frozen food I had bought inside my freezer. I wrote out a couple of checks for the bills that affect a man's credit report, got those knocked out, then flipped through the money I had left. I'd spent a good chunk of the money I'd just gotten from Scamz.

Itching hands and burning pockets.

The apartment was cold because I had the heat down to save on that gas bill. A dollar saved was a dollar earned. I had extra blankets on my bed to keep me warm through the night. I pulled on my gray sweats, put a sweatshirt over my T-shirt, then stretched out.

My phone rang. I let three rings go by before I picked up.

It was Jackson. He told me he was on the other line when I called a while ago.

I asked, "Were you talking to Robin?"

He said, "I was talking to Scamz. He called me."

"What he say?"

"I'm in with you tomorrow."

"Good." I paused. I pretended that I was happy to hear that, but in reality I wasn't so sure I was. I massaged the tension in my nose and asked, "You haven't talked to Robin?"

"Not yet. Think her and her Haitian crew are out at a Broadway play."

I was about to tell him. My mouth opened. The words made it as far as my tongue.

He did sound pretty stressed. Robin was right about him not needing one more thing. I convinced myself that it was about nothing, that she was just getting out to clear her head. I'd done that, hung out with a member of the opposite sex a time or two when whoever I was seeing gave me stress.

But I'd done a lot more than talked.

Jackson told me that he'd been with his kids all day. That after all the drama, at the end of the day he was still a parent and had to be bigger than the next man.

He'd got a friend to drive him around, had taken the kids to the zoo. Sabrina had already told the oldest one about the DNA testing, so he had to explain to the kid what that was all about. Had to explain that didn't mean he didn't love her.

"That was the hardest thing I've ever had to do," Jackson said. "Cree asked me, then why are you doing it? Even with the way their momma is yanking my chain, I didn't have an answer."

Cree was six years old, his oldest daughter. I listened.

He said, "Cree said she heard Sabrina talking to her spiritual advisor—"

"Who is her spiritual advisor?"

"This chick Juanita. Sabrina's landlord. Cree heard them in the hallway, and Sabrina was saying how messed up it was that she can have two kids for me and I turn around and marry somebody else."

"Damn. In front of the kids?"

"Yep. Then Cree asked me why I didn't marry Sabrina."

"Damn."

"She said Allen Iverson married his babies' momma; asked me why couldn't I be like Iverson."

"Double damn."

"What was I supposed to say, that we never loved each other? Tell her that her momma has played one game too many? Tell her how Sabrina would lie about being pregnant, just to see what I was gonna say? Psychological crap like that." He calmed down a notch. "I'll just keep on being the bad guy."

"I don't understand why Sabrina would wanna head trip you like that. I mean, damn, she had them take your driver's license. You can't even drive to pick up your own kids."

"Robin has to take me and Sabrina throws attitude about that. I know how I can get out of it."

"You ain't thinking about consulting O.J. or Rae Caruth and doing something crazy are you?"

"I'm pissed off, not insane." Then he said, "Sabrina told me how she could fix it."

"She can fix it? How can she fix it?"

"She can make it vanish with one phone call to the district attorney."

"She gonna do it?"

"Hell no."

"Then why she throw that in your face?"

"It's emotional extortion. I turned down her offer."

"What offer?"

"Don't matter." He paused. "I'd like to stick those arrears up Sabrina's rear."

That made both of us laugh.

Me and Jackson talked awhile longer. He needed an ear, so I loaned him mine. Just wanted to be an umbrella to shelter him from the rain. He'd do the same for me. Robin said that she'd been out tonight with another man because she needed an ear. Somebody to lean on in troubled times. And I bet Sabrina was doing the same. Everybody's life gets unbearable at some point. I didn't want Jackson to get to a point where dreams were better than reality, to where he'd rather give up and become an angel.

He said, "Look, I hate to ask you, but I need a big favor."

He told me that his wallet must've slipped out of his pocket when he dropped his kids off at Sabrina's apartment down in Leimert Park. He was trying to do as little driving as possible, plus if he went to get it he wouldn't be surprised if Sabrina called the police and had him arrested for driving with a suspended license. He didn't want to see her. Didn't feel like dealing with another guilt trip.

I was dead tired, but I told him that I'd make that run for him first thing in the morning.

I asked, "You sure you wanna roll with Scamz?"

He knew what I meant. Like I had told Pam, every job has its occupational hazards.

"I'm falling," he replied. "My prayers have been ignored. Feel forsaken by the people above me, and I've been deceived by the people on the ground. I'm falling, Dante."

"I feel ya."

"Scamz is my last chance before I hit the ground."

I let those words settle on me. We were all falling right now. I was thinking about that karma thing Jackson was talking about earlier today. Might be some truth to that stuff. Wonder what I did in my last life to make this one come out like this.

"Get some sleep," I told my friend. "We need to be rested."

"You too."

"Hey, bro. I know I ain't been through the same kinda stuff—"

"And I hope you don't ever have to. Get a vasectomy, jack off in a cup."

"If I get a vasectomy, jacking off in a cup will be futile."

"Dante, get serious for a minute."

"I'm listening."

"Always protect the sperm. That's your power. That's what I should've done."

"Just wanna say," I started, then slowed when a rush of thoughts of my mom's final days came and interrupted my flow, made some serious emotion catch in my throat and that mental speed bump slowed me down. "Don't give up, man. Whatever you do, don't give up. Call me anytime you need to talk, or if you want to get out and walk it off, I'll come by and walk with you."

"Get some sleep, Cool Hand Dante."

We hung up.

Took a while for that conversation to fade. His words and tone disturbed me, just like seeing Robin in her emotional state had bothered me. Had to put on my Levi Chen CD before I could move that drama out of my mind. Had to let my mind go where peaceful waters flowed.

Thought about better days. I thought about Pam.

I was itching for Pam the same way Jackson was itching for Robin. And Scamz was no doubt getting the scratching of his life all through the night tonight.

Doubt if Scamz ever went to bed or woke up itching with a fever. He's got it like that. Wished that had been me walking into that mansion just in time to see Pam getting out of that pool, naked for me, water raining from her skin like that. I'd drink the water from her flesh, lie her on her back, spread her wings, and take flight.

That image got me to itching so bad I couldn't sleep.

My hand went down my chest, to my soft bone, and held on. I squeezed, moved it up and down, felt its rising power. I moved my hand away. But it was swollen, re-fusing to go down to Bruce Banner size, begging for re-lief. I pulled my sweats away, touched myself, moved my hand up and down, slow and easy, until my eyes closed and I didn't care if the whole world was watching. I imagined my hand was Pam's soft hand, her mouth, any part of her that would take me on this journey.

My moan caught in my throat and I imagined that was her moan, that this was her pleasure. I could hear her whisper for me to go slow and easy. She said my name over and over. Slow and easy. I whispered hers as well, begged her not to stop. That desire rose and hu-midified my flesh. Pam kissed my fingers and pleaded for me to go faster, to go deeper. Her back arched, hips pushed up into me, and her moan was the sweetest sound I'd ever heard, and she sang out nonstop. It felt like I was in New Orleans on the Fourth of July, sweat-ing, the heat index in triple digits.

Heaven's ache came in bright colors, reds and yel-lows, a few shades of orange, hints of sky blue.

Then I lay there and let my ragged breathing even out. Let my heart rate settle.

When I looked to my left, when my eyes focused, I expected to see a wonderful woman with bushy hair and deep dimples in her cheeks, her face painted with plea-sure, but there was no Pam.

Those magnificent colors faded. Reality came back a breath at a time.

My sweats fell to my ankles when I got up. I duck-walked across my two-shades-of-brown carpet, stepped over a few scattered videos, went to the bathroom, clicked on a light, waited for the water to heat up, soaped up a towel, and stared at myself in the mirror while I washed away my sin. My mother's eyes stared back at me. My father's brief forehead. My mother's small nose. My old man's shallow eyebrows. My mother's grade of hair trying to grow from my bald head. Her complexion covered me. My old man's height. His build. We were all right here. All three of us.

I clicked off the light, let all of us get swallowed by the darkness.

It took a while of walking around in the dark—always left the lights off as much as I could to keep the electric bill down—but I crawled back in the bed, a mixture of relief and guilt under my skin.

Not sleepy, not wide awake, but not itching as bad.

I sat up, feet flat on the worn carpet, toes opening and closing, eyes staring out the window.

I was lonely, but I was feeling a little shaky too. It was all mixed up like a salad.

I stretched out in my queen-size bed that had no queen, stared at the off-white ceiling. Tossed and turned. Wondered what Pam was doing right then. Wondered if I had made her itch, so much as a tingle. Or if somebody was scratching her itch right now.

8

Oscar was tired and grumbling when I parked out on
Stocker at Degnan, right in front of a mauve-colored
apartment building that had an upside-down U-shape.
It was a two-story structure with a total of twelve units.
It was eight in the morning, and I was down in the center of black culture for Los Angeles. A group of people
were out jogging by the Baldwin Hills hoodrat mall,
moving by Founders Bank, up Stocker toward Valley
Ridge. People were out hustling R.I.P. AALIYAH and R.I.P.
TUPAC T-shirts. Others were walking their pit bulls, letting them hunt for Chihuahuas to feed on for breakfast.

Sabrina's red Ford Explorer was out front. The windows
still had dew on them. Two child seats in the back. A few
bumper stickers—all against some sort of injustice—were
fading. ABORTION STOPS A BEATING HEART and REPARA-
TIONS NOW were the newest and easiest to read.

I climbed to the second floor and knocked twice. Sabrina opened the door right away. The anticipation that
was on her face disintegrated when she saw that it was
me. That five-foot-tall woman with the young face and
the old hair had on peach satin pajamas and no shoes.
Smelled like sweet patchouli. She had a silver ring on
each of two toes. Her toenails were pink, which looked
odd to me. Too cosmopolitan and too girly. The silver
ring in her left eyebrow and the one in her nose both
looked more natural on her. A yellow bandanna with
silver studs covered her salt-and-pepper locks. She was
the sexiest queen mother earth from Compton to
Harlem.

She said, "Thought you were Jackson. He told me he was coming."

"He sent me to pick up his wallet. Hard for a man to get around on a suspended license."

"You say that as if I'm the one who suspended it."

"You didn't?"

"The court did that. I have no hand in what they do."

I didn't argue that point. "Thought maybe we could talk for a minute, if you're not busy."

Sabrina evaluated me, tried to read my intentions before she said, "Wait right there for a second."

While I stood in the door's cool cross breeze and looked down at my clothes, she turned on most of the lights, then blew out the scented candles. The door across the hallway opened. I looked behind me and saw a cute redbone with short blond hair stick her head out. Real pretty woman. She had to be pushing forty. Mature eyes and strong lines in her face, like life had forced her to make hard choices.

She introduced herself, "I'm Juanita. I'm the landlord of this building."

I was face-to-face with Sabrina's spiritual advisor. I said, "G'morning."

"Is there anything I can help you with, my brother?"

"Nah. Just waiting for Sabrina."

A young Latina woman stood behind Juanita. They regarded me with cautious eyes and shared a few words in Spanish. Juanita called Sabrina's name, asked if everything was alright. Sabrina called out and said that everything was okay. The two women disappeared back inside their apartment. I guess with no men around, they had to have each other's back.

When Sabrina came back, she had on long jeans, a baggy blue shirt, and big blue slippers. She'd covered up all the good parts. That made me feel a little more comfortable.

She motioned with one finger. "You may come in now."

A few toys, dolls with deep brown skin, African-theme coloring books, a small red-and-green slide, other kiddie things were in the living room. They weren't scattered everywhere, just neatly put in one section, over near a small board that had the ABCs in white letters. Looked like the warrior queen had some home schooling going on.

I said, "Didn't mean to get you out of bed."

"It's after eight. Been up for two hours already. Hard for me to sleep after six."

"A morning person."

"Kids make you into a morning person whether you want to be or not."

Her place had a peaceful glow. Cherry incense flavored the air.

She pointed toward the sofa. "Please, have a seat."

There was a peach-and-gray sofa and love seat that matched the light gray carpet. Pictures of her two daughters, Cree and Lisa, were framed and all over the place. She had a lot of pictures of Jackson up too. Too many. Some of them were from a while back and had just him and Sabrina, that was back when they first went out. Some were when Lisa, the youngest one, was born. Cree's birth was there too. All were nicely framed, a lot of them on the back wall closest to the kitchen, right in front of the smoked-glass dining room table. Her own little shrine.

I said, "It's quiet. Where the little women at?"

She hesitated. "My mother's. They're going to Adventure City with their cousins today."

Looked like breakfast food had been taken out and placed on the counter. The dining room table had two settings, not three like she and her two kids would have.

I asked, "Were you waiting on somebody?"

She smiled, but didn't answer.

Lots of mirrors were on the walls facing the window; their reflection gave extra daylight for all the plants and made the room look bigger. Ceiling-high plants rested on both sides of the window. She had a wicker basket in between the L of the sofa and love seat that was filled with stuff by Angela Davis, Stokely Carmichael, Huey

Newton, and Alice Walker. The top of the floor-model television was filled with pictures of her and Jackson.

She put Jackson's brown wallet on the table. I stuffed it in my jacket pocket.

She asked, "What's on your mind?"

"Well, you've got Jackson in a tight situation."

"You say that like my situation is much better."

A pot whistled and she hurried to the kitchen to click off the gas stove.

She asked, "Tea?"

"What kind?"

"Korean ginseng."

"Sure."

"Honey or sugar?"

"Honey."

After she made two cups, she walked over to the love seat and clicked on another lamp. She sat straight-backed at the far corner of her love seat, knees and ankles touching like two lovers on a honeymoon.

She pointed toward a container. "Coaster, please."

I took out two silver metal coasters that had Egyptian designs and soft bottoms and put one close to her end of the coffee table. After I moved my hand, she picked it up and moved it closer. When she took a short sip and cleared her throat for the talking, I interrupted her with a tired smile.

I said, "Your crib is tight."

"Dante," she said as she buttoned up the top three buttons on her shirt, "thank you. For your observation. But let us cut right to the point so you can finish your tea and be on your way."

"A'ight. Let's do that."

She said, "I know where you're going with this. Let me say this: Jackson needs to do the right thing. We have too many of our men who refuse to step up to the plate after they have started a family."

"What does 'do the right thing' mean?"

"It means what it means, Dante."

"Look, all I'm saying is that I know he's been kicking

you down cash. I've seen that with my own eyes. How
can you go to court and lie like that?"

"This isn't about money."

"Then what is it about?"

"Responsibility."

"Well, when a judge is asking for sixteen thousand, it
sounds like money to me."

She sipped her tea.

She said, "This situation makes me feel uneasy."

"Okay. Well, this ain't easy for me. Feel like I should
say something."

"Did Jackson ask you to be his voice, some sort of ar-
bitrator in this matter?"

"Nah. Just asked me to grab his wallet."

"I commend you on your undying loyalty. You've had
your say. Now, as for me, if I don't speak my mind, I get
too resentful."

"Okay."

"I don't want Jackson hanging out with you."

"Why not?"

"We have two kids and despite our situation, I don't
want him getting incarcerated."

"If you care about him so much, then why don't you
drop the charges you have against him? If you make life
better on him, that makes it better on the kids, then
everybody wins, right?"

"Well, if he did the right thing, we wouldn't have this
problem, would we?"

"If you did the right thing, you wouldn't have this
problem."

"What's that supposed to mean?"

I almost went off on one of those rants about how she
got knocked up with no wedding ring in sight, maybe
say that bear trap was part of a master plan that backfired, but I'd be speaking on things that I really didn't
know. I didn't understand women, and this situation
made no sense to me.

I said, "You can't blame the whole situation on him."

"The kids are here. You can't change that."

"Nobody said that. I'm just saying you should cut Jackson some slack."

She sipped her tea and waited to hear my argument. I sipped mine so I could get my words right.

I said, "Look, with his job laying off, and this court thing, Jackson is overwhelmed."

Sabrina said, "We have two beautiful daughters. I'm a full-time parent. Do you know how much energy that takes? From cooking breakfast to getting to the baby-sitter, to getting to FedEx on time, to driving a truck, loading and unloading boxes *by myself*, dealing with my customers all day, to picking the kids up, to cooking dinner, to reading to them before they go to bed, to ironing clothes, to potty training, to getting two children up in the morning, and it never ends. And if either one of them gets sick, it's chaos. Do you know what it feels like to be tired all the time? Every day I'm overwhelmed. I've been overwhelmed for years. While he's lying up with Robin, I'm overwhelmed. While he's making plans to get married, I'm overwhelmed. While they're out holding hands at jazz festivals, relaxing on beaches in Laguna, and walking around Universal CityWalk, I'm at Chuck E. Cheese and Discovery Zone, being mommy, and I'm overwhelmed. I'm doing what a mother is supposed to do twenty-four-seven, three-hundred-sixty-five. Not every Wednesday, not every other weekend, not on alternating holidays."

She massaged her temples, then made a motion that asked me to forgive her for that outburst.

She said, "Working at FedEx was supposed to be temporary, not a career move. I wanted to get back into nursing, get my degree, help low-income women, work in labor and delivery management, become a certified nurse and midwife, not throw boxes on a truck eight hours a day."

I sipped my tea and wished I had taken that wallet and run back to Sherman Oaks.

She said, "I know he's going to start another family. Men always do. Me and my girls will be left behind like yesterday's news."

I said, "Jackson's not leaving his kids. You know that."

She bobbed her head and looked at her feet. I looked around at all the memories she had on her wall. It was like seeing the inside of a woman's heart, picture by picture. With that many photos of her ex up, no way she was ever gonna let go and get serious about another guy.

She went on, "Requesting a DNA test was low. That was vindictive. Futile and vindictive."

"Well, you started the game of dirty pool. Like Jackson says, bad karma breeds bad karma."

"He said reprehensible things about me. Insinuated that I was a slut. Assassinated my character."

"Right after you slaughtered his."

"Dante, stop acting like you're the president of his fan club. Keep out of our business."

I sipped. She sipped.

"You love 'im?"

"He's the father of my children. I will always love him."

"Then stop trying to extort him and let him go."

"Don't confuse my affection for extortion."

"Don't confuse extortion for affection. What you're doing should be illegal."

"If it was illegal, the courts would tell us, now, wouldn't they?"

"It's not moral."

"How sweet. A con man is talking to me about morality."

I sipped and tried to think of what to say. Once again, I wished I was in Mensa, a member of that club for geniuses, somebody who had the power of persuasion. I wished I was Scamz.

She said, "The position he's left me in should be illegal too."

"But it's not. So you're just gonna go at him hit-'em-up style to prove a point."

She smiled at me. I could tell she wanted to slap me, kick me, burn me, stab me, drown me.

She sipped. I sipped.

"Sabrina, do you mind if I ask what you got against me?"

"To be honest, you're Jackson's friend, but yeah, I've always disliked you."

"I've never done anything to offend you."

"You're irresponsible. That's more than enough. But on the other hand, you're a smart brother and I'm watching you waste away your life. You fight and gamble and hang out with crazy people and pedophiles, befriend thieves and robbers, and don't have any friends your own age, and I think that's bizarre. Like most of our people, self included, you could use some therapy."

My tongue ran over my top gum. "So you think I'm crazy."

She said, "Don't you think you have some issues that need to be addressed by a professional before you come in my home, into the place I give love to my two little girls, and chastise me?"

We sat around like two chess players, waiting for the other to make a move. Legs crossed, eye to eye, matching sip for sip, wallowing in the quiet. Silence was a very hostile thing.

She sipped her tea and asked, "Everything understood?"

I thanked her for the tea, and then peacefully walked out the door.

9

The CLOSED/CERRADO sign moved when I cracked the pool hall's door open. I peeped in the square mirrors on the walls to make sure I didn't see Nazario's reflection before I crossed the doorsill. From the streets I could hear the CD machine thumping out Z.Z. Hill's "Down Home Blues" loud and clear. The door sensor sang out its intruder alert when I came in. Big Slim was roosting in the circular booth in the center of the room. He had a harmonica palmed in what was left of his hands and was jamming along with the blues.

He stopped playing and leaned forward when he saw it was me.

"C'mere, boy." He sounded as pleasant as the whine of a rusted metal door. Didn't look like he'd had much rest.

"Nazario passed by a while ago. Every time somebody step foot out that do', he ask'n 'em if they know where you live, if you been around. He mad because Scamz cut him out of some business and he blaming it all on you."

"Want me to raise up?"

"You here now. You safe on this side of that door. Other side, you on your own."

Behind me was the clacking of pool balls followed by curses or cheers.

Big Slim clicked on the light at table number fifteen then handed me a tray of pool balls. He sat back down and started playing his harmonica along with the blues.

Six other tables had players. People I knew I could

beat shooting eight ball. My mouth watered, but I swallowed that desire.

Big Slim bow-wowed my name as soon as I broke the balls. I went back over to him.

He asked, "If a man told you to suck on his johnson in front of a room full of colored women, would you let it be?"

"No, sir."

Big Slim's dentures slipped. He took a sip from his Dixie cup and the aroma of Johnnie Walker Blue rode out on the winds of his breath.

I asked him, "If you were me, would you give him the ring back to make him go away?"

"Never leave a debt unpaid," he said, a stiff frown etched in his face, "but never pay a man no mo' than what you owe. Don't let no man make you less than a man."

The door sensor went off. I jumped. Big Slim did the same. I held on to my pool cue. Big Slim was ready to reach underneath his counter and pull out his twelve-gauge peacemaker.

It was Pam. She made an entrance, sashayed in like she was the high priestess of the blues. People stopped shooting pool when she walked in. Men smiled; the ones who were wearing hats took them off or tipped them toward her. It was the Fresh Meat Factor. No one knew her. Every man wanted to.

She fanned some smoke away from her face, then took in the place, especially that ugly lime-green wall with the huge photo of Dorothy Dandridge. Pam was dressed the way I had told her to dress: dark skirt, dark sweater, her leather coat, all in classic New York blacks. Pretty casual, but pretty trendy. High-class for a place like this.

I headed back to the pool table. She made her way over to me, we said our good mornings. She reached out her hand and shook mine, then leaned against the wall and watched me shoot a game of eight ball by myself. I expected her to be impressed by my range of shots, but she didn't blink.

Pam told me, "You're decent on the pool table."

"I know."

"Not a compliment, just an observation."

"Think you can do better?"

"You need to work on your English. Your bottom spin ain't all that. The cue is supposed to stop on a dime. Your bad English is letting it roll a good two inches. That leaves you in a bad position for your next shot."

"Is that right? What, you're the Black Widow or something?"

"Just trying to help. But hey, shoot your own way."

The door buzzer sang again and I tensed. This time it was Jackson. His long hair was back in a ponytail. He had on a black suit, white shirt, dark tie, black shoes, and dark socks. Looked like a hip undertaker, but that was his chauffeur gear. He came over and handed me a box. I gave him his wallet and decided to keep the conversation I'd had with Sabrina to myself. Some of what she had said about me, the way she looked at me, all of that spiritual mumbo jumbo had rattled me.

I introduced Jackson to Pam. He looked at her, and this weird grin grew on his face.

Jackson said, "Didn't you used to hang out at the Golden Tail and Paradise 24?"

Pam laughed. "Oh, my God. You gotta be joking. That was way back."

"You used to have big hair, wore a lot of leather, most of the time a black leather miniskirt."

I put my pool stick away as I said, "Never heard of those places."

My favorite waitress winked. "Doubt if you were in middle school back then."

Pam wasn't sure, so I confirmed that Jackson was working with us.

That moved us toward business. Jackson went to use the head, then eased out the back door.

Over the speakers Dorothy Moore started crying her heart out, aching, bitching about how her world was upside down and her man made her feel "Misty Blue."

Pam went to the other side of the room and grabbed a soda. On her way back, she stopped on the checkered-tile part of the floor and started dancing, sang her lungs out and got the room's attention, worked her tail like it had sixteen switches, moved that mound of real estate front, back, side to side. An outdated disco globe was over her head, spinning and reflecting light like it was waiting for Donna Summer to come inside and do the Hustle.

Big Slim yelled from his booth, "Stop dancing all that nasty round here."

Pam stopped showing off. "My first time down here. Don't know the rules."

"Act like a woman, not a streetwalker."

She came back to me. "That dude with no fingers gives me the heebie-jeebies. Simon Legree's over there acting like we're up in Grover's Corners."

I didn't ask her what that meant. Business was on my mind. I opened the box Jackson had given me. Inside were a few "his" and "hers" wedding rings. I handed Pam a couple of rings to try on.

She asked, "What's this for?"

"Today you're my wife."

"Don't expect a honeymoon."

"Get serious for two seconds."

"Okay." She found one that fit. "How long have we been married?"

"What?"

"We should know that stuff, just in case. Do we have kids, how long we've been married, where did we meet, honeymoon, yada yada yada. You have to know your character."

"Pam, this ain't a play."

"Still, we should know." She glanced up at that huge picture on the wall. "Who's that?"

"Dorothy Dandridge. Don't you know your stars?"

"Better than I know my own family. That's not Dorothy Dandridge."

"Who is it?"

"Not Dorothy Dandridge, I know that much."

"It's Dorothy."

"Nope. Not Dorothy."

Both of us stared at the picture before we went outside.

Jackson pulled up in a black Town Car. Pam followed me to the ride so we could be taken through the canyon into Hollywood Hills. We stepped out on Ventura Boulevard, and a chill hit me. I looked toward Jinky's Café, toward Westwood Insurance, toward the tattoo and body-piercing joint, then back down toward the grocery store.

Pam said, "Who you looking for?"

"Nobody. Let's roll."

I was beyond uneasy. I didn't hear the roar from a ghetto-red ride with the plastic Jesus on the dash, didn't hear anybody bumping out Tupac. I knew that fool wasn't too far away. Something told me that I was being watched. Felt like a knife should come spinning through the air and break my skin.

I told Jackson to drive around a bit. I made sure nobody was trying to follow me.

Pam bounced her leg and picked her cuticles all the way.

10

Scamz's rental con sounded simple enough. He rented a place under a fake name, then acted like he was the owner and rented it out fifty times over to the eager. The renters would be anxious to get the crib because, one, it was Hollywood Hills, and two, it would be in the market at a bargain price for the area, but not cheap enough to make it questionable. They were asking everybody to pay with a money order for first and last month's rent in advance, cleaning fee, and credit check fee. The reason was simple: no one wanted to get a bad check. They'd be given a move-in date a few weeks away, and by then Scamz would be gone, leaving nothing but fake names and a shitload of pissed-off people who all showed up on move-in day with their lives packed inside a U-Haul.

I introduced Pam to Scamz. She was impressed. He looked more like a financial planner at AXA than what she had in mind. She expected to see a man who was thugged out to the max.

Scamz said, "So you're the queen of pickpockets."

She laughed. "I've done a little dirt in my day."

"Dante speaks highly of you."

"He speaks highly of you too."

"Let me show you around." Scamz motioned for us to follow his stride. "If you have any questions, now is the time to ask."

Pam looked around the place in awe. This one was a Tudor-style crib on Miller Place with views of the city from damn near every window. Three levels with a separate guest house. Unlimited amenities.

She asked Scamz, "Where are the owners?"

"Out of state."

"No way they can walk up in here?"

"We're covered on that end."

Pam nodded. She asked questions like a student in a classroom. "What if the customers decide to ask the neighbors questions about the owners?"

"In Atlanta or Tennessee that might be a problem. This is L.A.," Scamz informed her. "Neighbors don't know each other. People stay out of each other's business."

"Won't take but one to ID you. Or me. Or anybody up here."

"Not on this one. Molly did the face-to-face work. She's the front man. Won't nobody get a decent look at anyone but her. Then she'll be back in New Mexico this time tomorrow."

"What's her story?"

"Divorce ruined her years ago. Changed her life."

He motioned toward Molly. She was sipping on a bottle of Evian. Molly was the Bad Witch, the same woman I'd seen last night at the Comedy Emporium, the lady who wore the big hat and shades. She had passed some of Scamz's earnings on to him then, right before he had that one-sided fight on the side streets.

Scamz nodded. "She needs money to get back on her feet. There are things even a brother in a nice suit can't pull off without help from the other side of the racial tracks."

"I saw a lot of people next door. What's going on?"

"Movie," Scamz said. "They've been shooting over there all week."

Pam perked up. "Really? What studio?"

Scamz said, "They're renting that crib and making a porno. I did my homework and peeped in yesterday. They're out from Magic City. A few of the sisters over there can throw down."

Pam said, "Yikes."

Scamz said, "So, you're an actress."

"Not that kind, though."

"Good. Don't disrespect yourself. You in the unions?"

"SAG and AFTRA."

"That's great," he said. "Who did you study with?"

She told him that she had graduated Bennett College in Greensboro, North Carolina.

Scamz asked, "Where have you studied since then?"

She named a few places, mentioned some films, commercials, sitcoms that had come and gone.

He asked, "Done any Greek tragedies?"

"Uh, no." That threw her. "Stage, but no Greek tragedies."

"Nothing more challenging for an actor. Nothing like watching cataclysmic events being performed on stage."

She was impressed. "You're into the theater?"

"Of course." He nodded. "You read Homer's the *Iliad*?"

"Not yet. Read the *Odyssey*, though. That was back in college."

"It's great."

There was more talk about Medea and the Eumenides, the human emotions and foibles of Greek gods, then about the feet of the actors in L.A. not being big enough to fit the shoes of titans, something like that. All of the talk about mythology was outside of my world, so I stood to the side, stood not too far away from Pam, and listened.

Scamz told Pam, "To do the classics correctly, you have to have a vocal coach. You need the breath and stamina to pull off the long speeches. Not like this crap you see on television or in the movies. That's real acting. Bare stage, no second chances."

With a smile, Pam agreed. Her breathing had mellowed.

Scamz said, "What we do has no second chances. Understand?"

She nodded.

Scamz put out his cigarette. Pam was standing there

with her mouth partly open, stunned by Scamz's knowledge. I was impressed by hers.

Pam said, "So, you like the Greek gods."

Scamz replied, "Of course."

"Is that because men were higher than women?"

"Not a bad ordering of things, but not at all."

"Why you like them so much?"

"No consequences for their actions."

That chilled me. Had the same effect on Pam for a
moment.

Just when it got too frosty, Pam chuckled. Then Scamz
smiled a smile that said he was a god with a sense of
humor. His sneaky laugh softened the air. I studied him
and tried to understand what made Scamz who he was,
tried to find out how he could get to people so easily.
Pam's eyes had softened. Everything about her was
womanly, but flirty. That made me a little angry. Started
feeling that resentment the moment Pam smiled at him
the way she did.

I understood what Scamz had done. Calmed her. Saw
nervousness in her eyes, talked to her on a level that
made her feel safe, and left her smiling, almost blushing,
in the end. He knew where she was from, where her
family was, what schools she went to, and knew she was
in the unions. That made her traceable. Scamz's boyish
smile and mellow voice had bought all of that info for
free.

Then, with his mission accomplished, he went back to
business. Underneath a cool breeze and palm trees—as
if we were planning a picnic—Scamz gave us a little pep
talk, told us what to look out for, what not to say. I already knew, but he still liked to remind people, keep it
fresh in their minds.

Scamz asked Jackson, "You alright?"

"Yeah. Why you ask?"

"You're looking a little preoccupied." That charming
smile was in full effect, the one that masked his real
mood. "My friend, my brother, all of us need you to be
focused. Too much at stake up here. You have problems,

we all have problems. Be professional. Do like the rest of us do, check them at your door before you leave home. Deal with them when you get back."

Jackson nodded.

Scamz motioned me to the side. He never lost that smile. He said, "I'm only using Jackson as a favor to you. He's a loser. He's wrapped around his woman and his kids. He slips and falls, he starts pointing fingers to save his own ass, and he will point a finger like that at you too."

We had a short rehearsal, just long enough to go over the hand signals, signs to let people know if the police had been spotted, if this was to be shut down, if a certain mark didn't feel right and we had to call it off. A touch of the right ear, a rub of the nose, the opening of a purse, all of those signals had specific, significant meanings.

Scamz said, "Keep your energy up, but keep it simple."

He gave us our instructions, never repeated himself, then walked away. It was time to get rolling.

Pam chewed her bottom lip. "I'm nervous."

"Butterflies?"

"Like you wouldn't believe. Curtains about to go up and my bladder is acting crazy."

We headed toward our car. A brand-new shiny black Benz.

We heard people talking and looked back. A few fine women and ordinary-to-ugly-looking men were heading inside the crib next door, going to clock in at Porno World. I wondered if they ever got laid off from getting laid. They waved at us, maybe thinking we were part of that crew, maybe inviting us to come join in on the fun, then went to earn their paychecks. We went to earn ours.

Pam asked, "Was that Heather Hunter?"

"Think so."

"You see her bad-ass shoes?"

"Just saw the weave."

"She did kill a few ponies."

I pushed a button on the keyless remote. The lights

flashed. Doors unlocked. Oscar couldn't do any of those tricks.

She said, "Interesting friend you have. Very charismatic. Like Creflo Dollar without the Bible."

I didn't reply, just gave Pam the key to the donkey we'd be riding. She didn't hesitate to take it.

"Nice ride," she said.

She got in and started the engine. It purred. She eased the chariot into gear and we floated down the hill with so much grace and dignity.

Pam shook her head. "I'm gonna hate getting back in my bucket."

That gleam was in her eye.

I said, "Think of it as a prop. At the end of the play, it stays at the theater."

"Personal prop."

"What?"

"It's a personal prop. A prop is something on stage that you don't use. You use it, then it becomes a personal prop. This, Dante, is a hellified personal prop."

"Like I said, at the end of the play, this becomes a prop."

"You could fuck up a wet dream, you know that?"

11

Most of Scamz's clientele—his marks—were as plastic as Hollywood was cutthroat. Pretentious tribes who lived like life had no price tag. Cartoons and caricatures of human beings who faked the funk and existed on the wrong side of their true income. Image was their only reality.

The first mark was a potbellied wannabe movie producer. He was middle-aged, sported a ponytail, and wore an ill-fitting three-hundred-dollar jacket, two-hundred-dollar trousers, ninety-dollar boat-neck shirt. He bragged about the cost of his threads from the moment he cruised into the skylighted foyer of the house. His burlesque of a woman had on more makeup than Tammy Faye Bakker, and wore a cheesy leopard-print mini, stiletto heels, and silver broaches. Her hair was dyed the color of ripe carrots.

He asked, "And you're leasing this at seven?"

"That's right." That was Molly with a warm smile on her face. The kind of grin that made you think she made the best apple pie in the world. She was like Betty White off *The Golden Girls*. White-haired, fitted chartreuse suit, low heels, string of pearls, a brand of Elizabeth Taylor perfume. She looked like a poster child for old money. She led people up the hill in a limo driven by Jackson. The people were told to meet her at different locations and follow her up to the crib because she didn't want them to disturb her current tenants. No tenants were in sight, but with all the family pictures placed all over the house, a disorganized office with papers scattered here and there, kids' toys in the living room and on the patio, food left on the stove, it looked like Poppa Bear and Momma Bear had taken Baby Bear for a walk through a galleria.

Molly told the customers, "Seven thousand a month. Place next door is leasing for eight-five."

"This is a better place. Has great karma. I feel the positive energy in the air."

"Former home of Richard Wright, David Hockney, and the Beatles."

"All at the same time?"

"Ha ha ha ha ha."

The next man was from El Salvador and had more earrings in each ear than he had natural orifices. His lover-man was holding his hand and blushing the whole time. The Spanish man dressed like a *Soul Train* hip-hop dancer, his lover in struggling plaids and checks. They wore military boots. New York stage actors in the market for a local pad so they could label themselves bi-coastal.

There were a few others. People with no jobs and plenty of money, small intellect, and less common sense. All were brought up at one-hour intervals, and only stayed between thirty and forty-five. One couple was only up for fifteen. A very fast-paced scheme that matched their lifestyles.

Jackson stayed nearby. He had a cell phone on his hip and the earpiece in his ear, that line always open to Scamz's phone, picking up new instructions like a quarterback in the Super Bowl.

Scamz was stationed across the street, holding a briefcase, standing near a Land Cruiser. When things were ready, Jackson would cough twice into his headset. It was so subtle that nobody would think anything about it. That's when Scamz would play his short part. When Molly and the happy-go-lucky victims got out of the limo, Scamz would smile, wave, and say, "Hello, Molly."

She'd say, "Hello, Robert."

"Jonathan and Sally told me they were moving."

"Unfortunately. Next week is their last week."

"You're renting it out or you're going to move back in?"

"Renting. Since Faber died and our children moved away to start their own families, I don't need this much space. You on the way back to the studios?"

"Yeah. We're finishing up a script for Denzel. I've got a meeting with his agent fifteen minutes ago. Call my secretary to set up a day and we'll do lunch at Eurochow."

"I'll have my assistant call and compare our schedules."

Scamz got inside the Land Cruiser. "Have a nice day."

"Have a nice day."

A minute after Scamz pulled away, Pam and I would cruise up in the Benz acting like honeymooners in search of a place to get their freak on. Pam would be at my side, her hand in mine, so close I could smell every bit of her perfume. When I strolled in with her, every straight guy swallowed his wanting.

Pam would stand at my side, her arm in my arm, wedding rings in plain view. Then I'd talk to the owner in front of the patrons, tell her how much we wanted the house.

I'd say, "We changed our mind about the place."

"You want it?"

"We decided not to rent up in Malibu."

"Why not?"

"The houses we've seen don't compare in price. Plus, the more I think about it, I'm not crazy about driving across Malibu Canyon every morning."

Pam would say, "Tried to get here sooner; we went by Wells Fargo to get our cashier's check."

"Well, at your request I've already taken you off the list and have others in line. These lovely people are taking their time to come out, and I'm disrupting my tenants' personal lives by having them leave in order to make the property available for inspection."

"Look, I'm sorry to come up without an appointment, but we really want this place."

"You'll have to contact my assistant later in the day to see if anyone was interested, and if I accepted a lease, and if not I'll see what we can do. But I make no promises. Fair?"

I'd smile. "That's fair."

She'd say, "Like I said before, I'm only showing my property today and this is for the serious. So, if you are really serious and would like to leave your deposit, in the event that another application is accepted, it will be returned to you by the end of the week."

The owner would emphasize it was first-come, first-serve, and if the couple she was interviewing didn't want the house, she'd contact us. What we said always varied, but that was the gist of it. That one-minute act gave urgency, made the others feel as if they had to snatch up the property yesterday.

Each dropped down a cashier's check or money order in their next breath. The wannabe movie producer wanted the crib so much he expanded his pompous chest and put a cashier's check for an extra six months' rent on the marble table. The two men who loved each other like Romeo and Juliet dropped down just as much cash, and between exchanging back rubs and butt squeezes both held the gleam of redecoration in their twinkling eyes.

In between the second and third run up the hill, Pam asked, "Why don't these people ask a lot of questions?"

"They don't want to come off as stupid. They trust."

"Unbelievable."

I glanced at Pam. "You wanna go down on Third to the Little Door and grab some food later?"

"You asking me out on another date?"

"Yeah. It's a French joint. Real French waiters and everything. They have candlelit tables and open the ceiling and you can see the moon."

"Sounds nice and romantic, but no thanks. Don't like French food. I'm a simple girl."

"A'ight. Then we can hit Mo' Better Meaty Meat Burger."

"Getting a Mo' Better Meaty Burger is the last thing I should worry about."

"Whassup?"

"You ever wonder what might happen to us if we get caught doing this?" she said.

"All the time. I'm human. I get scared. You scared?"

"Scared of wearing prison blues and using a steel toilet."

"Sounds like you did some time."

Her voice lowered. "Few months."

"What happened?"

"Don't wanna talk about it."

"Where's your kid?"

She hesitated. "Why?"

"Just asking."

She stared at the wedding ring on her hand. "This ring is nice."

"Scamz says it adds to the illusion. Think he conned it off somebody."

"Being a good woman ain't the move, so I guess that's what I'll have to do to get one, huh?"

"Surprised you've never had one."

"This is a damn good ring." She let out an exhausted sigh. "You have kids?"

"None that I know of."

"Then you don't have as much to lose as I do."

My mind drifted. My thoughts were seven years behind. When I was fresh out of juvenile hall. On the West Coast without friend, family, job, or shelter. A brother who was getting knocked off bicycles and passing off rocks-in-a-box as brand-new televisions to make food money. I was down on Wilshire and Crenshaw when I spotted a BMW and did the bike trick. Timed it so he'd clip me as he turned. I hit the ground hard, but knew how to roll like a pro to keep from being hurt for real. A crowd gathered. The driver and an old man got out of the car. The old man limped toward me, but the driver told him to stay near the car. The driver came over. He didn't rush. Lit up a cigarette on the way. I shielded the

sun from my eyes and looked up into the face of a man
in a double-breasted suit.

That man was Scamz.

He asked me how much I wanted. That was the first
thing he said. He gave me twice what I asked. The second thing he said was that he invented that trick twenty
years ago. The third was asking me if I wanted to make
a few more ends in a way that wouldn't cause brain
damage or a broken leg. I was hungry. I left my bike in
the grass and rode in a BMW for the first time. Got in
the backseat with two of the finest women I'd ever seen
in my life. Both of them were dressed like attorneys.
They were introduced as Scamz's friends. Both were his
lovers. That was when he liked to double his pleasure.
And that old man with the razor bumps was Big Slim.

We ate lunch at Phillip's Barbecue down off Vernon,
then I was taken up to Sherman Oaks to the pool hall. I
asked him what was up with all the generosity, wondered if he was setting me up for something. He
laughed. Scamz told me that I reminded him of somebody—himself when he was my age. Then he told me
the story about growing up in Mississippi, a place he de-
scribed as the land of mosquitoes and poverty, with a
house filled with fatherless rugrats. I didn't trust him,
not at all. But with that story, he got me to tell him
about my life.

"Dante?"

"Huh?" I snapped out of my daydream. "Whassup?"

"I said, do you see how people look at us when we're
driving?"

I wiped those memories away. "What you mean?"

"With respect. With envy."

She wasn't lying. Men looked at me and gave me the
thumbs-up; women looked at her and did the same.
They thought that we were part of that upper ten per-
centile.

She said, "Damn near every car has an American flag
on it."

"Patriotism at its best."

"Oh, please. If they were giving those flags away, that would be patriotism. They've jacked the prices up and played on people's fears and emotions in the name of capitalism."

"On every corner hardworking Mexicans are selling American flags made in China."

"Yeah." She chuckled at my sarcasm. "America the beautiful."

I told her, "You're pretty funny, in your own way."

"You too."

We did that newlywed routine three more times. Each time Pam got better, acted like it was no big deal, which was some damn good acting. She led the way on two in a row.

Then came a problem. Something nobody expected.

An actress and her husband were the last customers. Me and Pam stepped out of our high-class ride and walked into the foyer of that house holding hands. We slid into our little routine.

Pam said, "Hi, Molly."

"You and your husband are back."

"Love those shoes. Jimmy Choos?"

"Ah, yes they are."

"We changed our mind about the place."

"You want it?"

"We decided not to rent up in Malibu."

The people with Molly were looking at the kitchen, and the moment Pam's voice carried, the woman peeped around the corner, saw Pam, and lit up. Pam's mouth dropped to the floor.

She beamed. "Pam? Girl, that you?"

I swallowed.

"Tammy?" Pam froze up. That was a very scary moment. Then she readjusted, pushed her lips up into some sort of a smile. "Oh, my God, I heard you had moved to Paris."

Her name was Tammy Barrett, and her writer-husband came out of the kitchen, was right there with her, holding their newborn. Tammy was a yellow gal with a nice shape and a little size to her. Her husband was thick, like a linebacker who'd become a couch potato. He was soft around the middle, very artistic and reserved, had short dreads, a beard, was dressed down in jeans and a leather coat.

Tammy was screaming like a teenager, "When did you get married?"

Tammy was damn excited and she went on and on, talking, jabbering, not giving anybody enough space to jump in. From her diatribe I picked up that her and Pam had done quite a few plays together down in Hollywood. And it sounded like it had been a while back.

"I'm just running my mouth. Darnell, you remember Pamela?" Tammy motioned toward her man and said to Pam, "I introduced Darnell to you the last night I was in *Who Will Be There for Us?*"

"Oh, yeah. He was—that night when everything got crazy?"

"He was married to somebody else back then."

"Girl, you are too scandal-lust. Seems like everything worked out."

Molly opened and closed her purse, a signal that the deal was being called off. This was too risky.

Tammy said, "Let me see that ring. When did you get married?"

I started, "Last—"

And I froze. Pam was right. We should've created a history. Her friends were waiting for an answer. I coughed like I had a dry throat to buy some time.

Jackson moved near Tammy. He'd grab her if Molly gave him the signal. I had sized up Darnell already. With a soft belly, one good blow could take him to his knees. Two more and it would be lights out until we could figure out what to do next.

Pam patted my back and stepped up to the plate with an answer. "Not long after you jetted for Paris. We met around the time when I was auditioning for *The Vagina Monologues.*"

Tammy asked, "You get the part?"

"They went with Robin Givens." Pam turned toward me. "You okay, sweetie?"

I said it was my allergies acting up.

That was when Pam had to introduce us. And women want the details. The when did she get married, where did we meet. Before they could get to asking too many questions, I cut in. "Sorry, but I have to be in a meeting pretty soon."

Tammy went on, "I'm living in Paris, but I need to be over here for a few months to do some work. I've got a part in a movie with Nicolas Cage, and I'm doing my first jazz album here in the states."

Pam asked, "Nina Simone stuff?"

"You know it."

Her husband smiled and added, "She's done three, but this will be the first one in English."

Tammy said, "Make sure you give her one of your new books. He has a new book out. It's on tape too. I read the female voice."

Pam chuckled. "Look at you. You are working your behind off."

Jackson was still in position. Scamz had to be on the other end of the cordless, evaluating the situation. If Molly ran her hand across her neck in a casual way, this would get ugly real fast.

Molly had her sweet smile on, but in a firm voice she said, "Hate to rush you, but we really must get moving."

Darnell said, "We need to go anyway. I have a meeting with some people at Trillion."

We were about to ease up, but that got Pam's attention. She raised a brow. "Whassup at Trillion?"

Tammy had a huge smile. "They've optioned his first book. He has to meet with the producers and the director to talk about doing the script."

Pam said, "Good for you. Hope you have a part for me."

"What are you in now?" Tammy asked.

"I'm working on a few things. Just finished *For the Love of Freedom*."

"Ben Guillory's play. Wonderful." Tammy said. She glanced at the car we were driving, saw Pam still had the keys in her hand, and went on with her assumption. "I'm so happy for you. Married. Doing so well. I used to worry about you."

Pam spoke up. "I'm fine."

"You sure?"

"Yeah. Everything is working out. I'm blessed."

They had one of those girl moments, one with eye contact that was high on emotion and no dialogue. Some information was being transmitted that only the two of them knew about. Pam's eyes became sensitive. For a moment it looked like Tammy was about to head toward the land of tears.

Then both of them laughed and hugged each other.

Tammy held on to her smile. "Now look at you. Both of us have come a long way, girl."

Pam smiled. "We sure have."

Tammy said, "I have to get your number before I go. We have to get together and do lunch. I'm hooking up with my old girls, Chante and Karen, and maybe you can meet with us at Spago."

"How are they?"

"Chante is on her second baby, and Karen is about to take the bar."

"Sounds like everybody is doing so well."

"We've all been stressed, blessed, and put to the test."

Pam went on, "If you're looking for a crib up here, you've passed the test."

I wanted to cringe. Pam had slipped and said "if you're looking" and not "if we're looking." That let her friends know we couldn't afford this crib. One slip could shatter the whole confidence game.

Fear was in Molly's eyes; her Betty White demeanor became more like Joan Crawford.

Jackson reacted too. That look was in his eyes, the one that said he'd take somebody out before he let anybody separate him from his kids for a four-year stretch.

Molly's hand went into her purse. She was about to

pull out her signature weapon. Hell was moments from breaking loose.

The child started wailing. Maybe he sensed trouble and was screaming for help. That got Tammy and Darnell's undivided attention. Made them drop everything and switch gears.

Molly's hand stayed in her bag, and that Joan Crawford look wasn't as harsh. Jackson backed down too. He nodded his head. He wasn't nodding at us, just reacting to whatever instructions Scamz was giving him through the earpiece.

I kept reading Tammy and Darnell for a tell that they were suspicious; didn't see anything. Darnell was preoccupied with the kid; Tammy was too busy talking to listen. But I didn't trust that. I heard shit and acted like I didn't hear it all the damn time. That was another way you played people.

Tammy made a baby voice and said, "Feeding time. Somebody hungry, ain't you, boo?"

"Since you've got the food," Darnell said, "we better get to our mobile restaurant."

Tammy said, "For the next five or six months, I am the mobile restaurant."

Laughter.

Tammy and her family headed toward a silver BMW X5. They had followed Molly up the hill. Jackson and Molly headed for the Town Car, their pace a little slower than ours, but they got in the car. They didn't drive away. I lingered with Tammy and Darnell, played the buddy role a moment to see what they were thinking. Had to know if something had fallen apart. If I pulled on my right ear, Jackson would come running back.

Darnell said, "I dunno."

His wife said, "Don't start with that."

Pam asked, "What?"

"Darnell thinks that this deal is too good to be true."

"It is," Darnell said. "Kinda weird that they won't take a personal check, and insist on money orders or cashier's checks."

Tammy said, "Why is that weird, Darnell? Geesh. If somebody moves in on a bad check, do you know how hard it is to get them out? Does the movie *Pacific Heights* ring a bell?"

He went on, "People shouldn't rush into a major contract like this. This is a lot of money."

"We can afford it and it's a write-off," his wife retorted.

"Besides the point."

"Always suspicious. You still have the mind of an esquire."

I kept my smile in full bloom and asked, "What do you mean?"

"Once an attorney," Tammy said about her husband, "always an attorney."

Darnell said, "I know what's up."

"What?" I was reaching for my ear.

He said, "It's because we're black. No matter how high we rise, we'll never rise above racism. They always want to see our money first. That's how Denny's ended up getting sued."

I wiped the sweat from my nose and put my hands back in my jacket pocket. "Yeah, right. Bet they're just asking the black people for that much cash up front."

Molly and Jackson were still in that car.

After the child was loaded up and phone numbers had been exchanged, Darnell gave us one of his books, signed that legal thriller to us as a married couple, then we said our good-byes and followed them down the hill. They turned left, we made a right.

I asked Pam, "You a'ight?"

Pam had a look on her face, sort of like disbelief. "Tammy, that girl used to go out to Rancho Cucamonga to sing at this two-bit restaurant with this two-bit band, and she got discovered. Became big in Paris. We stood side by side in the same play and she used to beg me to go out there and sing with her, and I didn't see the point of going to Rancho Fucking Cucamonga. Look at her. That driving out to West Hell got her a husband, a career that is growing like a weed."

I didn't say anything. That was the least of my worries. That had been close enough to make me realize how much I didn't want to go live in a free hotel that offered three squares a day. Didn't want to spend a few years counting stones in a wall or talking to cockroaches.

She said, "You know the difference between her ride and this ride?"

"This is a six-cylinder and they were in an eight."

"No. Theirs was legit."

The expression on her face and the heavy tone of her voice made it sound like her old friend had the life that she was supposed to have.

I wondered who had mine.

12

We drove around for a while. Burned gas until the c-phone rang and told us everything had been shut down, then instructed us where to go meet with the rest of the crew. I told Pam where to turn, what narrow roads to take up another hill. All the way I looked in the rearview, searched for trouble.

Then we were at the crib. Not the same one we had just used in the rental scam, but the one not too far away where Scamz had been laid out in a hot tub with Sierra catering to him. We wouldn't go back to the other crib. Sometimes tenants liked to double back, maybe bring a friend and brag about where they were gonna be living. That operation was shut down like Napster.

Pam said, "Is he doing the same scam at this crib too?"

"Don't matter."

She chuckled. "What, am I fired?"

We rang the bell and Sierra opened the door, still living in silence. She looked at me, then her eyes went over Pam, head to toe, did that evaluation thing that women do, before she stepped aside and let us in. Jackson was there already. He had a tall drink in his hand; the fumes from the rum were strong enough for me to know it wasn't diluted too much. At least a quarter of it was gone.

Jackson said, "That was too close for comfort."

I said, "I know."

He gave Pam a look that said she'd almost created a nasty situation. Then he headed toward the kitchen. Quite a few people were over that way.

I asked, "Where you going?"

"Gonna try to call Robin again. You better go see the boss man."

"He pissed?"

"See for yourself. He's that way."

We headed through two rooms toward a large sunroom. Voices came from around the corner, blended with the flow of classical music. Peaceful music like that always worked my nerves.

"—motherfucking amateurs." That was Molly's voice. It wasn't loud, but it was loud enough, too damned intense. She raged on, "I don't work with amateurs and you know that. Don't pull that shit again. If somebody works with us, they have to know what the fuck they're doing. When I give a signal that means to act now, not to fuck around exchanging numbers and shit, hugging babies and swapping recipes for homemade cookies. That bitch could've had us all living in a five-by-nine. And how in the hell are you going to use an actress? Actors are the most recognizable people on this fucking planet."

We had stopped around the corner. Pam gripped my hand like she wanted to moonwalk out of there.

Then in that calm tone, Scamz asked Molly, "You through?"

"Maybe, maybe not."

"Take a walk. Have a drink. I'll be with you in a few."

We stepped around the corner. Scamz was sitting at the piano that overlooked the city, playing like a professional. And he was pissed off. Not the kind of pissed off that threw chairs, but a very methodical irritation was in his face, the kind you'd have to know a man for a while to recognize.

Pam said, "Hey, if you have a problem with me, tell me to my—"

Scamz interrupted, "We don't work that way up here, Pam. All problems come through me first."

Molly marched by without a word. She'd already changed clothes. Dumped the Betty White gear and put on a studded blue-jean suit, pulled her hair back in a ponytail, scrubbed her overdone makeup off her face. She had taken twenty years off her appearance just that fast.

Me and Pam stood there a moment. Listened to him play. She was too impressed.

Scamz said, "Beethoven. Sonata in C minor. Written during his first period. Did you know he had an alcoholic, abusive father?"

My hands tightened; for a moment I heard a scream, saw the flash of police lights in my eyes. I blinked and it all went away.

Scamz went on, "And he overcame. He was a true survivor. For a while. His own brother refused to give him fire, wouldn't give him heat, and that led to pneumonia. And that pneumonia led him to his grave. Sad for a man to live like that, to be betrayed like that, to go out like that."

Neither of us answered. It was all rhetorical.

Scamz stopped playing and came toward us, drew his smoke as he told Pam, "They recognized you."

Pam looked twice as nervous. "That white woman was tripping."

"No room for racism up here," Scamz replied.

Pam stood there, waited for Scamz to finish his critical thinking and get back to us with his thoughts on the matter. I felt like a child waiting to be chastised. Reminded me of when I stood before my old man, trembling in fear, never knowing which way his mood was going to swing.

Scamz spoke. "Molly was right. She's been my friend for years. She's been on lockdown a few times. And she's at the age where she's afraid to be on lockdown again."

Pam's expression changed. She was a kid in the principal's office.

Scamz went on, "Reverse your point of view, disagree with yourself. In other words, put yourself in her shoes."

Pam said, "This was my first time."

Scamz made a motion that said that didn't make any difference to him at all. He said, "Fine, you're a new jack. Let's take it to your level. Maybe just imagine yourself on stage, in a master performance, where your name is in lights, where you've rehearsed for days on end, and one of the extras or cocky performers who refuses to be a team player just totally ruined the illusion you were trying to create. How would you feel about it?"

Pam nodded.

Scamz said, "Now imagine at least four years in jail as a consequence."

Pam swallowed.

Scamz said, "We went over the signals. You understood what you were supposed to do when it got risky. This is what happens when you bring in somebody, Dante. You pumped her up, made her sound like a pro, said she could handle this, not put us all at risk."

"I'm sorry," Pam said. Some tremble was in her voice—not the tremble of fear, but the edges of frustration.

"No, I'm to blame. I did Dante a favor. This is what happens when you do a man a favor. You take risks. Uncalculated risks. Your instructions were clear, who was to do the talking, who was to say what, what to do when trouble rose to the top."

Pam replied, "How was I supposed to know I'd see somebody I knew?"

I stepped up. "I'll cover it."

Scamz asked, "Why are you jumping into business that has nothing to do with you, Dante? Keep out of my fires."

I repeated, "I'll cover it."

Scamz paused. Our eye contact was strong.

"This is between boss and employee, Dante. This is early intervention and a performance review. Get your emotions in check and be professional. Not being able to master your emotions and control your moods is what got you on lockdown in the first place. Ain't that right, Dante?"

Again we gave each other prison stares. Scamz took a slow drag on his Djarum and smiled.

Then he told Pam, "Overall, you did an excellent job. You were really valuable to me today."

His words were pats on her shoulder, echoed respect.

"No sweat about your friends," he said with utter calmness and sincerity. "They were nice people. I watched them walk up. Saw them interact as a family. Picked them up talking through Jackson's earpiece. The way he was with his kid, have to admire that. Not many men are like that. Seen too many women struggling out there. Maybe one day I'll meet the right woman, slow down, and be like them."

That got soft laughs out of us, with Scamz's boyish chuckle leading the way. He was the greatest salesman in the world.

We followed Scamz back into the back part of the crib, near the sundeck. That was where a few of the others had congregated. At least twelve people had arrived. A few had been in on this scam in some way, others were just in the business.

Lobster scampi. Shrimp suzette. Crawfish étouffée. Gumbo. Crab cakes. Dinner salads. Salmon salads. Blackened catfish. Fried chicken. New York steaks. Clam chowder. Vegetables. Fruit. Most of the grub was Cajun food that had been catered from Harold and Belle's, down on Jefferson and Tenth in the Crenshaw District. That was the black man's Spago. A bowl of caviar was on the side. Fish eggs for people who couldn't hang with some of the best food in Los Angeles.

Pam grubbed on pretty much everything. Ate and drank like she had no food at home. I ate the same way, but took it easy on the drinks because I didn't want to wrap Oscar around a pole.

Pam said, "If we had some dominoes, this would be perfect."

"You play bones?"

"Please. I'm the queen of bones."

Sierra was serving drinks, taking coats, being the

silent hostess. Seemed like she loved that housewife kinda role because she did it with a subtle smile. She moved as if this were her home. Had no doubt picked out a room to be a nursery. Walking in her own land of make-believe, pretending that Scamz was her man alone. A projector was on and it was aimed at the pool, using the bottom of the pool as a screen. Somebody had popped in a risqué movie, a bootleg copy of a big-booty Latina girl who was now a mega movie star, a tape people said didn't exist. It had everybody's attention.

Pam said, "Damn. This is a nice party. People swimming and drinking champagne. All this food."

"Always celebrate a good day at work," Scamz said. "Never know when it might be your last."

He went from person to person, told them they did a good job, said things that made them all feel good about themselves, patted each on the back and slid each employee a white envelope. The eagle was flying and people were ready to go out and play.

Pam whispered, "When do I get paid?"

"After we finish swimming with the sharks."

"Should I ask—"

"Scamz does things his own way, in his own time."

"A control freak."

We mingled, talked about this and that, mostly people running down some short cons they had done here and there, doing that the same way I suppose people play catch-up at a class reunion. Pam held a drink in her hand, she was all ears. So much fascination was in her eyes.

There was a lot of laughter, a lot of drinking.

Pam asked, "Is there a school to go to learn all this?"

"Yeah, the School of Hard Knocks."

Laughter.

"Just don't get your degree at the county."

Pam had a sideways smile. "Been there, done that."

"Club Fed has a much nicer degree program."

"Now you tell me."

More people laughed.

Molly was still there, sipping on her second apple martini, eating caviar, angst in her expression every time she glanced at Pam, no respect in her eyes. Scamz made his way over to her, did it in his own time, massaged both of her small shoulders with his sturdy hands, whispered a few words in her ear, and a smile grew on her face. She laughed and became a beautiful woman. She let down her guard and her sensuality came through. There was some carnal history there, a connection that went back years, and it showed in her jealous eyes. The same look she had for Pam, she had for Sierra.

Scamz motioned for me to come his way. I did and followed him into a back room. We picked up Jackson along the way. He was in the hallway using the phone. He was on his second drink. He usually stopped at one.

Scamz asked, "Who you calling?"

He said, "Robin."

I asked, "Heard from her yet?"

"Not yet."

Guilt made my insides become a knot of fire.

We closed the door to the back room and had a short meeting.

Scamz had two shoeboxes. One was filled with credit cards. The other had green cards.

He said, "I thought that me and you could do it by ourselves, Dante. But I decided one more hand wouldn't hurt. Jackson said he wanted to be in on my runs tomorrow night."

Jackson looked at me and nodded. He'd made his own deal behind my back.

I asked, "Hot or cold?"

Scamz replied, "Smooth and guaranteed."

"What we doing?"

Scamz told me, "Easy night. Only two quick runs. Shouldn't take any more than three hours."

Jackson asked, "Where we going?"

"Westwood," Scamz said. "And Boyle Heights."

"Boyle Heights?" That was Jackson. "You're joking."

I was on the same page with Jackson. Hearing Boyle

Heights made that knot inside my stomach tighten. With all the stuff Scamz was doing over a few hours, he had to be wearing himself thin.

I said, "Don't you think you're taking too many chances?"

Scamz said, "I've done a lot more multitasking than this."

Jackson said, "Let me be straight up. I'm not so sure about this."

Our savior in a four-button suit put out his Djarum, then lit up another one, kept the air smelling like sweet cloves.

Scamz told Jackson, "So, your ex got you for sixteen large."

He nodded and lines came in his forehead, in his neck. He took a long sip of his drink.

Scamz had reminded Jackson where he was in life. That reminder was a low blow. That reluctant look in Jackson's eyes was still there, but the need to survive was overruling that apprehension. My problems, Jackson's problems, Pam's problems—Scamz could write a check and make them all go away. Like any good employer, he had us where he wanted us.

There was a lot of plastic in that plain shoebox. American Express. Visa. Unocal. That kind of plastic made the scam I pulled on Tommy Boy look like Amateur Night at the Apollo.

I said, "That's a lot of plastic."

"Sierra is doing her job better than anybody I've ever had on my payroll."

"Even Arizona?"

"Arizona never helped me line my pockets like this."

"Pussy and money."

He nodded. "She never hesitates to distribute either one."

That was why Sierra was so valuable to him. No doubt that she had gotten access to a shitload of credit card numbers at Wells Fargo. All Scamz had to do after that was pay a couple thousand for a small machine to imprint the numbers. The plastic needed to make a charge card was cheaper than a Big Mac. That plastic would be good for about thirty days, about as long as one billing cycle, so he had to move that product quick. He was more into fast sell, quick profits than using the cards to buy merchandise, then having to fence a lot of goods. Too many layers of work in an operation like that, too much that can go wrong. Plus, that kept his face away from the cameras at stores and banks.

I've learned a lot from him. Too bad I couldn't put that knowledge on a résumé.

I asked Scamz, "You worried about Nazario?"

He smiled a smile that said he wasn't scared of anybody, but he wasn't a fool either.

Jackson pulled out his own pack of cigarettes. He lit a Marlboro and asked, "We need a piece?"

Scamz shook his head. "I loathe guns. Loathe any weapon of genocide and mass destruction."

We concluded the meeting and went back toward the party. Jackson stopped at the phone again.

Pam was finishing up a glass of wine, her eyes glowing a bit, when I made it back to her side.

She asked me, "What's Scammy Boy up to?"

"Nothing."

"Don't snap at me, just asking."

"Sorry about that. Just taking care of some more business."

"What's he gonna do with the other crib we just left?"

I told her that by now a cleaning service was over there scrubbing the house from top to bottom. Scamz had already tossed the house keys to the winds. Not a fingerprint or a cobweb would be left.

Pam said, "I calculated how much he pulled in today. Seven thousand for first, another seven for last, then add in other fees, that was at least fifteen to eighteen grand. Then a couple of people paid for six months in advance. Now check it out, even with a discount, they had to drop down at least forty-four thousand. And two people did that."

"Whassup with you counting somebody else's chips?"

"That is a helluva lot of money. He must be the richest man in Babylon."

Scamz came back, asked me step to the side with him so we could chat again.

He told me, "Pam's got the right look, the one people trust, and she has a lot of potential to be a natural at this. Smart woman. Very smart woman. She can sound professional, or like she's from the other side of town, and that's an asset. She's beautiful without being distracting."

"She's a damn good actress."

"She acted like she was about to rip Molly a new asshole."

We laughed.

He asked, "You hitting that?"

"She's out of your age range."

"Who said I had a range?"

"Then she weighs too much."

"Not when you carry it like that."

He went to Pam, started a conversation. He asked her about her Puerto Rican roots and she said a few things in Spanish. Scamz did the same. Both shared a lot of smiles and chuckles. They kept their conversation on that Spanish channel for a while. I had no idea what was up, what they were talking about. That knot in my belly got a little tighter. Sierra was in the background, watching Pam have an old-school chitchat with Scamz. Her face looked just as tense.

Scamz asked Pam, "You remember Mingles?"

"Hell, yeah. Used to party there every Friday night. The Ramada Inn at LAX. Had the meanest waitress working there. Man, sister was mean."

Just like that he had wooed her. He was the best one-minute manager in the city. One-minute praises. One-minute reprimands. Then on to fun. Watching Scamz was like a lesson in psychology.

While they fell into their talk of yesterday, Sierra ran her fingers through her mane and left the room. She wanted some attention and she wasn't getting it. Maybe seeing

Scamz with Pam, listening to them talk, made her realize
how young she was. The same thing it was doing to me.

Jackson was on the phone again. Sipping, smoking,
and checking his messages. He was worried. I was about
to tell him that I'd seen Robin, but once again I struggled with the decision to be an informer, then let it go.
Told myself that now wasn't the place or the time. I'd
give it until tomorrow.

I went to the counter and looked over a stack of
rental applications. The ones people had filled out for
the crib we just abandoned. Each one asked for driver's
license numbers, social security numbers, and credit
card numbers. Enough information to wreak havoc on
somebody's credit before they had a clue. The application made the renter's rip-off look legit and kept one
scam feeding another.

Scamz asked Pam, "Was Tammy nice to you when you
two were friends?"

"She always had my back. She was so supportive.
Never playa-hated on anybody."

Scamz pulled Tammy and Darnell's application out,
tore it up, trashed it.

Pam smiled the warmest smile.

I wanted to ask him if he did that to impress Pam. If
anybody else had cost him seven grand, his mood
wouldn't've been so agreeable.

Then we were ready to go. Jackson had vanished.
Everybody was busy socializing and nobody had seen
him leave. We looked around every room, searched outside on the grounds and called his name, even looked to
see if anybody was floating at the bottom of the pool.
Scamz said he'd bring Jackson down on the next run. We
left that at that. Me and Pam got in Scamz's ride. I sat in
the back. Scamz played Mozart as he drove us back
down the hill, then back over into Sherman Oaks.

He asked Pam, "What about Currie's down in Long
Beach? Ever hang out there?"

"Ooo, that was back in my Cabbage Patch, E.T., eating Fatburger at three in the morning days."

I let them talk about the dinosaur age, back when Kurtis Blow was doing his Christmas rap and Lisa Canning was the sexiest DJ on K-DAY. Back when former police chief Darryl Gates had LAPD using a battering ram on crack houses. I just chilled out and absorbed the history lesson.

Pam told Scamz, "Straight up, if you can use me, I need some more work."

"Dante told me that you wasn't interested."

"Dante's not my agent. I speak for myself."

She glanced back at me. My expression was nonchalant, but I was getting pissed.

Scamz told her, "You're ambitious."

"Ambition got you where you are, right?"

He laughed his sneaky laugh. She laughed along with him. It sounded like a song.

Scamz said, "Everybody gets a nickname. We'll call you Pickpocket Pam."

"Pardon me if I don't get all teary-eyed," Pam said. "What's Dante's nickname?"

"Cool Hand Dante. Like Cool Hand Luke. Never cracks under pressure."

Pam asked, "What you call that Molly witch who snapped on me?"

"Sometimes we call her the Bad Witch. That's when she's in a good mood."

"What do you call her other times?"

"Switchblade Molly," Scamz answered. He took an easy draw on his Djarum. "And she has earned that name a hundred times a hundred."

"Yikes," Pam replied. "She ain't but two feet tall and couldn't weigh more than a buck-oh-five."

"And you don't want to mess with her," he told her as a warning.

I said, "She goes in her purse, you're out a quart of blood."

"And Dante's not exaggerating," Scamz said. "She won't hesitate to get Peckinpah-ish."

"I'll remember that," Pam replied. "Especially the Peckinpah-ish part."

I asked, "What's a peck and paw?"

"Peckinpah," Scamz said. "A movie director. Made some violent movies."

I said, "He could direct my life story."

We laughed.

Scamz dropped us off at Jinky's Café, right across the street from the pool hall. He took to Ventura Boulevard, mixed in those six lanes of madness and waved good-bye like he was the Lone Ranger.

Pam came near me. She asked, "We be done?"

"We be done."

I headed up Ventura, crossed over, and walked toward Moorpark.

Pam kept up. "I didn't get paid. Don't fuck me over."

"When we get to your car, check your glove compartment."

"What you mean?"

"Look in your glove compartment."

We got back to our spots and she chirp-chirped her alarm off, got in on the passenger's side. She found a plain white envelope with ten crisp C-notes stuffed inside her glove compartment. I had fifteen of the same dead presidents. I was parked two cars behind her. She hurried back toward Oscar; her bushy hair bounced with her anxious stride. Surprise was written all over her face.

"When did . . . my car was locked, alarm was on, how did—"

"Don't ask."

She had found something else on her front seat. A copy of the *Iliad*.

That was another subtle message from Scamz. One that shook her up and made her raise a brow and smile. Pam gazed the way her savior had left. "Scamz is scary. And smooth."

"He can swim in the ocean and not get wet."

She said, "Thousand bucks."

"Poor man's fortune."

"Not even. He pulled down all that cash, and we barely got a corner of it."

"You don't get to be the richest man in Babylon by being generous."

She shook her head. "Looks like he has a thing for cute little Pinays."

"Sounds like we have a playa-hater."

"Nope. Just surprised at how easy it is to do something like this."

"Takes a lot of work to make something look easy."

She held her cash and stared at that book.

Traffic zoomed up Moorpark. We stood there and watched the world go by. I was looking toward the pool hall. I didn't feel comfortable standing out here in plain sight. No sign of a ghetto-red car with a plastic Jesus on the dashboard.

I asked, "What you thinking about?"

"Tammy Barrett. We did the same plays, sang the same songs. Hell, I was the lead in one play and she was my understudy. I'm supposed to be doing as well as she's doing."

"Well, maybe her book-writing husband is making serious cash."

She chuckled. "Guess I should've rode out to Rancho Cucamonga. Don't get me wrong, I'm so happy for her. Just hate that I had to lie and say I was at the same level. So, next time I run into her, I have to lie again, I guess. Have to tell her I got divorced and you took everything."

"What do you think is holding your career back?"

"Everybody loves my reel, but when you're my age and don't have the credits like Vivica or Halle, when they want to put you up against somebody like Regina Taylor, you're a hard sell and it's a rough battle. You don't get as many calls. I'm sacrificing now. Have to show my agent how serious I am by being available, so that means I can't get a full-time gig somewhere, because that would wreck my chances. But at the same time, gotta pay my bills, and that keeps my pocketbook drained."

"Catch twenty-two."

"Twenty-four-seven. That time I took off changed everything."

"Why'd you take time off?"

She smiled and that was her shield. "Just did."

My eyes went over her brown skin once again.

She asked, "Why are you looking at me like that again?"

"I know this place over at Olympic and Robertson, Natalee's, a real funky art deco place with waterfalls built into the walls, and it has the best Thai food in the city."

"This is where we part company." She smiled. "Thanks for this hook-up. Time to bounce. Heading home."

I wondered if she was trying to tip back up the hill to Scamz-ville. Wouldn't be surprised if he whispered an invitation in her ear while I was mixing with the heathens. Bet she was headed to the land of charisma and caviar, ready to strip down to her skin and have intimate moments in a Jacuzzi tub to the sounds of Mozart and Beethoven.

. I said, "Take me home with you."

She moved away from me the way women do when they've heard the wrong words slip off a man's tongue.

She said, "Know when to be a Q, when to be an Alpha."

"That a yes or no?"

Her hips shifted again, this time like she was leaving. She put her hand on her car door, pulled it part of the way open.

I didn't chase her.

She turned her eyes back to me, then said, "I had a date tonight."

"Okay. Sounds like you got a man."

"Well, I'm not using all this ass as a paperweight."

"Why didn't you just say so?"

"Would you have hooked me up with Scamz if I had told you I had a man?"

"You never know."

"I doubt it. Look, I'm seeing somebody, yeah. But he hasn't called."

"What are you saying?"

"Do I have to spell it out for you?"

We stared until she motioned at Big Slim's joint.

She asked, "They gamble up in there?"

I nodded and told her a few of the rules.

She asked, "You wanna shoot pool?"

"You good?"

"Better than you."

"You wish."

"Wanna go inside Big Slim's joint?"

I thought about Nazario. He was out there somewhere. I said, "Anywhere but here."

"I know what you mean. That old man gives me the
heebie-jeebies."

"Wanna go down on Crenshaw? There's a spot by the
probation department."

"Nah. I know that spot."

"Scared you might run into a few of your men?"

"You never know. I have a thing for bad boys." She
laughed. "It's too wild down there."

"What about Gotham's in Santa Monica?"

"Club 360. Natalee's. The Little Door. All you know
are the trendy places, huh?"

"Tell me where and I'm there."

"I know another place. Follow me."

I cranked Oscar up. Pam hopped in her car.

I shadowed that beautiful woman away from the land
of broken dreams.

13

We took the 101 until we hit the 405 South, made our way to the 710 South, rode that stretch of concrete until it ended in Long Beach down near the *Queen Mary*. All the way Oscar did his best to keep up with Pam's ninety-mile-an-hour pace. We parked in a free parking lot that used to service the mall, then I followed Pam's lead and headed toward the Blue Café. It was a square building back away from the promenade. Downstairs it was a bar and deli, a wooden floor full of round wooden tables, had a stage along the front window for a blues band. Upstairs had gray brick walls, concrete floors, and darker decorations, pictures of dead movie stars and deader blues singers, like Robert Johnson.

About ten other tables had players, all into either nine- or eight-ball worlds of their own. Looked like mostly men and women about my age. Most of them had on shorts and CSULB sweatshirts.

She acted like it was Sadie Hawkins Day and paid our way in. That made it clear that this wasn't a date, that she didn't owe me anything. She led the way while we climbed the stairs from floor one to floor two, singing along with the blues song pumping from the wall speakers.

The waitress came over to see if we wanted to get some drinks. I wanted a whiskey sour; Pam wanted a pink panties. When the waitress carded her, Pam was pleased, maybe flattered. The waitress checked the DOB, smiled wide, and said a perky "happy birthday" before she left.

I said, "Hold on, whoa. It's your birthday?"

"And what a way to spend it."

"We're the same sign."

"Yep. We're both born under a bad sign."

"Happy birthday."

The right corner of her lip gave me some of that Debbi Morgan smile. Those dimples lit up the room.

I asked, "What we playing for?"

She raised a brow. "What you wanna lose?"

"Ouch. I smell attitude."

"Afraid of losing some of that money you just made?"

I shook my head. "Nope. Had something else in mind."

"Like what?"

"Kisses."

"Your young ass never quit, do you?"

"Scared?"

"Hmmm. Kisses? Oh, really. How does that work?"

"You open your mouth, I put my tongue inside."

"Uh, that's not what I meant."

"You miss a shot, I get to kiss you how I want, anywhere I want."

"Sounds like a no-loser for you."

"Only if you wanna."

"If we did play, hypothetically, what happens if I lose the game?"

"You get a room at the Astro Motel on Sepulveda and we get freaky deaky."

"Just when I thought you were a real adult, you've stooped down to making a childish dare."

"Call it what you like."

"Disrespectful."

I ran my hand over my chin. This was one of those moments I wanted to be as cool as Scamz. Wanted to talk about the Greek gods, and Beethoven, shit like that. But that wasn't me.

I went on, "Let me break it down for you. You're afraid a young buck like me might turn an old woman out."

She shook her head. "Kisses don't pay the bills."

"We can start with kisses."

"You're persistent."

"Let's compromise. We play for kisses, but whoever wins the game gets fifty dollars a game."

She ran her hand through her bushy hair. "Make it a hundred."

"Sure you wanna lose all your money?"

She smiled. "I get first break."

I racked the balls. Watched her move in a way that made me warm.

She said, "Smoking gun."

"What?"

"The music. That's a Robert Cray song from the eighties called 'Smoking Gun.' "

"You know the blues."

"I live the blues."

The waitress dropped off our drinks. Pam paid the lady, then grabbed a pool stick, moved her hips in that lazy bedroom rhythm, rolled the stick back and forth across an empty table to make sure it wasn't warped, then took a slow, sexy stroll up to the head of the table.

She took her jacket off, draped it over the back of a high chair, pulled her sleeves up, powdered her hands, gazed at the table, held her stick loose, left-handed, bent over toward me and I got a ringside view of her cleavage, dark lace bra, saw her breasts kissing each other.

She made a strong break, did that with an umph and a fury, like she was jabbing somebody in her mind. Balls scattered and ricocheted every which-a-way. Three fell in: two solids and one striped.

I sipped my whiskey sour and asked, "Is there anything you can't do?"

She hit her drink, then chalked her cue. "Solids. We're calling pockets."

"Yep."

"I wasn't asking." Her eyes were on the table, as if she were mapping out her next four shots. "I was telling you. Call your pockets. If you get a shot."

"I will if I do. Damn good break."

"Of course."

"You're good."

"At a few things. Other things I'm out of practice on."

"Things like what?"

"Things that your young ass will never find out about."

She re-chalked her stick between every shot.

Six shots later, when the eight ball landed in the side pocket, my lips were dry and lonely, and I was a C-note in debt.

She said, "Rack 'em up, shorty."

Chuck Berry was telling Beethoven to roll over while I racked the balls. Pam sipped her pink panties, checked her watch, did the same with her pager. I took my whiskey sour, went to a high chair, and sat down. Her face lost the professional stare, went back to a very feminine gaze.

She said, "Why do you keep looking at me when I bend over to shoot?"

"Can't afford to do nothing but look at you, so I'm looking at you."

"Looking at me ain't free."

"I didn't see a toll bridge."

"Whatever. Just make sure you have enough money to pay what you lose."

"This is gonna be an expensive kiss."

"What makes you think you're gonna get a chance to put your yucky saliva in my mouth?"

"Everybody misses sometimes."

She made three bank shots, two of them pretty difficult.

She chalked her stick. "You're not bi, are you?"

"Hell, naw. I love women."

"Had to ask. You know how men are in L.A."

"Like I said, I love women."

"Please. You love pussy, just like all the rest of 'em."

"Pussy ain't nothing if it ain't attached to the right woman."

"You ever turn any down?"

I laughed.

She said, "I rest my case."

She leaned over to take her next shot. It was an easy duck shot hanging in the corner. Pam missed the entire ball. She did that on purpose, then gave me a light shrug, a cute smirk. She moved over and stood right in front of me. Close enough for me to feel her warm breath on my cool skin.

I hesitated.

She licked my cheek. "Now look at who's scared. You're typical."

"Is that right?"

"You come to my job talking so much game. All day nothing but game. And now you can't back any of it up. Just pay me what you owe me so you can go play with the little girls."

My hand eased around her waist. Felt her nervousness when I brought her to me. I was fidgety too. We were trying to out-bold each other, playing truth or dare with nothing but dares.

Her lips parted and my tongue went into her mouth. I put my hand on her waist, eased her hips forward, brought all of that good stuff to me. My hand rubbed her back, her face, traced over her backside. That slow and easy tongue dance lasted a good minute before she pushed me away.

"Okay, Dante." Her hips shifted like she was trying put a fire out. "That's enough. Your shot."

I sank two balls, saw her looking at me. I missed the third shot. Missed on purpose.

She came over and kissed my neck, danced her tongue up to my ear, eased her warm, liquor-tasting breath back around to my tongue, moaned her way inside my mouth. I moaned too, started getting light-headed. This time her hand found its way around my waist, pulled herself up on me, her breasts on my chest, gave an easy grind which I gave back to her in double.

She said, "You're kinda smooth, shorty."

She missed her next shot. Didn't even try to hit it. We kissed some more. Held each other tight, like we were slow dancing on a Saturday night. I hadn't had a kiss that good in a long time. Took us a long while before we backed down.

I missed my next shot. Hard to concentrate when your blood flow has shifted south.

More kisses. I rubbed up against her, let her feel what had risen. She didn't shy down, even let out that orgasmic sound every now and then. Her hand drifted to my lap. Massaged what she felt.

I whispered in her ear, "Where do you live?"

"Mmmmm." She whispered back at me, paused, stopped the kisses, then started back with a little more passion, a lot more heat. Her eyes were tight, the way eyes get when hormones are taking over. She nibbled my lip and said, "I want you to understand something."

"What?"

"I've always made love on my birthday since I turned eighteen."

"Lucky you."

"Just never had to do it like this. With a stranger. So if I can't make love with someone who cares about me, I'll settle for spending some time with a good-looking man. That's my thing. Call it tradition. Part fantasy, part tradition."

"So this is part fantasy."

"Maybe. I've never done it like this. I just have to tell you the rules."

I said, "Okay."

"I'm not looking for the start of a new beginning that will eventually be another ending. We don't need to exchange anything but pleasure. And we'll leave your fluids inside a condom. And when we're done, while you flush those fluids down the toilet and wash my scent off your body, I'll leave quietly. I'll be home before the sun comes up."

"Before sunrise. You wanna be home in case your friend calls, right?"

"You're catching on."

"No cuddling?"

"One, let's not make this something it's not. And, two, if I'm going to feel guilty, I want to feel guilty alone. So I can't stay after we've done what we're going to do. That's if you can handle the rules. Understand the parameters. No attachment whatsoever. No putting on airs. Can you hang? If not, speak now and I'll move across the room."

"Nothing across the room but white boys."

"You think I'm not their fantasy?"

My hand was up under her skirt, stroking her front. I said, "Not even if it's good?"

"Shush. No more questions ... mmm ... no questions ... mmm ... Dante."

14

When we rushed up the concrete stairs and opened my apartment door, the crib was quiet as a church mouse on Easter Sunday. We were both winded and laughing. I was a little buzzed, but I think Pam was tipsier. The vertical blinds in the front room were closed, so the room was on the dark side.

Pam leaned against the front door and we became two shadows kissing.

She said, "I'm taller than you."

"You're talking vertical. Start thinking horizontal."

"Was hoping you'd be more creative."

"We should've stopped and picked up some Popsicles."

"For what?"

"Guess you'll never know now."

"It's stuffy in here."

I opened the front windows, cracked the blinds.

She said, "Leave it dark."

"I wanna see your body."

"Leave it dark, please."

I closed the blinds, but a corner of light slipped inside my hideaway.

She said, "Your place is a mess."

"Francesca took the week off."

My tapes and CDs were scattered in front of my television and twin CD towers. The two-shades-of-brown carpet looked like it could stand to be run over with a vacuum cleaner.

She gave me one of those clumsy smiles that was somewhere in between pleasure and unsure. She wasn't playing the Sharon Stone role anymore. I wasn't acting like a Denzel clone anymore either.

I kissed her some more. Felt her breasts, ran my hands up and down her legs.

She slowed my roll and whispered, "Let me tell you one more thing, sweetie."

"Whassup, baby?"

"I'm more than ten years older than you."

"A'ight. How much more?"

"Don't matter."

Her pager was blowing up. She looked at the number. I asked, "Who was that?"

"Guy I was supposed to hook up with."

I said, "Turn it off."

She did.

Then my phone rang.

She said, "Sounds like your booty call trying to hunt you down."

I didn't check the caller ID and I didn't answer.

Another phone chimed. It wasn't mine. Wrong tone. It was the cellular inside her purse.

She checked her caller ID and said, "I guess I can turn this off for a while."

"Leave it on."

"You're a bossy little bastard."

"In case your kid has an emergency or something."

An expression of uneasiness came and went; then gave me that warm smile. "Glad you understand."

"My buddy keeps his phone on. I understand."

The phone rang again. Again she checked the number, she made the same too-late-for-your-ass-to-be-calling face, then stuffed the phone back in her purse.

I went to her and kissed her again, wanted to keep her here and make her forget whoever that was. Kissed her face, took her breasts out and loved them. I pulled her skirt up, moved her thong to the left, and slipped my finger inside, not deep, just searched around and found that spot that gets harder than a button, did an easy massage on that.

"God," she let out another orgasmic sound that sounded like a sweet song of promise, "I was visualizing this while I followed you."

I kissed her. "Were you?"

"You have fat fingers."

"Thanks."

She sang that song again. "Deeper."

"Like that?"

She kept singing. We kissed and I stirred her like coffee.

"You just don't know, Dante. Almost zoomed away and went home."

She crossed her legs on my fingers, made her thighs rub together, put her hand on my hand, showed me where and how to rub.

She slowed her grind, nibbled her lip, and moaned, "Wait, wait."

"What?"

"Take your thing out." She struggled to open my fly. "Let me see."

I helped her get Mr. Happy out. She held him in her hand, rubbed it back and forth.

"Nice." She hummed. "Wanted to make sure we weren't gonna be wasting our time. Don't want nothing in me that can't touch at least two sides and reach the bottom."

"How tall do I have to be to get on this ride?"

"Oh, you're tall enough. But I have to look at it first. You mind?"

She led me over by the window, let the light fall on me while she became Inspector Number 5. I asked, "What you doing, sweetie?"

"Making sure Mr. Big ain't got acne. Don't want nothing with moguls on it going inside me."

"Let me inspect you too."

We played with each other. Her hand joined my hand, showed me how to do what she wanted done. She pulled me closer and I rubbed my hardness up and down against her wetness.

"How's does that feel, momma?"

"Get your condom, that's how it feels."

I hurried to the bedroom dresser and came back before she could change her mind.

She wanted to see the condom.

I asked, "Whassup?"

"She doesn't like just any kind of condom."

"She who?"

"Duh. The coochie."

"Don't 'duh' me."

"What kind is this?"

"Grape."

"Okay. Grape. What are you, one of the Fruit of the Loom guys?"

She helped yank my pants down far enough so she could put her foot in the crotch and stomp them down until they became a pool of material stuck at my ankles. I rolled the condom on then tried to pull her panties down.

"C'mon, you bad." She grunted. "Know when to be a Q: Rip 'em off."

I did. She kicked her heels off, came down to my level.

I left my shoes on. Needed that extra inch in the vertical.

I broke her skin. She was tight, but loosened up when I started moving. I traveled deep.

My phone rang again.

Pam bit me, clawed at me, pulled me. Standing right there, we fucked hard, made love hard, sexed each other hard. I turned her around, her face against the door, and I massaged her ass while my insides tingled with fire, rubbed and kissed on her while I loved her from behind.

Her hands were reaching up for the ceiling, then pulling at the door, moving like she was trying to climb the walls, like Spiderwoman. That look of good pain was all over her face.

She had a sweet conversation with God. Brought up my name a few times.

Her phone rang again.

She came. I watched that beautiful woman make the ugly face. Felt like I had conquered.

Her skin was so damn hot. Sweat growing over her brow.

She pulled her hair from her face, sucked my fingers. "Okay, okay, okay, I want you to come."

"Not yet."

She shuddered. "You think you're all that, don't you?"

"You tell me."

She pulled me out, pushed my back against the door, stumbled on one of her shoes and kicked the other one out of the way, told me to stay where I was.

I asked, "Where. You. Going."

She laughed. "Sounds like you're in the agony of coitus postponus."

Pam yanked off her bra, headed for the kitchen, and went in my freezer. She took out an ice tray and slapped it on the counter hard enough to shake free all the cubes.

I chuckled. "Oh, shit."

"Be afraid. Be very afraid."

She dropped the tray. Ice fell all over the linoleum floor. Then she came back to me, so arrogant and erotic, kissed my neck. Her fingers had an arctic chill. Ice was in her mouth.

"Mmmmm ... ooooo ... shit shit shit Pam ... mmmm."

She said, "Now you're making some real noise."

My shoulders. My nipples. She kept ice in her mouth and kissed me all over. When the ice melted, she grabbed another cube.

"Ooooo ... mmmm."

She said, "Noise is what I like. You were too damn quiet. You have to give me some noise, let me know you feel as good as I feel. Let go. Get sanctified on a sister."

She worked her way down to my navel. I lost my breath.

My phone rang while I was riding that stairway to heaven.

I made noises I never knew I could make. Saw so many colors.

She said, "Oh, yeah. You're about to claw your way through that door. Keep talking to Jesus. So, who's the boss, baby? Who is working who? Or is that whom? I think it's whom."

She pulled the condom off and took my penis in her mouth. Felt so good I almost went into shock. My heart-beat was a serious gallop. Her mouth was warm, smooth, wet. She did that with tenderness, was so good at it that I felt like a virgin all over again. That mixture of heat and cold had me jerking to get free. And when it became too intense, when it felt like my head was about to cave in because she had some skills, when I got to feeling too high, when I saw bright colors and heard birds singing "Kumbayah," I pulled her face away.

She laughed. "It actually tastes like a grape."

I caught my breath, pulled her up, put her back on the door.

She said, "Whoa, cowboy. Get another condom."

"Shit."

"Hurry."

I ran to the bedroom and came back dressed for the party. She was anxious, tried to rush me inside her. I slipped out a couple of times before we got it right. I wanted to back away and tease her until she went crazy, but it felt so good. I went deep inside her. We held it like that and kissed. Short movements. Just enough to let her feel me, but not enough to make me come too quick. We got to moving and I slipped out again, then had a hard time getting where I wanted to get. I put her legs around me, held her just like that and rushed her across the room to the sofa. We crashed down so hard the springs almost gave in. All of my weight was on her. A new look came over her face.

"You. Are. So. Fucking. Deep."

I had her knees up to her breasts, those long legs so

far apart she looked like a three-way intersection.
Showed her that I might be younger, but I don't play.

She wasn't laughing anymore. Just singing that sensual song like an angel in heat.

"Oh. God. So. Fucking. Deep."

We slid from the sofa to the floor, something that didn't give when I pushed my way deeper inside her, chased her as she tried to scoot away. That hard stroking was my ego talking to her. We turned, changed positions. Then I was behind her again, had Pam on her knees, leaning facedown into the sofa. I found that angle so I could roll deep, came out to the head, went deep again, gripped her hair and pulled her face up so I could watch that mixture of pain and pleasure all over her face. Then she was on the carpet, on her back, pulling me down on her, her other hand stuffing me back inside a place so wet and hot. Pam wiped sweat from her face, slapped my cheeks, mixed her sweat with mine and kissed me. She turned me over, sat on me, did a greedy and ambitious rise and fall, tongued me down.

"Gonna. Come. Shit. Gonna. Come. Again."

She did, and when she was done, she went limp like she was about to pass out. I pushed her back, took over, let her slap me some more, chased the feeling across the room, fell on CDs, pushed those out of the way, and we ended up in a scissors position, both of us twisted, her face near my feet, my feet near her face, me getting a firm position, holding her hips and pulling her back to me over and over, both of us looking at each other with tense faces and hungry eyes. My blood flowed and gave me more girth and length. Pam grunted and gave me a wide-eyed expression that made me think I had scared her with my pace and intensity. I thought she was hurting but she held on tighter, pulled me in deeper, let out sounds that rang out like a Negro spiritual.

Her phone rang. And while it rang, so did mine. We'd changed positions again, back to that good old missionary style. I was so far gone I could barely hear the overlapping rings and chimes. I don't think Pam heard; she was making enough racket to drown everything out.

Electricity ran up my legs, seemed like every hair on my body stood tall, muscles locked up as I strained to set free what was inside of me; toes curled and I gripped the carpet, her hips, pulled her hair so hard I thought I was about to snatch out a handful, brought her face to mine and we kissed so hard, kissed until we both got lost in what we felt and let out enough sounds to make the neighbor's three little dogs start barking like wolves underneath a full moon.

Then our opera faded, not all at once, each sound softer than the one before. So much sweat was on us, on our lips and brows.

We fell away from each other, yanked dank clothes away from our skin, lay in our sweat and panted, our chests rising and falling. She crawled toward me. Took her a while to get to me. She kissed me over and over. He body was still quivering. Small jerks. Twitches. Pam swallowed hard.

I asked, "You okay?"

She coughed. "That gets a high-five."

I raised my hand. We missed by inches. She held my wrist and slapped her hand against mine, then our hands fell like rocks.

Her hand crept my way, reached for my penis. "Want me to take that raincoat off for you?"

"I got it."

I thought about Jackson's advice. Had got so caught up in the moment that I had forgot what I was supposed to do. Protect the sperm. A man should always protect the sperm. I took it to the bathroom myself. Flushed the reminder of my pleasure into the Pacific Ocean. Then flushed again just to make sure it was on a one-way journey.

I looked for my reflection. I smiled at myself.

I went back to Pam. She was in the dark, resting on the floor.

She said, "God, that was good. Can't feel my legs."

"Wanna get in my bed?"

"Nope. Remember the rules."

"Guess that would be too much like a relationship."

"Leaving as soon as I can get up. Soon as I can shake some of this sleep off me."

I grabbed a pillow and a blanket, then got down on the floor with her. Pam put her bushy head on me. I rubbed her hair. Clothes half on. Sweat on our faces. She kept her back to me while she wiggled out of her clothes and got more comfortable. We rested flesh to flesh. She put her face on my chest, her breath mixing with mine, both of us dehydrated and too tired to move.

She whispered, "Happy belated birthday, shorty."

"Yeah. And happy birthday to you too."

I held on to this complicated woman I didn't know from Eve.

Like Joe Average, I dozed off. It was a beautiful dreamless sleep.

I jerked awake.

Not much time had gone by. No more than twenty minutes. I sat up. Looked around me. Couldn't find my clothes. Pants, shirt, shoes—all of my gear was gone.

Pickpocket Pam had grifted me, taken all my lunch money and run for the border.

A rugged whisper came from the kitchen.

I got my head straight and saw that Pam was standing in the dark, on her cellular phone, arguing with who-ever. Sounded like she was getting grilled on where she was and where she had been.

She said, "What, I was supposed to spend all night waiting to hear from you?"

Her voice was low, a touch on the mean side, but pretty much the fragile skeptical way you talked to somebody you cared about and didn't want to care about, somebody you wanted to hear from but were avoiding at the same time, somebody you missed but had put up with enough of their bullshit.

I stood up and looked at her. I walked over to her. She

had my clothes on. All my clothes, right down to my shoes. And they looked better on her than they did on me.

She winked at me.

I winked back.

She handed me the glass of water she had in her hand. I drank most of it, then handed it back. She had her elbows on the counter, that soft butt arched up and looking so good. I moved behind her, massaged her breasts, kissed her neck, rubbed her crotch while she argued with her man. She moved against me, licked my hands, my fingers, then smiled back at me and winked again.

I went to my bedroom, came back with a strawberry tuxedo on Mr. Happy.

I unsnapped her pants. Let them fall. I tried to unbutton the shirt but she wouldn't let me.

I dipped and eased inside of her. She lost her breath for a moment.

She was still on the phone, her words getting thick. The more she talked, the more I moved. Had a steady in-and-out flow. Her body weakened at the knees. She put her free hand down on the counter, held herself up. Her breathing changed with every stroke. She was pulling her lips in, very excited, and trying to hold it all back.

She bit down on her bottom lip, tried to muffle her moans.

"Let. Me. Call. I'll. Call."

I rocked her soft and steady; soft became hard.

"Look. Call. You. Back. Lemme. Call. Ya."

She fell into a sanctified moment; she was pushing at the buttons, trying to cut off the phone. In. Out. She moaned. In. Out. Her pretty legs quivered. In. Out. I kept giving it to her just like that, kept stroking like Clarence Carter until she let the phone drop on the counter. It bounced on dirty plates and forks, fell into the sink.

"You. Ain't. Right. Dante. You. Know. You. Ain't. Right."

We did it right there, me behind her, skin slapping against skin, her leaning on the counter, reaching for things, knocking plastic cups to the floor, chanting to Jesus, his father, and me.

When I was done, I caught my breath, slipped out of her, kissed her back, and staggered away, fell back into the refrigerator, dizzy as hell.

She held her hand up. "That gets another high-five."

I staggered back to her and slapped her hand.

She said, "When did you put a condom on?"

"Between the *ooo* and the *ahhh*."

"Was I loud?"

"Yep. Think you scared all the roaches out the building."

"Oh, boy. You got roaches?"

"Was a joke."

"Damn. Oh, damn."

"What?"

"Not sure if I hung the phone up."

"Who was that?"

"This guy I'd been dating. He was supposed to take me out for my birthday."

She said hello a few times, cycled power, then started punching in digits at a nervous pace.

I checked my caller ID to see who had been ringing my phone off the hook. It was a 562 area code with an 803 prefix. That was east of L.A., down in Cerritos or Lakewood. I knew a few women down that way I used to kick it with, but a name didn't pop up and I didn't recognize the number.

Pam said, "If you need to make a call, handle your biz. I won't bust you out and act a fool."

"The same for you."

I left the room, went to send this package to the ocean and gave her some talking space. Left wondering if Pam moaned and moved like that when any dick touched her clit, or just mine. Wanted to make her feel so good she'd always come back to me. I put the stopper in the tub and let the water flow like a Toni Braxton song. The tub was almost filled before Pam came in and saw me in the raw.

She grinned. "Feels like I just had ten shots of Jose Cuervo. Still can't feel my limbs."

"So, I was a good lover?"

"No such thing as a good lover; just good couples. Something about you brings out something in me. Maybe because you're younger, that makes me feel younger. Wilder. Freer. Know what I mean?"

"I guess."

"But I'm not wilder. Freer. Or younger."

"C'mon, now. You can be as young and free and wild as you wanna be."

"I wish. My life is pretty complicated."

I nodded. Tried to think of something to say, but no words or phrases with any depth or any real wisdom came. I was wishing I could be as cultured and literate as Scamz for about fifteen minutes.

Pam checked the time on her watch, did that in an obvious way, sending me a message. Lust abandoned her eyes and a stark look of reality took its place. She'd hit it and was ready to quit it.

Pam started getting herself together, hand-combing her wild hair. She went into the living room and changed back into her clothes.

When she came back to the bathroom, she said, "A little Comet will do wonders on that toilet."

"I'll tell Francesca."

I didn't want her to leave, but I wasn't gonna ask her to stay. I'd just put another notch in my bedpost and she'd add me to the list of jockeys who ridden her to heaven.

I said, "You know, we could do this a lot."

"Do what? Rob people of their riches? Shoot pool? Have sex?"

"Hook up. Hang out."

"Could we? You're offering me . . . Exactly what are you offering me?"

"A woman needs to feel like a woman sometimes."

She shook her head. "Shorty, I've spent all my life sleeping with the wrong men."

"How do you know they were wrong?"

"Look at where I am."

I didn't know how to take that, so I didn't. I was so tired from running from spot to spot. From hanging out in court to scamming Tommy Boy to getting my life threatened to partying at 360, then into this long day I had today, I was tired as hell. Almost too tired to stay awake, and too exhausted to sleep. And today would be just as long. Not like I could call in sick or take a vacation day. I had made promises, and those promises had to be kept.

She asked, "What do you do besides this kinda stuff?"

I told her that I had worked at a widget factory in Culver City, did some work as a tech head on a special line of widgets, Widget II, an older Pentium II–based widget, but now with the Widget IV out, all the technical peeps on Widget II were kicked to the curb.

She said, "Why don't you take classes?"

"Short on cash. Will soon. Have to catch up my bills first."

"Catch twenty-two."

"Catch twenty-two."

Her eyes came to mine and she stared at me for a while. Stared in silence.

Pam spoke in a soft tone. "Hungry?"

"Yeah." I looked at the clock. Hours had gone by since we were up on Sugar Hill pigging out on caviar and Harold and Belle's Cajun cuisine. Guess I'd worked off that meal. "You hungry again?"

"Starving." Again, she paused and thought. "You have anything to eat up in here?"

"Some food in the fridge. Most of it is stuff you have to cook."

"You cook?"

"Some. I gets by."

Another thoughtful moment came and went.

I told her, "Don't think of this as a one-night stand.

Every time I came to your job, when you waited on me, it was like being out on a date. Hope you don't think I'm tripping, but that was the way I felt about it, no matter how corny that sounds. So, when you get home, don't feel bad about tonight."

"That was sweet, Dante."

"Am I trying too hard?"

"Sometimes corny is what a woman likes to hear."

"And will it be cool if I still come by Ed Debevic's from time to time?"

"Free country."

I didn't press it.

"You're remarkable." She yawned. "You've hooked me up in so many ways. And the last two days have been fun. Look, let me cook you a little somethin'-somethin' before I go."

"Sounds cool. And I have a better idea," I said. "Wanna work together?"

"Whassup, Cool Hand Dante? Your friend has more work you can get me in on?"

"Not talking about that kinda work."

"What's on your mind?"

"Not much you can't do, so I guess you can cook too, right?"

"And?"

"So I waste a lot of money eating out."

"Your point?"

"Maybe I could clip the coupons and buy the food, and you cook enough for me, you, and your kid. Nothing fancy, just some get-by meals until we all get our financial situations under control."

"What you gonna offer me next? To clean out your toilet in exchange for a roll of two-ply?"

She pulled at her hair, did things that made her come off as a little agitated.

"Dante, I was asking to cook you a snack, maybe make a peanut butter sandwich, that was all."

"I say something wrong?

She took a hard breath. "Let's cut to the chase."

"Okay."

"Dante, you're one day into being twenty-five, so in my book you're still twenty-four."

"Twenty-five."

"Fine. With no kids."

"As far as I know, right."

"At some point you'll want a kid."

"Okay, now you're Ms. Cleo."

"I'm being serious." She hesitated. "I can't have kids."

"Did you get fixed?"

She nodded. "My point is, let's not start something that's gonna be drama."

I asked, "Why you get fixed?"

"Women do a lot for Hollywood." She ran her hands over her face. "I'm talking way too much."

She laughed and shook her head.

"What's the joke?"

"Not a joke, just thinking of how ironic it is," she said. "Damn shame when a woman gets fixed, she still has to do it with a condom."

"I guess the same goes if a man has had a vasectomy."

"You had a vasectomy?"

"Nah, was just saying."

"Yep. A damn shame."

I asked, "What does any of that have to do with my proposition?"

Again she paused. "Look, once again, let's cut to the chase."

"A'ight."

"You wanted to fuck me and I wanted to fuck you."

"A'ight."

"Anything after that can be the worst thing to happen to us."

"One more time, what does that have to do with—"

"I don't want pity and I don't need handouts." She snapped when she said that. Her pride had risen to the top and showed what motivated her, what made her a do-what-I-have-to-do kinda woman. She backed down, massaged her face, and glanced my way. Her voice was a lot easier when she said, "No handouts. No welfare for the kid."

"It's bartering. Not a handout. An exchange of services ain't welfare."

"No, thanks. Told you once, I'm not looking for no new ties."

"Think about it."

Pam turned off the light before she kneeled by the tub, pulled one sleeve of the shirt off, touched the water with her elbow. All I could see was her silhouette.

I asked, "Why you like the darkness so much?"

"Afraid of the dark?"

"Nah. Not if you gonna keep me company."

She played shy-girl and kept her back to me as she got naked. She did a little sensuous dance, made those hips move the way she had done for me at Ed Debevic's, only this time she wasn't belting out a corny musical. I kept my eyes on her backside, on her legs, saw how it all looked like a smooth road to pleasure. Nothing like a woman with curves, breasts, all the things a man likes, the things a man can touch and make him feel like a man.

She said, "Now, close your eyes."

"You're not going after more ice are you?"

She sounded nervous. "Close 'em."

I did.

She slid into the tub with me, relaxed with her hands across her belly.

She tilted her head, gave me her tongue. My hands rubbed her breasts. Played with her nipples. She rubbed her back against my penis, did that, closed her eyes and hummed. Licked her lips and smiled.

She said, "You're off the hook, shorty."

"Thanks for inviting me into the land of the jolly green giants."

She laughed. "That was some serious Kung Pao sex. Most men think they're laying it on me, but I need a vibrator to finish what they start."

I wondered how many men there had been. Then I

wondered why I cared who she'd been with, especially
since she wasn't sweating me to do a roll call of the
women I'd been with.

Not like she was my woman.

"This thing you do with Scamz," she started, "it
bother you?"

That caught me off guard. Moved me away from
peace.

When I think about it, it scares me. Every fucking day
I'm trying to survive. Make it from Monday to Sunday,
then I start all over again. When trying to do right
doesn't work out, to keep from having to sleep on a concrete mattress with cardboard pillows and a comforter
made of yesterday's newspaper, I do what I have to do.
I do shit I'm not proud of. But I make it from Monday
to Sunday. And along the way I try to help a few people.
That takes some of the edge away, dulls the guilt from
some of the wrong I've done.

Some days I want to go back to being that kid in Arizona, the one with the algebra book in his hands. Some
nights I want my momma to call me and tell me what to
do. Some nights I want to talk to my daddy and ask him
a thousand questions. I want everything to be better. I
want to have a regular family. Want to stress over other
things, like finding a baby-sitter, or trying to juggle work
and my kid's karate practice. I want a boring and pre-
dictable life. That kid from Arizona, that ain't me no
more. Maybe that never was me. Maybe I dreamed that
all.

I did my best to relate all of that, then I asked, "What
about you?"

"What you mean?"

"Dunno. You're hyped. Today must've done something to you."

"I was scared as hell. Almost didn't show up. But it was,
dunno, exciting. We were like Steve McQueen and Ali
MacGraw in *The Getaway*."

I didn't like what I was hearing. Hoped she was just
talking out of the side of her face.

Pam went on, "Most of it was like doing improv. Some of it scripted, but not much. Everything was on hit, everybody hit their marks and played off each other, almost like doing a play and Scamz was the ultimate director. Just like a director, he was in charge of the play, but he wasn't in the play. He was almost unseen. Smart man. I could do that on my own and pull down all that money he got. He made mad, ridiculous money in a few hours. All I need is a little help, could do that and keep the big bucks."

I didn't say anything. What she just said, I didn't like. And she was asking me to help her go that route. She didn't understand how much had gone into setting up that confidence game. How Molly was the sacrificial lamb. That's why she was paid a larger cut for being up front. Her face was the only face that they'd try to remember. Everyone else was a passing stranger. Pam didn't understand how the people working in the background on this operation had got the ball rolling a while back, had found a house to rent, one with the owners living far enough away for them to not be a problem, how they had found those marks, how they had gained their trust, and how much risk was involved.

She whispered like she was still high, "Surprised at how easy it was."

"Don't."

"Don't what?"

"What you're thinking. Don't. Leave it be."

"It could be my way to success."

"Put your kid first."

She shifted, touched her face. Bringing up her kid made her uneasy. "I've got to make a living."

I pressed on, "Must be hard being a single mom."

Her brows knitted and her breathing thickened for a few moments. She rubbed her face, wiped away that bad expression and replaced it with a worn smile. Her eyes didn't mask her true mood.

She said, "Been a long day. Have to get up early to get my little boo. Have to let this . . . this go and get back into mommy mode. Have to pay my rent, buy my kid a couple of new VeggieTale videos, a few things from the sale rack at Old Navy, and get back to my master plan."

"Sounds like you have your hands full."

"I don't have a husband, a movie deal, or a BMW."

She sounded like Jackson. Like she was walking on a tightrope with a noose around her neck.

Pam told me, "I do what I have to. Like that song by City High. Hear them singing what would you do. That video is exactly about what we are talking about. That's where we are."

The water was sauna hot, had plenty of heat to soothe my muscles and relax her mind at the same time. Her eyes were closed. She was between my legs, her back on my chest. She got quiet. I fell into conversational hiatus as well. Pam hummed an Enya song about calling you. The acoustics in this small room had a nice echo. She owned the voice of an angel and the body of a devil. She sang, hummed, rubbed my skin, and sniffled. Rubbed her nose. At first I thought she was catching a cold, but a tear rolled down the side of her face and splashed into the tub's water.

15

"What is your fucking problem?"

I had staggered back into a corner, felt like I had been kicked in my gut by a mule. Pam was on the other side of the room, shivering. Her eyes were wide. Her bushy hair was lopsided and she held her mouth where I had hit her. She had taken a pretty hard blow.

Things had changed so fast.

I said, "Pam . . . ?"

"What's your fucking problem?"

"I'm . . . I'm . . . sorry."

I moved toward her; she backed away and stumbled to the wall. She slapped on the wall switch. I saw her body for the first time. All evening she had clung to the darkness and kept most of her clothes on while we had sex.

After we bathed, she got out first and pulled a towel around her body, then she clicked on the lights and handed me a towel. Gave me kisses. Asked if she could sleep a few minutes before she made that drive home. Wanted to get the edge off her sleepiness before she wrestled with the drivers on the 101.

Guess she had gotten like women do after sex and was too wired to sleep. All I know was she had done something that she shouldn't have done. Maybe she was watching me sleep; maybe she was touching on my face; rubbing my chrome dome; maybe even kissing on me. But during her playfulness, when she was trying to wake me up, she yanked the covers up over my head, covered me the way men did other men in prison right before a violation was about to happen.

Being locked down. All of those screams.

I started fighting for my life. Felt five, maybe six of them covering me in the darkness, hitting me, beating me. I came to screaming and swinging, jumping and swinging, grunting and swinging in the darkness. I hit somebody and felt them fall back away from me, stumble across the dark room.

That somebody had been Pam.

I blinked and blinked. Stared at her through opaque eyes.

I was huffing, puffing, slobbering, confused, terrified.

I remembered where I was.

I remembered who I was.

Then I remembered who she was.

My breathing was heavy, but my fists relaxed into open hands. Pam was trying to recover. She held her face like she'd taken a good hook to the jaw.

I caught my breath. "You . . . you alright?"

"Hell no. What is wrong with you?"

My eyes adjusted to the light. That was the first moment I saw her naked. Full frontal nudity.

My eyes went to her stomach. That part of her stood out. The skin at her waistline, extending right above her navel, looked like a balloon that had lost all of its air; like the flesh of an old woman, darker than the rest, just didn't match the rest of the beauty and sensuality that surrounded it. It was like that part of her was the repository for all of her tears and suffering.

Pam's hands came down from her face and slapped over her belly.

She said, "Geesh. That was pretty . . . telling."

"What?"

"Your expression. You looked seasick."

I rubbed my temples. Those screams were fading and the phone was ringing again.

I said, "It doesn't look that bad."

She spoke over her nervous laughter. "God, I feel . . . feel . . . naked . . . like shit right now."

"No . . . it's . . . I was . . . surprised."

"We all can't have Janet Jackson bellies. Sorry to disappoint ya."

"Didn't say I was disappoint—"

"You don't have to say what's written all over your face."

"Let me see your face."

She didn't come toward me. "God, I'm gonna need some ice and an Advil."

She covered herself and went to the kitchen.

My phone rang again.

She said, "Somebody is trying their best to get over here. Can't say I blame 'em. Tell 'em I'll be the fuck out of here in a few minutes and they can come be your punching bag for the rest of the night."

I heard her breaking more ice, then her hard steps took her by the bedroom into the bathroom.

"Where's your Advil or whatever?"

"Tylenol. Second shelf, I think."

I heard her open the cabinet. "I see Preparation H, NyQuil, Desenex, Magic Shave—everything but Tylenol."

"Look under the counter."

She found the Tylenol, then I heard her drinking water from the faucet. She had to be hurting pretty bad to drink California hard water. That filthy stuff could kill cockroaches.

I called out, "You okay?"

"Sure." Her tone was stiff. "Think my lip is split. Oh, yeah. That swollen lip will look real good at an audition. My ass'll walk in looking like an abused wife from a Lifetime movie."

"Damn. Sorry—"

"Love the way you pillow talk."

All I could think of to say was "Look, sorry . . . it doesn't look that bad."

"Pick your lie. My face or my stretch marks?"

"Your . . . tummy."

"You're joking right? This is the kinda zebra skin men look at then run to the bathroom to puke."

I asked, "Is that why you need six thousand?"

"Yep. Tummy tucks ain't cheap. Between four and six grand. I have a friend who knows this doctor in Beverly Hills. Six grand to get it done right. Then maybe I can get some decent work."

We stood there for a moment, in that artificial light, both of us looking down at our feet, like two people whose darkest secrets and biggest fears had been exposed.

She asked, "What happened to you to make you scream like that?"

A shiver ran from my feet to my skull. "Nothing."

"Nobody wakes up trying to beat somebody down because of nothing."

"Leave it alone."

"You're too young to have been in Vietnam, so I know it wasn't a flashback, or the side effects from Agent Orange. You're probably too young to have been in Desert Storm too. I know you ain't Muhammad Ali, so you couldn't be having Joe Frazier flashbacks."

"Nothing. Let it go."

"I saw your eyes, that paranoid look in your eyes."

"I'm not paranoid."

"If I hadn't being moving back when you swung at me, you would've killed me."

"Nothing, nothing, nothing. Pam, let it go."

"Whatever. And don't think I didn't notice how you tripped when I offered to take your condom off for you. What did you think I was going to do with it? Hustle your baby juice on the black market?"

"You're . . . you're tripping."

"Be real. You've got a few issues, shorty."

"Sounds like you have issues, too."

"I know I have issues. I'm tall; I have big feet; I'm a black woman in a white man's business; I'm not a size negative two—the list goes on and on. And I have scars. I have reminders of shit that didn't go right. I have more strikes than Rodney King has felonies."

"At least you can tummy-tuck your scars away."

"Knew I should've left the first time you nodded off."
I snapped, "Maybe you better go."

"Such a gentleman. Yeah, beat me down, then kick me out."

"Pam. Hold up."

"You know what? Your expression, I mean, damn. The way you looked at me verified that I need to get that six-G. Don't need another man looking at me like I'm a piece of crap."

"I didn't—"

"Let's not lie any more than we have to, Dante."

"It's not bad."

"Look, try that psychology move with the young girls. I know better."

"Don't do this. You know what? Forget it. You wanna go, then go. Your loss."

"More low-level psychology. Yep, you're twenty-five."

"And this twenty-five-year-old worked your old ass like a pork chop at a pit bull farm."

"You think you're the first? Don't fool yourself."

"Yep, gave your old ass some vaginal rejuvenation in a major way."

"Please." She chuckled. "Not like you had a nine-inch dick, you know?"

I nodded. "Anything else?"

"So you got the oochie coochie and we had a booty-slapping good time until you flipped out and damn near beat me down."

I sat right there while she got dressed.

"And stop coming to Ed Debevic's."

"Don't like that food anyway. Who wants to eat with y'all singing all that whacked musical-show-tune shit? I should be at Roscoe's Chicken and Waffles recycling my black dollars."

Not another word was said as she walked by me and went into the living room. I followed. She stopped at the door and frowned back at me. I wanted to tell her that I was accumulating too many moments in my life that I wished I could take back.

I said, "I'm feeling like shit right now."

She turned away. "And I feel like Miss America."

I grabbed her hand when she reached for the doorknob. She stopped and faced me again.

"Let me go, please?"

"Hold on for a second."

"Dante, don't dog me out and try to play me so close."

"Can I see you again?"

"Thought you were going to Roscoe's to recycle those black dollars."

"Can I see you again?"

"Nope. This was our first and last night."

"Just to talk?"

"What part of no can't you comprehend?"

We stared at each other.

She asked, "Vaginal rejuvenation?"

We laughed.

Pam said, "That was too funny. Where you come up with that?"

"Saw an ad in the *L.A. Weekly*," I said. "And what about booty slapping the oochie coochie?"

"I don't know where that came from."

That Debbi Morgan smile came back. She came closer. I looked at her face.

Again I asked, "Sure you're okay?"

"Been hit harder. I'll survive."

"It was an accident."

"People die in accidents."

I said, "Here, you can hit me back."

"A freebie?"

"Go ahead. Hit me as hard as you want."

She drew her arm back, then said, "Nah, if I broke a nail, it would really be on and popping."

We went back into the bedroom. She yawned a few times. I started undressing her. She let me strip her from the waist down, but when I reached for her shirt, she stopped me.

Pam asked, "Do you mind? I'm not that comfortable right now."

After all we'd done over the last hour, I didn't understand that.

I said, "Whatever makes you comfortable."

She turned the lights off again. She kept her top on. We cuddled up. I was behind her.

She whispered, "You did some time, huh?"

"Something like that."

"What got you yelling and swinging like that, was it real bad?"

"Yeah. Lot of fights. Too many to count."

There was a long pause. She took her shirt off. Her skin felt good next to mine.

I gave her the *Reader's Digest* version of my incarceration, told her how I had spent months with murderers, sex offenders, child molesters, and none of them were old enough to vote or buy liquor, most of them weren't old enough to pop a good nut. That was my boot camp, the catalyst that led me into the world I was chilling like a villain in now. Talked about that military-style life with lots of blacks and Mexicans and very few whites. About how I read books by Mario Puzo and Jackie Collins. Being locked up made everything on the outside so romantic: women like her, cars, even fresh air.

I said, "Guess I'm kinda messed up in some ways."

"Don't let it get you down." She talked to me like she was an older woman giving a young jack some sage words. I let her play that mother role. I needed somebody to fill in that void, even if it was only for a few minutes, every now and then. "Everybody's messed up. That makes us normal."

She reached back and ran her fingers up and down my skin, became my lover again.

She asked, "You have a lot of support?"

"Nah. People like me don't get support. You?"

"Me either. Just people who criticize."

"We must be related."

I played in her hair. Liked the thickness and strength it had.

I asked, "You have a boy or a girl?"

"Shhh."

That made me feel like I was getting too personal. That's the way people were; sex was less personal than other things, didn't have the same value. I understood because I was the same way, didn't want her to start asking me personal questions. Didn't want to get exposed, not too much.

My hand moved over her skin. My fingers got close to her tummy, she jumped and didn't hesitate to clamp her hands over her stomach. Tried to smother and hide her Achilles' heel.

She said, "I've tried vitamin E, olive oil, cocoa butter. Did a million sit-ups. That one spot irks me. In this business, it's hard to compete with women who can walk around with their tummies out."

I moved her hand away from her belly, turned her over, kissed her, her breasts, made my way down south. She jumped at first, tightened up, then relaxed, and her breathing loosened up. I kissed her a hundred times. She closed her eyes and hummed. She let me rub and kiss that part of her stomach. She pulled me back up and I kissed her breasts some more, got her comfortable with my touching her and moved back down south, went from her breasts down to her pubic hairs.

She sighed and the tension fell from her body.

Then I put a pillow under her butt, moved her long legs apart and went lower. I licked and nibbled and fingered until her back arched and she pushed her vagina in my face and called for God.

She rolled over on her belly and asked me to get behind her because she liked it like that. She pushed back into me and we rode slow and easy. Heaven's ache came back to visit me in the brightest colors I'd seen in a long time. Colors I'd never been able to see when I took that journey by myself.

I flushed the condom, then came back and got as close to Pam as I could. Would've crawled back into her womb if she had invited me.

"Please tell me you're done. A sister gotta work in the morning."

"Well," I said, "you're gonna have to promise me a chance to finish what we've started."

"Whatever you want, just let me get some sleep or I'll be dead on my feet."

"You can't spend the night."

"Why not?"

"The rules."

"Enough with the yak-yak, shorty." She yawned. "Need to nap for an hour or two."

She cuddled up. Her breathing became heavy. Light snores came in no time flat.

I was dead tired and wide awake. Too scared to sleep. Afraid to find out what dreams would come this time. The screams hadn't faded. Not yet. Not sure if they ever would.

My phone rang again. Pam moved around, made a face that said she really needed her sleep.

I looked at the caller ID, saw the same 562 area code and 803 prefix pop up. I answered because I was getting a little irritated and wanted to know who had been ringing my phone off the hook. I heard Robin's frantic voice. She sounded like she was deep into phase II of her emotional overload.

I left Sleeping Booty and hurried into the kitchen so I could talk and find out what was going down at four in the morning. Jackson's fiancée had never called me before. That was a violation of brotherly protocol. If Jackson's woman rang me up during the graveyard hours, this had to be serious.

I knew what was up before she told me.

Jackson had found out that she wasn't in New York. He knew she wasn't playing home alone. He was at her front door, banging and waking up half of Downey. He refused to leave. Jackson was at her apartment acting like a fool, and she wanted me to come get him before she had to call the police.

Robin shrieked. "He just tried to kick down my front door. He's lost his mind."

I threw on the first clothes I found, headed out the door, and got to Oscar as fast as I could. Time was of the essence. Matters of the heart were in full bloom. Blood pressures were way up. I was dead tired, but had to set that aside and beg Oscar to make a forty-minute drive in under fifteen. Had to hope that CHP was off at a doughnut shop. Felt like this was my fault already. I'd betrayed my friend. Should've told Jackson last night that I'd seen Robin chilling up at 360. This was the kind of stuff that made a man do unforgivable things that would keep him from ever seeing the light of day again.

16

It started when we were still at Scamz's after-party. I remembered seeing Jackson when he was using the house phone to call his woman. The Hollywood Hills number must've showed up on Robin's caller ID and made her think that it was safe to answer the phone. That's my assumption. Jackson wasn't calling because he thought she was home. He thought she was busy flying and getting ready for that defibrillator class. Guess he figured if he couldn't talk to her now, he could get some stress off his back by listening to her voice on her answering machine. Let the sound of her voice satisfy one of his senses.

Then somebody fumbled with the phone and answered, sounding sleepier than hell.

"Yes?"

"Robin, you home?"

"Jackson?"

"Yeah. Why didn't you call me and let me know you were back?"

She faltered. "What's that noise?"

"I'm at a little get-together with Dante."

"Who's giving a party?"

Later on Jackson would tell me all of that, plus the rest. Would tell me what he went through and how he felt when he had looked back at us—me, Pam, Scamz, and the others who were walking around on marble floors. And part of him wondered why he was here in this den of thieves, a place that couldn't make his situation any better. A place that could have us all longing for sunshine and singing the Folsom Prison Blues if we stayed on this train long enough. It went against his up-bringing. How he was lounging with people who had done wrong to others, then at the end of the day were laughing and talking and pigging out on Harold and Belle's.

He wanted to lie and say he was somewhere else, but he didn't like lying to Robin. That would set a bad precedent. Move him away from the kind of relationship he was trying to have.

He answered, "Scamz."

"Oh. Glad you and Dante are kicking it tonight. Tell him I said hi."

"Let me come by and crawl in the bed with you."

It got quiet for a moment.

She took a difficult breath. "It would be crowded if you did."

He paused. "Crowded?"

The phone connection between Hollywood Hills and Downey broke.

Jackson dialed Robin's number again. She didn't answer.

We were so busy that we didn't notice him hurry for the door. He caught a ride with somebody else and got dropped off down by Eight Ball. That's where he had left his little blue pickup truck.

Jackson had zoomed from the 101 to the 110 to the 105 to the 605 and screeched to a halt at 10000 Imperial Highway just east of Compton in the city of Downey. He didn't worry about buzzing her, just parked in visitors' and went into green-beret mode, jumped the six-foot wall and made his way inside a complex of close to a thousand units. Robin's silver Passat was still in her stall, the hood of good old EYE FLY 4 U cold, the windows of that Volkswagen frosted over enough to let him know she'd been here with her company for a while. Made his way toward building E, looked up and saw a light go on and off in Robin's place before he marched up the stairs and stood outside apartment 313.

Sweat fell in his eyes as he knocked and knocked and knocked.

"Robin, open up the damn door."

No answer.

Soft knocks grew into impatient strikes.

"Robin. Open up."

The third-floor hallway was narrow and dark. Each apartment on both sides of the light-green corridor was staggered, so no front door faced another. Shoddy fluorescent lighting made the industrial, dark-brown carpet appear closer to black. The kind of place where crimes were committed.

There was movement. Mumbles. Stumbles. The music was lowered. Then muted.

"Robin, open up."

Down the hallway a door jerked open. Light hurled out and shone on the wall like fire radiating from a cave. A woman with a big face and thin neck stuck her head full of many-colored rollers out, twisted her lips, shook her head, mumbled a nasty phrase starting with "loud-ass motherfuckers" and ending with "people trying to get some goddamn sleep."

Jackson snapped, "Then go to sleep and get out of my business."

She made a "humph" sound and slammed her door.

Finally, through the door, he heard Robin's voice: "Please, this is so humiliating."

"Open the door."

"I can't."

He knocked some more. Knocked until he heard a rattling behind the door. Like something out of a horror movie, that door started to open. As soon as it did his emotions took over. He pushed with the flat of his huge hand, tried to rush the door open, but the thick safety chain was on.

He smelled her Bijan perfume. He smelled the fruity oils she had been burning to set the mood for her deception. And he smelled her perspiration from anxiety.

He demanded, "Let me in."

"Baby, don't make me call the police."

"You'd call the police on me?"

"Okay. Move your hand so I can get the chain off."

He backed up.

Robin closed the door. Clicked the dead bolt on, engaged the other lock, turned the handle to make sure it was secure, begged him to go away.

Jackson kicked the door. The building shook.

That was when she went into another emotional meltdown, freaked out, and called me.

Jackson waited. There was only one door. Somebody would have to come out at some point.

Down the hallway the elevator whirred, clattered, and opened.

He tensed, got ready to face Downey PD, maybe the sheriff's department. Decided they would have to drag him out of the building in handcuffs.

A twenty-something couple got off the elevator, yawning, flirting and holding hands. She adjusted her midnight-colored mini, pulled it down toward decency. Her royal-blue pumps were in her hand, his cherry-colored jacket on her shoulders. Her brick-hued lipstick smeared on his face. The front of his wool trousers protruded with a hearty erection.

Their eyes met Jackson's. All quieted.

They went to the next apartment. They mumbled some things to each other. The girl took out her keys, opened the door, and then let her beau walk in first. Jackson raised his head and saw she was still in her doorway, watching him.

She waved with her fingers.

"He's been there since late last night. Maybe after three, almost four this morning. Thin walls, you know. I hear it if she coughs, and I say bless you when she sneezes. Your girl is a helluva moaner, and a serious screamer right before she comes."

Jackson frowned. "Why are you telling me some shit like that?"

She chuckled. "I was about to give you your props. My

bad. Thought that was you over there working her out last night."

"Why are you . . . why are you telling me this, doing this to me?"

"*I don't like her.* She calls the front office when I play my music too loud, which ain't loud at all, then calls the office if I double-park for a few minutes just to bring my groceries up. If I can't have a couple of drinks and a little fun, fuck her. And she moves my clothes out of the dryer. I don't like negative people putting their negative energy in my clothes. I have to wash them again."

Jackson stared at the girl.

She blew him a kiss. "Have a nice night. Tell her I send my love."

With that, she closed her door.

By then I'd left Pam at my crib, run out without leaving a note, and once again I was putting Oscar to the test, had him coming down the 110 going close to a hundred. At about sixty, the front end started shaking like my old reliable had a bad case of Parkinson's. Oscar could stand an alignment.

By then Jackson felt it coming on. The shortness of breath. He leaned back against the wall. A dizzy spell came. So did pain in his chest. He got down on his haunches and sat next to Robin's door.

My buddy got up and banged on E-313 again. Each beat became the hailstorm to punish all hailstorms. Doors opened up and down the hall. People stepped out cussing and fussing.

Down the hallway keys jingled. A radio squawked. Two uniformed security guards were running toward Robin's den. Both were young, short, and needed to lift a few weights. Both had bad skin: one with acne, the other with a pockmarked face.

Robin opened the door. She had on black jeans and a Minnie Riperton 10K T-shirt.

Jackson faced her. She was crying.

One of the guards asked, "Is there a problem?"

Robin said, "I've got it. There's no problem."

"Ma'am, we can't have this sort of disturbance—"

"It's under control."

"We're calling the sheriff."

"No, please, that won't be necessary."

"We need you to clear the hallway."

That's the sideshow I saw when I hurried down the hallway. It had taken me thirty minutes to get to Downey, breaking almost every rule of the road along the way, and another good five minutes to find building E in that maze of stucco, concrete, and steel in her city-size complex. There was a lot of noise, rambunctiousness I had heard from the ground level. I had imagined a fight was going down, that maybe homeboy and his posse were trying to beat Jackson down, or Jackson was slapping somebody in the face with a shovel. Then I heard the radio's squawking and I knew the police had shown up.

Jackson was outside the door, half of his hair down and covering his face, looking tattered and frowning like he was the bringer of death and destruction. Robin was in the doorway in wrinkled clothes, no makeup on her beautiful dark-brown skin, hair in a ponytail, shaking, tears in her eyes, coming apart like a cake in the rain. Security guards looked ready to rumble and earn that minimum wage. Damn near every door in the long hallway was open, at least twenty heads sticking out, people mumbling, talking to each other, pointing.

Robin saw me and sighed. I'm not sure if she regretted calling me, or if she had hoped I could've gotten here sooner. She lowered her head, hid her face from all the eyes that were watching her, said, "Jackson, Dante, step inside. Too many people are up in my business."

One of the guards stared me down, his flashlight gripped in his hand like it was a club. The other looked at Robin, asked, "You sure everything's okay?"

Robin exhaled. "Yes."

We went inside and she closed the door. The room smelled like sweet oils had been burning.

A noise came from the bedroom.

Jackson and me looked toward the noise, then back at each other.

I said, "Whatever way the wind blows, I got your back."

Robin's brows crinkled. "Please, don't act a fool in here."

Jackson asked, "Who is the motherfucker?"

"God, Jackson. You're drunk."

"I'm not drunk."

"And you smell like cigarettes."

"Want me to tell you what you smell like?"

That shut her down.

"Who is the motherfucker, Robin?"

"Dante, can you calm him down?"

My attention was on the door that separated the tiny living room and kitchen from the bedroom, waiting to see what kind of trouble was waiting back there. "You're the one who got this ball rolling."

Darkness was behind her. Vertical prison-bar shadows from the venetian blinds were on her beige sofa and love seat, lay across the smoked-glass dining room table. The refrigerator hummed.

I stood there. Wasn't anything I needed to say right now.

"Shit, Robin." Jackson's voice cracked. "This shit hurts."

"I didn't mean to hurt you, Jackson. You know I can't hurt you without hurting myself."

"Don't give me that shit."

"I'm tired of Sabrina." She snapped out her truth hard enough to rattle us all. She caught her breath, ran her hand over her hair, then spoke in a soft and honest voice filled with frustration and pain. "I'm tired, Jackson. I can't be what you want me to be to you. I can't. I wanna be your friend, and I need you to understand that. I've been wanting to tell you that for a while."

"You don't love me?"

"I'm not happy. I'm miserable."

"Tell me you don't love me and I'll leave right now."

"I'm miserable. Sabrina has made my life a living hell and I can't deal. I'm falling apart."

Robin ran her hands through her hair, cleared her throat, and looked toward the archway that separated the living room from her bedroom. Her tears were falling.

Jackson moved toward the bedroom door. I went to grab his arm because we didn't know who was back there or what he had as an equalizer. Jackson jerked away from me.

Robin hopped in front of him with her palms out. "Don't, please, don't, Jackson no."

"Move or I'll move you."

Again she exhaled, dragged her fingers through her hair, and massaged her neck.

He was bigger and stronger, but he didn't try to run her down.

She said, "We might as well get this over with."

Robin called for the guy to come out. The bedroom door opened.

A short, thick brother sporting a short haircut, his jeans pulled on, but not buttoned, stepped into the dim lights. Waited on the peach carpet. Gold chain around his neck. Golden bracelet. The same brother I'd seen her with at 360. He looked at Jackson's wild expression, then at my pisstivity, sized both of us up, and decided he was on the short end of the stick. His eyes went around the room the way a man searches for something to use as a weapon. Or looks for a way to escape. He focused on a brass lamp. When his eyes came to me, I shook my head, told him to not even think about going that route.

Robin went to the end table. Her hand was unsteady. It took her a few tries to turn on a light.

Her voice was quivery. "Now, do we drink tea? Do we talk? Is there a Robert's Rules of Order for this situation? Do you call me names? Do we fight? Do I scream and throw things? I've never been in this kinda situation, so where does this go?"

The guy opened his mouth, but before a word could come out, Jackson screamed at him, "Don't say shit. Don't say a word. You say one word, I'm all over your ass."

He closed his mouth. I'd never seen a man look so afraid.

Silence. Robin's midnight lover looked toward her, then back toward me. I never took my eyes away from him. He inhaled, I was there. He exhaled, I was there.

No intelligible words came from Jackson's mouth, just a low sound of a man in pain.

That hurt me.

Jackson took his anger toward the brother. Fear popped up in homie's face. Jackson stopped after two steps. He looked down at the brother's crotch, then at his feet. They were wet. He was having a bladder problem. A puddle of old beer and wine escaped down his leg into the carpet. Somebody was gonna need a dry vac and some Carpet Fresh.

The brother said, "Man, I didn't know, I didn't know, I didn't know. Ain't like she had no pictures of you and her up around here. A woman should have pictures up when she got a nigga. Big pictures. A lot of 'em too. In every room. Know what I mean?"

I told the brother, "Give me your wallet."

"What?"

My look let him know that I wasn't going to repeat myself.

He tossed me his wallet. I pulled out his driver's license and I threw his wallet back to him. He was too nervous to catch the wallet. It slapped his forehead and bounced to the floor. He picked it up.

He asked, "Whassup with my license?"

I read the name, address, then stuffed his property in my back pocket. I said, "Raymond, from Willow Street down in Long Beach. Think you'll ever come back this way?"

He shook his head.

Robin was crying, rocking. "Dante, don't threaten people in my home."

"When did you hear a threat?" I chuckled. " I just asked the brother a simple question. Actually, I think he's ready to go."

Raymond nodded. "Look, man, look . . . just let me leave. That's all I'm asking."

I went to the front door and opened it. Raymond ran like a roach.

I closed the door. Stayed right there. Waited to see if they wanted me to go or mediate.

I asked, "That's the same dude I saw you with last night, right?"

Robin nodded.

Jackson said, "You saw Robin last night?"

I clenched my teeth and hated myself. I said, "In Hollywood. At a club."

"And you didn't tell me?"

Betrayal flashed in my friend's eyes. He was my friend, my mentor, my daddy at times, my brother at others. He'd loaned me twenty dollars when he only had thirty in his pockets. My body felt like a boulder had been put on my shoulders, sinking me into the ground. I couldn't deny what I felt right now. I had betrayed him, had allowed his woman to talk me into violating one of the basic Rules of Brotherhood. I'd just have to add that moment to that list of moments I wanted to do over.

I rubbed my eyes. "Y'all wanna talk alone or what?"

Nobody answered.

He asked, "You like that guy?"

"No. It just sorta happened. I needed somebody."

"Then why—"

"I was escaping, Jackson." She let out some of her own frustration. "Guess I just needed to escape. I needed to have fun. I needed to dance. I needed to laugh. I needed to feel some things you used to make me feel. I needed to forget. I needed to pretend."

"You needed to get away from me."

"I didn't say that."

"Were you going to tell me?"

"I've been trying to tell you for a while."

Silence.

He asked, "So it was just sex? That's all it was, right?"

Robin bounced her foot.

He said, "I can deal with the pain of infidelity, I've done that before. I just need to know if you love the guy, if you don't love me."

A few tears ran from Robin's eyes. She wiped them away with the back of her hand.

Jackson told Robin, "You know this is what Sabrina wants. We've stumbled, but we don't have to fall. We have to be bigger."

"Stop, Jackson. It's her fault you have to go to the doctor all the time."

"We have to be bigger than this."

"I can't handle this, Jackson. I really can't. I love your kids. I love how you are with them. I respect how hard you work, how hard you try to make everybody happy. I can be your friend forever and I'll help you out forever, but I can't be this deep in this thing with you and your ex. It's killing me."

Jackson said, "You're giving in to Sabrina. This is exactly what she wants to happen to us. She wants us to break down. To go at each other."

I was so tired I couldn't stand it.

She said, "Tell me something."

"What?"

"You're smoking again. Drinking too. Are you back on the grift as well?"

Just like that, she put Jackson on the defensive.

"I'm trying to dig myself out of a hole."

"By getting yourself in a deeper hole. Doing that thing at the DMV was one thing—"

"Of course," Jackson said with mucho sarcasm, "because you needed that, so that was cool."

"Jackson, that guy Scamz gets into some serious stuff."

"Remember when your Cherokee kept breaking down and it was out of warranty, and you couldn't handle your car note and a huge mechanic bill at the same time."

"Jackson, that was different."

"I'm not done. I set it up to make it look like your Cherokee was broken into and stolen, then took it down behind the Goodyear and set it on fire so you could get out of the note and get the insurance money. *I* took that risk for you. Because you needed help. What, that wasn't serious?"

"That was different."

"Of course. What was I thinking? It was just arson and insurance fraud."

"Scamz takes money from people. That's wrong. Think about your kids."

"If I didn't have kids, then I wouldn't be in the situation I'm in today."

That stunned everybody into silence.

Then she said, "I want to have kids, Jackson. Do you want to have kids with me? Be honest."

"Why are you bringing that up now?"

"Because I need to know now. Maybe if I had known yesterday, we wouldn't be where we are today."

"I told you that I don't know."

"What am I supposed to do until you figure that out? I can't sit around and wait for your answer to be the answer I want, the answer I need. What if your answer isn't the answer I want? Then I've wasted all my time. I'm not a man. I can't wait until I'm fifty to decide if I want kids. I don't mind being a stepmother, but hell, I want my own kids too."

"Is that what this is all about?"

"It's about a lot of things. Mainly Sabrina, but I'm not gonna lie, that's one of them. And it's high on the list. Between that and Sabrina, I wonder why I even bother."

"It's because I don't have a job right now, right?"

"I don't care about that."

"Look, I talked to some people down in Cypress at Mitsubishi. They can get me in, I just need to get my license so I can drive to work. Either that or I can move to Orange County."

"Is that job guaranteed?"

"No."

"And even if it was, Jackson, the moment you start working, Sabrina is going to snatch eighty percent of your paycheck. You know what she wants."

"So, it's about the money."

"It's not about that. I can get both of us by. I've been doing that with no problem. I even offered to let you live with me, but you said Sabrina wouldn't let you bring the kids here overnight."

"The market will turn around and I'll be back at work again."

"Or you can get back into school and change fields. I don't care. I could take money out of my SEP and pay that bitch off. But you have to let me know if you want to have a kid with me."

"I don't want your money, not to give Sabrina. Never mess with your retirement money. Never. I told you that. Don't end up ready to retire and not have a dime."

"You're skipping over my question. Kids. Or just one kid. Yes. Or no."

Silence.

She said, "You can have two kids with a woman you don't love, but can't decide if you want to have at least one with the woman you claim you love. How's that supposed to sit with me?"

Silence. The first sound I heard came from Jackson. It was a brief grunt with layers of pain. Sounded like a vice grip was tightening around his head. It was subtle, but I heard it.

Robin said, "No answer, huh? Maybe you should take Sabrina up on her offer."

"Don't go there."

"Serious. Maybe you should. It would get you out of your situation."

"And free you from me, huh?"

Silence. I wanted to ask what offer, but I stayed out of the conversation.

"I love you, Robin. When this gets settled, we can have a kid. We can have two."

"Don't patronize me. Don't offer me a pity baby. Let's just be honest with each other."

"I just ran somebody out of here and you're talking to me about honesty?"

Silence. I went to the kitchen and got a bottled water.

Robin asked, "Will you please leave, Jackson?"

"What if I wanna stay?"

"I want you to go."

Jackson asked, "You're putting me out?"

"I need some space. My head is hurting. My heart is hurting. I need to be alone."

"You're putting me out."

After rocking and shaking his head a moment, Jackson opened his mouth to tell her something, then changed his mind and headed toward the door. Robin followed. I followed her. They didn't look at each other. When Robin's front door opened, all the neighbors opened theirs. Security was still in the hallway, tense and ready to rumble.

The way all of them looked at me made me feel so hollow. All of this disturbance. This craziness. This is my life. All of this madness.

Jackson kept moving.

One of the guards was asking Robin if she was okay. The other guard trailed us downstairs. We walked through that maze of concrete and palm trees. Jackson's head was down the whole way.

I'd parked in visitors' parking, a space over from Jackson's truck, then Robin had buzzed me in the front door. That was out near Imperial Highway, on the other side of the metal security gate. Jackson got to his truck, then stopped. He patted his suit pockets, turned his pants pockets inside out.

He said, "Can't find my goddamn keys."

I peeped through the passenger-side window and said, "They're in the ignition."

Jackson cursed, held his head back, and yelled at both the fading moon and the rising sun.

He picked up a brick that had fallen from the base of

the complex, flung it through the driver-side window. His alarm went off. Then he saw that the door wasn't locked.

He cursed and shook his head. He chirp-chirp-chirped the alarm off.

He sat on the driver side and banged his head against the steering wheel a good ten times. He said, "Sabrina has caused all of this."

"Let's roll somewhere else. Security all over our asses."

He snapped, "Why didn't you tell me you saw her last night?"

That caught me off guard. I had no real answer. "Bad judgment."

Again he snapped, "What?"

"Look, man, I wanted her to tell you. She told me she was out trying to clear her head."

"What does that have to do with you telling me?"

"Let's get away from here. Come to my crib. Crash. We can talk it out or something."

"How do you talk something like this out?"

"I dunno. We just . . . talk."

"Talking can't do much for me right now. If I had that sixteen thousand, then I could straighten all of this out. I'd throw every dime in Sabrina's face and laugh. Sabrina wouldn't be able to hold anything over my head. Outside of dropping off the kids every other weekend, I'd never see her damn lying-ass face again. If I never saw her again, that would be alright by me."

"You said she could make it all go away. Whassup wit dat?"

"Yeah. With a phone call to the district attorney."

"What do you have to do to get her to do that?"

"Marry her."

"What? Whoa, where did that come from?"

"That's what she told me. If I marry her, then it'll all go away."

"Emotional blackmail."

"She said that's what a man's supposed to do. Marry the mother of his children, no matter what. Maybe she's right."

"That's what they did a millennium ago."

"We've had two kids. Sabrina asked me how I would feel if my daughters got knocked up twice by a man who wouldn't marry them. Wanted to know if I'd hope the man would do the right thing."

"But y'all don't love each other."

"We don't. Too bad God didn't make it that way, that you could only be sexually attracted to somebody that you were in love with. That's why we're so fucked up. He missed that one detail. I guess since it was only Adam and Eve, that little switch just wasn't on the list." He stared back toward Robin's building. "Wish people could only have sex with that one person they were in love with. And you didn't think about sex until you had met that person. Or at least have it so she could only get pregnant if both of you wanted the same thing. Then that line at Superior Court would be so damn short, they'd be laying those gut-busting, insensitive court people off."

"Extorting you for a ring."

"That's the way I see it. She's on a mission."

"Sabrina won't let go, huh?"

"I keep asking myself how it got to this point. Seven years ago, we were breaking up, then instead of me just leaving, we had one of those emotional, one-for-the-road nights. Two months later she called me. Pregnant. I had to break up with this other girl I had just started seeing, nice southern sister named Gerri Greene. She's hot in real estate now. Bad move on my part. Sabrina never worked out. We never got along. All we had in common, all that was good was the sex, and that is the worst thing to base a relationship on. We broke up again, moved on with our lives. Then one Friday evening, right before Christmas, I went to pick up my little girl. Sabrina came to the door and told me that my daughter was with her mom and she'd be back home in a little while. She invited me in to chill, then offered me dinner. Just so happens she had made my favorite meal, chicken and brown rice. That girl can cook if she can't do nothing else. Her and her boyfriend had just split up. We talked about it, like two adults. She was being real nice to me. I thought her being all happy was just the Christmas spirit. Talking about all the good times we used to have, half of 'em I didn't remember, but I played it off like I did. I think those memories were better to her than they were to me. Then while I'm eating the last of my chicken and brown rice, she tells me she's going to get my dessert. She leaves the table and comes back in the room butt naked with whip cream all over her breasts."

"Damn. You should've told her you were lactose intolerant."

"Should've. But she can be pretty aggressive. She does what she has to do in order to get what she wants. That was another one-shot deal. Six weeks later, she tells me she's pregnant again. Pulled me into her web again. We tried again, and it didn't work out. Sour milk is always sour milk."

"Can't argue that."

"When something goes bad, it stays bad. You don't put sour milk in the refrigerator one day, and take it out the next and expect it to taste sweet. We don't have that kinda chemistry."

My eyes were on the security guards. They were ten yards away, watching. I was ready to get away from this hot spot, but needed Jackson to wind down, to get to a point where he could drive without slipping into road rage and tearing up half the city.

Jackson said, "All because of my motherfucking dick. Hope you learned something from this, Dante, from all of this."

I was so exhausted and overwhelmed that I didn't know what I was supposed to learn.

I nodded at the rent-a-cops, then made a motion asking them to give us another minute.

Jackson said, "I'm creating my own bad karma. I've created my own hell."

Jackson stared back toward Robin's building for a moment.

I asked, "You think she's been playa-playa for a while?"

"Nah. She was celibate for three years before she met me. That says a lot. I ain't had no drama from her. No drama from her family. She's a peaceful woman. Not many women gonna accept a man over forty with two young kids. This stress . . . stress makes people do some desperate things, Dante. A drowning man, a drowning woman, we all cling to anything that looks like it's gonna keep us afloat."

I absorbed those words.

He said, "I've put her through a lot. Didn't realize how much damage I'd brought to her world."

His expression had changed. His anger had dwindled, replaced by love and worry for Robin.

He smiled. "We better get some rest. We have a long day ahead of us. Scamz doesn't like tired people showing up to work with bags under their eyes. I've gotta make a lot more money before I can buy my freedom from massah and go north."

I watched him. Had no idea what to do.

His eyes darkened and that warrior look came back. He said, "I work hard and legal, and this is what I get. A motherfucker like Scamz, that psychopath don't give a fuck about nobody but himself, and look at his life. Living on the top of the highest hill. He had friggin' caviar. Hanging out with women who have room-temperature IQs. He's like Teflon. Nothing bad ever sticks to him."

"Be careful with the glass. Don't cut yourself."

He chuckled. "This damn window'll cost me another two hundred to get fixed."

That misplaced laughter, that misplaced smile, all of that bothered me. Scared me a bit.

I got in Oscar. It was traffic time and would take me forever to get back home.

Another thought came to me.

It had taken Jackson over an hour to get to Downey from Hollywood. That was plenty of time for Robin to have gotten her friend out of there and cleaned house. But she didn't. I wondered why.

Jackson fired up a cigarette before he started his engine. He looked like he was having a hard time breathing, like a panic attack was coming on. He just didn't look too good.

I woke up Oscar. He coughed twice, then eased into a smooth rumble.

Security was still there, still staring us down.

Jackson's truck bucked over the speed bumps. Oscar's tires squealed as we tried to keep up. Jackson's truck flung bits of broken glass as he zoomed into the traffic on Imperial Highway. I ran a red light to match his pace. Jackson hit the entrance to the 105, jumped in the carpool lane. Riding alone, he was risking getting a $271 ticket. And he was driving with a suspended license. That would have him locked up in no time flat. He left me and Oscar in the dust. My friend vanished into the morning.

17

Pam was gone when I got back home. I had kinda hoped I'd walk in to the fresh smell of salmon croquettes, homemade biscuits, and grits. Once again, my queen-size bed had no queen. Pam had put her dark lipstick on and kissed the mirror on the medicine cabinet as her good-bye.

Jackson and Robin were heavy on my mind. I didn't take my clothes off, just crawled in bed and yanked the covers over my head. My sheets smelled like traces of Pam and winter-fresh Tide.

That was how I stayed until after two. I hadn't slept that late in a long time. When you're hunting for a job, you have to get up with the early risers and chase that worm. I made myself get up and read the classifieds, then read the front page, finally took my clothes off, brushed my teeth, and showered.

By then it was a little after 4 p.m. The day was almost gone.

I called Pam. Left her a short message.

As soon as darkness began to shadow the bad and smother the city, the skies became restless. That made me uneasy. I neatened up and put on my gray suit.

The weather changed from chilly to cold. Clouds had moved in a little at a time. Dissension was in the sky and the dry air was turning humid. If I were superstitious, I would've called it an omen.

I changed my routine and hid Oscar near the over-priced condos on the backside of Jinky's Café. Made sure he was well hidden before I took the long way around the block. I came out by the Ralph's grocery store, crossed over, and eased up on Eight Ball Corner Pocket. It was calm. No sign of Nazario.

I opened the door and saw that wonderful picture of that beautiful woman on that ugly lime-green wall. That had to be Dorothy Dandridge.

Pam was down here. She was on table number three playing a dude in a game of eight ball. By the look on his face, she was whipping him deeper into the land of poverty. She slowed her determined roll long enough to wink at me, then went back to her game. On her next shot she dropped the eight ball. Her opponent shook her hand, so much disbelief in his eyes, and I could see him slide her a fistful of greenbacks to settle his debt.

I went over and asked, "What you doing up here?"

"Getting my hustle on. You bailed on me last night."

"Had an emergency."

"The way your phone was ringing, hope you had enough energy left to make her happy."

"Not that kind of emergency."

I moved like I was gonna hug her, but she stopped me.

"No PDA, shorty. Don't take it personal."

I said, "I need to know when to be a Q and when to be an Alpha."

"Right."

"A'ight, playa."

I took a deep breath, stuck my chest out, and went over to the circular booth, to Big Slim, asked where Scamz was. Big Slim said that Scamz was back in the Money Room, that he wanted me to sit tight and wait for him. I grabbed a seat at the bar and watched Pam's reflection in the mirror.

Sierra came out of the yellow door to the Money Room, opened the blue door across the hall, and went into the bathroom. A minute passed and she came out of the bathroom and went back into the Money Room. She was dressed in jeans ripped at the knee, a shiny halter top that stopped an inch or two below the curves in her breasts, and she had on some sort of funky black, almost military-style boots. She looked like one of the girls they allowed to sit on stage on *Comic View*.

Big Slim left his station, headed toward the back rooms.

A lot of activity was jumping off back there.

The door sensors went off and the double doors opened. A small Indonesian man in a white satin-studded jacket walked through the front door, peacocked in like he owned the joint. His white silk shirt was open to his navel, like he'd just been thrown off the set of an old John Travolta movie. He strutted over to the CD jukebox, stopped right between the NO DAMN GAMBLIN' sign and the St. Ides clock, stood there shaking his ass to the beat, smirking at people. Two minutes later, he was sipping on a Sprite and chomping on ranch potato chips, eyeing everybody playing, checking out their style, nodding his head and smiling like he was about to make a killing.

Pam was two tables over, all by herself, pretending she couldn't shoot worth a damn. The three ball was a sitting duck in the corner. She concentrated like she was really trying and missed the shot twice.

She was shooting right-handed.

The small Indonesian man drifted her way. He pulled out a big wad of money, counted off a few bills. He looked toward Pam and raised up one finger. Pam raised two. He nodded and tried to hold back his smile. A few people gathered around to watch the show. They'd seen Pam play already. They knew what was up. Pam and the small Indonesian man shook hands and flipped a coin. She got the first break. And she did a lousy break. The man was smiling and winning the first two games.

Pam stopped shooting right-handed and started shooting left-handed.

Twenty minutes later, the small Indonesian man yelled and broke his pool stick across his knee. He slung the pieces across the room, almost hitting men sitting at the bar. His shouts were in broken English. Pam had already beaten that man out of a poor man's fortune.

"What's the problem?" That was Scamz. He had walked in without making a sound. Sierra was standing in his shadow. Scamz motioned at the man, spoke in a soft and easy, almost hypnotic tone. "You're not conducting yourself like a gentle man. And I do say that in two words. Gentle and man."

The Indonesian man let out a few choppy curses, yanked up a pool cue, and marched toward Pam.

A shotgun cocked and silenced the room.

Everybody flinched but Scamz.

Big Slim was standing in the door frame that led to the back, his shotgun aimed at the small Indonesian man. I knew how they knew what was going on out on the floor. Cameras were hooked up out here and they had monitors in the back, equipment that Big Slim had bought off loco Nazario.

Big Slim's voice sounded as crude as a rusty door. "What you thank you doing? Put my damn pool cue down then pack up'n move on outta my place of biddness."

The Indonesian man froze.

A loyal customer picked up the broken pool cue and showed the pieces to Big Slim; his lip quivered.

The small man asked Big Slim, "How much I owe you?"

"Hunnert damn dollars." Big Slim barked. "Plus eight and half percent sales tax. That comes out to two hunnert and forty-five dollars. Plus reparations for insulting a colored woman in my place of biddness. That comes out to almost a thousand dollars."

The man didn't question the math, just dropped the five-dollar stick like it was hot coal and started rifling through his pockets. He pulled out a pack of gum, a peppermint, a rubber, and some change.

"That's bull," Pam snapped. "Where's that bankroll you had?"

He threw his wad on the table too. It was a five-dollar bill wrapped around a roll of cut-up paper.

Damn near everybody in the room laughed. They already knew. That was one of the oldest tricks in the book, and Pam had fallen for it. That took her ego down six notches.

Pam snapped, "Five dollars? You better come better than that."

The player had been played by the player.

The Indonesian man took off his gold watch, dropped it on the table like he was offering a present to King Solomon. Scamz stared at the man's trembling hands, then he looked at Big Slim.

Big Slim hobbled closer. He was an old knight ready to defend Pam's honor. "Well, what's the good word, young woman?"

Pam moved out of the way. "I don't know the rules at your place of . . . uh . . . biddness."

"You mocking me? I know your fast tail ain't mocking me."

"Can I get a break? Geesh. For the last time, I don't know the rules up here."

Scamz checked his watch. "Blow his brains out so we can move on."

"Soon as you done scooted over," Big Slim grumbled. "Don't wanna bloody up your suit. Where'd you get those Sunday clothes from?"

Scamz said, "Had it shipped out from New York. Want one?"

"Nah. Your clothes too fancy for my taste. Like mine plain. Too old to be dressing like that." He waved the muzzle of the gun. "Scoot down li'l mo'."

When Scamz moved down, the grifter yelped and tripped over the end of the pool table, bumped face-first into the concrete support pillar, and stumbled out the door; cars screeched and the man almost got run down and pancaked by an RTD. That reminded me of the way Raymond from Long Beach had fled Robin's place last night.

Big Slim uncocked the gun and belched. Pam was furious.

Scamz picked up the watch and the condom. He waved the blue Trojan and said, "It's a regular-sized one. Too small for me."

A few chuckles warmed the smoke-filled room. A couple of the women gave smiles that said he wasn't lying.

Scamz tossed the condom to one of the guys shooting nine ball. "Probably too big for you."

The whole room laughed.

Pam asked, "What if he calls the police or something?"

Somebody said, "A criminal gonna call the po-po 'cause he got busted trying to rip somebody off?"

Laughter doubled. This world had its own rules.

Pam laughed, but I saw it in her eyes. She wanted to get that money so bad, that six thousand she needed so she could feel perfect. So Hollywood would smile at her and give her a chance.

Pam headed back across the room, got herself a soda.

Scamz gave the watch to Big Slim. After he looked the timepiece over, he let the shotgun rest over his shoulder while he put the watch on. He already had three watches on that arm. It had been a good night for him. Everything was back under control. He limped away and went inside the room next to the Money Room. Once again he took out his keys and unlocked the dead bolt, then limped inside his private room so he could count all the fingers he'd collected.

I went to Scamz. We started talking business. Sierra walked away. She went to the bar and sat down, ate peanuts and sipped on an imported beer.

I felt sorry for her. She acted like she had everything, but she had nothing.

The door sensor sang and Jackson walked in.

Scamz looked at his watch. Jackson was ten minutes late.

Scamz said, "We don't do CP time down here."

Jackson acknowledged his chronological sin with the nod of his head and an expression that said he was doing the best he could. Scamz's expression said that excuses weren't accepted, not now, not ever.

I went over to Pam. I asked, "Whassup for the rest of the night?"

"Why are you inquiring about the activities listed on my day planner?"

"Palm Pilot. Step into the new millennium."

"Whatever."

"Thought you might wanna see me."

"For?"

"Don't play games."

"C'mon. Straight up. Where'd you go last night?"

I nodded toward Jackson. "He had a crisis."

"Sorry to hear. He does look wound up a bit."

"Stress."

"I'm the queen of that club."

"Get some Popsicles and let me de-stress you later."

"You really think you're all that."

"Is that a yes or a no?"

"Nope. Last night will hold me for a while. Don't need you getting sprung."

"Thought you said we could hook up again."

"Okay, look, Energizer Bunny, last night I was so tired, I'd say anything to get you to shut up and let me sleep."

I nodded. "Don't get sprung down here."

I went over to Scamz and Jackson.

Pam went back to shooting pool. Missing almost every shot. Not putting any real English on the cue ball. The buzzer sounded. Somebody new walked in. A woman who hadn't been here in a while. She watched Pam a few seconds. She got Pam's attention and raised up one finger. Pam raised up two.

Jackson said, "I gotta go drain the snake before we get to rolling."

When he left for the bathroom, Scamz pulled me to the side. Nazario's name came up.

I said, "He's sweating me over a debt I don't owe."

"Just be careful. Nazario doesn't rationalize the same way a normal person would."

Scamz told me that Nazario was from an Ecuadorian ghetto called El Guazmo.

He said, "Nazario grew up doing everything from car-jacking to home invasion robberies like it was a nine-to-five. Where he grew up, they'll cut off your hand to steal your watch."

I nodded, tried to remain cool and unaffected.

He went on, "Ecuador has a very beautiful side as well, waterfalls and tropical forests. You could go to the Galápagos Islands and see the iguanas, pelicans, and blue-footed boobies. The sea lions aren't afraid of you. Or take a rafting trip down the Rio Upano. I could go on and on and still not do it justice."

The memory of that land was in his eyes, and he pronounced each Spanish word with beauty and perfection, the way the newscasters with roots in Spanish-speaking countries did on the evening news.

I said, "You know a lot about Ecuador."

Scamz smiled the poetic smile of a true grifter. He was an old-school player who refused to get conned in a conversation. He knew that I was trying to read him, figure out who he was and where he was really from. He always had his shields up so nobody knew. If anybody knew, nobody ever said.

Scamz said, "I speak four languages. I know about a lot of places."

"But you don't talk about the other places the way you talk about Ecuador."

"I'll make a note of that." That elusive expression came back again. "I'd love to take you down to the equator one day. Beach weather every day. You could tan until you were as dark as your shoes."

"That's out of my budget."

"Whenever you're ready to make some serious cash, I can set you up with a bank card. At any ATM, you can withdraw three hundred in cash every day—but it would be up to you to withdraw the money every day. I'd set you up with a car. You'd stay at the luxury apartments in Fox Hills."

I did think about that offer. Thought of all the shit I could do. Watched Pam shoot her game and imagined her with me in a million other places.

I told Scamz, "I wanna see London. Momma always talked about going there; never did."

"Why not?"

"Momma got pregnant with me when she was seventeen and her parents were some strict holy rollers and they pushed her into an old-fashioned shotgun wedding."

"How old was she when she died?"

My voice softened to that of a kid. "Almost thirty-six."

"You said it was a car accident."

"Yeah." I cleared my throat. "Car accident."

He asked, "Was she driving or a passenger?"

We made eye contact. He was studying me.

My lips went up into an awkward smile. "Whatever I told you last time."

He nodded. "Young woman."

"Yep. Momma was young."

I wondered if I'd stay on top of the soil as long as she did. A lot of days I didn't care if I did. Some days I wanted to live to be one hundred plus fifty; other days whatever time I'd already served down here in this hole was more than enough.

Scamz asked, "How old was your dad when he died?"

"He'd just turned forty-four." I pushed my lips up in a smile and went back to talking about London. "Read that it was pretty funky in London."

"British women are remarkable."

"Yeah?"

"Yeah."

"When they are having an orgasm, do they scream 'I'm coming' or 'I'm arriving'?"

Both of us laughed that time.

"Three hundred a day to start." He took out a golden ATM card and showed it to me. "The code to the ATM is on the back of the card. It's good for around thirty days, then you'll get another one."

"Every month?"

"Every month."

The temptation made my mouth water.

Jackson came out of the head. Scamz put the card away.

Scamz said, "Think on it a few days."

I nodded and we headed toward Jackson and the back door.

Scamz took a long draw on his smoke, then exhaled slow and easy; blessed the air with the aroma of sweet cloves. "When I was your age, I'd seen half the world."

"I'll travel." A smile of hope came over my face. "That's one of my goals in this lifetime."

"Too see the world?"

"To escape from the one I'm living in."

Jackson walked behind me. I followed Scamz. We strolled out the back door of the pool hall.

Scamz slipped out of his four-button coat and asked, "You alright?"

I said, "I'm cool."

"Was asking Jackson."

Jackson made a rugged sound and lit up another cigarette. He coughed.

I said, "Why don't you take it easy on the smokes."

"Funny, I don't hear you telling Scamz to put his out."

Scamz looked back at Jackson, then moved on.

I asked, "Everything a'ight, Jackson?"

Scamz said, "Check your problems at the door. They'll be there when you get back."

"Sure, boss man," Jackson responded. "Whatever you say."

An old, dull-gray Volvo was parked out back in the alley. The kinda car that wouldn't get too much attention. I took to the front seat. Jackson took to the back. Scamz was going to drive. When our savior in a four-button suit got in, he put the radio on KUSC.

Scamz drove by the miles of specialty shops lining the boulevard. Plenty of people were out on the streets, both in cars and on foot. We got on the 405 and blended with the road rage heading south. I cracked my window to let some of the fumes out—needed cool air on my face, tried to wake me from this madness. A couple of drops of water appeared on the windshield. Dripped down like tears.

Jackson flipped his cigarette out the window. He coughed again and I heard some wheezing.

I shook my head.

Scamz said, "Jackson."

"Yeah, boss man?"

"Don't be a liability."

Jackson fired up another cigarette.

Fifteen minutes later we crossed the Sepulveda Pass. We passed the Getty Museum, took the Wilshire exit, and headed north into Westwood. A twelve-story-tall mural of firefighters, the American flag, and the Statue of Liberty with a tear running from her eye stood on the side of a building.

Being in the highbrow district made me look at how I was dressed. How all of us were dressed. Scamz was dressed in a dark pin-striped suit that made him look like a cross between a real estate tycoon and a fashion king. I had on my black jacket, loose-fitting gray slacks, soft black shoes. Jackson had on a brown tweed coat, white mock turtleneck, and tan pants, all of swap-meet quality. I dressed for business because to some a black man in jeans looked like a suspect and got no respect. Scamz dressed for the hottest commodity in the area: women. Jackson dressed so he wouldn't be naked.

We parked across from a high-rise with dual peppermint-striped awnings stretching from the front door to the curb. A middle-aged, chubby attendant dressed in a golden Sergeant Pepper's–style uniform and black cap was posted out front. He stood military style, arms folded behind his back. When a car stopped out front, he molded a plastic smile, opened the passenger door, let the brunette rider ease her long legs and miniskirt out. Then the attendant dashed to the driver's side and did the same with the Asian man in the ripped jeans.

I said, "I wonder what Asian women say about their men doing a Kobe."

Scamz asked, "What you mean?"

"Making bank then hooking up with a white woman."

Jackson said, "Bet his woman gets pregnant as fast as she can and take him to the bank before they can cut the umbilical cord. Then she'll be getting alimony and child support like a motherfucker."

No one replied to that. We let Jackson marinate in his own issues.

Scamz passed a small McDonald's bag over the backseat and said, "Jackson, this one is yours."

Jackson said, "Ain't you coming along with us, boss man?"

"Dante's got your back."

Scamz told us the name and the unit number.

Jackson flipped his cigarette out the window. "No problem, boss man."

I hopped out. Jackson followed me. My guts were churning.

The interior of the place was an architectural masterpiece: pastel marble, towering plants; an indoor stream gave the relaxing sound of running water round the clock, and mirrors did the magic of reflecting light and making the peaceful space look larger. I strayed by the shoeshine stand and stood by the sign that said this was a no-smoking lobby, waited by the vegetation and river stream and kept my back to the receptionist. Jackson went over to the hotel desk and used the courtesy phone so the customers would know we were on the way up. He came back and we headed for the golden elevators.

I coughed. "You talk to Robin?"

"Why? You seen her again? No, wait. If you did, you wouldn't tell me."

I let it go.

While the elevator took us to the thirtieth floor, Jackson waited like it was my turn to contribute to the dialogue. I didn't wanna go that route. I folded my hands across my crotch like an usher boy and stayed quiet. My heart thumped as I watched the red digital numbers light up from floor to floor. We were going up, but my insides felt like they were going down.

Rahel Mengistu was a beautiful woman. Maybe twenty-five, about five-eleven, barefoot with flawless, reddish-brown skin, dressed in a white body suit with a yellow-and-blue sarong wrapped from her waist down to her calves. Full bottom lip, thin top lip, generous forehead, keen eyes. She had jet-black, wavy hair that was pulled back into a ponytail.

Rahel greeted us with a beautiful grin and a nine-millimeter.

We greeted her by raising our hands over our heads.

A constant whir blending with click-clacks and heavy breathing and moans echoed from around the corner. The noise was sensual and orgasmic, a steady, repetitive rhythm. We stepped in. Rahel moved a footstep back and yelled, "Seble! *Metu!*"

The noise stopped. A second later another woman hurried in from the other room. She was a year or two younger, similarly shaped face, and even more lovely. Spunky. She was about five-four with her butt-length, wavy reddish hair pulled back into a long braid. Diamond earrings. Sweat poured from her face, from underneath the brim of her worn Brazil World Cup Championship baseball cap, down over her black croptop, into her midnight spandex shorts. She looked at us, took her cap off, frowned at Rahel and said, *"Guhnah ahun metu?"*

Rahel nodded. Seble dabbed her face with her towel then came over and patted us down better than LAPD ever would, ran her fingers up every crack and crevice like it was nothing but business, then walked back over by Rahel and nodded.

Seble stared Jackson up and down and twisted her muggy face. They said more things in their language, then they laughed. I didn't see shit funny, but then again I didn't have a gun. Seble pointed a finger at me. Rahel smiled and licked her lips. Seble trotted away giggling. A second later I heard the fast-paced clicks and whirs mixing with Seble's grunts and moans.

"Gentlemen," Rahel said, "please put your hands down."

Jackson coughed and frowned.

I kept my game face. "You always open the door with a gun?"

Rahel ran her fingers through her hair. "A girl got raped on campus two nights ago. That's the fourth I've heard about this semester. Who knows how many others have been assaulted."

Jackson scowled. "So you open the door with a gun."

"Pardon my paranoia, but I take no chances."

Jackson didn't hide his pisstivity. My expression didn't wane.

She said, "If something like that were to happen to my sister . . ."

Seriousness blanketed her face for a moment.

My face owned the same expression.

She laughed and waved her hand at me before she pinched my cheek like I was a baby. "Kill the stoic attitude, handsome American. Tonight, I do business with you."

I gave Jackson a rigid glare, snatched the McDonald's bag from him, and followed Rahel through the foyer. Their high-rent retreat had green Italian leather furniture in the front room. One wall was filled with vanity shots of Seble and Rahel, modeling and mingling with white people involved in either politics or the movie industry. Not a photo of a regular old Negro in sight. Their balcony windows were open to the city's lights west to the beaches of Santa Monica.

I wondered why life had allowed her to have so much and given me so little.

She clanked her gun down on the mirrored coffee

table, right next to a broken line of white powder and a razor blade. The powder and blade were next to a magazine with her picture on the cover, in a white dress, standing on the white sands of a beach with clear waters. More magazines were on the table. To my right, Seble was on a StairMaster, pumping up and down at a constant pace, light weights in each hand working her biceps, her face wrenched with the pleasure of pain, her harsh breathing in sync with each step.

Jackson asked, "Mind if I smoke?"

"Smoke?" She frowned. "How dare you ask me if you can smoke. It would have my home smelling for a month. That was rude."

"And shoving a loaded gun in my face makes you Miss Congeniality."

He put a cigarette on the tip of his lip and held a match in his other hand.

There was a moment when I thought she was about to go for that gun.

Jackson put the cigarette and the matches away.

Rahel backed down a bit.

I put the bag on the table and got back to business. "Here's your Happy Meal."

She opened the McDonald's bag and dumped the insides out on the table. About ten credit cards, ATM codes, and IDs. She looked at the ID and platinum cards and smiled ear to ear.

She beamed. "Just in time. Nordstrom's shoe sale starts tomorrow."

She picked up a sealed white envelope on the table and politely handed it to me. The paper felt like a wealth of dead presidents. Enough dead white men to pay my rent for the next year or two.

I looked down and saw something that troubled me more than the gun, the cards, and the powder. Me. My eyes felt trapped when I saw my reflection in the mirrored table, I saw my mother's eyes, her brown skin.

"Excuse me for a moment." Rahel laughed. She ran her baby finger through the grains on the table then rubbed her pinky across her gums. She smiled like her senses had been flooded with an aphrodisiac. "Tell Scamz Seble said hello and to come visit her sometime. She misses him desperately. You can come too and keep me company if you wish."

I looked at her without any expression. A thick wedding ring was on her finger. Her eyes followed mine to her ring hand.

Rahel said, "He's in Addis Ababa. He won't be here until after I finish my Ph.D. program."

Jackson grunted.

She put some happy dust on the tip of her finger and held it out toward Jackson. "Since I can't give you an enema, here's a little something to calm you down."

Jackson looked at her like she was the devil.

I put my hand on her wrist, eased her hand back down.

She smiled like she was having fun toying with Jackson.

I got up and walked away. "I'll tell Scamz you said hello."

She chuckled. "Don't forget my invitation."

When we got out into the hall, I asked Jackson, "What's wrong with you, man?"

"I asked if I could fire up a Marlboro. Problem with that too?"

"You know better."

"She had a table filled with the white horse, trying to fuck around on her husband, and she tripping on a smoke?"

"Smoking ain't socially acceptable in L.A."

"But cocaine and adultery are."

"Pretty much."

He said, "That's twice in twenty-four hours you've punked out on me because of a woman."

"If you got a problem with me, be a man about it."

"What the hell you know about being a man?"

"I'm learning a lot. You're the teacher. But then again, looking at your situation, that and the way you're tripping on me, maybe it's time for me to drop outta this class."

"We're being straight up?"

"The only way I know how to be."

"You let me down, Dante."

"What did I do?"

"You coulda told me about Robin. You were supposed to call me on the spot."

"I was with Pam."

"Wait. You punked me out because of some old-ass nappy-headed woman you just met?"

I slapped the envelope deep into his chest, then stepped on the elevator.

He followed. "Uh oh. Is Cool Hand Dante losing his cool?"

"Look, let's get something straight. It ain't my fault Sabrina got you in a trick bag with Superior Court. Not my fault you trusted her. Not my fault you didn't have receipts. Not my fault you got laid off. None of that is my damn fault. I don't blame my problems on you, so don't dump your shit on me. Not right now. I've got my own problems. I'm between jobs, just like you. Can't handle this now. Leave that mess alone until we're off the clock. Can you please do that? Everybody gets tired of listening to you whine about your drama twenty-four-seven."

He smoothed his hand over his ponytail. "Tell me this: how much did Scamz pay you yesterday?"

I took a breath. I knew where this was going. I said, "Fifteen hundred."

"He gave me one thousand. Paid me like I was a bitch."

"Take that up with him. That's more than you had when you woke up."

"Well, after paying my rent and my phone bill—and of course I gotta replace that window in my truck—that'll be gone. So what's the point of all this?"

"Don't blame me for your bills. I got too many of my own."

"He used to give me top dollar. Looks like you're his right-hand man."

"These are my last few runs, then I'm cutting all of this shit loose. I don't have OPP like you got."

"OPP?"

"Old People's Problems. I'm not six thousand or six-teen thousand in the hole. I don't know what the fuck I'm doing here in the first place."

"You here because you're trying to get in Pam's drawers."

"Come off that nonsense."

"Man, everybody can see that shit. That's all Scamz and Molly and everybody else in on the rent thing was laughing about yesterday. How your young ass was try-ing to act like Big Willie."

"I'm not doing shit for Pam. We were standing out in front of Superior Court and you're the one asked me to get you a hook-up. Guess you forgot that. If I wasn't try-ing to help your ass out, I'd be at home filling out my college application so I could get a better life than the shit you bitching about."

His body jerked, lips tightened. I'd said too much. He doubled up his fist, but he wasn't stupid enough to jump to me. Jackson cleared his throat, wiped his face, and stepped to the far side of the elevator. Anxiety had him going insane. He yanked out his smokes, ripped the tip off a Marlboro.

I said, "C'mon, Jackson. This is a no-smoking building."

He fired it up.

Jackson adjusted his virgin wool jacket, wiped his nose, and snapped, "I see what's up. Didn't see before, but I see it now. You think you're better than me."

I didn't say anything, just opened and closed my fists.

"Nigga, you ain't shit," he said. "You let me down. Just like everybody else."

We made it out of the lobby without letting people see any more than the backs of our heads. I gripped his shoulder hard enough for him to cringe and said, "Jack-son, we're friends. I'm sorry for my bad judgment. I did my best, but point-blank, I'm not the one who stuck his dick in your woman. And if Robin was gonna fuck somebody else, wasn't no way you was gonna be able to stop it anyway."

"Don't talk about Robin like that."

"You were the one who told me that a woman could give away more pussy in fifteen minutes than a brother can get all year."

"I never said nothing like that."

"Maybe it was Scamz."

"Don't know and don't care. Don't ever insult my woman, not even in your dreams. If you do, you better wake up and apologize. Matter of fact, you need to apologize now."

"Let me tell you something. You can chastise me all you want, but if you call me a nigga again, things'll change between us. I'm serious. You can take that to the bank."

"Don't start writing checks your ass can't cash."

"Plenty of money in my kick-ass account. Anytime you wanna make a withdrawal, step up to the ready-teller. Just be ready to rumble when you do it."

18

It was a twenty-minute drive to get east of downtown Los Angeles. Scamz drove on Mission Road toward the projects in Boyle Heights. There had to be at least ten different buildings; all were three floors of sun-beaten, earthquake-chipped, mauve stucco. The trash Dumpsters at both ends of one building were overflowing. Cryptic street art was all over the Dumpster and sprinkled on the foundation of the building, looking like a roll call for the local gang.

Scamz said, "Years ago these used to be Jewish apartments."

I said, "Down here?"

"Yep. That was back when a black man couldn't get a haircut in Westwood."

We passed by a petite, dark-haired girl who was strolling by herself, dressed in a red skirt and high heels. She tried to look into our car, but we kept moving.

Scamz stopped across from the complex's parking lot. There were overlapping conversations, plus mixed English and Latino music coming from a few of the apartments. A few natives headed in and out of the worn complex at a snail's pace. They were at home. We were in the dark, so nobody could see our faces. Nobody knew we were visiting without an escort or a barrio version of a ghetto pass.

All I knew about this hood was what I saw on television, and that was usually a news clip of somebody laid out with a sheet over their face, shell casings at their feet. They never showed the positive. If what was on TV was all they knew about black people, we could stumble into a thick situation driven by cultural misunderstanding. I'd be just as nervous if we were dealing with our brothers and sisters down off the 105 in Nickerson Gardens or Jordan Downs. I wouldn't feel any easier. Same skin color, different gang, same danger. Just like in the motherland, all of our tribes didn't revere each other back then, and still don't respect each other right now.

Scamz left Jackson in the Volvo. His job was to watch over a box of bogus green cards. After we hooked up with somebody named Pedro, all I had to do was walk up the way with Scamz, get the money, then walk out to the car with Pedro's homeboy and pass on the box. Scamz said we were supposed to meet Pedro on the old bridge that crossed over the railroad tracks and led into downtown Los Angeles, right near the middle by the stairs and under the lights.

The temperature had dropped twenty degrees and landed in the fifties. Car after car zoomed by while we waited twenty nerve-racking minutes. A speeding truck backfired twice. I almost did a stop, drop, and roll. I kept my hands deep in my pockets, stepped back and looked around.

Scamz touched my shoulder. "Nervous, Dante?"

I motioned at the colorful tribal markings on the brick walls, then at the side of a small store with all of its broken neon signs in Spanish. "Why would I be?"

His laughed his creepy laugh. "Don't fuck with them, they won't fuck with you."

We waited ten more bone-chilling minutes, which was thirty minutes past the deadline. Scamz's cell phone didn't ring to let us know what was up. When we turned around to leave, shadows and voices were moving toward us. They quieted, then sauntered out of the darkness into the streetlights.

A squad of seven men strutted up. Ribbed T-shirts, flannel shirts, tattoos, sagging pants. Most had that penitentiary build: hard upper body and weak legs camouflaged by their chinos.

"Either we're in the remake of a Michael Jackson video, or we've got some trouble."

"Quiet, Dante."

I became Cool Hand Dante. Scamz counter-marched over to the bunch, face-to-face, hands showing. I stayed close to Scamz and held my tongue. My job was to be quiet and intimidating. Besides, worse came to worst, I'd hate for them to find our bodies too far apart.

Scamz threw his head back: "*Qué pasa,* fellows? We're meeting Pedro."

The one wearing a fishnet, his upper body tattooed with fire-breathing dragons, took charge and spoke. His friends fell into buffalo stances, folded arms and sideways glowers. We were dressed in neutral colors and styles that signified we weren't representing a gang, but it looked like they were starved for some trouble.

Jackson and our getaway ride were parked down the hill and around the corner. I held position so we couldn't get cornered.

Scamz spoke Spanish to one of the smaller, thicker guys, one that had his shirt unbuttoned so he could show a snake tattooed across his hard pectorals.

The stranger raised his voice. I tensed and hoped this was just some local ritual and the situation would ease up. Scamz kept his hands open, but didn't back off. Backing down would be a sign of weakness. Running would be worse. You'd lose respect and leave your back open for whatever.

The guy with the snake on his pectorals said something to his partners, then to Scamz, called him a *puto,* which meant asshole. He pointed at me and snarled something about the barrio.

Scamz said, "Then we'll be on our way."

A car passed by, clicked its lights high to low, and that made me jump. Thought they had backup. But that car sped away and disappeared on the entrance to the Golden State Freeway.

While I was watching that car, a fist smashed into my chest. The one in the flannel shirt had rushed and hit me.

I staggered away from the blow, did a bob-and-weave move that would make Billy Blanks proud. The one in a ribbed T-shirt smashed his fist into my back. My spinning back fist crashed into his eye. My connection was good enough to send his baseball cap flipping over the edge of the bridge. Flannel shirt charged at me. I sidestepped and swept his foot; he stumbled and smashed into the curb. My breathing had already doubled, and sweat sprouted on my brows. The stairs were clear. But Scamz was too far away, and I wouldn't leave him.

A bottle crashed, somebody screamed. I flipped one off me, looked that way in time to see Scamz mule-kicking another.

I looked for an escape route. Up the bridge, narrow concrete stairs spiraled down into the darkness and led to the railroad tracks. That could lead to a dead end. Our car was in a siesta at least a hundred fifty yards away.

I tried to get closer to Scamz, but I got cut off by a charging body. My hook connected with his windpipe. He gagged, stumbled, his sagging pants slipped to his ankles and tripped him up. His wardrobe was on my side.

We threw blow for blow. Like a man in a war, I had no idea what I was fighting for; didn't know how to break the idiocy down and say it wasn't necessary. So I did like men had always done when they were out of intelligent words: I kicked ass to make my point. Kicked ass to keep from getting my ass kicked.

Another swung and clipped my ear. It stung like a hundred bees. He swung again, a very unsure punch that let me know he was the weak link of the group. I bobbed, stepped forward, shoved him into the bridge, eased inside his arms like the night air was lubricated for my pleasure, and sent six hard hooks. He fell wheezing, woozy and winded.

The one with the wild goatee tackled me. I slammed the rail hard enough to bruise my left arm. I elbowed backward and connected with the bridge of his nose, then threw a side kick to his stomach. When he dropped like a rock, an open knife flew from his hand. Seeing the blade terrified me. I rolled and made it back on my feet close enough to the stiletto knife to snatch it up.

Death was whispering.

Scamz had his hand clamped around somebody's neck. The one he had mule-kicked was still on the ground, rocking back and forth, holding on to his ribs. Scamz shoved the man back to the rail, socked him in the face until he weakened, then pushed him until he almost went over the edge.

Scamz told the others, "Back off."

He dangled the guy over the concrete rail. An easy shove, their buddy would drop like a rag doll for the next hundred feet. He was upside down, grasping for any and everything. Nothing was in reach. His partners stopped and raised their hands up in the air, but didn't move away. Scamz faked like he was letting the boy drop. The boy screamed, a low whimpering yell that had the flavor of pure fear. I don't know what he pleaded, but his friends stepped back.

Everybody quieted. The wind stopped blowing. Clouds quit moving.

Harsh breathing echoed in my chest. The open knife I held became part of my hand. Fear made me anxious to hit somebody, cut them like they wanted to cut me.

I had a knife. Scamz had their friend. The next move was theirs.

They said something to Scamz, once again in Spanish. Scamz replied in their language.

They backed away about twenty yards.

Scamz yelled at them again.

They backed away ten more yards.

Scamz yanked the man up by his checkered shirt, then shoved him away. His posse exchanged stares. I held the knife in my fist, the blade pointing away from my body, ready to fight. But they dashed down the spiraling concrete stairs into the night. Not one bolted toward the apartments.

Without a word, we hustled toward the car, our shoes click-clopping in a jogger's rhythm all the way down the hill, a sprint that sounded like the beat of one drum.

I was winded. I'd panicked and inhaled too much cool air. I grimaced and grabbed my side. A runner's stitch crippled my stride.

Scamz said, "You okay?"

"Don't fuck with them," I said, not hiding my anger, "they won't fuck with you."

His face tightened over my pissed-off words.

The Volvo was about forty yards away, but my heavy legs and the sweat stinging in my eyes made that seem like a country mile. Scamz slowed a bit; we checked out the shadows. He popped his left knuckles with his right hand. Blood was clinging to the corner of his lip. His sneaky laugh, gone.

I flexed my hands. A sadness crept into my stride. Men I didn't know had tried to hit me for no reason but the color of my skin. Skin two shades darker than their own.

"They were talking a lot of shit," I said. "What they say before they bum-rushed us?"

"Wasted trip." Scamz answered his own thoughts before he got to my question.

Sweat had mixed with his hair lotion as it ran down his skin, made his face shine. I knew sweat had crowded the wrinkles in my forehead, waiting to ride down over my nose or into my eyes.

Scamz finally answered, "They claim Pedro got shot last night. Said he got jacked by some brothers when he was selling some hot DVD players down on Whittier Boulevard."

I asked, "What you think?"

He looked at the rips, rumples, and soil he'd gotten in his pin-striped suit. "I think they were tripping. Thought we knew something about it. Wanted to take it out on somebody."

"It was a setup."

He glared toward the apartments. His mouth tightened, but his thoughts slipped off his tongue. "Fools killing each other over some roach-infested, tore-down real estate they don't even own."

"Brothers do the same."

"A fool is a fool." He spat again. "No matter what the damn color."

I wondered what that made us.

More clouds had swooped in, covered the moon and stolen its glow. Humidity had jumped up. The air was colder, with pockets of warmth blowing by, swirling trash and dirt. Tejano music was blasting out into the empty streets. I couldn't see Jackson's shadow in the backseat as me and Scamz hurried toward the car. I was just as mad as I was scared. As long as we'd been gone, he should've driven up to rescue us from the mouth of madness.

Headlights clicked on us, blinded us, and we both jumped and doubled our fists. I shielded my eyes with my right hand and got ready to open the knife. A carload of laughing young girls pulled out of the parking lot and screeched toward the 101 freeway. Their Chevy backfired, they accelerated, then they were gone.

A few feet from the rear of the Volvo, Scamz gestured and we slowed to a stroll.

The doors weren't closed. Jackson was gone. So were the green cards. Keys dangled in the ignition. I touched the handle of the back door and felt something moist and sticky. I knew the feeling. Knew that stiff odor of copper too well. I stepped to the side for better light to check out the color. Red. More red smeared the backseat next to his pack of cigarettes. I looked at the sidewalk. Broken light showed dark spots splattered six feet toward the direction we'd just come from.

Scamz said, "Two of the tires are punctured, damn near flat."

"Make that three tires. Air's seeping out of this one too."

We looked up and around and didn't see shit but a three-story apartment building and its bright eyes looking down at us. We listened for trouble. Somebody was jamming a Spanish version of Elvis Presley's old song "Suspicious Minds." Somebody else was jamming hip-hop on Power 106. The overlapping Spanish and English music sounded louder. Sudden death was out there dancing somewhere. Scamz looked at me and I saw something I'd never seen in his face: fear. It was controlled, but the fear was there. The first steps to a man becoming unraveled.

We hopped in the car, rode down under the 101. By then those three tires were flatter than Texas.

He said, "We're gonna have to bail."

I swallowed, looked around to see if that cavalry was coming back with reinforcements.

We left the windows down. Doors unlocked. Keys in the ignition. Scamz didn't say a word, but he had to be thinking the same thing I was. We'd been set up. He'd been ripped off. A poor man's fortune was gone with the wind.

The petite dark-haired Mexican girl strutted her short, red skirt, and high heels by us on the other side of the street. She put her hands on her breasts, adjusted her tools and continued her midnight hunt, peeping into every car that exited the freeway and passed her way.

Scamz took out his pocket cellular while we watched each other's back. He called Sierra. At least he tried to. He couldn't catch up with her. Nobody was answering at the pool hall. It was after hours and Big Slim only answered if he felt like it. Scamz started calling other numbers.

We were trapped.

We hurried up another half mile or so before I needed to slow and catch my breath.

But catching your breath down here could be the last thing you did, so we kept moving.

Arizona's light-brown Hyundai screeched off the 101 freeway. The bass in her radio led the way, thumping out J.Lo and Ja Rule's groove through the closed windows. Arizona clicked the car's headlights from high to low so

we would know it was her. We had sandwiched ourselves between an abandoned building and a storefront
Catholic church. When the headlights shifted high to
low, Scamz jumped out of our crevice and waved her
down. Arizona hit her brakes and backed up. She rolled
down her tinted window and killed the music. She
clicked off her headlights and did the same with her mobile phone; Scamz flipped his cellular closed. He had
used it to tell her where we were, then both of them
stayed on the air in case we had to move because of
trouble. Scamz had asked her to turn her radio down a
few times, but she didn't.

Before she stopped, I heard the angry side of her Filipino accent coming through the window. "What the
hell you doing out here?"

Scamz yanked open the front passenger door. I
hopped in the back. Before she could pull away, tires
squealed, flashing police lights turned the corner and
zoomed toward us. Arizona's eyes widened; her round
face lost all of its softness.

Scamz commanded, "Down."

Arizona leaned to the right and dipped down deep
into the front seat. Scamz ducked on his side. I crouched
deep in the back.

The sirens came on. Rainbows were on top of us.

Scamz was unmoving.

Arizona whimpered something desperate in Tagalog.

The squad car's wails passed us by.

The wails died, but the lights were still flashing.

A hundred yards from us, the police stopped a Monte
Carlo. Two male passengers were spread-eagled on the
curb. A few girls were against the wall with their hands
over their heads, felon style. They were getting stalled
out for DWB, Driving While Brown. This brown community and my darker one had something in common.

Arizona pulled out and screeched a U-turn. Both officers jumped like they'd had a little too much caffeine
with their jelly rolls. Their eyes widened and their hands
moved closer to their holsters.

The bottom fell out of my stomach.

We left the police behind us. No shots were fired our way.

Arizona glanced at Scamz. "Why didn't you get Sierra to come out here and get you?"

"Don't worry about it," Scamz said. "Slow down."

Arizona was African-American and Filipino. Her skin was smooth, the shade of a lioness. A small top and shapely legs. The kind of legs that a woman thinks are too big, but a man admires. Most of the time she wore a smile brighter than a Vegas night, a smile that said it was possible for all of a man's dreams to come true. Not tonight. Her eyes were dark, hard, and wicked, her look discouraging. The way she had been yelling at Scamz over the phone, I was surprised she showed up at all. The way she sounded now, I knew she hated that she had come. But she was the kind of woman who would risk incarceration for her man. A ride-or-die kinda woman.

I said, "Whassup, Arizona?"

Her eyes butchered me in the rearview, then turned back to Scamz to give the same treatment. She said to him, "Like I said, we need to talk."

"Later." Scamz lit a Djarum. "Run me to Big Slim's."

"What about Jackson?" I asked. "We gonna ride around and look for him?"

"Wake up, Dante. Jackson had a hand in this."

"I don't believe that."

"You better get a new religion and start believing."

"He's not that kinda brother."

Arizona jumped in. "Thought we were heading out to Mo Val to my place so we could talk."

"Get me to Big Slim's," Scamz said, then asked me, "How bad you hurt?"

"Hands hurt. Back hurt. Ain't nothing that some ice and Tylenol can't fix."

"I asked you a question," Arizona said to Scamz.

Scamz asked me, "You get cut?"

"Don't think so. Can't tell. Don't think so."

"Check."

Arizona said, "Scamz, don't ignore me."

He told her, "Dante needs to get back to his side of town."

I said, "We should be worried about Jackson."

Arizona told Scamz, "On the phone you said we could go talk about this situation. About us. About Sierra."

Scamz was becoming more unraveled. "Well, there has been a change of plans."

"In other words you lied to me."

"Respect me, Arizona."

"Respect you?" Arizona spat out. "You're demanding respect and you're sleeping with Sierra."

"Can you be quiet for one moment?"

"Why Sierra, of all people? I bet she's sucking your dick."

Arizona was doing almost eighty, and rising toward ninety, looking like she would get this starship up to warp factor nine if she could. The Hyundai had been shaking with a bad alignment since she crossed sixty miles an hour. The lights of Hollywood came up on our right, the old Capitol Records building, the Knicker-bocker, and the huge illuminated head of a lion for *The Lion King*.

"Middle of the damn night," Arizona said. "I'm getting tired of this mess. I don't know what I'm doing messing with your old ass in the first place. Maybe you and Sierra should be together."

I said, "Scamz, why don't you drive?"

"Dante," Scamz said and rubbed his fingers like money. "I'll tighten you up when we get back to the pool hall."

"I'm not worried about the money," I said with force. "Look, man, we need to be riding around looking for Jackson."

"Did you hear Jackson scream? Did he call for help? You better wonder why."

"Did we scream? Did we call for any damn help? Hell no. There was blood all over the car."

"What's blood got to do with it?"

"He got ambushed just like we did. He could be in-jured, bleeding to death, needing help."

Arizona *tsk*ed, shook her head and mumbled, *"Tu-migil ka nang nigirilyo sa akong tabe."*

Scamz said, "Blood don't mean nothing without a body."

"C'mon, Scamz. He could be out there dying."

"Or somewhere with my merchandise trying to cash in so he can solve his own problems."

"That's cold, Scamz. Damn that's cold."

"If you want to get out and walk around, let me know and I'll have Arizona pull over."

She asked, "You want to get out, Dante?"

"This is cold-blooded."

"Cold world, Dante," Scamz said. "You better wise up. Jackson just flipped the script."

"When in the fuck has Jackson ever done anything like that?"

"Stand down, Dante." His voice was tense. "You're crossing a line."

Arizona raised her voice: *"Tumigil ka nang nigirilyo sa akong tabe."*

Scamz lit up a Djarum and asked her, "What was that?"

"Stop smoking around me," she yelled. "Second, I'm tired of your shit. Third, this shit is tired. Fourth, that's what the fuck I said. Fifth, I'm tired of your old ass always—"

Scamz slapped her.

She shrieked.

I screamed.

We swerved two lanes to the right, skidded left, horns blared from every direction, almost clipped the back end of an eighteen-wheel big-rig, she wrestled with the steering wheel, then almost hit the concrete wall at the Melrose/Normandie exit.

Scamz didn't say a word while Arizona struggled to keep from crashing. He switched the radio from a bumping beat to classical music from KUSC, lowered the volume and relit his smoke.

My legs were up to the back of her seat, so when my heart stopped beating inside my throat, I felt Arizona's body trembling through her seat's springs. Her body was an earthquake. I thought she felt my knees shaking because she looked at me in the rearview mirror. Water came to her shame-filled eyes, but she didn't blink it out or wipe it away.

My arms flexed. I glowered at the back of Scamz's head, took a few breaths, then opened and closed my fingers.

I asked, "You okay, Arizona?"

Scamz said, "Leave her alone, Dante."

"I was talking to her."

"I was talking to you."

"I was talking to her."

Arizona whispered, "Leave me alone, Dante."

My hands were shaking. Arizona looked at me through the rearview, then turned the glass away so I couldn't see what emotion she held in her light-brown eyes.

She muttered, "Sierra got you twisted."

"Don't give me the jibber-jabber right now." Scamz rubbed his temples. "Arizona. Please."

She replied, "I hate you."

A moment of nothing sounded so good.

I asked, "What are we going to do about Jackson?"

Scamz said, "I'll handle it."

That scared me. "What does that mean?"

"Back off, Dante. It's been a rough night, I need to think, so back off."

Arizona rolled her window down, shoved in a tape, and cranked the volume up.

It was that trifling "I hate you so much right now" song.

Scamz pushed eject. The tape popped out. He tossed it out the window. I wanted to applaud.

She reached into her purse and took out another tape. Popped it in. It was the same song.

The speakers were rattling and squealing right behind my head. Scamz leaned over and touched the side of Arizona's face, sweet and soft. She leaned her face into his hand, got lost in his touch before she rubbed his hand, then moved his fingers away. She turned the music off.

Scamz closed his eyes, exhaled, went back to thinking. It was quiet for a moment.

In a soft voice, right above a whisper, a tone mixed with confusion and love, she asked Scamz, "How can you make love to me, then turn around and sleep with my sister?"

He didn't respond.

Arizona went on, "What you did to my brother, that wasn't necessary. You broke his nose."

"He assaulted me."

"He was looking for Sierra. He's trying to protect us, that's all."

Now I knew what that was all about at the Comedy Emporium, when that dude in the Mustang ran up on Scamz. It was a family thing. Nothing to do with a scam, but just as dangerous, if not more.

But then again, sleeping with two sisters was the ultimate scam for some men.

Her tone changed, became filled with hate and pain. *"Namumuhi ako sa iyo."*

She turned the music back on.

19

Arizona jumped off the 101 at Woodman. She was driving calm as she went underneath the overpass by Fashion Square car wash and the line of apartment buildings leading to Ventura Boulevard. She was too calm. Driving at least ten miles under the speed limit, acting like a little old lady from Pasadena, just to irritate Scamz. She took the alleys to the back door of Big Slim's joint.

I asked, "What are we gonna do about Jackson?"

No reply.

Scamz got out. I did the same. Arizona had her lips fastened virgin-tight. She'd been quiet for the better part of fifteen minutes. Scamz told her he'd be right back. She stayed in the car. When we walked away, she turned the music down to a whisper. That was when I heard her sniffling.

After a few steps, a car door slammed. I glanced back. Arizona had gotten out and leaned against the passenger door. Her breath fogged the night's air as she folded her arms. Her hair hung down her back and she was shivering. Underneath the streetlights her face looked hot enough to evaporate the tears that wanted to roll from her eyes. I didn't see Arizona anymore. I saw my past. Saw my legacy. The landscape changed, and I saw my mother standing out in front of our home in the desert; I cringed. A pain shot through my wrists, the same injury I felt when I was handcuffed too tight.

My throat was on fire and I had to speak my mind.

I told Scamz, "Don't hit Arizona anymore."

Scamz stepped back toward me. "What was that?"

We stood in the stench of the Dumpsters that were on either side of the back door.

I walked closer to him. "You heard me."

"You stepping to me, Dante?"

"Talking man-to-man."

I'd planned for my words to come out smooth, more on the brother-to-brother tip, but my voice carried too much resentment. Too much of my past. My father had slapped my mother on the way home from my grandfather's AME church, hit her because she had the flu and didn't feel like cooking. He said she wasn't too sick for church, so she could cook. She asked him to pick up something on the way home. He shoved her head and dared her to talk back to him. I told him to stop, then cringed and took the slaps that made him quit hitting Momma. I didn't raise a hand. That was the first time I ever wanted to kill somebody. This was the second.

He said, "Remember, you're the one who begged me to let Jackson in on this."

"You think I had something to do with this?"

"I hope you didn't."

"You threatening me?"

"I'm wondering things."

"Raise up off that noise, man. I was jacked just like you. I almost had involuntary surgery."

"C'mon, Dante. Game recognizes game."

"Look, whatever. Don't lash out at Arizona."

"Act like a man."

"I'm a man. Guess I'm more of a man than you."

He stood in his own anger. I stood in mine.

"You know the difference between you and me?" Scamz asked me. "I'm not weak for women and don't get sprung."

"Fuck you."

Again we stared. Prison stares. I didn't know which way this was going to go.

Scamz swaggered away.

I followed. "I'm serious, Scamz."

"We had a tense night—"

"No shit."

"—so I'll assume that's why you're tripping." He held the back door open for me. "Don't ever front me again and we'll be straight. Worry about what's yours and I'll worry about what's mine. Remember your past. Jumping in another man's fire won't do anything but get you burned."

He walked on. His strut had a don't-challenge-me-again rhythm, like the theme from *Shaft* should've been playing to match his stride. I was right behind him.

Inside the hallway, Big Slim passed by us. He stopped me, handed me an envelope.

He said, "That fast gal who was nasty dancin' and causin' a ruckus left this for you."

Inside was a note from Pam.

He said, "Tell that fast gal I ain't no delivery service. Next time use FedEx."

"She cause you any problems?"

"Two fights. Big-leg wimmen in short skirts always cause problems."

Big Slim moved on, each step so heavy. I caught up with Scamz.

We strolled up the narrow hall to the Money Room. The setup wasn't extravagant, so at a glance it didn't look suspicious. A couple of six-inch monitors with split screens showed both the outside parking lot and the game room. Many evenings they used soft-voiced women and ran telemarketing and credit card scams from back here. Scamz used to run tele-frauds by having a few honeys call people and act like they were working as investigators with the FCC. They'd tell people some bull and get them to give up their calling card numbers, pretend they were investigating a fraud on their phone line, then ask to make sure they paid their phone bill until the investigation was complete.

That was how Scamz met Arizona. She showed up, broken-down and hungry, looking for work, anything to put some food in her stomach and take care of her missed-meal cramps. She was hungry and homeless enough to compromise. And for a woman with a tender voice that sounded like nothing but trust and friendship, the work was easy. Outside of English and Tagalog, she spoke Spanish, pidgin, Japanese, and Vietnamese. She was an asset in more ways than one.

Before long Arizona was resting her bones in Scamz's lap, and the long-legged twenty-year-old who was wiggling there before her had been given severance pay and thrown on the 10 eastbound.

Now Arizona had been replaced by her own blood.

Or was refusing to be replaced.

Scamz opened the safe and gave me six hundred dollars in crisp twenties. He didn't offer me any reimbursement for the damage that had happened to my suit. Or for the damage that had happened to my body. This job didn't have workman's comp or anything for work-related expenses.

I counted the money to make sure neither of us made a mistake. I said, "How much you lose?"

"Forty."

"Thousand?"

"Close to."

I stared at Scamz. He said that in a way that said he knew Jackson had something to do with that, that Jackson was doing what he had to do to save his own ass.

He asked, "We straight?"

It wasn't as much as I deserved for a night like this one, but I said fuck it and nodded.

My ear ached. My arms ached. Fists were swollen. But there was no broken skin; no blood.

I asked, "What about Jackson?"

"Jackson'll show up, one way or the other."

"Let's call up a few people and go look for him."

"That area is too hot. Besides, do you really want me to find him right now?"

My head ached. Couldn't think straight right now. Couldn't stop sweating and I couldn't think.

I asked, "You think Pedro got shot or the homies

lied? A drive-by in Boyle Heights wouldn't make the papers. Not unless white people from Europe were involved."

Scamz was so far gone I was rambling to myself. I was jittery, high-strung, and he was in a mood as well. People who scheme hate getting played or grifted more than anything else. With his disposition, might be a bad night for any of his women. Might be a bad night for a few brothers too.

Somebody banged on the door, hard and strong.

"Scamz," Arizona yelled, "why you leave me sitting in a nasty alley?"

"Stop beating on the door."

Arizona kept knocking at a machine-gun tempo. Scamz got up and headed for the door.

I said, "Don't hit Arizona. Next time you need to hit somebody, come see me."

His face darkened and he frowned like he wanted to shoot, stab, and drown me. Felt like I had signed my own death warrant. I stayed firm and cool on the outside. His look passed by like a cloud floating in the winds. He nodded and said, "I'll buy her some vanilla ice cream and a Barbie doll and tell her I'm sorry. Cool by you, Cool Hand Dante?"

"Damn, bro. Her sister?"

"Sierra came to me."

"Blame the victim."

"Everybody's old enough to vote."

I said, "As long as they have grass in the front lawn."

"That's right. There are no victims, only consenting adults."

"Look, she's upset. Be cool with her."

He glanced back before opening the door. "You better find your friend before I do."

He left the room. I waited a few seconds, rubbed my burning eyes. My damn chest ached too. Took some hard blows. Part of my face was swollen.

A good minute went by, a minute of me thinking what I should do, before I headed out into the smoky hall. I was gonna go back down to Boyle Heights by myself. I'd keep my Louisville Slugger in my lap and take my chances. That's what I was telling myself I was gonna do. Jackson had a fiancée and two kids. I couldn't leave him out there by himself.

The front of the pool hall was empty, most of the lights were off. The green-and-yellow St. Ides clock had the best glow in the room. Big Slim had put on some music to suit his southern taste. John Lee Hooker sounded as hurt as my stride; lamenting about covering the waterfront, waiting for his baby.

Scamz was close to the front, standing in the shadows, under a ceiling fan, kissing on Arizona's neck. He was slow-dancing with her, rubbing her backside. She flipped her hair out of her face, then held him and kissed him with so much passion.

She had his attention.

Guess she was as unconcerned about her sister as her sister was unconcerned about her.

Part of me wanted to watch. Not for pleasure, but to see what made Scamz Scamz. To understand his power over his women. To understand what made somebody like Sierra betray her own sister to wait on him hand and foot, then turn her eyes away from me like I wasn't worthy of a decent hello. To understand why Arizona was so hurt and betrayed, but still she couldn't walk away from this insanity.

"Pack up and move on." That came from behind me. It was Big Slim. He said, "Your biddness done here for tonight."

I glanced behind me. Arizona had taken Scamz's hand, was leading him deeper into the darkness of the room, away from the lights of the hall. I heard her laughing, sounding happy.

I passed by Big Slim without a word.

He said, "You making fun of my walk?"

I shook my head. "I'm hurting, man. Damn, can't you see I'm in pain?"

"Serves you right to suffer."

With each step I hugged the wall and made sure I didn't bump into him. He was the type of man who got offended when somebody accidentally touched him. Something horrific had to happen to a man to make him hate the world the way Big Slim did.

He said, "Hurry. Nigger, I ain't got all night."

"Dante," I said.

"Don't start wit dat 'I ain't a nigger' shit again."

His words singed the hairs on my neck. His breath reeked of hard liquor and bad memories. And his body odor was rising like a hot air balloon. I hadn't been this close to him in a while, but it smelled like he hadn't had a bath in a few days. He didn't look too good. Not at all.

I asked, "You a'ight?"

"Bastard invited me to suck his johnson."

He was talking about Nazario. That angst had cost him a lot of sleep, I could tell by the bags under his eyes. He hadn't been the same since Nazario slung those words of disrespect his way.

Big Slim said, "I need yo' help with somethin'."

I knew where he was going with that. I shook my head. "I'm keeping out of other men's fires."

"When Nazario came hunting for you, I let you slip out my back do'."

"Thank you."

" 'I see,' said the blind man." He rubbed his razor bumps. "Okay, boy. Name your price."

He said that like he thought I was a dime-store whore, ready to get pimped by anybody if the price was right. I gritted my teeth and loaned him a frown to match his own.

I said, "Deal with your own fires. I'm tired of getting burned."

He said, "All y'all turned your back on me. All y'all."

"That's life. That's what people do."

I left, that envelope from Pam still in my hand. The door club was put on as soon as the back door creaked closed. I glanced up at the surveillance camera, that single eye pointing down at the cold ground. Sirens were in the distance. Dogs were barking down the alley. I stared at the graffiti tattooed on the walls and fences and wondered what kinda world I was living in.

Clang Clink

Somebody kicked an aluminum can; it scraped across the asphalt, whined, and rolled to a stop.

I turned around, fists doubled, heart thumping. "Who that?"

Somebody was in the shadows.

Again, a lot harder and louder, I said, "Who that?"

"Dah-dah-Dante."

"Nazario."

"You have my wife's r-r-ring, no?"

I was beat down and exhausted, not in the mood for bullshit. I yelled at that fool, "I pawned the damn ring. Now leave me the fuck alone."

"You p-pawn my w-w-wife ring?"

"What, you blind in one eye and deaf in both ears?"

He charged at me with the grace of a rabid dog, moved at what looked like slow motion, but still going way too fast for my exhausted mind to figure out where the hell he came from or what to do. I moved—more like tried to move—and realized how tired and beat down I already was. Damn tired. Too beat down. My legs were too heavy to sprint, too tight to get ready to throw a decent kick, arms too stiff and hands hurting too bad to throw a blow. I wasn't ready for a fight, but I was in one. Before I found enough coordination to sidestep, he tackled me. Knocked my wind away. I had to let my body roll with the blow and tumble across the concrete away from trouble.

We scrambled to our feet at the same time. Both of us huffing.

The back door to the pool hall opened. Big Slim saw us. Before I could go that way, Big Slim closed the back door. Put the locks back on. Turned his back on me. Sent me a firm message.

It was between me and Nazario.

I fell into a boxer's stance and moved toward his blind side. He charged at me. Again, it was like I was

scampering in slow motion, like I was moving inside another dream. Weariness, hunger, surprise all had me un-
coordinated. I met his charge with a growl and ran into
him Wrestlemania style. That move was as smart as an
SUV going head-on with a freight train. We collided and
I bounced off him like a pinball, hit the concrete wall
and ricocheted against a Dumpster, stumbled over beer
cans, shattered bottles, used condoms, slipped to the
piss-and-oil-smelling asphalt. My hands burned from
where the concrete took off a layer of skin. I'd just have
to add that new pain to the other ones I'd accumulated
tonight.

He stood near me, glaring the best he could with the
solitary eye he had left inside of his empty head. I almost got hypnotized by the empty socket. I blinked and
scooted away.

"You g-get me the r-ring. You th-think this is a game or
s-s-somethin'?"

Nazario pulled his shirt back, showed the pearl handle jutting from his waistband. He was stepping to me
with a loan shark attitude. Two hundred damn dollars'
worth of trouble.

And Alfalfa had been slaughtered over fifty.

Bright lights came from around the corner and covered us. Startled me. Made Nazario's solo eye open wide
enough to get a panoramic view of the alley. The lights
went from low to high beams. Nazario grimaced up at
the car. The beams clicked from high to low again.
Nazario ran off in the other direction.

The bright lights stayed on me.

The car door opened. Somebody got out. The lights
were in my eyes, so for a moment all I could hear were
footsteps. Heels crunching over loose asphalt, light
steps, a slow stroll.

Dressed in all black, floating through the darkness, it
was Sierra.

She stopped and stared when she got close to me;
once again she caught my eyes, then she walked on by,
did that like she didn't care. She stopped in front of Ari-

zona's car. She spat on it. Then she picked up a brick and threw it into the driver's side of the windshield.

She stood and waited. The back door to the pool hall didn't open again.

Nobody came.

She walked toward me again. So many tears in her eyes. She passed by me and lowered her head, put her hands deep in the pockets of her leather coat, got back in her chariot, and went back the way she had come from.

I picked up the envelope I'd dropped at some point, the one Big Slim had given me, and I hurried the way Sierra had gone. My hurry was a painful run. Every old ache and every new ache were teaming up to slow me down to a crawl. I clung to the darkness like I was its original owner, made my way over to the residential area, tiptoed and watched my back for what seemed like a nervous man's eternity.

When I thought the coast was clear, I rushed toward Oscar. I could depend on my car to fire up those four cylinders and get me out of this area as fast as he could. My eyes were all over the road as I came out on Ventura Boulevard, trying to see what was ahead, and always peeping back over my shoulder, never slowing down, doing my damnedest to get away from trouble as fast as I could.

A police car was parked near Oscar. I thought The Man had come to get me and escort me to a five-by-nine so I could start counting bricks and making friends with cockroaches. What stopped me from turning and running was seeing a big red fire truck parked down that way too. Lights were flashing from all directions, American flags were on all the service vehicles, looked like Mardi Gras with all the people gathered around.

Smoke was pluming from under the hood of my car. It had the stench of an electrical fire.

I ran to my ride. They didn't ask for any ID, but they asked a lot of questions. The passenger window had been broken out. Battery acid had been poured all over the seats; the hood had been popped and the same damage had been done to the engine. Enough acid to melt through the wires.

The officer told me the obvious, "Your car is totaled."

I leaned against Oscar with my face in my hands; groaned and cursed a thousand times.

They watched me. Read my reaction. Saw more anger than surprise. They asked me if I had a scorned lover out there somewhere pulling a *Fatal Attraction* on me. I shook my head and wished I did.

The officer asked me, "What happened?"

"What you mean?"

"Your car has been vandalized." He waited for me to start confessing. "Want to talk about it, son?"

"Nothing to talk about."

"We're just trying to help. You're pretty banged up."

I used one of my momma's old lines: "I tripped."

"You tripped quite a few times."

"Clumsiness runs in my family. We fall down a lot."

He didn't like my answer.

He asked, "You want to stand over here and show me your ID?"

"For what? My car has been vandalized and you're treating me like a criminal."

"Nobody said you were a criminal. We need information for the report."

I limped to the sidewalk, my scraped hands in the open so they wouldn't flip out and start acting like Dirty Harry. My heart beat harder. Sweat poured from my forehead like rain. My eyes went to their squad cars. Already I could feel the cold plastic from those hard seats on my skin.

I gave him my driver's license. He handed it off to another officer. They were about to put my info into the system and see what came up.

A heavy bass line vibrated through my body before I could make out the lyrics to another one of Tupac's songs. Once again my heart tried to beat its way out of my chest. A ghetto-red tricked-out Trans Am came from the direction of the mini mall that housed Jinky's Café, eased up the peaceful, tree-lined avenue with that silver eagle sparkling on its hood, that plastic Jesus wobbling side to side on the dashboard, and those two furry black-and-white dice dancing and swaying to their own rhythm. He had American flags flapping on both sides of his ride, looking about as "God Bless America" as they came.

Nazario was taunting me by returning to the scene of his crime.

I wanted to scream and charge at that fool with fists of fury. I had to grit my teeth and stay put.

One Time asked, "Friends of yours?"

I shook my head.

Nazario wasn't alone. He was riding three-deep. I recognized both of his friends. We'd all met a while back on a bridge in Boyle Heights.

Nazario slowed and we mean-mugged each other. He hit the switches in his car and made it pop-lock. All the rainbows made him look like a star at the circus.

He dared me with a smile. His boys did the same.

Nazario cruised by, bold and easy, made a left at the end of the block, and vanished.

One Time didn't find any warrants, not even an unpaid parking ticket, so they had to let me go. Then they suggested that I get to an emergency room and have my bruises checked.

Finding Jackson was in my heart, and putting a hurting on Nazario was on my mind. That motherfucker was insane. Then another thought hit me in the gut. My heart sped up and I rushed to look in my glove compartment. It had been broken into with a screwdriver. My car registration, all of my paperwork, was gone.

All of that had my address on every page.

Now that one-eyed psychotic bully knew where I lived.

The fire department left. A tow truck came. Paperwork was signed. The driver knew a salvage yard. I paid him. He was no doubt getting a kickback from that salvage yard, but I didn't have time to haggle with that hustler. I patted Oscar a few times, told him I was sorry for the way shit went down.

I pulled my Louisville Slugger out of my trunk and started walking.

20

Pam's note was an invitation to come by her crib and cuddle up for the rest of the night, maybe add another chapter to what we had started at my place last night. She lived right off the 101 in a huge complex called Premier. I didn't have a c-phone, didn't wanna risk stopping at a pay phone, so I made that three-mile journey as fast as I could. Every step hurt more than the one before.

After I was buzzed in at the front entrance on Woodman, I was lost in a maze of three-story buildings, outdoor grills, volleyball courts, basketball courts, and exotic shrubbery. The compound was like a small city. Took me a few minutes of limping around to find my way over to structure F.

Pam opened the door and lost her grin. She had on a Victoria's Secret number that didn't hide much of her secrets. She let me into a candlelit room and said, "Damn. Let me look at your bruises."

She clicked on the kitchen light and looked me over. I did the same with her. Her bushy hair was done to perfection. Perfume was rising from her pulse points. Nails and toes done in glittery polish. Plum-colored lipstick told me that her lips were ready for a lot of kissing. She looked very sensual, but I was in too much pain to enjoy the view. A bottle of wine and a bowl of fresh fruit were on the counter. The apartment smelled like exotic fruits, things like fresh mangos and kiwis.

She said, "Your clothes are jacked to the max."

"Tell me something I don't know."

"Looks like you got your ass kicked."

"You should see the other guy."

She was at the refrigerator taking out an ice pack. She cut her eyes at my baseball bat.

I answered her unspoken question, "Every job does have its occupational hazards."

"Yep. Even the Pope got shot at."

Her kitchen was to the left, right inside the front door. A couple of bar stools were at the counter. Candles were lit and a mood was set. She blew out the candles and turned on the lights. That was when I saw the real estate section of the *Los Angeles Times* valley edition on her counter. She had circled a few listings in red and had written down a few names. Prices were jotted down as well. Looked like she'd already made a few phone calls on those properties.

I asked, "Whassup with this?"

"We'll talk about it later. Put this ice pack on your face."

Pam hurried me into her bathroom and I leaned against the counter icing my wounds. We had to walk through her bedroom to get to the john. A golden silk scarf was laying across her white sheets; six fluffy pillows were there too. Massage oil and a pack of condoms were resting on the nightstand.

I said, "Damn."

Pam made an *oh well* sound and said, "C'mon to the nurses' station."

Pictures were Scotch-taped to her wall-length mirror: Halle Berry's abs in *Swordfish*, Janet Jackson dressed to the nines, and Angelina Jolie in her *Tomb Raider* gear— all stunning women with the bodies of death. Women with perfect stomachs. There were cut-out articles from magazines like *Essence* and *Cosmo* on how to lose weight, how to tighten your tummy, how to do makeup.

Pam got out a bottle of peroxide and wiped me down while I looked at myself for the first time tonight. I'd taken a few good blows. Enough to swell my left eye a bit. Ear was still stinging. Face was bruised more than I realized. Clothes had seen better days.

I could've died ten different ways since sunrise. The

way things were looking, I'd be lucky to make it to the next sunset. That didn't sit too well with me.

Pam looked at my face and hands the way a mother looks at a child, then pulled out a first-aid kit.

She said, "A Band-Aid might not cover this cut."

"Do what you can with what you got."

"Mind if I put a napkin on it?"

"A napkin?"

"Feminine napkin."

"Hell yeah, I mind."

"They absorb—"

"I'll bleed to death first."

"Then bleed to death."

"With dignity."

"You smell, Dante."

"I know."

"I mean really smell."

"Hurry up."

"Don't snap at me, shorty. I'm not the one who kicked your ass."

I told her I needed to borrow her ride. She grabbed some cotton sweats from her closet. She didn't say it, but her body language told me that she didn't know me well enough to be loaning her car out, so she was going with me.

She said, "You need to let this go, Dante."

I shook my head. "I don't want you in this."

"It's too late for that, don't you think?"

"Hurry up, then."

She kept her back to me, still timid about that part of her.

I said, "Mind if I get some water?"

She motioned toward the kitchen. I headed that way. When I opened the fridge, I saw that she had a yellow sheet of paper Scotch-taped to the front. It was a long list of things that a man must have to be her Mr. Right. Financially independent and cashing in around six figures a year. Spirituality came in behind that financial desire. Good family values. Good with chil-

dren. Good in bed was underlined. No more than one
kid. At least five years older and ten years wiser. At
least six feet tall.

Pam walked up behind me. "Sorry. Meant to take that
down before you got here."

"Nice grocery list."

"That's the best way to shop. And if it's not written
down, then it's not a goal."

Two days ago, before I'd ever touched her or shared
dinner and a few dances, I knew what I wanted from
Pam. I didn't have to write it down to know that I
wanted her to have a key to my crib. To go hiking and
skiing. Rollerblade on the beach. To meet me for lunch
and see an art house movie a couple of times a week. To
surprise me by showing up at 2 a.m. and crawling in bed
with me. Lots of laughing and lots of cuddling. To have a
drawer at my crib. Her favorite food in my cabinets.
Most of all, I wanted her to have a toothbrush at my crib.
That might not sound like much, but when I woke up
and saw her toothbrush I'd know she was coming back.
That it was more than a fuck-and-go thing. That would
tell me that we were working on something real.

Takes a long time to make something real happen.
Takes a long time to meet somebody you want something like that to happen with. Long time to find somebody you could trust to not walk away when they knew
all about you. Learned that from Jackson. Maybe
watching my buddy struggle was why my list didn't have
all that other Cinderella mess. I don't know if men were
ever afforded a chance at fantasies like that. I had issues
I needed to deal with, but when I read over Pam's wish
list, I didn't have those kinda issues. Maybe because I
was only a day into being twenty-five. I had street
smarts, but at times I'd had to admit that I was still a
babe and naive in my own way. If I were her age, my list
might be just as extensive.

Right now I was too busy trying to make it from sun-
down to sunrise.

The ice pack warmed up. Pam reached in the garbage

and pulled out three plastic grocery bags from Ralph's. She layered the bags, put ice inside, and handed them to me.

I said, "Looks like you just got back from food shopping."

She tied a purple bandanna around her hair. "Yep. Guess I bought Popsicles for nothing."

She grabbed her keys.

Pam drove the 101 east toward downtown. I told her almost everything.

She said, "Jackson is sixteen thousand in debt with the courts?"

"Yep."

"Well, that'll make you slap your momma."

I told her that the girl I'd seen at 360 wrapped around that dude was Jackson's fiancée.

"That'll make you slap your daddy."

Then I told her that Jackson had busted Robin with that dude the next night.

"Now we're slapping Grandma. Wanna go for Grandpa?"

Then I told her about us getting jacked and Jackson vanishing along with the green cards.

"We're slapping ancestors back in Africa now."

I told her that Nazario had ambushed me. And he had killed Oscar.

She asked, "Who's Oscar?"

"My car."

"Your hoopty was pretty much on its last leg anyway."

"That's not funny."

"My bad. You're sensitive about your car. I'll make a note of that."

Boyle Heights was still bumping when we pulled off the Golden State Freeway. People were driving back and forth, music filled the air. I was jittery. My hands ached. With that knot throbbing in my back, Pam had to drive. My plan was to get out of the car, Louisville Slugger in hand, and search for Jackson. That wasn't much of a plan. If something went down, I told her to speed away and don't worry about me. I'd pretend I was the next Barry Bonds and hit a few home runs until I got back to home plate.

"Shorty, don't start thinking just because you're mad you're invincible."

"I've got my bat."

"Well, Batman, they have guns."

"I can hold my own."

"You never played paper-scissors-rock, did you?"

There was no dark-haired woman adjusting her tools and strutting her real estate up and down the avenue. The Volvo was gone. Pam pulled over and I dumped my ice bag, went and stood by where we had left Scamz's car. No way for it to have made it far with three flat tires. One Time could've had it towed, but I doubted that. This wasn't Beverly Hills or Malibu; in urban areas a car could sit disabled for days and get ticketed every day, but not get towed.

I had Pam ride back over the bridge and turn around where the fight went down. That area was dark and calm. No signs that a fight ever took place. I let my window down and asked myself what I would've done if I couldn't run up the hill to help my friends. I had Pam drive in the direction I thought that Jackson might've fled to get away from whoever attacked him. There were a few spots that somebody could've crawled into and balled up in pain. I stuck my head out the window and called Jackson's name a few times. No answer. I took a chance and looked in a few nooks and crannies. Nothing. It was late, a lot of time had passed, enough for him to have lost enough blood to pass out.

Pam said, "He could be anywhere by now."

I didn't know what to do.

Pam slid me her c-phone and said, "Maybe you should call his girlfriend."

I dialed Robin's number and got her machine. Asked her to call me or have Jackson call me if he was with her. After the way things were the last time I saw them, I doubted if they would be together. Not this soon. But in matters of the heart, you never knew. A lot of fear and craziness was in my voice. I squashed as much as I could, but desperation was still in my tone.

Then I called and checked my messages. Nothing.

Pam said, "What now?"

"Dunno."

"Riding around in circles ain't gonna solve anything."

"Let me think for a minute."

That shook me because I swear I heard Scamz's irritation coming out of my mouth. My mind took me back to my old man's funeral. I hated him in some ways, but still loved him in others. Time to time, he did help me with my homework. He did keep a roof over my head. He did buy me clothes. He brought us to Disneyland. Took us to church. And he was my father. His blood ran through my veins twenty-four-seven and he was on my mind three-sixty-five. The last image I had of him was when I was standing in front of his casket. I imagined Jackson's kids doing the same with Sabrina at their side. I saw Robin there too.

A moment went by. I said, "Okay, whassup with the real estate section of the paper?"

"You know what's up. Nothing's changed."

"Find another hustle. Look at me, will you? I'm beat down like Rodney King."

"Look, Dante, keep it real. I need something that can pull down some nice cash. That rent thing was off the chains. Outside of bumping into Tammy Barrett, it was so damn smooth."

"What if you bump into somebody again?"

"Dunno. Guess I do what I have to do."

"Your friends almost . . . It almost got ugly up there."

"But it didn't," she said with force. That showed me corners of her other side, the one that would cut you a hundred ways to heaven or a thousand ways to hell. Pam quieted long enough to let out a determined sigh. That dimpled smile came back. "It didn't get ugly. It was like doing a play."

"This ain't a play. You don't get beat down in a play. Ain't no jail when the curtain goes down."

Pam pressed on. "Everybody had a part and it was organic, ever changing, getting revised, improvising, and getting better every time. You guys were the perfect cast, a team, had hand signals that were so slick. And everybody was in on it but the people who were dropping off cashier's checks. Everybody had everybody's back."

I asked, "Would you have been willing to hurt your friend and her husband to get what you want?"

She slowed her verbal roll. "Stop focusing on that glitch."

"You saw Molly reaching in her purse. Scamz wasn't lying."

"Nobody got hurt. Outside of that, people gave up tons of money just like that."

I took a deep breath, held it, let it go real slow. My head wanted to explode.

Her voice remained soft. "Just once. That's all. Hit it and quit it."

"Is it that important?"

"To me it is."

"Why?"

"Like Ally McBeal said, my problems are important to me because they're my problems. My insecurities are important to me because they are my insecurities."

"Look, I'm out here looking for Jackson because of the same thing. Hell, if I had stayed at the car and he'd been up on that bridge fighting for his life, I could be the one missing. Or whatever."

Her voice turned tender. "You think he could be dead?"

I didn't say anything. My mind refused to go that route.

I had Pam get off the 170 at Magnolia and head toward North Hollywood High. We took the back way, eased up Colfax and cruised down the side opposite my beige stucco apartment building. The train tracks and palm trees separated northbound and southbound traffic. My living room was upstairs and faced the streets. Had to check out my apartment, make sure no loco idiots had set the building on fire. I couldn't see much from where we were parked, so Pam went down to Laurel Canyon, made a U-turn at the 7-Eleven and came back down Chandler on my side. I stayed low in the car and looked around for trouble. Pam didn't see a ghettored Trans Am anywhere in sight. We circled the block a couple times. The next time she slowed to a crawl as she passed my crib, and I looked up. Didn't look like any windows had been broken out of my place. Didn't look like anybody was lying in the cut waiting for me to show my face. But in a war you never knew where the land mines were planted.

We kept going beyond the high school and stopped near the 170 overpass.

She said, "Want me to go up to your place and act like I'm looking for you?"

I shook my head. I already had one injured friend out there, and that was more than enough.

Jackson had me on edge. Scamz had me scared of what he might do. Nazario had rattled my cage big time. Home was the last place I needed to be; that was the first place trouble would come hunting.

I told Pam to start back driving. I wasn't comfortable sitting in one spot too long.

She asked, "Where do you want me to drop you off?"

"Can I crash at your crib for a little while?"

"Guess you need a favor."

"Just need to rest and think for a few."

"Sure, shorty. My sofa is your sofa."

Pam changed out of her sweats, put that black Victoria's Secret thing back on, and got in her bed.

She asked, "Need me to do anything?"

"Just need to use the phone."

"The cordless is in the kitchen."

I called a few hospitals. Called Robin again. Called Jackson's crib. Nobody was answering.

From the kitchen counter, I had a straight shot of Pam. She was on her stomach, her mound rising high, her head turned the other way, the white sheets coming up to the bottom of her butt.

She must've felt me staring because without looking she asked, "Any luck?"

"Nah."

"I have an extra blanket at the foot of the bed. Grab a pillow. Get some sleep."

"I'm funky as a donkey. Need to clean up a bit."

"Extra towels are already hanging by the shower."

I headed for the shower, took my soiled and shredded clothes off as I limped that way. Turned the water up hot enough to humidify the place. Cotton balls, Q-tips, Noxema, candles, and twenty things that smelled like a fruit garden were all over the counter. A big orange towel and a matching face towel and one of those bright yellow scrungy things were there too.

I asked Pam, "Got an extra toothbrush?"

"Right-hand drawer. Should be a purple one."

"Is it new?"

"Brand-new. Bought it this afternoon. Toothpaste is on the counter."

After I flossed and brushed, I grabbed the scrungy, got in the shower, adjusted the water to a cooler setting. Used her liquid Neutrogena to scrub myself clean.

My eyes were on her while I dried off. White sheets on Nubian flesh. Tingles in my groin tussled with my pain. That elusive creature was a work of art, as exotic as the African photographs by Uwe Ommer.

She said, "Pick a pillow. The big ones are hypoallergenic. If that red blanket's not heavy enough, I have another one in the closet. If you get too cold, thermostat's on the wall by the bookcase."

I asked, "Mind if I turn some music on?"

"I made a blues tape. It's already in the stereo."

I pushed play and let the blues fill the air. It was slow bump-and-grind music.

I made a hurting sound when I sat on the bed. It was

nice to be on a soft pillow-top mattress covered with sheets that smelled as clean as the first day of spring. This was a peaceful room and Pam was a fine woman. I ran my hand over her butt. She didn't say anything. I pulled the sheets down and ran my fingers over her skin. She didn't move. I picked up her scarf, wrapped it around her eyes.

She didn't slap my hands away or question what I was doing.

I headed for the kitchen cabinet, got a glass, and filled it with ice, then looked in the refrigerator, let that coolness creep over my wounded and naked skin as that light brightened up her living room. There was enough glow in the room for me to see she had beige furniture on beige carpet, a small kitchen table with two chairs. Headshots and acting résumés were all over that table. She ate pretty healthy. Very little meat was in the fridge, no red meat or pork, and plenty of fruits and vegetables; strawberries and grapes, cucumbers, asparagus, tofu, turkey meat, tomatoes, lettuce, other things to make a nice romantic snack after a night of loving by candlelight. I grabbed a bag of frozen peas out of the freezer part, rubbed that over my hands and face. Then I saw a big box of grape Popsicles; the long, narrow kind. I got another glass, dropped two of those frozen sugar sticks inside, and went back to Pam.

I let the ice make my hands cold, then ran my fingers from the bottom of her feet up and over her butt, made a trail until I got to the arch in her back.

Pam held on to her pillow and shivered; Etta James sang "At Last."

I kissed Pam in the same places I had touched her. She squirmed, pulled her lips in.

I turned her over. Undressed her.

My hands traced the sides of her face, over that blindfold, around her neck, rubbed her shoulders, around her back, then cupped and massaged her breasts. She started to squirm.

I took one cube of ice. Slid it up and down her legs,

over her calves, over the soles of her feet. She was panting, tensing, pulling the sheets. Did that until Etta went
away and B.B. came on to let us know there must be a
better world out there. I licked the water that was left behind, then grabbed another cube. The ice clinked on the
glass; Pam tensed. I put this one on her inner thigh, ran it
up to where her legs met, rubbed it there. My finger
slipped inside. That tall drink of water was wet and hot. I
put the cube on that tender red meat, held that ice right
there. Her back arched, she pressed down on her palms,
lost her breath, squealed, and tried to get away. I pulled
her back, told her not to fight it because I'd follow her.

I said, "Open your mouth."

Her trembling mouth opened like a little bird ready
to feed. I put a Popsicle inside.

"Suck this, Pam. Don't stop."

She caught her breath. I made sure her scarf was on
tight, then ran ice up and down her again, put that
frozen water on her breasts, watched her nipples rise,
stand strong. I teased until the Popsicle in her mouth
had been sucked away and nothing was left but the dark
purple stains in her sheets.

I opened the other Popsicle.

Pam moaned, "Damn. Dante."

I ran it around her nipples, down over her navel. She
jerked when I got close to her pubic hair. I eased it between her legs. Her breathing sped up and she made an
ugly face, but she didn't stop me.

I put my tongue where the Popsicle was. Used my soft
flesh to heat her up and used the Popsicle to cool her
down. Juice melted and created a sugary puddle from
her thighs to her sheets.

My stomach growled. Didn't realize how hungry a
night of fighting and running had left me until I started
feeding on her. She arched her back, panted, held the
pillow so tight I expected it to burst. Looked like she
was about to come; I backed away and let her ache. Left
her squirming.

She groaned, asked, "What are you doing?"

"Coitus postponus."

"Jocking my style."

"I'm a quick study."

I dropped my towel and went to the kitchen. Opened the fridge and looked back at Pam. Her legs were moving up and down, rubbing each other. I checked out her food. Saw what I wanted to feed her; went back, touched her there, rubbed that wetness.

"What are you putting . . . putting . . . putting in me?"

"Shhh."

Her back bowed and Pam let out the sweetest chant I'd ever heard. That sugarcoated hymn both stirred me and surprised me as she rolled her hips into what I had in my hand. She had a short talk with God and a long conversation with his son before she cursed in a voice so sweet. Pam's legs started to wobble, reminded me of a rolling earthquake, and she sucked her lips in, did all she could to lower the volume on her song. I whispered for her to let me hear and not hold back. Nothing like watching a beautiful woman make that ugly face. She did that until she slowed down; her bottom lip quivered. Pam reached for my penis, searched for it like she had to touch it, feel it, squeeze.

I moved her hand away.

I said, "That ain't ready to become a personal prop yet."

I looked around her room while I fed her strawberries. Checked out her life while I gave her grapes. Posters from black movies were on walls in the front room, I'd seen those when I came in. In this den, pictures of her were on the dresser. Looked like family pictures were there too. All adults. Some were photos of her and B-list actors and actresses from the black side of the Wood. Most of those were group shots. No photos in sight of anybody who stood out as a lover. Not one photo of her child.

I rubbed cold juice on her. Licked every drop off.

She was on the other side of wet and ready. Needed her on the edge before I slid inside her. I leaned over to the dresser and opened the condoms. Hand throbbed a bit as I rolled one on.

I moved her legs apart, climbed on top of her, and let our weight sink into the mattress; kissed her face, sucked on her lips, did that until she reached down and put me inside of her; she pulled her knees back to her breasts, had her legs over my shoulders, allowed me to hold her butt with a firm grip, go deep and look at the glow on her face, the way her skin was set on fire.

I filled her up the best I could and held it right there. I moved down in her, and she moved up against me with the looseness and smoothness of a dancer. I did my best to move like she did. We took that groove and loved through Little Milton and Bobby "Blue" Bland and Bo Diddley. That music got under my skin in a good way. Heaven's ache crept up on me in so many wonderful colors. Pam kept grinding and held on to me for life. Her right leg quivered and she jerked around for a while. I was still hard enough for her to feel something, hard enough to make her come like that again.

When we were done, she raised her hand. I gave her a high-five.

She moved her nappy mane from her face. "Can I take my blindfold off now?"

"Sure."

She needed me to get up so she could change the sheets. These were ready for the washing machine, and the mattress had to be flipped. I turned the mattress, then went to flush the condom.

Pam said, "You're moving like my granddaddy."

"Doing my best."

"You've gotta be hurting pretty bad."

"Yeah. But that made me feel better."

"Tylenol is in the cabinet. Eight-hundred milligram."

I popped three, washed them down with tap water. She grabbed a set of sheets from the closet.

I watched her make up the bed. I said, "I'm chasing one man while another man is chasing me. Anybody I'm with might be in trouble too. What you want me to do?"

Her eyes told me she knew what I meant. I had too much drama following me around.

She said, "Crash and regroup if you wanna."

"You're not scared?"

"Shorty, I've been in trouble all of my life. Told ya, I was born under a bad sign."

"Just like me."

"Yep."

"Just need a couple of hours and I'll be okay. What time you getting up?"

"You're not gonna flip out and sock me upside the head again, are you? Lemme know so I can put on my racquetball goggles and Rollerblade helmet."

She chuckled. I didn't.

I got in the bed first, closed my eyes, and asked the tension in my shoulders to fall out of my body and vanish into the softness. The room wasn't that big, so I heard her in the bathroom singing the blues and emptying her bladder. She washed up and came back, crawled in the bed next to me.

The tape clicked, then turned over to play side B.

I asked, "More blues?"

"Nothing but Billie Holiday on this side."

I moved closer to Pam. Her body was warm.

She ran her hands up and down my body. Touched my stomach, slid her fingers across my flesh over and over. She asked, "What you gonna do about your friend?"

"Dunno." My headache came back just like that. "Just have to find him before Scamz does."

"What if Scamz already has found 'im?"

"Doubt it. Scamz was wrapped around one of his women."

"Then wrap yourself around me."

I relaxed. She scooted closer, bounced her foot and sang along with Lady Day for a while.

I said, "Think twice before you try to run that real estate thing. That's serious business."

"You say you're out, then stay out, shorty."

I stared at the ceiling and thought about the night.

Pam kept shifting like she was waiting for me to change my mind about helping her and talk.

She bumped me with her leg, whispered my name in the timbre of an angel, "Dante?"

"Whassup?"

"Sleep?"

"Nah. Too much on my mind. You?"

"No sleep for the weary."

"Bet."

"Hurting?"

"I've hurt more."

"Can you hook me up one mo' again?"

"You need some more horizontal recreation?"

"And vaginal rejuvenation."

That got a decent laugh out of me. "Back hurts. So I have to take it easy."

"I like it when you move slow like that. That was better than yesterday."

"What made it better?"

"Well, yesterday you were like the typical man. Acted like you had something to prove. Think banging me, jumping up and down in the coochie and making me scream is all a woman needs."

"A'ight. What I do different this time?"

"You were passionate. Was more like making love than fucking. Know what I mean?"

She kissed my hand, my face, then eased down and used her mouth and hands to help me get rigid again. She had passion and skills that were to be reckoned with. Never felt anybody work it like that. She wasn't afraid to be affectionate. Pam relaxed, took as much of me as she could, did that in a gentle way with a lot of energy. Don't think I'd ever moaned that loud in my life, not from feeling good. She looked up at me, had a little smile on her face, those dimples in full effect, then made love to me in a way that made me think I was the only man on the planet she ever wanted to touch.

When that bone had risen and turned into wood, she helped me roll a condom on. She brought all of that real

estate to me, got on top, shifted, elevated her hips, found
her position, and came down on me a little at a time, let
out a delicate sigh that invited me to move deeper.
Nothing like that split second when a man broke a
woman's skin, when her face glowed and she lost her
breath, almost like she was drowning in good feelings.
She went into a rise and fall. I lost my breath and began
drowning too.

I hit the right spot and Pam wasn't trying to move so
slow anymore. She was gone. Pam touched her breasts,
pulled at her bushy hair like she was going insane, went
into a steady ride toward paradise. That slow trot became a gallop severe enough to make her pine headboard slap back and forth against the wall. Somebody in
the next apartment tapped on that partition a couple of
times. Pam slowed down and stuffed a pillow between
the headboard and the wall. Did that in a smooth motion, like she'd been given that same signal and done
that move countless times before.

Billie sang us into another place and time.

Pam moaned a thousand times. "God. That. Feels. So.
Good."

My pain was slipping away. Not gone, but tolerable.
Tingles turned my body into a living ball of fire. Our
harsh breathing and steady moans added some alto and
baritone harmony to Billie's blues.

Pam was bucking like a rodeo queen. I wanted her to
ride me until hard times got better.

"Oh. God. Dante. Oh. Jesus."

I slapped her backside over and over. Slapped her
real estate and had to admit that no matter how much
she infatuated me, I didn't know a lot about Pam, only
what she'd said and what I'd seen.

"Coming. Coming. Coming."

All of what she told me about herself could be true,
or all of that could be the biggest lie ever told.

"Come. With. Me. Dante. Come. With. Me."

I held her hips, let my rhythm meet with hers, and I
knew this much: she was a thief and a liar.

"Don't. Stop. Dante. Don't. Believe. This. Coming. Again."

Those bright colors overwhelmed me and I joined her in that orgasmic song. It took her a while to stop her hips from moving. Then we lay there with Billie's voice covering us like a blanket.

Heaven's ache started to fade; my mind was somewhere else.

"Damn." She caught her breath and kissed me a few times. "I came too hard."

I swallowed.

"I had to sound like a nuclear warning," Pam said, and fell away from me. "My neighbors are probably running for a fallout shelter."

We raised our tired arms and struggled to do that high-five thing again, then she staggered to the bathroom. Caught a glimpse of her stomach before she pulled on a T-shirt and covered herself up again.

If Pam didn't have those stretch marks on her belly, I'd say that she was lying about being a momma just to keep her skills at deception sharpened. She didn't know me, so she didn't owe me the truth. Outside of needing six grand to erase those scars, something was going on with her.

She came back and pulled the condom off me, wrapped it in the damp towel I had left on the floor, then took another end of that towel and wiped me down, did the same to herself. She tossed the towel toward the bathroom and got back in the bed, slid her hand over my chest, down to my groin; held my shrinking personal prop in a tender way. I looked toward that towel. Felt a bit uneasy. I told her I had to go take a leak and grabbed that towel along the way. Shook that condom out as I emptied my bladder, then sent all of my fluids to the Pacific Ocean.

Pam watched me the whole time. Saw her studying me when I moved to the sink.

While I washed my hands, I looked at her counter. From living room to kitchen to bedroom, something wasn't right about this place. I went to the kitchen and used the phone again. Called to check my messages. Nothing. Called Robin again. No answer. Called Jackson's crib. No answer. I massaged my chrome dome and looked around the living room; it took me a minute but I figured out what was wrong with this place. After that revelation, I got back in the bed with Pam.

My mind was troubled in six directions. I kept my tone light and even, the way Scamz did when he made you think that he knew more than he really did. "Tell me the truth."

She let out a lover's laugh. "What truth you looking for?"

"Whassup with your kid?"

She stopped laughing, got quiet.

Back when she ran into her girlfriend Tammy and her husband, Tammy didn't ask Pam about her kid. Women always fell into Oprah-mode and jibber-jabbered about kids and lovers. If they had done that many plays and all those rehearsals together, then Tammy had to know about Pam's little boy. No kiddie pictures were up in this den. Yesterday she said that she had to get Veggie-Tale videos, and I know those are for preschoolers. No toys from a Happy Meal scattered here and there, nothing like the proud and cluttered atmosphere at Sabrina's crib. Even Jackson had kiddie sketches on the refrigerator and other junk out in the living room at his pad. Pam's kid could be older and that would erase that doubt, but this was a one-bedroom. Her clothes were in both sides of the closet. Her feminine stuff was all over the counter, not just on one side. Not even a jug of Mr. Bubbles or a yellow rubber ducky in sight.

I told Pam all of that. Expected her to jump in and correct me. She listened without moving.

I asked, "Was he taken from you or something?"

She turned her back to me and tensed up. I thought she was about to tell me to get the fuck out. I moved away from her a bit. She reached back and pulled me close, took my hand.

I told myself that it didn't matter, that my mind was

in the wrong place and I had other things to worry about. I let that go and asked myself if I had done all I could do tonight, then tried to think of what to do at sunrise. My body was worn down and I managed to doze off. Fell toward the edges of a nightmare, but pulled myself back with a jerk.

I sat up. Startled. Disoriented.

Pam wasn't in the bed. I walked to the doorway that separated the bedroom from the living room. Pam had taken a pillow and the blankets. She had wrapped herself up like a child in a nursery and was sitting on the sofa. Crying. Pictures of a baby were scattered on the coffee table.

21

Pam's voice thickened with sorrow when she said, "SIDS."

"What's that?"

"Sudden Infant Death Syndrome. Crib death."

I didn't know what to say. She motioned for me to come and sit near her.

Pam said, "Died in his sleep. Just stopped breathing."

"Sorry to hear that."

She was smiling at pictures of a baby. His hair was light brown with soft curls, and his complexion was about ten shades lighter than Pam's.

"It defies the natural order of things." She sucked her bottom lip in. "A parent is supposed to die before her kids."

"Why did you keep saying you had a kid to get home to?"

"Why did I lie to a bunch of felons who lie, cheat, and steal to make a living?"

"Since you put it that way . . ."

"C'mon, now. I don't know you guys. Somehow I don't think that Scamz's real name is Scamz, know what I mean? And I doubt if Big Slim is that maimed guy at the pool hall's name. And if Molly's real name is Molly, then I'm Colonel Sanders. For all I know, your name might not be Dante."

"True."

Pam went on, "Why should I tell you the truth when I don't know what's the truth about you?"

"I told you enough about me."

"And it doesn't add up, shorty."

"Like what?"

"You did that much time for getting in a fight with your daddy? I don't care if he was a police officer, I can't see you doing that much time, not almost two years, just because you got in a fight."

I closed my eyes and saw me and my old man fighting again. Guilt and shame numbed my wounds. Saw how we went at it from wall to wall in that living room. Destroyed everything that wasn't nailed down. For the better part of five minutes, violence begot violence and you could've bought two fools for the price of one. I gave my old man back what he had taught me.

I told Pam, "I pulled his gun on him."

"Get the fuck outta here. You pulled a gun on Porky the Pig?"

"Yep."

"Wow. You shoot him?"

"It went off. Blew a hole in the wall."

"Wow."

"Scared all of us so bad, the fight just ended. Daddy ran out the back door. I dialed 9-1-1 and sat on the porch with my momma. Held her hand while she put ice on my bruises. Waited for One Time so we could tell 'em what went down. Four or five cars showed up at the same time. They all pulled up like it was a scene out of a movie. Drawing their guns and ready to blaze me."

She closed her photo album and put her pictures away. The blue shadows outside her window were fading. The sun was struggling to come up outside. I'd made it to another day.

I asked, "What you do time for?"

"Passed a few bad checks."

Pam told me that she used to be married, back when she was my age.

I said, "You said that you'd never worn a wedding ring."

"I'd hardly call that piece of shit he gave me a wedding ring. It was about the same as that cigar band that Luke gave Laura."

"Who?"

"Never mind."

She said that she had a bad marriage to an actor who couldn't act his way out of a paper bag with a hole in the bottom. Said that they got married because she was pregnant, and they lived out in Simi Valley. Told me that it was hard living and loving in a small apartment that had one ego too many, no steady income, and a lot of fighting. A lot of living hand-to-mouth. She got married. Had the baby. Lost the baby. They split up. Along the way she found out her hubby was a small-time crook and he showed her a few things.

She said, "He talked me into kiting checks. You know what that is?"

She told me how he got her to open three accounts at three banks with small balances, then talked her into writing big checks from one account to the other. She did a check for ten grand from bank one to bank two, then did a fifteen thousand dollar check from bank two to bank three, then wrote a larger one from bank three to bank one.

She said, "I had enough imaginary money long enough to pass a few bad checks."

"I'm hip to that."

"Ever done it?"

"I've schooled a few people on it, but I don't do that. That's supposed to be hard to catch."

"But I got caught."

"And you did it?"

"Love makes you do some crazy shit. Besides, I had to eat, you know."

"Where did you learn how to pick pockets?"

"Same guy."

"He taught you to shoot pool too?"

"Got that from my dad. He ran a pool hall."

"You're good."

"Not good enough for the pros, but I can hold my own."

"How much time you do for the bad checks?"

"Lost six months of my life. That's a year sentence with time cut in half for behaving like a nun."

"How long ago was that?"

"Long enough for people to forget, but not long enough for me to stop remembering."

"Not a lot of jobs you can get with a felony on your record."

"Oh, please. Nobody cares about an actor's past. That's why Robert Downey Jr. and the rest of the rehab crew keep getting major work while the clean and sober file for unemployment."

She leaned up against me, pulled some covers over us. My hand was in her hair, fingers massaging her scalp. The room had the kind of darkness and quiet that helped people reveal secrets.

Pam told me that she was skipping her shift at Ed Debevic's because she had a meeting to get to. She was meeting with a couple of people she knew. People who needed to make some cash. She was moving ahead with her own plans, trying to put her own little scheme into motion. She told me that she had made a few contacts when she was lingering and gambling at the pool hall.

I said, "You don't waste no time networking."

"Time ain't on my side." She chuckled. "I had my reality check last week."

"What happened?"

She told me that she had gone to meet with a new agent. Said that she'd taken her reel, film of all of her best performances. The agent looked over her work and told her that she was a great actress.

Pam said, "He was brutally honest, flat out told me I was too old."

"You don't look old. How old are you?"

"That don't matter. The point is, once the word gets out about your age, especially if you're a woman and over thirty and don't have the credits to make you salable, your career is pretty much over."

"Then why bother with ... why bother worrying about dropping six-G on an operation?"

"The stretch marks." She took a breath. "It's okay to say it; it's not a bad word."

"Why bother?"

"I'm not young like you, Dante. I don't have the same kinda time left that you do. You're a man. If you were in this business, you could do like George Burns and work until you were damn near one hundred. A woman's acting career doesn't have the same life expectancy, and a woman of color, we don't have that many roles from the get-go, so that makes the our shelf life shorter than a loaf of bread."

I didn't understand that business, so I just listened to what she had to say. More like half-listened. Hard to keep your mind focused when your thoughts are racing in too many directions.

She said, "My old agent told me in no uncertain terms that if something didn't happen soon, since I'm no longer young enough to be on *Buffy the Vampire Slayer* and *Clueless*, that he was going to stop wasting his time and energy trying to get me work. That's the nice version of what he said."

"He's gonna drop you."

"Like a hot potato. Getting a new agent when you're over thirty and don't have credits like Vivica Fox or Halle Berry is next to impossible. That's when a lot of actresses vanish and do whatever they do when they realize Hollywood has put them out to pasture and started milking the new cows."

"Why don't you do something else?"

"I never planned to fail. I have no backup plan. I can't turn back. I can't start over."

"What if you run your scam, then you get famous? It'll come back to haunt you."

"I'll take that chance. Maybe they'll think it's funny."

"Nobody thinks getting scammed is funny."

She shrugged. "Maybe I'll keep their names and send them their money back, with interest. I just need . . . I need to do this. I can't go back now."

She cuddled up closer to me. Her body was warm and that touching felt better than sex. Moments like this were what I had in mind when I used to look at Pam, used to wonder what it would take for us to be like this with each other. That was back when I was scared of how she would react if I ever told her the truth about me.

"I like you, Pam."

She reached up and ran her hand over my bald head, then touched my face in a soft way.

"Twenty-three," Pam said.

"C'mon. You're older than twenty-three."

"No." She kept touching my skin. "You've sat at my station twenty-three times."

"Damn." I chuckled and looked at her. "You counted?"

"Yep." All the sadness and angst that had been in her tone was gone; that smile came to life. "Twenty-three orders of turkey burger with a side of fruit. Wrote it in my journal too."

"You were so quiet. Outside of taking my order, hardly got a word outta you."

"I was really nervous being around you. Still am, you know."

"You didn't seem nervous in bed."

She laughed a little and blushed a lot. "Everybody down at Debevic's knows your young ass has a thing for me, shorty."

"They cracking on me for macking on you?"

"Nah, they're just haters. That Asian girl has the hots for you like you wouldn't believe."

"You about to do a puff, puff, pass with my ass?"

"Hell, no." She laughed. "I made it known that I sorta like you, too."

"Sorta?"

"You look at me like, I dunno, it scares me and excites me at the same time."

The way she said that made her seem exposed, made me keep my eyes on her. Made me wanna drop my guard and become just as vulnerable as she had let herself be, made me wanna say things that were straight from the heart.

I told her, "You're the kinda woman I wanna kick it with, Pam."

"And what does 'kick it with' mean? Soccer or on the Raiders special team?"

"You know what I mean. That we, you know, spend some time, get to know each other, get into that love thing and be a couple."

"Dante—"

"Serious."

"I'm not twenty-five, Dante."

"I can play older."

We laughed at that Hollywood line.

She said, "You rocked my headboard, but outside of that you don't know me, shorty."

"I know you. Knew that I wanted to spend a lot of time with you before I knew your name."

"Oh, God. Don't start talking like that."

"You're the kinda woman I wanted to be in love with and love me, you know."

She said, "There's a difference between loving somebody and going to bed with them."

"Maybe if we go to bed enough, we'll wake up loving each other."

"You know, no matter whether you're twenty-five or sixty-five, all men think the same way. You want sex without love and companionship without commitment."

More laughter came after that. It was a strange kinda laughter though, the not-real kind that helped make the truth seem like a joke.

"Wish I didn't know about love," I said. "Maybe that's why my life is where it is now. If I didn't love, didn't try to help people, my shit would be tight. I could be out of college by now."

"Not too late for college, shorty. No kids. Not married. You have room for second chances. If I was your age, I'd have so many options that it would make my head spin just counting them. I've got a lotta history under my belt. Some great, some not so great. Not too late for you, not at all."

I sighed. "It is when you feel this old. People my age are already done with college."

I'd helped Pam because she was another wounded lamb that I had wanted to save from life's slaughter. I'd only pulled her deeper into the lion's den. The same thing that I had done for Jackson.

She told me, "You're out of jail now. Don't create your own prison in your head."

"What you mean?"

"You can't blame your daddy, your momma, the white man, the cat, or the dog."

I rubbed my palms together.

She said, "Life is short, Dante. Twenty years go by just like that. And those years gonna go by anyway, so be wise with your time."

"A'ight. What do you think I should do?"

"Give your mind some direction. Write down your goals. Write down who you really wanna be five or ten years from now. Game plan and try to become him."

"Guess I need to change my focus."

"You need to get focused."

"You do the same. Not too late for you to wise up."

"I am. As soon as I do what I gotta do, I'll pray for forgiveness and get back to my master plan."

22

At first glance, it looked like the door to Jackson's apartment had been left part of the way open, then I saw scratches around the lock and splinters of wood on the floor. Looked like somebody had tried to pick the lock, then forced it open. I pushed the door wide open and let the morning's glow fall across the room. It was overcast, but the filtered light helped take away a lot of the shadows.

Cigarette smoke stood strong; almost as strong as the fumes at Big Slim's pool hall.

I called Jackson's name. No answer. No movement came from inside.

Cushions and pillows were off the sofa. Drawers were left open and their contents scattered on the floor. It was right at eight in the morning and his apartment had already been tossed like a jail cell.

Pam said, "We shouldn't be around here."

"Why not?"

"If something did happen to him, the last thing you want to do is leave your fingerprints all over his place."

"I'm here a lot. My fingerprints are already here."

"Then you might not want to be seen here by the neighbors."

"If he's in here hurting, I can't leave him messed up like that."

She was behind me. A dark scarf was over her head. She had on gray sweats underneath her black leather coat. I had borrowed one of her T-shirts and had her gray-and-maroon UNC sweatshirt on top of that. Out-

side of that wardrobe change, I still had on the same
beat-down pants and scuffed shoes from last night. I
wasn't going to swing by home until there was plenty of
light out, not until prime time for drive-bys had given
way to a working man's day.

I stepped inside the apartment. Clicked on the
lights. Pictures of Robin were all over the place. Pictures of them in Vegas, skiing up at Mountain High,
walking the beach at Malibu. He had twice as many
pictures of him and his kids. The want ads with a lot of
jobs circled, then crossed out, were on the kitchen
table. And so was his Wells Fargo bank book. That letter from the D.A. asking for his blood, sweat, and tears
was in that stack too, right up under a green ashtray
overflowing with Marlboro butts. An empty fifth of
Bacardi 151 was on the table. That had cigarette butts
in the bottom. By the way the gook inside the bottle
had dried out and hardened, it had to be a few hours
old; maybe this was his last supper before he went to
see Scamz. A straight-edge razor was on the table as
well. Right next to that was another stack of pictures
of his kids and all of his insurance papers. A glance at
those policies let me know that my friend was worth
more dead than alive.

Slow and easy, I moved from room to room, peeking
in like a bandit before I walked into each one. Checked
every closet. Nobody was here. No blood was on the
floor, no stained rags in the bathroom or the laundry
basket, no sign that Jackson had ever been here. I
didn't expect to find him here, but I had to check to be
sure. His truck wasn't parked outside, but I didn't expect it to be. It had to be parked somewhere down by
the pool hall.

My thoughts refused to settle on anything logical. I
didn't know if Jackson had made it here before the
break-in, but I doubted that because he was a warrior
and wouldn't go down without a fight. This joint was
tossed, but not the way a room would look after a struggle for your life.

Pam had come in behind me. She looked down at the papers from the district attorney and whistled. "Sixteen thousand is a lot of money, shorty. A helluva lot of money."

"What are you saying?"

"Everybody has a sell-out price."

"Not everybody has that Hollywood mentality."

"This ain't got nothing to do with Hollywood." She motioned at the things on the kitchen table. "From what you've told me and from what I see, these are the signs of a desperate man."

"How would you know?"

"You've never been so overwhelmed that you just wanted to end it all?"

I hesitated. "No."

"We all have. Nothing to be ashamed of. Lot of days I get mad because I woke up again and had to go through another day."

"Don't talk like that."

"It's the truth. We react to stress and loss in different ways. Some people use a lot of meaningless sex as an escape!" I wanted to look at her when she said that. I didn't. Wanted to, but I didn't. Pam went on talking, said, "Some people use liquor to numb the pain and make them forget. We all pick our own poisons to try and kill our little problems."

"Don't start acting like an armchair therapist."

"Whatever you say. The evidence is on the table, shorty."

"That crap don't mean nothing. He's not crazy. And he's not a sell-out."

"Dante, somebody's coming this way."

I limped to the kitchen to grab something sharp. "Is it Scamz?"

"A sister and a couple of kids."

The stairs rumbled under the weight of Sabrina and her crew. Jackson's baby momma had both of his two little girls, Cree and Lisa, with her. The kids had on pink sweats and long colorful coats, hair in a double-twisty

styles. Sabrina had on her deep-blue FedEx uniform—
long pants and long sleeves—her salt-and-pepper locks
covered in a red, white, and blue bandanna that had
stars and stripes.

Sabrina slowed her stride, looked at Pam with ques-
tioning eyes until she saw me step all the way out into
the open. She saw my bruised face and looked horrified.
She peeped in and saw the place was tossed, then
blocked that view of pandemonium from Cree and Lisa,
told her girls to bundle up in their coats and go back to
the top of the stairwell and wait for her.

"Why, Mommy?"

"Mommy needs you to cooperate, Cree. You're the
big girl, set the example." Queen Mother's firm voice
trembled as she smiled at her little girls. "We talked
about cooperation, didn't we?"

"Yes, Mommy."

The kids obeyed Sabrina. Pam's cell phone rang. She
stepped to the side to answer.

Sabrina came to me, and worry covered her face.
"What happened?"

I told her bits and pieces, just enough to let her know
that Jackson was either hurt or in trouble. And somebody was looking for him because of some money matters. Didn't tell her everything that went down, just
corners of the problem, as much as she needed to know
right now. If I wasn't freaked out on the inside, I
wouldn't have told her that much.

She wanted to know, "How serious is this?"

"It's serious."

"Dante." Pam said my name, stepped back toward
me, and handed me her cell phone. "Somebody in the
513 area code named Robin said she's calling you back.
Said she's Jackson's fiancée."

I'd called Robin again when we were on the road.
Had told her to hit me at Pam's number.

Sabrina started pulling out her cell phone. "I'm going
to call the police."

I told her, "Wait."

Sabrina held her cellular phone at her side, headed inside, and went from room to room.

Robin asked, "Was that Sabrina?"

"Yeah. Where you at?"

Robin told me that she had just made it to Cincinnati and called home to check her messages. She hadn't heard from Jackson, not since we ran her maintenance man out of her apartment.

She said, "Sabrina never comes over to Jackson's apartment. She trips on our pictures."

"He didn't show up to get the kids this morning."

Robin asked, "What's going on?"

"Nothing."

"You've called me ten times; something is wrong." Her voice fractured. "What's going on?"

"Look . . . it's complicated . . . let me . . . I'll call you back in a little while."

She was upset. Took me a minute to get her off the phone.

Sabrina's mental state wasn't too much better. She had looked over the insurance papers, liquor bottle, and razor, and come to her own conclusion. As soon as I hung up, Sabrina ran up to my face and asked me if I'd called the police. I shook my head. That simple motion and her distressed tone added to my headache, made it hard to think of what to do next. Hard to think straight when sleep hadn't been your ally and every limb felt like a twenty-pound weight was attached. My bruises were looking worse. My feet felt dried out and were so tired that I couldn't tell where my shoes ended and the ground began.

Sabrina said, "I'm calling the police. Tell them—"

I shook my head. "I'm not staying."

"I'm calling and you need to be here when they arrive."

"Can't stay. Not looking like this. And don't bring my name up."

"Like hell I won't." She grabbed my arm. "Don't walk away from me when I'm talking to you."

She'd said that like I was one of her children. I jerked away. "Look, I gotta go."

"What do you know that you're not telling me?"

"Don't call the police. Not yet."

She raised her voice. "Was he doing something illegal?"

I did the same. "He was doing what he had to do."

"Mommy," both kids said at the same time.

"Mommy's alright. Cree, Lisa, stay where I told you to stay."

"We're scared."

"Mommy will be there in a minute, baby." Sabrina lowered her voice but didn't diminish her tone. She blocked me from leaving. Her eyes dared me to move her. "What does that mean?"

"Means what it means."

I was pissed, and she refused to back down or move out of the way; almost called her out of her name, but I caught myself. That was my own frustration rising to the top. Each word from her mouth was barbed wire raking across my conscience. Jackson's phone rang and saved us from making the scene any uglier than it already was. I headed for the kitchen; Sabrina rushed by me, stepped over things scattered on the floor, and answered.

It was Robin. She'd hung up from talking to me and dialed Jackson's number to see what was going on. Sabrina was curt with her words and hung up on Robin. Then Sabrina dialed three digits at the speed of lightning, yanked her bandanna off her mane, let her locks tumble down into her face, caught her breath, and let her free hand grip a section of her hair for a moment before she started rocking and talking with her hand, telling the dispatcher that there had been a break-in at her baby daddy's apartment. She said my name, told them that I was here with another female when she got here, that she didn't know who the other woman was and we were trying to leave, that I knew something about the forced entry and where Jackson might be and wouldn't say what had happened.

Pam's cell phone rang again.

She told me, "Same number that Robin just called from."

I gritted my teeth and made a rugged motion that told her not to answer.

Sabrina stepped to Pam. "What are you to Jackson?"

"I'm with Dante."

"And your name is . . . ?"

"On my birth certificate."

Beautiful rainbows were on the way.

I had to raise up outta here quick, fast, and in a hurry.

Pam followed my lead. I left Sabrina talking to the dispatcher and looking at the way Jackson's apartment had been left. I ignored my headache and put on my best smile, the grin of a hypocrite, spoke to the little girls, ran my fingers over their hair, gave them each a hug, told them I loved them. My words felt like a farewell speech. Cree was the six-year-old. Her body was stiff with fear. She was an emotional kid. Her tears had been set off because there were too many unhappy faces and unfriendly tones. Kids can tell when something isn't right.

Cree asked, "What's wrong, Uncle Dee? Why can't we go in?"

I didn't have an answer. Both of them had oval heads and sweet faces, just like their mother, but the oldest one had features like Jackson's. The youngest one was the one he had doubts about. I felt for her, hoped that Jackson was her daddy just so she'd have one less issue to deal with growing up.

Lisa was the one who had just turned three. She asked, "Uncle Dee, where's my daddy?"

Cree wiped her eyes. "And why was Mommy yelling at you?"

A lot of tears would be dampening the ground by the time LAPD showed up.

I kissed both of their foreheads and headed down the stairs. Left those two little girls standing side by side, holding hands, protecting each other, silenced by their own fear, wanting their daddy.

Sabrina called Cree and Lisa like I was the last motherfucker she wanted around her kids.

Pam was right behind me.

I hadn't said anything to Pam when I was up at Jackson's apartment, but when I had pushed open the front
door, I smelled sweet cloves, the scent of Scamz's
Djarums.

23

It took an hour to get from Culver City to North Hollywood. The skies were overcast and a few drops of rain
had fallen. Droves of high school kids passed by in their
Dockers and Gap gear. I'd had Pam stop around the
way from my apartment. Trouble or police, I didn't want
her to get caught up.

She said, "Be careful, Dante. I need you to be
around."

"For what?"

"Might need you to take me to the museum on
Wilshire for jazz next Friday."

"You asking me out on a date?"

"A woman needs to have a man around. Never know
when I might need some furniture moved."

I leaned over and put my finger in her right dimple.
She smiled a bit and kissed my hand. I grabbed my
Louisville Slugger from her backseat and grunted when
I got out. Pam sent me a worried smile, like one a
mother would give a child. I gave her one that told her
that I was a grown man and everything would be cool. I
told her that I'd find Jackson, that he'd be okay, and this
misunderstanding would get ironed out by the time the
sun had set in the west.

She said, "What about that dude who burned up your
car?"

"I can handle Nazario."

She was scared for me. "Hide out at my place tonight,
if you need to."

"I'll page you."

I stared at her. I was a young man and I fell into fantasy at least ten times a day. I saw a beautiful woman like Pam and she was perfect to me. Perfect because I didn't know anything about her. The absence of knowledge creates the image of perfection. Getting to know a woman always busted that bubble.

Pam's been through the kinda shit that would make Joe Average shy away. But I'd never been Joe Average. Not even his second cousin. Pam's imperfections made her perfect to me.

She gave me another kiss before she pulled away from the curb and headed off to her own meeting.

ALFALFA LIVES HERE had been etched in my front door with a knife. Nice to know that Nazario didn't stutter when he fell into graffiti mode. Piss was drying on the door, leading to a small puddle on the pavement. He had marked my territory and upped his threat ten notches.

His message was clear. We were at war.

My phone was ringing. I heard the chimes when I came up the stairs. The ringing stopped, then started back by the time I unlocked the door. I pushed the door open with my left hand, then got my Slugger in position, let the light from the gray skies fall across the room. Just like at Jackson's apartment, I smelled smoke. I had company.

He jumped and sat up when I came in the room.

I said, "Whassup, Jackson?"

He didn't say a word. Just looked scared as hell.

Before he could say anything, I asked him about my door.

Jackson said that the etching on my front door was there when he got here in the middle of the night. That meant that Nazario had come here while Oscar was getting towed. Nazario had been pretty busy.

I moved across the room at an injured stride and poured myself a glass of OJ.

Jackson said, "Look like you took a few blows."

"Looks like."

I was waiting for Jackson to tell me what happened on his end last night. That box of green cards was sitting on my kitchen counter. I stared at those in disbelief. Part of me wanted to know and part of me didn't wanna know. I needed to hear a miracle story right about now, about how he had fought off ten or twelve guys and the only reason he didn't come and have my back was because they had tied him to a Monte Carlo and dragged him up and down Interstate 5. I wanted him anywhere but here. Wanted to hear anything to take the edge off my thoughts. If Jackson had been laid up in a ditch busted to pieces it would've looked better than him being holed up in my apartment. It would've looked like he had been hurt trying to save us.

I didn't ask him how he got in. He was in that fraternity of thieves, so there was hardly a door that he couldn't get through, one way or another.

From where he was, Jackson took a stare at my injuries. He sighed and his shoulders slumped. Whatever lie that was about to roll off his tongue dissipated like smoke in an open field.

"I was counting the number of women in my life," Jackson said. "Sabrina. Robin. Cree. Lisa. That's a lot of women to have to either answer to, or be responsible for, or have to deal with the rest of your life. A lot of women. A lot of energy. Lots of expectations. Hard to be everything to everybody."

"I don't wanna hear about that."

He was on my couch. His shoes rested at the foot of my sofa on my two-shades-of-brown carpet. His right arm was wrapped up in rags, bloodstains all over his sleeve and pant leg. Jackson told me that he was attacked at the car and had beat two guys off him, then took off running.

I shook my head. "You want me to believe that you left us out to dry?"

He lowered his head, ran his hand over his ponytail; his hair came loose, fell and hid his eyes.

I pressed on, "How much was Nazario gonna kick you down for those cards?"

"Enough to clear up my debt with Superior Court."

"Sixteen thousand."

"A much better payday than Scamz offered. He paid me like I was a bitch. I've been working with him for years, I've had his back for years. You'd think that he'd come through on this for me. But instead he takes advantage, knows that I need the money, and uses me like I'm a bitch."

I paused when I heard somebody coming up the stairs. The footsteps went right by my door. I heard voices from the neighbors who lived two doors down.

I asked, "Who set up the ambush?"

"Nazario."

"Nazario?"

"He's pissed because he set up the deal with Pedro to fence the cards, then got cut out over that shit that went down between him and Big Slim."

Jackson said that Nazario convinced him that he could make it look legit, that Jackson would get paid and nobody would question a damn thing.

I raised my voice. "You telling me you sold me out to punk-ass Nazario?"

He rocked and lit up another Marlboro. "You let me down, Dante."

"Because of that crap that went down with Robin?"

"You just don't know how much that hurt me."

"They tried to kill me."

"It wasn't supposed to go down like that. You wasn't supposed to get hurt."

I asked, "What about Scamz?"

Jackson didn't offer me an answer. That told me a lot. He knew Scamz wasn't stupid, he was seasoned at this, and that had Jackson scared. All of his words were numb. He didn't know what to do.

I said, "You left me out to dry."

"Those guys were supposed to hurt Scamz and make it look legit."

"What about me?" I took the knife out of my back pocket, the one our attacker had dropped, and slammed it on the table. I said, "They tried to take us out."

He picked up a clear plastic glass at his feet. Jackson took a mouthful of juice, swished it around before he swallowed.

I said, "Scamz is gonna take you out, you know that."

"Oh, I know that."

"I should take you out. You left me in fucking Boyle Heights."

"I wouldn't stop you if you tried to take me out."

"Is that what you want?"

He drew his smoke, let the fumes cloud around his wild mane.

I told him that I'd been to his apartment hunting for him, that his place had already been broken into and tossed. Told him I'd seen the insurance papers on his kitchen table, like he'd left them in plain sight, so if anything happened to him nobody would have to hunt for them.

I snapped, "Don't you care?"

"I don't know anything anymore," he yelled back at me. "Yeah, I care. At the same time, I want this over with. Seems like every day I have a problem bigger than the one I had the day before."

"What are you saying?"

"I'd thought about doing it myself."

"Doing what?"

"You know what I'm talking about. If anybody knows, you know."

That halted my rage.

"I was close. First I was gonna use a razor. Backed down. Then I had my sleeping pills." His voice left him, then came back a little at a time as he said, "But that wouldn't be right. That could mess my kids up in the head knowing their old man took his own life. And insurance doesn't pay on suicides."

"Shut up shut the fuck up." I exploded. "Don't talk like that. Do not talk no crazy shit like that."

"So I'm getting somebody else to dig my grave for me."

"Shut up, Jackson."

"I'm damn near fifty years old, dammit. I'm tired of having nothing. Hell, I went through layoffs and shit back in the early nineties, and now this shit again . . . I can't keep living like this."

"Shut up."

"If Scamz took me out, my kids still get the insurance money. They'd be taken care of."

"Are you crazy or are you just crazy?"

"I'm just fucking tired, man. I'm tired. My spirit is all messed up. I don't want to live like this. I don't want to borrow money the rest of my life, or run to Scamz every time I need to get by."

I heard more footsteps coming up the stairs. Sounded like a couple of big people. Whoever it was walked up almost in silence. I tensed and stood up. Had no idea what I would do if that wood flew off the hinges. Sounded like they stalled at my front door, but then they sped up and kept walking by.

I told Jackson, "You're fucked like a ten-dollar hooker on Sunset."

He lowered his head, tugged at his hair. "I need to know how to fix this."

A police siren wailed outside. Both of us stilled until the sound faded.

He raised his voice at me. "How do I get out of this?"

"Ain't enough dirt in the world to fill this hole."

I let him know that Robin was pulling out her hair, that Sabrina had flipped out and called One Time. Told him that his kids were there too.

I said, "Everybody knows."

"How do I get out of this?"

"Is that why you came here?"

"Yeah. I need you to get me out of this."

24

I walked into the pool hall and everybody stopped their games. People sitting at the bar stopped looking up at the four televisions anchored to the walls. All eyes stared at me like they had seen a wounded and blood-stained ghost carrying a Louisville Slugger.

I nodded. Nobody spoke. Word had spread about last night, and there was a new vibe up in here.

I ignored all the eyes and cut through the smoke, allowed my strut to show no pain and went straight to the circular booth in the center of the room. Big Slim stood up when I got close to his watchtower. He slammed his mangled hands down on the counter and regarded me with angry eyes. I stood underneath him at an angle that showed off more razor bumps than I'd seen in a lifetime.

He grunted. "Your boy done got hisself in a world of trouble."

"I know."

"People say you with Jackson. That makes you a marked man too."

I asked where Scamz was. Big Slim told me without playing any games. Scamz knew that I'd be back by here. He always knew your next move before you did.

I said, "Was cold-blooded the way you left me out in the alley with Nazario."

He made another unfavorable sound. "I asked you for help and you turned your back on me."

"Look, man, we have a common enemy," I said. "That should make us allies."

"We ain't friends."

"We don't have to send each other Christmas cards."

"Whatcha need, boy?"

"What make you think I need something from you?"

" 'Cause you up in my face."

"Okay, I need something from you."

"Kinda figured that when you walked in here."

"You know everything that goes on around here."

"Uh huh."

"You sit around here all day watching and listening."

He nodded his agreement. "I knows thangs that most people don't. Whatcha need?"

"Nazario. Get me an address, a phone number, something so I can track him down."

"The hunted wanna become the hunter."

"I'm gonna kick ass before I get my ass kicked."

He rubbed his razor bumps and tilted his head to the side, his eyes telling me that I was the biggest fool he'd seen in a long time.

He said, "You can't do nothing for me, but you can ask me for a favor."

"Ain't nobody else I can ask for nothing around here."

"They ain't dumb. And what kinna fool you think I am?"

"He's our enemy, Big Slim. He stood in this room, in front of your customers, in front of a room filled with ... colored women, and told you to put your mouth on his—"

"That's enough, boy."

I shut up and waited.

He studied me. "And if I can get that?"

"Then get it for me."

"Ain't nothing free inside these four walls."

"Okay. How much it gonna cost me?"

He told me his price. That reminded me that nobody in this world had ever done anything for me, not even at cost. I agreed and he held out his mangled hand. His huge hand swallowed mine and we sealed the deal.

Once again, I was dining with the devil and I didn't have my long-handled spoon.

Big Slim sent me to Hollywood Hills, the same house where we had partied after the rental scam. The only thing different was that Arizona opened the door and let me inside the marbled foyer. She was barefoot, had on a white housecoat that slipped enough to show me one of her nipples. She pulled her clothes back together, did that in a modest way. Her butt-length hair was wet, smelled like a fruity shampoo. Her mane was dripping water on the marble and dampening the back of her housecoat. She didn't comment on my bruises or my stride. Angst was in her face. She had her own tribulations.

I asked her, "You okay?"

"Everything is working out."

"I saw your sister brick your car last night."

"I know."

That was when Sierra walked up the hallway. She strolled like she was on a catwalk in Milan. A cigar-size joint was in her hand. I'd smelled the ganja she was having for breakfast before I saw her. She was braless, in a sheer housecoat, wearing thong panties. She was the lighter of the two. Seeing them this close together showed they had similar eyes and lips; Arizona looked better because she owned at least fifteen more pounds. That gave her the build of a woman in training.

I spoke to Sierra. She looked at me with eyes that said I was worthless in her world.

I regarded Arizona again, said, "Hope I'm not interrupting a family reunion."

Arizona ignored my statement and motioned for me to follow her. "Scamz is back this way. He wants you to wait until he's ready to see you."

I took a slow stroll and followed her placid sashay through the mini-mansion. Sierra had gone back outside to the heated pool that stood high over the city. She slipped out of her robe, pulled off her thong, and dove in, started stroking like she was in the Olympics.

Arizona's eyes tightened. She mumbled, "Manipulative bitch."

Arizona had me wait in the living room, the same area where we had pigged out on Harold and Belle's Cajun food and caviar two days back. The big screen television was on Ricki Lake. WILL A DNA TEST PROVE THAT HE'S THE DAD? flashed across the screen as that segment of the show ended and went straight into a promo for the next show: I MAY BE WHITE BUT I KNOW ALL ABOUT PLEASING BLACK MEN.

Arizona picked up the remote and surfed the channels, stopped on CNN.

She said, "They dropped food on people in Afghanistan and the government ain't even dropping food on the people who are starving here."

Her eyes came to mine.

Arizona said, "I was homeless for a long time, both me and my sister. I'm sensitive about that."

"You got family out there?"

"My sister and my brother."

I made a grunting sound that could've meant that I didn't know that or that I didn't care, maybe a combination of both.

She asked, "You got family?"

"Nah."

The same grunt of indifference came from her.

She pulled her damp hair away from her face then clicked over to Sally Jessy Raphael. SECRETS, SEX, AND BETRAYAL. I don't think she liked that topic; she went right back to Ricki Lake.

She rocked. I was uncomfortable. Didn't know what I could do to get Jackson out of trouble.

I asked, "What you been up to?"

She shrugged as if to say not much, then added, "Got a job a while back."

"You stopped dancing?"

"Over a year ago. Quit when this girl, Cinnamon Delight, got attacked on stage."

I asked, "What you doing now?"

"Working at Northwest now. Flight attendant."

"You should get combat pay for doing that shit now."

"Or at least a few Tae Bo classes. Need to be a ninja these days."

We shared a polite and phony laugh. A lot of nervousness was in hers.

She said, "Jackson's fiancée is a flight attendant too."

"You know her?"

"She works for American. Does a lot of flights back east, just like me."

"Didn't know you knew her."

"We've met a few times." She gave me a strange grin. "Heard she got caught rocking somebody else's boat and Jackson went crazy. Tried to kick down her door in the middle of the night."

"What else you hear?"

"Heard that you're some old chick's boy toy."

"Uh huh."

"Outside of that, ain't heard much."

Ricki Lake came back on and saved us from talking. Some guy who didn't protect his sperm was complaining about having to pay child support. A woman in a shiny silver outfit was sitting between two guys, waiting for the results so she would know whose sperm fertilized her egg. The guy on the left found out he wasn't the dad and turned cartwheels. The guy on the right was the dad. He was happy about it, but the baby momma was pissed. She wanted the other guy to be her baby daddy.

Arizona said, "Thanks for ... you know, jumping in and saying something."

"You're too smart for that."

"Sometimes you have to push his buttons to get his attention."

"Rough game you're playing."

"Yep."

"So, you and Scamz and Sierra are ... I mean one minute your sister is bricking your car, then you and Scamz are ... y'know ... and a few hours after that both of y'all are ... Whassup?"

"That's our personal business."

Sierra was in the doorway, puffing on a joint like she was Afro Man. I didn't know she was there until that ganja smell pulled me that way. She had a white towel wrapped around her birthday suit, another around her wet hair. She motioned at me with one finger. That meant Scamz was ready to see me now. I left Arizona with Ricki and that baby-momma-drama-filled show and followed her sister's damp footprints and vanishing trail of smoke.

I said, "I see things are working out in your favor up in here."

Scamz said, "I'm an excellent negotiator."

He was getting out of the bathtub. Candles and classical music filled the room. Scamz had bruises on his back and shoulders, but he stood strong like he was the Black Panther. I matched his stance, put my injuries and exhaustion on hold, folded my hands in front of me and stood strong.

Scamz drew his Djarum. "You know I have a reputation to maintain."

"I know. We all do."

"A man is only as good as his reputation."

"So, how you gonna handle Jackson?"

"What do you suggest?"

"Give him a pass."

He said, "Just let him go."

"All of us go way back."

"A man steals from me, tries to kill me, and I should just let him walk."

"He didn't give the cards to Nazario."

"You can't undo what's already been done."

"He didn't go through with it."

"Don't try to minimize the situation."

"Just asking for you to put yourself in his shoes. He's dealing with a lot of situational stress."

"Don't beg, Dante. Never beg. Begging shows lack of self-esteem."

"I'm not begging."

"I've befriended and trusted him for ten years."

"Cut Jackson loose. Just cut bait and don't deal with him anymore."

"I see. Hand me those pants."

I grabbed a pair of tan linen trousers. "Here."

"So, let Jackson get away with a double-cross. What about Nazario?"

I shrugged. "Kick his ass. Fuck him up big time."

"Shirt, please?"

A matching linen shirt was on the back of the door. "Here."

"Keep one fish in the boat and toss the other back in the waters. You know I can't do that."

"You're the boss. You can do anything you wanna do."

"First, tell me this. You with me or you with Jackson? You can't be with both of us."

"You sound like Bush talking about terrorists."

"And you're Pakistan. Pick your side. Make sure you pick the right one."

"If I get the green cards back to you, all of 'em, can you let him slide?"

"You know where he is?"

"No idea. I called a few hospitals. Called the police. He vanished."

"Sure about that? He's got two kids. A fiancée. How far do you think he'd go?"

I kept my poker face.

"What can I do to get Jackson free and clear?"

"Why would you have to worry about getting him free and clear if he's an innocent man?"

"No games, Scamz. What do I have to do?"

"Why do you always do that, Dante?"

"Do what?"

"You're always trying to save the lamb."

Scamz picked up his cellular, dialed. He told whoever answered, "Put him on the phone."

Then Scamz handed me his cellular.

The bottom fell out of my belly, and I hesitated taking the phone. I said, "Hello."

"Dante?"

"Jackson? Where are you?"

"At your apartment." He was trying to sound cool, but was breathing too hard, had so much distress in his voice. "Two big motherfuckers are here. They rushed up in here soon as you left."

"How big?"

"Big enough to make Suge Knight look like Baby Huey."

Me and Scamz remained eye to eye. I said, "At least talk to the man, Scamz."

"Did he try to talk to me, or did he just act?"

"A minute. Just listen to him for a min—"

"Dante, Dante, Dante." He was grooming his hair. "He's blown his chance to talk."

I asked Jackson, "You a'ight?"

"Naw. They roughing me up. Beating me down like I'm a piñata on Cinco de Mayo."

"How bad?"

"Gonna piss blood for a week."

"What are they doing now?"

"Waiting for word from Boss Man."

"Help me out." I struggled to keep my breathing even. "I don't know what to do."

"I wanna see my kids. I miss my kids. What the fuck have I done?"

Jackson was breaking down and Scamz reached for the phone. I gave it to him.

Scamz told me, "When you're negotiating, you have to bring something to the table."

"I've got the green cards."

"Not enough."

"What's your price?"

"Work for me."

"We're back at that again."

"Life always goes full circle."

"Why me, Scamz? Why do you want me to work for you?"

"You've got a lot of potential, Dante. This can benefit us both."

"If I don't take you up on that offer?"

"You don't have to. No pressure, you know me."

"What happens to Jackson?"

"That won't be any of your concern. Between me and Jackson."

My head ached, was ready to pop. Jackson was at my apartment being treated to a serious beat down. If it went beyond that, I'd be going home and finding what was left of him in my front room.

I said, "Let Jackson go and I'll work for you."

"You'll do the hot work too, right?"

"No problem."

He stood there and read my face, became a human lie detector before he put the phone to his ear. I extended my hand to him and he accepted it. With a gentleman's handshake our contract was signed. After that he told Jackson in a stern voice to give the receiver to one of the men in the room with him.

Scamz told whoever was there, "Have a nice day." Then he hung up.

The green cards were out in the truck. I went outside and hiked halfway down the hill to where I had hidden the truck, then drove back up. I'd picked up Jackson's truck after I stopped by the pool hall. He'd left it parked on Calhoun. The box was tucked underneath the seat. I grabbed the goods, went back inside and played that mental game one more time, waited to be sent back to Scamz again. By then he was sitting in front of the baby grand, playing a classical tune to relax his mind. He knew that I was in the room. He didn't look up. Left me waiting like a pauper at the feet of a king.

I stood to the side and looked out at the city, didn't interrupt him. I caught my reflection and saw another version of me. I was fifteen and a half again, sitting in a hard plastic seat, rainbows dancing across the earth-tone stucco houses. Remembered how I was held hostage under a calm sky. There weren't any squad cars, no handcuffs cutting in my wrists, but I owned the same feelings right now. That same fear of the unknown was stealing my breath and heating my blood again. That desire to turn back time and do a few moments all over again was there too.

My eyes focused on Scamz's reflection. He played that piano like a pro.

When his mini-concerto was finished, I handed him the merchandise.

He said, "Jackson damn near got you killed too. Remember that."

I didn't say anything. I was too numb to feel anything.

He said, "Since the day you fell off that bicycle, I'm the one who has always had your back. I've always lived up to my word. I've never let you down."

I nodded. "I'll remember that."

"Jackson's ex got him in a trick bag and we all became expendable."

Scamz extended his hand. We stayed eye to eye and pressed flesh to seal our contract. He gave me a golden credit card, the ATM code.

He said, "This is good for thirty days."

Then he told me the rest of the package—the apartment in Fox Hills and a car—would be set up in the next few weeks.

I wasn't impressed. I'd been fine with Oscar. He had never let me down. And I liked the crib I was living in. It didn't look like this mansion, but it was legit and it was my castle. But Oscar had become a casualty in this war, and the crib that I was living in was no longer a safe haven.

I asked, "What about Nazario? You getting him served the right way?"

"Don't sweat Nazario."

"Nazario is the one sweating me."

"Master your emotions. Control your moods."

"Like you did with Arizona."

"Nobody's perfect. At some point every man is going

to meet at least one woman that brings out that side of him. The one that makes him lose self-control. Same goes for a woman. She'll meet a man that makes her act like a fool. Maybe you haven't met yours, but you will. It will get ugly and you will do things that are beneath you and you will not like yourself, but it will happen."

He'd said all of that with the ultimate smoothness. His logic wrecked my cooltivity.

I asked, "Why you always back down when it comes to Nazario? He insults Big Slim, you don't do nothing about it. He rips you off, you don't do shit, but you beat Jackson down."

"It has nothing to do with you. I make the decisions, so let it rest."

"Nazario totaled my car, jumped me in the alley, and he's stalking my crib all over a debt that I don't owe. I need to know if you've got my back on that or what."

"I don't get in another man's fire."

"Part of that fire is your fire."

"Not from where I'm standing."

"Sounds like you're scared he might cut off your hand to steal your watch."

"I fear no man."

Scamz's lips curved up into a smile. Mine did the same.

Sierra came in and sat on his lap. Scamz said a few words to her in that honeyed tone that he always used with the honeys. Sierra smiled like she was Marie Antoinette sitting on her king's throne. Scamz touched her cheek, her lips, and that simple contact made her eyes tighten with lust. She kissed him and straddled him. She was still naked.

He asked, "Wanna stick around for a while, Dante?"

I shook my head.

He said, "I'll be in touch."

I found my way back toward the front, passed by Arizona. She stopped watching Ricki Lake long enough to ask me to wait a moment. Said that Scamz had wanted her to give me something before I left. Her dark lips were saddened by sibling rivalry. She went into another room, came back and gave me a palm-size cellular phone. A perk of being a full-time employee. My electronic leash. We regarded each other like we shared similar sentiments, both for our situations and our employer.

She said, "The heart plays by its own rules."

I said, "Guess you love 'im more than you realized."

"Thin line between love and hate, Dante." Her lips created a shallow smile. "Very thin line."

I headed for the front door. Gray skies were brighter than what was in this place.

I called my crib as soon as I started driving down the snaking hill that led into the heart of Hollywood. Jackson answered. He was breathing hard, a combination of smoking too much, drinking too much, and being scared shitless for hours on end. Sometimes a man had to get close to death, had to stare that demon in the eyes before he realized that death wasn't his friend. What they had given Jackson was worse than death. They'd put the fear of Scamz in his heart. I asked him if they'd beat him down some more. He told me that those two big motherfuckers had stopped kicking his ass as soon as Scamz had given them the word, then those soldiers marched out my front door cool and calm, chatting about Halle Berry's sex scene in *Monster's Ball*.

I asked, "Can you stand up?"

"Lemme see. Those Magilla Gorilla–looking bastards did a number on my leg." He groaned, made a lot of painful sounds. "Okay. Yeah. I'm on my feet."

"Now get the fuck out of my apartment." My anger was deep and certain. "*Now*. If you have trouble walking, start crawling."

"You've got my truck."

"You're tripping over this truck? Not like you have a damn driver's license."

He fell into his own misery and shame.

I went off. "Can't believe you turned your back on me

because Robin fucked you over. C'mon, man, speak the fuck up. You're the teacher. Help me to understand that. Break that problem down to its simplest terms so I can comprehend, because I'm tired, my head is hurting from getting beat down, so I'm not fucking comprehending right now."

Not a sound came from him.

I couldn't stop cursing. My words were so thick with emotion that I choked. "Be outta my apartment when I get back. I don't wanna see your face again. Never. If I do, I just might pick up where those two big mother-fuckers left off."

Finally, in a voice so pathetic it sounded as if he had withered away, he said, "Okay."

He held on to his end of the line like he was waiting for forgiveness. I held on to mine, giving none.

"Kiss your kids," I said, my voice still bad-tempered. "Tell 'em I love 'em. Tell 'em Uncle Dante won't be coming around anymore. Those two little girls are the only reason I didn't sell you out."

I hung up.

25

I'd sealed two deals with just as many devils in less than two hours.

I drove my anger and disappointment around awhile. Clear plastic was duct-taped to the passenger window that Jackson had broken out that night outside of Robin's apartment; it rattled like a warning in the 40 mph wind. Hours went by and sunlight faded.

Pam was on my mind too.

I paged her. She called me back about an hour later. I was aimlessly cruising the city.

She said, "Somebody page me from this number?"

"It's me."

This time she sounded excited to hear my voice. If I wasn't so numb I would've liked that.

Pam said, "Sounds like you're in Africa."

Sunlight had abandoned me by then. I had landed in Leimert Park and meter parked Jackson's truck in the heart of that Afrocentric haven down by a coffee-house and strolled up to the Dance Collective. An African dance class was in full swing. About twenty women and a couple of men were doing their best to follow the instructor's straight-from-the-motherland moves. Another crowd was across the street at the World Stage. Corner to corner, it was crowded and thunderous—in a spirited kinda way—and filled with energy from positive people. Everybody down here was touched by the spirits of the ancestors. My insides were hollow and I needed all of their energy right now.

I took a deep breath and told Pam, "I need somebody to talk to."

She hung up and made it from her complex in Sherman Oaks to Leimert Park in thirty minutes. She was dressed in black jeans and a turtleneck sweater, midnight colors that magnified mystery. She'd changed her hairstyle since this morning, most likely did that to have a different look from the one she had when we did that rental scam. Her thick mane was in cornrows that ran from her forehead back. She smelled good. Probably the best fragrance I'd inhaled in this lifetime.

I hugged her awhile, then said, "I don't wanna conversate right now."

"I'm here for you, shorty."

We held hands and walked the block, passed by people selling incense and African knickknacks, moved by a few people offering nothing for spare change too. Everybody was invisible to me. I held Pam's hand like I was afraid to let go. Was scared that I'd fall off the end of the earth. She didn't complain. We went by the museum and crossed Degnan right in front of World Stage. Her heels made her a lot taller than me tonight. She didn't mind, and that vertical advantage didn't bother my ego. We stood outside and listened to a couple of people throw down some verse before we moved on.

We made our way back to Lucy Florence. Pam knew the owners. Their intimate setup used to be in Hollywood, at the Hudson, a ninety-nine-seat theater where Pam did a few plays. The owners talked about a few people who were doing well, said that J. Anthony Brown's comedy night was off the hook, then they brought Tammy's name up, said that she had come through last week with her husband.

Pam kept the conversation short and we headed for the stairs.

Pam said, "Tammy paged me twice today."

"You call her back?"

"Nope. And I felt bad for dissing her like that because I wanted to hang with my girl, but I know I can't call her back, not after that big-ass lie. If you tell one lie, you have to tell another, so I'd be lying all night long, and at some point that house of cards would cave in."

We took our high-end coffees and looked over some art on the walls before we copped a squat upstairs, found a corner with some comfortable furniture and let that be our own little Garden of Eden.

Pam asked me, "What do you know about vending machines?"

"Thought you were setting up a rent scam."

"That's long term. Have to work that the right way so I can get long dough."

"I see."

"But the problem is, I'll need a nice chunk of change to set that one up."

"Right."

"A vending machine thing is going down in Lancaster and Palmdale."

"That's skinhead territory. Brothers get attacked with machetes up that way."

"So I've heard."

"Scamz's gig?"

She shook her head. "Not this one."

"Uh huh."

"A quick in-and-out thing, you know."

"Uh huh."

"Just drop them off, tell a few lies, collect the cash, then back on the freeway."

"Uh huh."

"A quick hour drive to the high desert and I could pull down a few more bucks and be that much closer to that six thousand I need to get hooked up."

"Uh huh."

"Is 'uh huh' all you have to say?"

"Uh huh."

"Do better than that. Drop some knowledge."

"That's an old game."

"Yeah. Okay, so what you know?"

I told her that the vending trick got wannabe entre-

preneurs to invest their hard-earned cash in a few use-
less machines, used somebody to give a phony lie and
hype it up by saying how much cash they'd made by
having the machines on their property. After you took
the money and promised to get them established at a
high-money location, everybody disappeared like L.A.
smog after a rainy day.

She said, "No matter what kinda scam I mention, you
seem to know a lot about it."

"I was educated by the best. That makes me an asset
on any team."

That was part of the reason Scamz needed me. He
had his hands in so many pockets; I could help him get
his hands in just as many more.

I said, "Why don't you pass on it?"

"Don't start with that. Told you, my time ain't as long
as yours."

"Just do this. Look at me. Think about Jackson."

"I don't wanna think about any of that. I have to be
positive. Your boy Scamz pulled down at least forty-four
thousand on his grift."

"Grift. Great, now you're using the lingo."

"If I get half that much, I'd get the operation, take
classes, get my plan moving at full speed, be straight for
a minute. You have to remain positive if you want anything to happen."

"While you're being positive, be real. Imagine what
could happen to you."

She made a motion with her hand that asked me not
to try to talk her out of it.

I was about to offer to use the golden ATM card to
get her what she needed. I didn't. Maybe I didn't like
the indentured servitude that the card represented.
Didn't like being pimped.

I asked Pam, "How much they offering you?"

"A thousand for a few hours' work."

"How many machines they hustling?"

"They're dropping four at two locations tomorrow."

I said, "They'll be making at least eight Gs a pop."

"Damn."

"Give or take."

We sipped our coffees. Lines came and went in her forehead, so many thoughts were bouncing around in her head. Her face was like a movie screen and I had a front-row view of every scenario that she came up with, every combination and permutation of how shit could turn out for her. Sometimes a sly smile was there, the look that she would have if she had her belly done and Hollywood lowered its bridge and let her cross the moat. Other expressions didn't look so pleasant, like she was imagining slipping into the moat and being attacked by the alligators.

She drummed her fingers on the side of her cup. "To be so young, you're pretty smart."

"What you mean?"

"Was just thinking about this other girl, this actress friend of mine. Her agent didn't like her chin, said it stuck out too far. Guaranteed her more calls if she got her face fixed."

"Uh huh."

"She paid a grip, had a surgeon break her face and jaw, remove some bone, push it back so her teeth came together, cut her tongue and staple her nose. She couldn't eat for months. Had her jaw wired."

"She working?"

"Yeah, at Ed Debevic's with me. The Asian girl."

Silence for a moment. I was amazed at the crap some people do out here.

Pam said, "The vending machine thing. I'm gonna pass."

"What about the rental thing?"

"Passing on that too."

"Good."

"I'll get my belly fixed, but it'll be for myself, not for Hollywood."

"That makes me feel better." That was the truth. Something I had done or said had actually made a difference in somebody's life. Felt like I should get a gold star. I asked, "Why the change?"

"Dunno. I talk shit, but I'm scared."

"We all are."

"I'll be patient. Somebody out there has to recognize talent and be willing to take a chance. Maybe give this acting thing two more years."

"Then what after two years go by?"

"Guess I'll see then, you know?"

Pam got in her car and followed me over to Blair Hills. I left Jackson's truck parked on the street out in front of his house. Left the keys under his front door-mat. I didn't knock on the door. No lights were on. Didn't wanna see him anyway. Couldn't face him with my anger sending me on a rampage.

My castle still wasn't safe, so I went home with Pam. We took a nice long shower in water hot enough to hu-midify the whole apartment, put lotion on each other's back. She walked around with her housecoat closed, made us turkey sandwiches and fruit, then we sat at her small table and ate like we were a family. After that snack she looked at my bruises, played nurse and made sure I was healing.

She said, "You worry about me, but I'm really wor-ried about you, shorty."

"Couldn't tell."

"Don't wanna get too attached to you too soon. That's been my downfall."

"I understand."

"Geesh."

"What?"

"You're all up in my crib. This was supposed to be a one-night stand."

"See what happens when you miss a few shots on the pool table?"

"And don't forget you still owe me a C-note for that game."

We got in her bed and snuggled up in spoon position.

She said, "I like your company. You warm my spirits."

Every time she touched me I wanted to make love to her, wanted to hide myself inside her, but I couldn't tell

if she wanted me like that. Guess I was feeling like that
song by Jaheim, wanted to make love to her again just
in case I didn't make it through the night.

She went to sleep smiling. I felt good. She had backed
down from her grift. I had saved her.

Around two in the morning, I pulled her face to mine
and kissed her, gave her my tongue and told her I was
about to raise up. I told her that I had wanted to make
love to her when we got in the bed.

Pam mumbled, "She was right here waiting for you."

"Was she?"

"Just as an FYI—"

"Uh huh."

"I love making love."

"Really? If we were together five days in a row, how
many times would you wanna do it?"

"Once in the morning, again at night."

"Women always say that and then put the coochie on
lockdown."

"I haven't met any man with the same sex drive I
have."

"That a warning or an invitation?"

"Both."

"I might be able to match that."

"When I have a man, I take care of him in all ways.
I'm an old-school momma from North Cakalaki.
Brought up to please my man, cook, clean house, all the
stuff that would make a member of NOW puke. Just
don't have nobody in my life right now taking advantage of all I have to offer."

"Can I get an application?"

"You've already filled one out."

"I get the job?"

"We'll see."

Her sweet words were little more than mumbles. She
struggled with the sandman and told me to be careful. She
didn't ask me where I was going and I didn't bother
to tell her.

I slipped out of her bed, and the chilly air almost

chased me back under the covers. Hated to trade her softness and warmth for the cold, hard world. With her hair in braids, every inch of her face stood out. She looked older when she slept. Maybe because she was relaxed and that smile and those dimples weren't teaming up to hide the subtle lines in the corners of her eyes. I didn't mind those lines. That showed she'd been living. Age was supposed to mean wisdom, but age didn't always bring wisdom as fast as you needed it. She was a misfit just like me.

I got dressed in the living room, then peeped back at her before I let myself out into the brightness of her long, narrow hallway.

26

The steel door groaned and the business end of a sawed-off twelve-gauge came out to greet me. It put thirty hostile inches between me and Big Slim.

"Whoa, hey, man," I said. It was right above freezing. Every word left my mouth in a puff of fog. "It's me, Dante."

"The nigger who ain't a nigger."

"Let's take that up some other time."

The light thrusting down from the back door of the pool hall gave Big Slim the advantage. I couldn't see all of him, but I inhaled an inhospitable smell, the combination of old age and hard liquor. I sniffled and hoped I wasn't coming down with the flu. Walking three miles in the desert night had numbed my fingers and put a serious chill on my head.

The old man gruffed, "C'mon in."

"You got that information?"

"C'mon in 'fore you make me mad."

"A'ight, a'ight. You need to lighten up on the cappuccino and try decaf."

He slammed the metal door and it echoed like a fortress being sealed. Big Slim moved by me and pushed some buttons on a panel. There was a beep; a yellow light changed to green. The security system was activated and I was locked inside. The hairs on my arms stood up. I didn't trust Big Slim, but he had the information I needed to settle my score.

I said, "What you find out?"

"Come this way."

That aging buffalo limped down the dim hallway. There wasn't any cigarette smoke, but that nicotine odor lived in the walls the same way smog lived in the skies over Los Angeles. Big Slim smelled like he hadn't had a bath in four days and hadn't washed the crack of his butt.

He said, "Word is, your friend got busted up pretty bad."

"Bad news travels fast."

"That wasn't news. That was a message to everybody round here."

He limped away in his boxer shorts and mismatched socks—one was black, the other blue, both drooping. His left leg was ashy and hairy. The right leg was a prosthesis from the knee down. He had a brown steel-toe shoe on that one. I didn't understand why he had a sock on a plastic foot. Especially since it couldn't get cold and it wouldn't blister.

That old man stopped underneath a rattling ceiling fan and scratched his scalp. He wore a beat-up stocking cap on his big head. Big Slim pointed at the door to the Money Room.

"Gotta take care of some biddness," he told me. "Wait over yonder."

"Just give me the info."

"In due time. Clap till I come get'cha."

"Clap what?"

"Clap your hands, nigger. Can't touch nothing if ya clappin'. If ya stop clappin', you either stealin' or meddlin' in somethin' that ain't nunna yo' biddness." He held up what was left of his hand and two red shotgun shells appeared. He palmed them into the twelve-gauge and flipped it closed like he was the rifleman. "Start clappin'."

My hands started slapping each other. He went into the bathroom and closed the door. The toilet seat dropped. I clapped away from his funk.

The room he had told me to go in was the Money Room. On the way, I had to pass by the door to his private room. He'd left that green door cracked. Light brightened the edges of the door, but I didn't hear any sounds. I didn't think he'd have a woman laid up with him. Big Slim was too old for fornication as his recreation, but you never knew what a little Viagra could do.

"Where you at, boy?"

"Heading down the hallway."

"Keep movin' and clappin'."

My hands kept slapping each other and I moved on to the Money Room, bumped that yellow door open with my foot and I went in clapping up a storm.

The off-white walls and beige carpet became too bright, too soon. I covered my eyes.

"I don't hear no clappin'."

I went back to slapping my hands together.

Big Slim stopped singing the blues and I heard a rotating, rattling sound. The toilet flushed. I kept clapping and tried to move closer to the door. The bathroom door flew open.

Big Slim shouted, "Where you at?"

"Right here."

Big Slim rushed into the Money Room, shotgun at his waist. His freshly created fertilizer odor whisked in behind him and covered me like tear gas. He needed to change his diet.

He said, "Stop that damn clappin'."

I did and wondered if he ever used a decent tone when he talked to folks.

He pointed me to the hard-back Kmart chair and limped over to a softer one. Big Slim kept the twelve-gauge resting over his right shoulder, pointing up at the ceiling like a hunter.

Big Slim said, "What you plan for Nazario?"

I answered, "Eye for an eye. Like you said, never pay a man more than you owe him."

"I see. So the devil wanna collect his due from the devil."

"No games. No small talk," I said. "Do you have his address or what?"

"Maybe I do, maybe I don't. Told you the deal and we shook on it."

Big Slim wanted to get his own eye-for-an-eye with our Ecuadorian friend. I emphasized each word. "It's too dangerous and you're—"

"I'm what."

"You're a cripple, Big Slim. You're a poster child for handicap parking."

His expression told me he was offended. "I can handle myself."

"You're too old to go with me looking for somebody. Especially a fool like Nazario. You're slow and I don't need no dead weight. I'll get him back for the both of us. And Oscar."

"Who Oscar?"

"My car."

He made a sound that said he didn't give a shit. "How you got that planned?"

"I just said that I don't know yet. Was gonna sneak up on him like he did me."

"A real man ain't gotta sneak up on nobody."

"Eye for an eye, Big Slim. That's what it's all about. Beat 'im down to the ground and do as much damage to that car of his as I can. Have to show him I ain't no punk."

"Then we should understand each other. A man handles his own affairs."

I took in a lot of air and let it out in one sharp burst. "Nazario can break you with one punch, old man."

"Old man, huh? You thank I ain't no mo' than a old gimp."

"Next time you pass by a mirror, stop and check out the reflection."

His frown became as deep as an ocean.

He said, "If I can't go get my justice, that's a deal breaker."

I was exhausted.

He said, "He gutter talked me in my place of biddness. Said foul and nasty thangs to me no white man ever did say. Look at these hands, boy. Look at what's left of this old man."

A chill ran over me when I stared at that horror.

I asked, "What happened to your hands?"

Big Slim gazed at his hands like he could still see his missing fingers. Then his mangled hand reached down and touched the prosthetic like it was something he'd never get used to.

"Ain't your biddness."

I didn't press the issue. I didn't really care. Didn't care because I didn't want anybody pressing me for answers about my past.

I said, "Gimme the info on Nazario and we'll talk about the rest."

"I ain't no fool. I give you that and you don't need me."

"I don't need you."

"The way I see it is like this," he put his twelve-gauge across his lap, "you don't know where to find Nazario, I do. I can't get to 'im myself 'cause I can't drive. I got a van, but my hands, sometimes they cramps up too bad. We can be a team. You can drive us both to 'im."

I headed for the door. "Thanks for nothing."

He barked, "Same to you, nigger."

I got to the back door and waited for him to catch up and let me out. He got close enough for me to get another whiff of his body odor and alcohol.

He said, "Come back here, boy."

"For what? You're playing games and shit."

"Don't cuss at me."

"Don't play games."

"Listen to the old man. Just listen and you decide."

It took a moment of thought before I went back to the Money Room. Big Slim came in behind me. He eased a silver flask out of a desk drawer, took a sip, wiped his lips, then offered me a hit.

I declined.

I sat back down and he pulled out a chair. That fake leg that was molded out of some kinda hard plastic, those mangled hands with fingers that wiggled like baby worms—all of that looked unreal. He was a Mr. Potato Head without all the parts.

I leaned forward, put my head into my hands. "Quit playing. Whassup?"

He went on, "Scamz ain't done nothing to rectify that situation."

"He cut Nazario out of a big deal. He shut down a lot of his money."

"That gets Scamz respect, but that don't get me no respect. Money can't buy the kinna respect I need. I need the kind people have when they walk in that do' and stand under that picture out front."

"You need to talk to Scamz."

"Scamz too worried about getting money in his pocket or sticking his thang inside a woman young enough to be his chile than to look out for me."

His anger was deep and dangerous. Traces of a huge powerful man were still in him, but his muscles were like a balloon with not enough air, sagging and wrinkled. He had a gut that spilled over his belt. He could barely stand up to hobble around this place.

Big Slim had brought his problem to me. Scamz kept customers coming through that front door. And I'm sure Big Slim was getting a kickback on the activities that took place under this roof. The bottom line was that Big Slim didn't want to bite the hand that paid his light bill.

He said, "I got ridiculed 'cause I kept that boy from putting a hurting on you."

My stomach caught on fire and my belly fell to my groin when he said that. He was telling me that he had befriended me, protected me, might've even saved me, and I'd become his Judas.

My voice was soft and easy. "I know. Yeah. You right."

He waited for me to talk up, but I didn't have much to say.

He asked me, "You scared?"

"As hell."

He rubbed his hands together. "I'm so old I done forgot how to be scared."

"Now would be a good time to remember. Let me go this one by myself."

"Our deal was for you to take me along. I ain't asked for no more than that."

I nodded. I did owe him.

He stood up. I did the same. That old man gazed at me.

I said, "Get dressed and we can roll."

He grabbed some clothes and told me to wait in the hallway while he changed.

I added, "Just don't slow me down or get in my way."

"Start back clappin'. Don't miss a beat this time."

Ten minutes later he had on dark pants, a dark sweater, and a dark trench coat. His pencil-thin mustache had been touched up. That twelve-gauge was with him.

"Stop that clappin'."

We left the back way and headed to our left. His van was in one of the back lots over near the library. It was bright yellow thing about forty years old, dents here and there, and looked like the Mystery Machine from Scooby Doo cartoons.

Big Slim's ride wasn't a pretty woman, but after she coughed her way to life, her ride smoothed out and she hummed a sweet song. Just like Oscar used to.

Big Slim wouldn't tell me the destination, just where to turn. We hit the 101 east to the 110 and took that south toward San Pedro, only we didn't go that far. I did like Big Slim said and pulled off the 110 at Vernon. The edges of South Central. We were in a world the flip side of the valley. When the sun set on this shopworn part of Los Angeles, gas stations bolted their doors and did all transactions through a rude metal tray that slid in and out of a bulletproof window.

Big Slim coughed and spat out his window. "How we gonna do this?"

"What you think 'we' should do?"

"We oughta go up to the do' and call him out."

"Oh, really? How many of his loco people you think might be inside?"

"We'll find out one way or another."

"You're crazy. He just had seven of his fresh-outta-lockdown cousins attack us in Boyle Heights."

"Sound like the nigger-that-ain't-a-nigger scared."

Gunshots rang out. Three shots with very little pause in between came from the east side of the 110. Everybody stopped and looked toward the sounds.

Big Slim said, "Somebody's piece bucking like a mule."

He rolled up his window like he thought bullets were allergic to glass.

I asked Big Slim, "Where Nazario live?"

"Right there." There were only three houses on the block connected to the 110 freeway. He motioned right across from us. He said, "Yessir. That's the house he live in."

It was hard to tell what he was pointing his nub at, so I had to ask, "The purple house or the yellow one with all the piñatas out front?"

Big Slim frowned. "The purple house."

A yellow porch light glowed at the front entrance of the two-story wood house. It had black-trimmed windows that made it look spooky. We passed by Nazario's house at a slow pace. I didn't see that ghetto-red Trans Am anywhere.

I asked, "You sure that's the house?"

"Sure enough. Been here with Scamz a few times."

I parked in the gas station lot. As soon as we stopped, a street-corner entrepreneur ran over holding a bottle of Windex filled with dirty water, asking to wash the windows for spare change. While I dealt with that capitalist, Big Slim grunted and struggled to get out as fast as he could. I tried to get him to wait so we could talk this out, but that fool kept moving, hobbled his way across the lot toward the streets. Traffic was rumbling, trucks were going by, sirens were punctuating the background, so I had to shout and ask Big Slim where he was going.

The old man yelled back, "Ain't got all day. Have'ta get back to my place of biddness."

I caught up with him.

I said, "You going to the front door?"

"You can stay 'cross the street and listen to rap music and wait if you wanna."

I walked with him. His trench coat barely hid that twelve-gauge.

I said, "This is crazy."

Big Slim made his way up the four steps. A dog started barking. That old man knocked on the front door like he was a UPS delivery man. Nobody came, and he started ringing the bell.

I stepped off the porch because I wanted to see how many rooms lit up.

Nobody came to the door. Small miracles made me glad. Big Slim turned the doorknob. It was locked. He went around to the back door and knocked out a windowpane. The barking dog followed us from front to back.

I asked, "What are you doing?"

"Reach in and get the do' open."

"I ain't putting my hand in there with that dog."

Big Slim stood to the side. I kicked the door. I didn't believe that I was doing that, but I did. It gave on my first shot because neither one of the dead bolts was on. Either somebody was careless or somebody had just walked out and didn't plan on being gone long. The Rottweiler barked and didn't waste any time coming right at us, teeth first. I jumped off the porch and yelled for Big Slim to get out of the way, but that old man moved up and stuck his fake leg out. The dog clamped down on Big Slim's prosthetic ankle; Big Slim stumbled back a half step before he grabbed the door frame for support. The dog shook and chomped like it wasn't letting go until whatever it had gripped on was dead.

Big Slim balanced himself the best he could, put a

hand against the door frame, raised his other leg, and brought his steel toe down on the dog's head until it went unconscious. He reached down and grabbed the dog by the scruff of the neck and gently put the mutt to the side, did that like he was an animal activist at heart. He had more grip with those half-a-hands than I had realized.

I said, "You did that like you've done that before."

"A time or twenty."

"You know this is breaking and entering. Nazario could have us locked up."

"If you scared, go back and listen to some rap music."

He went in twelve-gauge first, calling Nazario's name like a nuclear warning.

No answer.

The house held the aroma of Old English 800 and spoiled chicken coming from the trash can at the back door. None of the vinyl chairs at the wooden kitchen table matched any of the others. I went to the front room. Pictures of Nazario and his wife were all over the place, from wall to wall, all up and down the hallway. They looked like the happiest family on this three-house block. Other than three brown beanbags, there were about fifteen boxed-up stereos, just as many VCRs, twice as many boxed-up TVs. Laptops, Palm Pilots, CD-writers, and other electronic equipment lined the hallway. Somebody had been on a shopping spree with more than a few credit cards.

I said, "This place looks like a damn distribution center."

Big Slim said, "Still thank he gon' call the po'lease?"

He turned around and headed toward the back door. His steps were slow and labored.

I tried to think of my next move. Didn't know what to do.

There was a crash in the kitchen.

"Big Slim," I called out.

I rushed back to the kitchen. Big Slim had collapsed in one of the chairs, knocked the salt and pepper shakers from the table to the floor. He was sweating big time, looking at his ripped pant leg and chewed leg. "Messed up . . . messed up my Sunday clothes. Had this suit now going on twenty years."

He was flushed. Taking short breaths. Blinking a lot like he was trying to stay alert.

I said, "C'mon, man. We gotta get the fuck outta here."

He tried to get up, then fell back into his chair.

My voice trembled when I asked, "You a'ight or what?"

"Too much excitement done stole my wind. Lemme catch my breath and we can go."

"Get across the street and catch your breath; we might catch a bullet on this side."

The Rottweiler woke up and ran back in the house barking. The dog saw Big Slim leaning over and sweating, propping himself on the edge of the kitchen table, and stopped barking just as fast as he had started. He made a U-turn, jumped off the porch, and bolted down the alley.

Big Slim tried to get up again, but had to sit back down.

Right about then we heard footsteps coming down the driveway.

Big Slim held his twelve-gauge, but he looked frightened. He said, "You was right. Ain't as young as I useta be."

"Now would be a good time to shut up."

I pushed the door closed. Big Slim made it to his feet and moved to the side, still breathing so heavily that it sounded like one of the Three Stooges snoring. That old man was going to get both of us killed.

Keys jingled, then they stopped. I thought they had heard us inside, but they must've seen the damage to the back door and halted. Whoever was out there stalled. We waited. Somebody tapped on the window and said a few words in Spanish. Waited, tapped again, then they tried the door.

It opened; it wasn't Nazario.

The woman with the big breasts saw me and yelped, did the same when she saw Big Slim about to pass out. I closed the door behind her. She was shivering just that fast.

"You're the men from the pool hall." She'd given the Budweiser garb a rest and was dressed in yellow jeans and a black sweatshirt that had EL POLLO LOCO across the front. "What are you doing here? You're trying to steal from Nazario."

I asked, "Where's Nazario?"

"Answer me, *puto*. What are you doing in here? You and *ese viejo cojo y aspestoso* best to not be here when he gets back home, *muchacho.*"

Pictures of Nazario and his wife plastered the walls, but this woman stood there like we were in her territory. Big Slim struggled to get out the back door and down those three concrete stairs.

I asked the girl, "Where is Nazario's wife?"

"She left him after he took that ring from her to pay you. She went back to Ecuador. I'm gonna be his wife now. He wants that ring back so he can give it to me."

I said, "Glad to know he's recycling."

"I want that ring, *muchacho.* That was his mother's ring. It has sentimental value. *Mi papi* promised it to me when his wife left him."

A steak knife was in the sink. I grabbed it. She made a high-pitched *eeek* noise, then jumped back and raised her arms up like she was getting ready to block the blows with her flesh and bones. There were no blows. I went to Nazario's back door.

I carved him a message: A-A-ALFALFA KNOWS WHERE U L-L-LIVE.

Eye-for-eye and door-for-door. My heart jumped with every letter. I couldn't let him punk me. His car would be next when I found him. Never let any man punk you. It didn't matter whether or not you could kick his ass, the point was to show him that if he brought you a battle, you'd offer him a war. He could kick your ass, but he'd have to kick it every time he saw you, and he'd better hope he saw you first.

It was easy to catch up with Big Slim. He wasn't moving fast. He stumbled, but he didn't let go of his shotgun. If I hadn't caught that old man, he would've hit the ground hard. He gripped my arm with his hand. I moved him along as fast as I could. It took a lot of energy but I helped him across the street and into the van. My eyes were on Nazario's house. Expected to either see that ghetto-red ride or hear Tupac blasting our way at any second. His woman was out front on a cordless phone, lips moving at the speed of sound.

Big Slim let his window down. Stuck his face in the wind the way a dog does.

He wheezed. "I needs my medicine."

"You're not doing too good. Let me call Scamz—"

"Don't—"

"I need to get you to Daniel Freeman."

"I ain't gonna go to no hospital."

"You're sick as hell, man."

"Just get me . . . get me back to my medicine."

Traffic was a bear going back through downtown L.A. and Hollywood, so that ride took the better part of an hour. Big Slim wasn't too much better when I pulled up at the back door of the pool hall. He was sweating and looking like he was about to check out. He gave me the keys and stayed in the van. I opened the door and hurried back to get him. Took a while to get him inside. A long time of me being vulnerable back in that alley. He had me step in first. He didn't have enough strength to pull the damn door closed. I had to do that too.

He leaned against the wall and turned off the alarm system.

"Look in my room. My medicine on the tele . . . tele . . . television."

I hurried down that way. The padlocks were on that door. I fumbled with the keys before I got the locks off and the door open.

I opened the door to the room that nobody went in

but Big Slim. Where people said he kept his missing fingers, the missing digits of others who had done him wrong, and God knows what else.

It was a boxy room with one small window on the back wall near the ceiling. It wasn't carpeted and had chipped, dark-blue walls. A six-by-nine that was crammed with a lamp, a twin bed, a small television, and VCR. It wasn't much, but it was clean from wall to wall.

Panic was in my voice when I called back, "Where your medicine?"

"On the TV."

I moved across the room and saw an empty, worn carton for the movie *Carmen* on top of the TV, next to a bottle of Johnnie Walker Blue. Seven bottles of medicine rested next to that. I grabbed all seven and rushed back to the old man. He was where I had left him, leaning against the wall, hadn't moved an inch, his chest rising and falling at a harsher rate.

"Which one?" I yelled. "Which one you want?"

"Gimme one of everythang you can find."

"Sure you can take these and you been drinking?"

"Gimme the medicine, son."

I gave him one of each. He pulled his teeth out, put them in his jacket pocket, and put the pills in one at a time. Made a nasty face and swallowed them all dry.

A few minutes went by.

He said, "Get me to my bed."

His eyes weren't open. I helped him find his way down the hallway.

My legs were tired from walking down here, had never recovered from all the running and chasing and loving I'd done over the last couple of days. Since my phone rang and Scamz was on the other end, sleep hadn't been my friend. I wanted to sit for a second.

His bed had crisp white sheets and dark covers. A small nightstand was at the foot of the bed; a faded yellow margarine bowl sat on the edge, half-filled with red beans and rice.

Big Slim lay down and kept his eyes closed. He made a sound like it was his last breath.

I watched his chest rise and fall and mumbled, "Don't die on me."

He mumbled something back.

Worry made me fidget and pace a bit. Then curiosity rose to the top and I looked around his room. Didn't see any pickled fingers. The wall in front of me had a Negro League poster thumbtacked to it: Satchel Paige in pitching position and a group photo of the Kansas City Monarchs.

Something caught my eye and I took two steps across the room.

The other nightstand was polished and had two small framed pictures on the edge; both were cheap dime-store pictures that came out perfect. Both were in black and white. One was a wedding picture. A slim man with the biggest smile I'd ever seen. It was Big Slim a long time ago. He wore a dark suit. He was with a woman in a white dress. She looked like Dorothy Dandridge with thick black hair and a southern Vaseline press and curl. The other picture was a black-and-white photo of that same woman wearing a dark dress with a fancy, flowery collar and a double string of pearls.

Next to the photo was a 1966 program that had the same woman's smiling picture on the cover. Same young and beautiful face. It was an obituary from Natchez, Mississippi. Her name was Annie Mae Cooper. The difference between the birth and death dates was twenty-one years. That picture on that obituary was the same one blown up on the huge poster out front, the one that rested on that ugly green wall and looked down on the front door in the pool room.

Big Slim's voice caught me off guard. "We was in a band."

I looked back at him. His eyes were halfway open, but he sounded better already.

I said, "What was that?"

"We was in a band . . . down in Clarksdale. Me and Annie Mae. Back when I was younger than you is now.

Back then we worked in a foundry and sang the blues at night. Was six of us. Big Red, he was from Lula. Bubba was from Alligator. Harmonica, he was my baby brother. Sara sang from time to time, but Annie Mae was our little bluebird. Had the voice of an angel."

"Didn't know that."

"Don't talk about it. Played the guitar, like Robert Johnson. Riley King, Howlin' Wolf, and John Lee all tol' me I was just as good as they was, if not better."

I nodded. I thought he was delirious, about to drift off, and I asked him a couple of questions. I did that to keep him talking. His chest didn't have much of a rise and fall when he breathed. The last thing I needed was for him to slip off into an endless sleep, so as long as he talked that was cool.

"Everybody—" he said, then coughed a little. "Everybody wanted Annie Mae, but she was mine from the moment we laid eyes on each other. She sang and birds got jealous. She stole my heart with a smile. Met her on a Monday and by the next Monday we was at the courthouse getting married."

"She looks like she was a nice woman. Real pretty smile."

"I was the happiest man on earth or in heaven when Annie Mae was my wife. Best four years of my life. Ain't been a year like that since. We was in a blues club, this juke joint down in Miss'sippi. Nightriders was out one night having their kinna fun."

"Nightriders?"

"The Ku Klux Klan. The devil's children. They started shooting in the air and throwing rocks and bottles of kerosene through the windows of the sugar shack we was all at."

"Why they do that?"

" 'Cause we was colored. They tried to burn that sugar shack down with all of us in it. All of us piled into my Packard and they chased us up that dirt road for miles. Ran us off the road down near Clarksdale, over near Alligator Town. Car went down through the woods and hit a tree. Left all of us hurt. We ran into the woods as fast as we could. A couple of the others in the band got away. I tried to get Annie Mae to go with the rest of 'em while I got the Nightriders to chase me. I was fast back then. Fast and strong as any man around. Annie Mae wouldn't ever leave my side, no matter how bad thangs got. Always looked to the Lord to protect us. Yessir. Everybody else got away. Not Annie Mae. Me and my Annie Mae didn't. We ran right into a pack of flashlights and trouble."

He stopped talking for a moment. His good leg shook and I thought he was about to slip into some sort of seizure, but he reached up and rubbed that crop of razor bumps underneath his chin, rubbed them a thousand times, before he went on. "I fought 'em the best I could. Too many of 'em to count. They hit me in the head with the butt of a rifle, and when I came to, they had tied me to a tree, did what they wanted to do to Annie Mae right in my face. All while she screamed my name and I screamed hers. Killed her when they got through."

He had my attention. My mouth was hanging open, weighed down by empathy.

Big Slim glanced at what was left of his fingers. "They cut me up, took a hatchet to my leg, beat me, let a dog eat me alive. Chewed what man outta me he could."

He stopped again. He opened and closed his hands over and over. Looked like he was coming back to life one piece at a time.

A chill ran through me. I wanted to be back in Pam's bed. Wanted this to be a dream.

Big Slim sat up. He pulled a handkerchief from his pocket, said, "They left me for dead. Right next to my wife. The woman I swore I would protect all of my natural days. She went off to New Jerusalem without me. Yep, left me here to suffer."

Again he paused. I had no words to give the old man.

He said, "Left me here to get disrespected by young bastards."

I cleared my throat, said, "Everybody said that you were in on a scam that went bad."

"People always speak on thangs they don't know."

"Just know what I heard. And I know you used to do things for Scamz."

"I don't steal. Did some thangs I wasn't proud of when times got rough, but I ain't never stole nothin' from nobody. I just try and run my li'l biddness."

"You some kin to Scamz?"

"No more than you are."

"You been here since I've know you. Ain't never seen you leave this place."

"Ain't much else I been able to do over the years. They took my fingers 'cause they knowed I played the guitar. They took my leg. Some cold bastards out there walkin' round. No sir. I ain't got much of nothing left. Now Nazario tryin' t'take my respect."

"Big Slim—"

"To have some young bastard stand up in my face and tell me to put my mouth on his private parts, have him stand in front of a room fulla my customers, to make fun of me and gutter talk me in front of colored wimmen, right under Annie Mae's picture and disrespect the both of us like that—he talked to me like I was less than a man, and that hurts me like no other hurt I done had in a long time. No sir, I can't live another day with letting that be."

He made it to his feet.

That old man went on, "That bastard said those thangs to me right underneath Annie Mae's picture. That's the same as disrespectin' her."

He rocked a bit, stumbled a step. I reached to help him get steady, but he waved me away. He was a buffalo again.

I said, "You a'ight?"

"Lord willing and the creek don't rise, I'll make it through another day."

A shared fear rested between us. What we had done couldn't be taken back.

Knocks came from the front door. Customers were showing up.

I said, "Nazario gonna be down here looking for trouble."

"I know. You can go now. Our biddness done."

I headed for the back door.

He said, "Don't tell nobody you done been in my room, understand?"

I nodded. More knocks came from up front. Customers were anxious to get their day going. Already people were here to see if Scamz could offer them a way to make their ends meet.

"Disremember all we done done today," Big Slim said with force. The deepness had come back to his voice and he had his game face on. "Disremember everything you done seen."

I nodded.

He said, "Learn to answer people with words."

"A'ight. I'm disremembering."

"Shaking your head don't mean nothing to me. Nobody cain't hear your head rattling."

He held out his mangled hand. Once again his huge hand swallowed mine. He had a good grip, enough to let me know he could do some damage back in his day. I didn't know if that handshake meant I was making a deal to keep my word, or if he was saying thank you or if somehow we'd become friends. Maybe all of that, maybe none of that. Might've just been a handshake.

I said, "You smelling a bit."

He sniffed his armpits. "Am I?"

"Yeah. Clean yourself up before you open up."

"When it's time. When everythang's all right in my place of biddness."

I left that old man behind me and hit the alley.

I'd seen Big Slim's room. It wasn't that big of a deal to me, but it mattered to him that I'd seen things he shared with nobody. Had seen his ghost and her name was Annie Mae.

27

My message box was full. That meant I had twenty-five messages since the last time I checked. I was still on Ventura Boulevard, miles and miles from my nice warm bed, walking at a worn-out pace with my cellular phone glued to my ear. Sabrina had called ten times since I'd left her at Jackson's place. Robin had called just as many times since then too. She had made it back to the West Coast and was looking for Jackson. Everybody sounded either angry or about to explode from the stress.

No trust was in my heart for that militant midget Sabrina and her warped sense of righteousness. She probably had called the police and given them as much information on me as she could. Wouldn't doubt it if One Time was waiting for me to get back home. That was another reason I hadn't been in a hurry to get back to North Hollywood.

I called Robin.

She told me that Jackson was hurt worse than I had imagined. That halted my stride.

I asked, "How bad?"

She let me know that he was at Daniel Freeman, the hospital with a clear view of the Inglewood Park Cemetery. Sabrina was down there with him, and Robin had made it back from the Midwest and rushed there to stand by his side. Just like Scamz, Jackson had two women who loved him, only his situation wouldn't have the same resolution.

Robin asked, "Where are you?"

I had to think, read the street sign to get my bearing. "On Ventura Boulevard."

"Can I meet you somewhere?"

I told her where we could hook up.

There were a thousand spots to hide and meet. I walked up to Mel's Drive-In—a *Happy Days, Laverne and Shirley* kinda place where customers could stick a quarter in the box on their tables and play Beach Boys or Elvis Presley music. Old black-and-white photos of white celebrities who had died slower than their careers were all over the walls.

All the booths were taken so I copped a squat at a green swivel chair at the counter and waited for Robin over a Melburger and some chili fries. Things had been moving too fast for me and I needed to sit down and think. Needed to feel normal.

Out of habit I grabbed a paper and went right to the classifieds, started looking to see if any widget factories were looking for widget masters. Nothing had changed overnight.

Robin got here faster than I expected. She looked haggard, but even with those bags under her eyes and her black hair underneath a dark-blue NYC fireman's baseball cap, that Haitian woman was prettier than a motherfucker. Her full and curvaceous frame made those toothpicks that Scamz dealt with look like the children in a Sally Struthers commercial.

Traffic had been in her favor today. I put the paper down, moved it to the side. She still had on her flight attendant uniform, the pants and shirt, under a dark wool jacket. Her eyes were swollen and red, with hints of more redness around her cheeks, and her dark skin needed some lotion. Looked like she'd rushed back to Cali on the midnight express. She didn't smell as fresh as she usually did, so I doubt if she had showered at all. The first thing she did was comment on my battered look.

I borrowed one of Pam's lines. "I'm auditioning for a Lifetime movie."

"Not funny, Dante." She took a hard breath. "I might not have a job tomorrow."

"They laying off?"

"I left Cincinnati and dead-headed back here without calling anybody. Went AWOL."

I was waiting for bad news, thought she was about to say her man had more internal bleeding than he had realized and had died from his injuries, but that didn't happen. He was hurt pretty bad, but he wasn't near death, just had a near-death experience. His ribs were bruised, not broken.

She said, "Sabrina was out there."

"With the kids?"

"Her landlord-slash-spiritual-advisor was there too."

"You're talking about that redbone chick from across the hall?"

"Yeah, Juanita. Juanita left when I got there, but Sabrina didn't."

"Y'all talk?"

"In a way. She got in my face. We had a few words."

"What happened?"

"Later."

It took me a moment of getting beyond anger and irritation to ask, "How was he looking?"

"Bad. Real bad. He's busted up, but he won't be there but another day or so."

"So, he's not doing that bad."

"No, it's an HMO. And when they say you gotta go, you hit the do'."

I ran my tongue over my teeth. My breath had to have a decent kick.

I told her, "Your eyes are puffy."

"I know. I look like a raccoon. I couldn't stop crying, y'know."

She wanted to talk, but the words weren't there yet. I waited. I expected her to try to explain how she ended up in bed with that dude from the club, try to get me to understand that her one-nighter didn't mean she didn't love Jackson, that she was running away from her emotions if anything.

She didn't, but the stress from that night was still embroidered in her beautiful skin.

She said, "He told me he stole something from Scamz, but that was all he'd say."

"Yeah."

"That and because of you, those guys Scamz sent, they let him go."

"Pretty much."

"What did you do to get Scamz to back down?"

I told her about my contract for indentured servitude.

She said, "You're joking, right?"

I shook my head.

The saddest look came over her face, like I was doomed.

She said, "You seem pretty cool about it all."

"That's why they call me Cool Hand." I smiled. "It's cool."

"He's still in debt with Superior Court."

"Yep."

It was easy to see that Jackson was all she cared about. The yin and yang of her emotional strain. She sipped her water and we let the noise around us entertain us until she was ready to talk some more.

She said, "We got into a fight at the hospital."

"You and Jackson got into a fight?"

"Nope. Me and Sabrina."

"What?"

"I asked her to step outside."

"That's how fights usually start."

"Just into the hallway. Thought it was time we had our words. I told her to take a good look at the trouble that she had caused. I was cool about it, considering." She pulled her lips in. "I offered her the sixteen thousand to drop the case and leave us alone."

"You're joking."

"Told her it was her fault Jackson was laid up like that. She'd almost killed him."

"What happened?"

"She started yelling at me, calling me a home

wrecker, all kinds of names. Her spiritual advisor couldn't calm her down. Sabrina was crying and cursing. Good thing her kids were down the hallway. I was about to slap some sense into her ass. Nurses came. Doctors came. Security came."

"You gotta be joking."

"She told them that she was the mother of his children, blah, blah, blah. I told them I was his fiancée. Too many sharp objects were in my reach, so somebody had to leave."

"They threw you out?"

"I just left. It got to be a bit much."

"You were right. Too many sharp objects around there for y'all to be trippin'."

"Trust me, if I could've reached a scalpel . . ." She ran her tongue over her lips. "Look, I don't know if I should tell you this—"

"Tell me what?"

"Jackson has been having attacks."

"He had a heart attack?"

"Not a heart attack. Well, a couple of times he thought he was having one, but it was a series of panic attacks. Shortness of breath. Throwing up. Thinking he was about to die."

"Like that girl . . . uh . . . the attorney on *Soul Food*?"

"Yeah, but it's worse in real life. Watching him break down . . . that was heavy on me too."

"He ain't never said nothing about having panic attacks to me."

"He won't tell anybody anything about himself that'll make him look weak. I had to stay with him at night, almost every night. He would sleep about an hour, then walk around frowning. You ever wonder why he was always up whenever you called him in the middle of the night?"

"Not really."

"He hadn't slept but a couple of hours in weeks, so that meant I hadn't had too much rest myself. The only way I got rest was by going to work, and then I couldn't rest because he stayed on my mind."

"Anxiety attacks. Like when you had pulled over downtown?"

"Yeah. Think I had one when I almost had that accident." She dabbed her eyes again. "Guess I know how he felt when everything avalanched down on him at the same time. He can't get a job, and it's not like he ain't trying. Hard on a black man. Society says a man without a job is a failure."

"I know that firsthand."

"Jackson has worked since he was eleven, so to be unemployed at this stage in his life . . . it's rough on a man's ego, rips him apart from the inside." She sipped water. "Sabrina has him stressed."

"No doubt."

"Hate that bitch more than anyone will ever know." Her voice thinned out, became almost nothing. "I feel so powerless."

What she was doing was obvious, but what she really wanted was unknown. Robin was Jackson's woman and we weren't the chitchat kinda friends. Right now there weren't too many people I trusted. She wanted something and was trying to create a soft spot to dig in.

My tone remained firmed by pisstivity. "Bottom line why you drove all the way out here."

She wiped her eyes and pulled out her checkbook before she put her hand on mine.

Robin said, "I know how you must feel right now, but I need a favor."

"No promises."

She asked, "Can I write you a check for sixteen thousand, and you cash it and find some way to give it to Jackson without him knowing it came from me. He won't take money from me."

I shook my head.

She said, "This is really important. Those anxiety attacks . . . if you had seen him you'd understand what he was going through."

"Not my problem."

"Please?"

"Hell no. If I cashed a check for over ten thousand the IRS would be all over my ass."

"Dante, please. I'm pleading with you. I can break it up into three small checks under ten thousand each so the bank won't report it to the IRS."

I said, "We're not gonna have that kinda contact anymore."

"Dante—"

"Are you done?"

She sucked in her bottom lip. "I guess I am."

Robin had ordered fries when she came in. They were dropped off. She ate a few and washed them down with pink lemonade. She chewed like a woman who was defeated.

Robin said, "I have so much guilt right now. It's eating me alive."

"Guilty because you got busted?"

"I didn't come here to get persecuted."

"You came here because you needed to use me for something."

Somebody dropped a quarter in the jukebox and played an Elvis Presley song, daring peeps to step on his blue suede shoes. Everybody wanted to fight over nothing. It was hard for me to hear most of it because my mind had gone white and a thousand phones were ringing inside my head.

She asked, "Honest, what do you think of me?"

I rubbed my temples. "You don't wanna know."

"And Jackson?"

"You don't wanna know."

I was mad, disappointed, pissed off because he'd gone Judas on me. If I had a million dollars, I wouldn't loan him enough to buy a Krispy Kreme doughnut. I wanted to hate him. I think I did, but not enough. He'd been my mentor. My brother. We had a history, and remembering how he'd helped me out from time to time kept the hate from getting as deep as it should. I wasn't as merciless as Scamz. Wished I was. Life was so much better for the heartless.

I asked, "How did you come up with sixteen thousand dollars?"

"What you mean?"

"You don't make that kinda disposable cash serving peanuts to the Mile High Club."

She drank some water before she confessed, "I did some work for Scamz."

"What kinda work?"

"This is the part where you're supposed to sound surprised."

"Not much surprises me anymore. What kinda work?"

"I'd fly packages to wherever."

"A courier."

"Just charge cards and things I could slip on the plane in my carry-on without being questioned."

"You still working for him?"

"Stopped back after Nine-Eleven. Security started searching everything, and a sister having sixty or seventy charge cards with nine or ten names was a little suspicious, especially with terrorists having fake IDs, so I told him I couldn't do that anymore."

I didn't know at first, but now I understood what Arizona was doing for Scamz. And I knew how she knew Robin. I knew Arizona's relationship to Scamz, but I hadn't known Robin's.

I asked, "You fuck 'im?"

She chuckled and shook her head. "Don't believe you just asked me that."

I asked, "That a yes or a no?"

"You really think I'm a ho', don't you?"

I asked, "Jackson know what you were doing?"

"Nope. He never knew. I did it off and on because I needed the money."

"For what?"

"Where did you think I was getting the money to help Jackson out?"

I shrugged. "Why would I care?"

"Now you know about my cash flow. I was helping

Jackson and saving for our wedding." She took in some air, and when she exhaled, a tear rolled down her face. She laughed and wiped that tear away with a napkin. "He's a good guy in a bad situation. He wants to work and take care of his family—and me. I believe in doing my part. I stand by my man."

"Uh huh."

Then she added, "As long as I can."

"Sounds like always ain't forever."

"Guess I wanted this Cinderella thing I'd always dreamed of. Wanted to make sure we had enough money to get into a house so we'd have room for our kids. Kinda silly, huh?"

"It's that Ally McBeal thing."

"What Ally McBeal thing?"

"Y'know, that 'my issues are important to me 'cause they're my issues' thing."

She sighed and pulled at her cap. "But he can't tell me if he wants another child with me. Nobody likes feeling like they're being dragged along by an emotional rope."

I let her wallow in her thoughts before I tossed my kerosene on her fire. "Sounds like that kids thing is a deal breaker. No need throwing a drowning man a glass of water."

She winced.

The cellular phone rang. It was Scamz.

He said, "What's this I'm hearing about you and Big Slim going out to Nazario's place?"

I responded in a light tone spiced with laughter. "C'mon, now. Keep out of my fires and I'll keep out of yours. That's the way it works, right?"

There was a moment of silence. I could visualize him pulling a thin brown Djarum out of a cigarette pack, reaching for a silver lighter, and firing up before he responded. That cool psychological move that rattled so many others did nothing for me, in person or over the wire.

Scamz said, "We have work to do today."

He told me where to meet him and we hung up.

Robin was ready to go. We headed out to the parking lot. I was dead on my feet and eight miles from home. I asked Robin to give me a ride to North Hollywood. I expected her to turn her nose up at me, but she motioned for me to follow her. She hit the remote, the lights flashed on EYE FLY 4 U, and we both got in her silver Volkswagen.

We didn't talk at first. Both of us were thinking.

I rubbed my temples again and said, "Something's bothering me; maybe you can clear it up."

"What?"

"Why didn't you get that dude out of your house before Jackson got there?"

"Why do you keep going back to that? Jackson's in the hospital, I just finished dealing with Sabrina, and all you want to do is make me feel like the Ho' of the World."

My reply was "Why?"

She took a hard breath. "Don't know. Now, can we drop that?"

"You had plenty of time. At least an hour. You know why you didn't."

"Sounds like you know more than I do, so why don't you tell me?"

"You wanted Jackson to see the guy."

"And why would I want that to happen?"

"You wanted to end the relationship, but you couldn't end it on your own. Like when some people do suicide-by-cop because they don't have the balls to pull the trigger themselves, you wanted Jackson to pull the plug on the relationship."

"Where do you come up with crap like that?"

"Am I lying?"

She asked, "And why would I call you?"

"To keep it from going too far."

She paused for a moment. "You're pretty smart sometimes."

"So I'm right. No harm, no foul. This is off the record."

"I thought he'd get upset and quit me. That's the way they do it in books and in the movies."

"This ain't no movie, this is real life. Jackson ain't reading no script; he has real feelings."

"I saw Jackson and changed my mind. By then it was too late to get my friend out of the house."

I said, "That dude had no idea what was going on."

"None at all. He was sleeping when I answered the phone. Didn't wake up until Jackson tried to kick down the door."

"You put him in a trick bag. Somebody coulda got hurt real bad in a permanent way."

"I know. Wish I could unring that bell, but what's done is done. My heart is with Jackson. That man loves me like no man ever has or ever will."

I'd tried to make a lot of things complicated when there were all simple answers.

I said, "You gave Scamz my phone number."

"What?"

"You heard me. I wondered where Scamz got my number from. I know Jackson didn't give it to him because Jackson hadn't talked to Scamz."

"You needed work. Guess I was looking out for you."

"Jackson gave you my number?"

"He called me from your house one day. It was on my caller ID."

I shook my head. "And if I got work, then Jackson could get work."

"You're one of Scamz's favorite people. Jackson used to be until you came along. And now Jackson is your best friend. You look out for him. I knew that you'd hook him up one way or another."

I said, "You set me up."

"I didn't know this was going to happen. Why would I put everybody in jeopardy? Why is this my fault and not Sabrina's fault? Don't forget who set all of this in motion. I just tried to help."

"Well, you know now. Jackson's blood is on your hands, not mine."

Robin's voice cracked. "No way I can talk you into helping a sister out?"

I made a sound that let her know she was insane for asking. "Not in this lifetime."

"Think about Cree and Lisa. Help their daddy out for them."

"Robin, don't ever play me like that."

"I'm not playing you. I love those kids."

A few minutes later she was on Chandler, pulling over in front of my building. Before I got out, she looked at me as if she was waiting to see if there was some message I wanted to send Jackson.

I told her, "This ends our friendship."

She tightened her hands on her steering wheel.

I thanked her for the ride and watched my back as I strolled away. Teenagers were on the courts playing tennis and shooting hoops at P.E., but those noises couldn't drown out Robin's wants. Her energy was there, hitting me in heated waves, begging me to look back and change my mind.

My wounded stride didn't change until I heard her car pulling away, zooming toward the 170.

My legs were boulders. Somehow I had to sleep. I headed up the stairs to my apartment.

ALFALFA LIVES HERE.

Nazario had fucked up my car and stalked my place. Had raised his hind leg and pissed on my world. His stench met me before I made it to my door. I owed him for that. Part of the reason I'd hunted Nazario down was because of Jackson. Robin gave Sabrina the blame for all that was wrong in her life. I was making mine Nazario's fault; he had been the snake that offered Jackson that apple.

I called Pam again. She didn't answer. I paged her.

I went inside and hit the shower, kept my baseball bat and a butcher knife nearby.

Nazario would come after me. Like Pam had done in Leimert Park when she was playing out all the combinations and permutations of how her scenario might come to an end, I stood under that warm water and did the same. My heart wanted another battle, but my body was telling me that it was too hurt to fight. Nazario was human. He wasn't invincible and I could hurt him. The reality was that no one had hurt him in a showstopping way. He had his eye gouged out and kept on fighting until he won.

Maybe having Nazario coming after me over a debt I didn't owe would be a godsend. If I ended up crippled like Big Slim, then there would be no way I could do anything for Scamz.

28

It was cool and peaceful, a perfect L.A. night filled with cold runs.

After a couple hours of working, Scamz drove his chariot to a hot spot in Beverly Hills called Reign, one of the better meat markets on Robertson, where the Talented Tenth congregated in between AA meetings. Scamz had a few charge cards to drop off there too. His clients were some beautiful Latina and Middle Eastern women who had a thing for black men and designer shoes. I sat back in my leather jacket, turtleneck, and black slacks and checked out their flow. They were all over Scamz. His black four-button suit was the best in the room.

Then we hit Sunset Boulevard and swung by Dublin's, a hip-hop spot where it was too packed to think. Arizona and Sierra met us there. I kept my distance and watched them compete for Scamz on the dance floor. After that I followed Scamz to the bar and he ordered drinks. Arizona and Sierra went to the other side of the room. Me and Scamz copped a squat and watched all the asses on parade. Scamz never ceased to amaze me. He fit into this world too. He was like vodka; took on the taste of whatever he was in.

All evening I'd been wondering if he would've killed Jackson. Right now you'd think that nothing bad had ever happened in his life. That nothing had gone down in East L.A.

He asked, "What's on your mind?"

I sipped my cognac before I replied, "Arizona and Sierra are some beautiful sisters."

"No doubt."

"Beautiful women. Nice cars."

"All at my disposal twenty-four-seven."

"You've been living large since I met you."

"You've always wanted to be like me."

"Never."

"You lie. You get a rush from all of this."

"Forget a rush."

"What do you see when you look in the mirror?"

"I don't see you."

We were having fun hanging out right then. He was my brother. When I think about it, he'd always looked out for me. Couldn't think of a time when Scamz hadn't been a man of his word.

He watched Arizona for a long while. He was in thinking mode.

Scamz said, "Let me show you something."

"What?"

He motioned toward Arizona and Sierra. "Who do you think is the prettiest?"

"Would have to go with Arizona. Sierra could stunt double for a toothpick."

Scamz laughed a little, then motioned for Arizona to come to him. She smiled like she was the chosen one. Sierra's expression didn't change. Looked like she was high on E.

Arizona had on a tan skirt that was just long enough to hide the cheeks of a firm butt. When she walked, her dress crept up with each step until it exposed as much thigh as legally allowed. Her nipples were erect and she smelled like she had been dipped in sensuality. Makeup done like she was ready for a photo shoot.

Arizona sat down between us and spoke in a soft tone, "Yes?"

Scamz told her, "Kiss Dante."

She was surprised. That caught me off guard too.

She didn't move.

Neither did I. Scamz had a glass of cognac in his hand.

He took a sip. Arizona's hands were slowly opening and closing. The tigress in her had become a cub, and that cub in her reduced to a clawless kitten.

Arizona leaned toward me, her lips parting and her tongue easing toward me.

I backed away.

There was a look of reprieve mixed with rejection in her eyes.

He told her to go back to the bar and wait with her sister.

She did. Her walk had lost its strength. She was disturbed.

I said, "Enough of this bull, Scamz. Stop dogging Arizona."

Scamz sipped again. "You were always weak for women."

"I just don't look at women through the eye on my dick."

"Your dick has you sprung on Pam."

"Maybe." I sipped my cognac. Hennessy was a truth serum that loosened the tongue. A sweet buzz was knocking at my door. "Women are more faithful to you than they are to Jesus."

"That's because some women allow men to be their god. That's their weakness."

"You're the expert."

"Why didn't you kiss her?"

"I wouldn't do that to your woman."

"I knew you wouldn't betray me."

"So that was another loyalty test."

"I wasn't testing you. I never test you, Dante."

"Who you testing?"

"Arizona. She failed." He sipped. "Trusting has been my greatest flaw."

"So she betrayed you because she would've kissed me."

"She betrayed me long before that."

"What did she do?"

He sipped his cognac, processed a thousand thoughts before he said, "Boyle Heights."

"What about it?"

"Arizona rescued us."

I said, "No doubt."

"She got there in thirty minutes."

I said, "Felt like ten hours."

"She said she was at home. Mo Val is an hour and a half away in no traffic."

Both of us looked at her.

I asked, "You think she was at some dude's crib, then bounced him to get to you?"

He stared at her. Just when I thought he was pissed, he smiled and let out that boyish laugh. But I could tell that he was troubled. That smile couldn't hide the tribulation that was swirling inside his belly.

Sierra came over. She kissed Scamz and took a sip from his glass. Her eyes said that she was ready to end the night and go back to that mansion overlooking Hollywood. Scamz told her that we were still talking. She looked at me like I was less than zero, then went back and sat near her sister. Arizona was watching. Jealous eyes were over her beautiful smile.

I said, "That girl cares a lot about you."

Scamz said, "Friends close. Enemies closer."

I playfully bumped him with my elbow. "Which am I?"

He didn't answer. Just kept smiling at Arizona. She had her eyes on him too. She winked and blew him a soft kiss. In a few hours all three of them would be riding a crowded stairway to heaven.

I asked, "You ever think about having kids and shit like that?"

Scamz paused for a moment, then shook his head. "My life isn't conducive toward the Ozzie and Harriet way of living."

We relaxed, worked on getting buzzed, and watched people for a moment.

Without a warning, Scamz started thinking out loud. "I would have. I couldn't do that myself, couldn't stand to see him after what he'd done, so I sent a couple of low-end workers who only understand violence. It would have hurt me because I always considered him my friend, maybe even my family, but I would have. It would've been business. Nothing but business."

I looked at him and kept my surprise in check. He said that like he could read the lines in my face and see what I was really thinking, that my mind was on Jackson too.

Scamz didn't talk for a while. He was in thinking mode and he was uneasy. At last he spoke in a human tone that I'd never heard come from him. "When a friend betrays you, you feel violated. Raped."

I nodded. Keen howls echoed in my mind.

We rode through Hollywood. Headed down to Highland and Hollywood. That area had been redone and was the best part of the strip.

I said, "You never answered my question."

"What question?"

"Why me?"

"I trust you, Dante. You remind me of me. And every man wants a son."

"Fine, then adopt me and send me to Grambling."

He laughed his sneaky laugh. "I want you to realize your full potential."

"I see."

"Just trying to get you to understand the value of the skills you have."

"A'ight. The way I see it is like this, with all this you're doing in a short amount of time, you're doing green cards one day, closing out a rental scam, doing it all in the same city and you're never suppose to shit in your own nest, so you must owe somebody some long dough."

He nodded and drew his smoke, cool and unruffled. "Lost a lot of money back in September. Stock market did a number on my investments."

"How much?"

"Seven figures."

"Damn. You're broke?"

"Not by your standards, but it costs a lot of money to run my operations. Have to maintain a certain lifestyle. Cars, payoffs, the people I take care of, all of that puts a lot of hands in my pockets."

"You have a serious overhead."

"I'm not a ninety-nine-cent-store kinda guy."

"Maybe you should start clipping coupons. It works for me."

He chuckled, once again the way a man laughed at a child who has said something amusing. He went on. "You're versatile, from fighting to thinking fast on your feet, you're good. I have others I can either use only as muscles—"

"Like the peeps you sent after Jackson."

"Right." He lost his smile and drew his smoke. "When you fell off that bike, you were still slurping your soup, using toothpicks in public, leaving long strands of spaghetti hanging from your mouth, reaching across the table, supporting yourself with your elbows—"

"Yeah, yeah, yeah."

He chuckled. I did the same.

I never stole much more than I needed to get by, so I guess that was my way of justifying what I did when I had to do wrong. But a sin was a sin. Momma would probably tell me that a man *kinda* being a thief was like a woman *kinda* being pregnant.

He said, "I'm going back to Ecuador when this season ends."

I said, "That's where you're from, ain't it? Not down south like Alabama, but from down south by the equator."

He smiled the smile of a career grifter, one that offered no real answer.

I bumped him. "Oh, yeah. Nothing like a vacation in the land where they cut off hands."

That sarcasm got a laugh out of him. "You should come."

"Can I bring Pam with me?"

"Why her? You'd be taking sand to the beach. You could lose your virginity every night."

"I . . . I like her, that's all."

He shrugged like it would be my loss. "Bring her."

A lightness took over me. A new apartment would be mine in a matter of days. And a car. Moving uphill financially for once gave me some clarity. Working for Scamz could be the best thing for me. Maybe I could pass on the luxury apartment and get a house. One of the two-bedroom single-family homes in Sherman Oaks. Get a big Jacuzzi tub put in the bathroom. I bet Pam would like that. We could sit around sipping on wine, eating raw oysters, and move on up like George and Weezy.

I moved a bit. Tested to see how damaged I was. Had more injuries than I could count.

We landed back at the pool hall around one in the morning, just when the city was fluffing its pillow and getting ready to call it a night. Traffic was easy. Ventura Boulevard was cold and calm.

Big Slim opened the back door, that twelve-gauge in his free hand. He had on his steel-toe shoes, dark slacks, a white shirt with a T-shirt underneath, and a button-up sweater that was the color of old ketchup. He smelled like ham, Aqua Velva, two shots of Johnnie Walker Blue, one beer, and old age. We made eye contact and exchanged greetings with nods of heads. I was glad to see that he was okay. I guessed he felt the same way about me.

Lights came down the alley. A car was coming our way fast, and another one was on its heels. Sirens came to life out on Ventura Boulevard. My heart rushed to my throat, and I expected to see rainbows covering me at any moment.

I said, "Trouble."

Scamz replied, "Be ready."

The vehicle in front was a pickup truck. A car with yellow fog lights was on its ass.

The horn blew over and over.

"Dante," a voice called out before the truck came to a complete stop.

It was Jackson.

Big Slim said, "Somebody's shopping for a tombstone."

I agreed with a nod.

Scamz had become cold. He took in a lungful of air, blew it out, and his mood changed, switched from noon to midnight. His jaw clenched and a vein popped up in his neck.

The car that was riding Jackson's bumper came to a stop and pulled to the side of his truck. EYE FLY 4 U was on the front plates.

Robin hopped out of her silver Passat and ran up to Jackson's window. She still had on her flight attendant gear. I guess that meant she hadn't had time to slow down since her plane landed.

They had words, the kind of words that were filled with love and stubbornness, the kind of conversation a man and a woman had when she wanted one thing and he wanted another.

Robin had been chasing her man across the freeway and down the streets, trying to stop him from coming down here. I picked that up from their conversation.

She begged him to stay in his truck.

"Jackson, baby, don't—"

"Move over, Robin."

He told her to go away and let him do what he had to do. Jackson was determined, so was Robin, but she couldn't stop him. Jackson had a hard time getting out, almost lost his balance, then reached back and pulled out a metal crutch. His left knee was in a brace.

Big Slim bounced that twelve-gauge he was holding against his fake leg.

Scamz told Big Slim, "Step back inside."

"Don't want no mess, young man."

Scamz said, "Won't be any mess."

Big Slim stopped bouncing his twelve-gauge, gave up a thick grunt, then moved deeper into the pool hall. Scamz stepped back to the door, stood there with one hand on the edge, and stared at Jackson.

Jackson ignored Scamz's coldhearted gaze and kept his eyes my way.

"Scamz," Jackson said. "Let's talk like men. I want to settle my bill."

Scamz didn't reply.

Bad blood was flowing like the Nile. All the friendship that we had shared over the years was gone. Couldn't find a trace of it in my heart. There was nothing but hatred between Jackson and Scamz, between me and Jackson, between Scamz and Jackson. The animosity created enough energy to light up the Las Vegas strip.

Jackson was wearing gray cotton sweats. His right arm was bent and he held it like he could hardly move that side of his body. From where I stood his face looked swollen too.

Scamz said, "Dante."

His tone told me what he meant. I headed toward Jackson. Robin was right there, at his side. I ignored her and let this be between men and former friends.

This reminded me of when I had to stand up to my old man. The scenario was different, but the torment was the same. That same anxiety has visited me so many times since that day. I was scared then. I was scared now. Those were two different brands of fear.

I pushed him hard, made him stumble back against his truck.

Jackson didn't come back at me with anger, just looked hurt and sad.

I clenched my teeth and said, "Look, man, raise up. Get home to your little girls."

Jackson said, "Dante, don't be his bitch."

I pushed him again.

Robin screamed and cursed me. Jumped in between us. My heartbeat was unsteady, breathing uneven. I

imagined that this was the way a sniper felt right before
he pulled a trigger.

Sirens were still screaming a few blocks away, an un-
usual sound for this part of town.

Those wails didn't distract me from my stare-down
with Jackson. I could've been stabbed in the heart because of him. Felt like I had.

I had sold my soul to set him free and he wouldn't let
that be.

Then I thought about the things he had left out in his
apartment, about his depression, and that damn compas-
sion got the best of me, frustrated me. I tired to conjure
up every image I could to take me back to anger, but my
heart wouldn't let me get to that point. Kept thinking
about my mother, those final moments before she ceased
to exist, and tried to understand Jackson's agony.

My voice started to crack. "Go home to your kids,
Jackson."

I turned around and marched away.

"Scamz," Jackson called out. "We need to talk. Let
Dante go and let me pay my debt."

I strutted across the piss-stained alley to the back
door.

Scamz asked me, "You hear anybody call my name?"

I shook my head. "Nothing in the alley but trash, and
trash can't talk."

Scamz closed the door. Locked Jackson out in the
alley.

We took the dim hallway, each step the smoke getting
thicker and the sounds of Etta James singing about a
party in a basement getting that much louder. Lots of people were down here, the way it was when unemployment
was high and money was low. Scamz walked in before me,
Djarum in hand, and all eyes came to him, people waiting
to be chosen for the next job, or one down the line.

My eyes went up to Annie Mae's beautiful picture.
Now I understood a little more about that old man.
About his pride. Most of it had been decapitated, and he
wanted to hold on to the rest.

Scamz kept moving through the crowd. I meandered by the pictures of Robert Johnson, Bessie Smith, Billie Holiday, and all the rest of the ghosts that watched over this place.

Sierra and Arizona were both there. Sierra was near the small stage where the house rules were posted. Arizona had her eyes up at one of the Sony TVs, watching CNN. She looked toward me and shame reddened her face. She turned her eyes from mine, picked up her drink, and took a hard swallow.

Both of them looked toward Scamz, waiting to see if he was going to come their way.

Big Slim sat at his circular booth and went into warden mode, slammed his twelve-gauge down on the counter to let people know who was large and in charge. He pulled out his flask, sipped, and sat back, his eyes perusing the room. His lips moved, singing along with the song that was playing.

Twenty minutes of chatter and peace went by.

The buzzer went off and four people walked inside. That was the crew from Scamz's vending machine swindle making it back from the high desert. Two men came in first, followed by two women.

The last woman was dressed in all black. It was Pam.

She halted her stroll when she saw me. We broke eye contact and she headed for a table. She raised a finger, and a player accepted her invitation just like that. They knew she had just come in from a grift and wanted to get a shot at making that extra income.

I went to her. "Let me talk to you for a minute."

"In a minute, shorty. I'm about to work a bit."

"Now."

She saw how serious I was and put her stick to the side. I had her follow me down the hallway. We stopped in the darker part, near the bathroom.

I said, "Why did you lie to me?"

"Why are you trippin' and frontin' me in front of all of these people?"

"Because you lied."

"I didn't lie to you."

"You said that you were passing on the vending machine thing."

"I changed my mind, then I changed my mind back."

"Why didn't you tell me?"

One of the guys came down the hallway and went into the bathroom. I moved Pam closer to the front. People could see us, but nobody could hear us over the blues.

"Look, shorty," Pam said with one hand on her hip. "I like you, you're cute, but I don't have to get my schedule approved by you."

"So it's like that."

"God, I never should've slept with you."

"Elevate your mind. This ain't about fucking."

"If we never *fucked*, then we wouldn't be having this conversation."

"Pam—"

"I've put a lot of time and energy into all of this, and I told you, I don't have an alternate plan to come up with the money."

"Why didn't you tell me?"

"I didn't want to argue." She shifted and her voice softened. "I didn't want you to worry."

"You're right. You never should've slept with me."

We stood there a moment, our eyes away from each other.

Pam said, "I was watching television this morning, guess it was a few hours after you left because the sun had come up. Was restless when you bounced out in the middle of the night. This commercial came on. A national commercial for orange juice. Guess whose face was smiling at me across my room. Tammy Barrett. Tammy was in it. Movies. CDs. Her husband's book was on my nightstand. Him signing to us as a married couple didn't help me forget that little white lie I'd told her. Everywhere I go there is something there to remind me about her, and every time I see her success, I see my failure, and I don't like the way that feels. I don't want to be a has-been before I've ever been."

I shifted and listened, but didn't understand why she would want to chase a business that didn't give a damn about her. She was upset, using her hands to emphasize, drawing some attention our way.

Scamz was watching. So were Sierra and Arizona. Big Slim was studying us too. Everybody in the room could tell that Pam was talking down to me, building up her reputation by denting mine. My rep was on the line. I should've gone back at her with a fury, but right now I didn't care.

"I have talent, shorty. I'm so fucking good it makes me mad every time I see a fucking movie. I can't sleep on my career." Pam said all that, then stopped and took a breath before she made her lips go up into a reluctant smile. "So, if we were to play make-believe and kid ourselves into thinking that the age difference didn't matter, that just because we had good sex a couple of times that we could give it a shot, then at some point it came down to choosing between my career and you, you'd have to go."

"You've mapped it out."

"That's what adults do, Dante. Children just act; adults consider the consequences."

The guy who was in the bathroom came out. Big Slim got up off his seat and came down the hallway. He said, "Y'all might wanna take that outside."

He hobbled by us and went into the john.

I said, "Consider this while you're in that considering frame of mind: everybody down here is gonna end up dead or in jail, me included."

Pam didn't look at me again.

She said, "We had sex. It was fun. Let's leave it at that."

"Do me a favor?"

"What?"

"If I call you, as soon as you hear my voice, hang up. If I knock at your door, don't answer."

"You do the same."

She didn't think twice before she walked away and

headed to the pool table. She added some sway to her hips and happiness was in her body language. A great actress who could hide her real mood in public. I bet she had left a lot of men in her day. Left them before they could leave her.

Watching her leave was like watching the sun set—sad and wonderful all at once.

I wasn't a pretender. I stayed where I was, caught between the light and the shadows.

Pam had photos of women with perfect bodies up in her bathroom. Everybody had the life she wished she had. Had to deal with the death of a child. Couldn't afford to pay her rent but she wanted a six-thousand-dollar operation to make her body look better, like getting her stretch marks removed was a shoo-in to winning an Academy Award. She was getting old and still wanted to be a star.

I felt sorry for her. I didn't think I could be in love with somebody I pitied.

The buzzer at the front door went off again. Jackson came inside. Everybody stopped shooting pool and scowled at him the way people of a clandestine group regarded an unwanted visitor. They didn't give a shit about his injuries.

Robin came in right behind him. She looked worn to the bone and frustrated.

Jackson saw me and shouted my name over the music. That didn't help my mood.

He stood there for a moment, waiting to talk to me. He felt the coldness in the room, did an about-face, and went back outside. Knowing him, he'd sit out there and wait for me.

Big Slim came back out of the bathroom.

There were too many faces in the pool room I wanted to forget.

I asked Big Slim, "Mind if I take the back door out?"

He hadn't seen Jackson come and go, so he assumed it was all about Pam. He nodded like he understood. "Go 'head. I'll double behind you and make sure it's locked good in a minute."

I turned around and headed back down the hallway. Expected Pam to come running after me or call my name, but that kinda soap opera shit never happened in real life, not to me.

I stepped out the back door, left that smoke behind for night air that was crisp and clean. Heavy thoughts slowed my stride. If my mind had been clear, my senses would've been working and I would've heard Nazario rushing up behind me.

29

Nazario thundered out of the darkness. My mind screamed and told my body to duck, but that cognac I'd been sipping kept my body from moving as fast as my thoughts.

His thick fist caught me in the back of the neck. I cursed and tried to go with the pain, but everything went bright red. My legs wobbled and didn't know which way to go.

"Y-y-you break in my h-h-house?" He fumed. "What, you c-c-crazy?"

I struggled to get situated, tried to see if he had his crew with him, but I didn't hear anybody else back here. Nazario charged at me like a raging bull. My feet squared off and I tried to get into boxer mode and swing at that eye, but his anger tackled me and lifted me in the air. I was airborne, went down hard and landed square on my right shoulder, rolled and the ground kissed my face. More bright colors came to visit me. Couldn't yell; he'd knocked the wind out of me.

"You m-m-mark on my door."

My legs moved like pistons, but I went nowhere. Hurting too bad to get back up anytime soon.

"You know how m-m-much a door cost at Home Depot?"

Step by step, that one eye came closer to me. Hypnotized me. My face and stomach knotted.

"And you scare my p-p-puppy."

He faked at me and I jerked. He kicked at me, I scooted back. Arm hurt too bad to let me bounce back up. He taunted me over and over, toyed with me the way a cat fucked with a mouse.

He let me get halfway up before he tackled me again, laid me on my back.

"You t-t-talk bad to my girlfriend and n-n-no give me my wife ring."

A thousand chills ran through me.

"Y-y-you cost me a l-l-lot of m-m-m . . . cash."

The back door opened up and the sound of the blues covered me. There was a low growl that sounded like a rabid dog on the loose. Light came out and Big Slim's silhouette appeared. I expected Scamz to come out too, but that old man stepped out all alone. He didn't have that twelve-gauge with him.

I tried to shout, "Get back inside, Big Slim."

My garbled words didn't come out as loud as I'd hoped.

Big Slim's growl grew deeper. He hobbled out into the alley and let the steel door groan closed behind him. There was no way to open that door from the outside. There was no handle to grab on to.

"Move 'way from that boy." That was Big Slim. "He too hurt t' be scuffling with you, boy."

"F-fuck you, *pendejo*."

Big Slim moved as fast as he could and pulled Nazario away from me, just like he had done before. Nazario hit that old man, knocked him back, made him stumble to the ground with one blow.

"S-s-suck my mudderfuckin' dick, you fat big slimy cripple."

Big Slim got up and went after Nazario. That one-eyed ox met that old man halfway.

The back door to the pool hall creaked open right about then. Somebody had finally looked at the monitors and seen that a war was going on in the alley, and a few people came out to watch.

I was on the ground, my eyes clouded with pain.

I said, "Somebody help Big Slim."

At least six people were out here. Nobody moved. They were all spectators.

By the time the tears of pain cleared from my eyes and I was able to focus, I didn't see what I had expected to see. Big Slim had death-gripped Nazario's neck with the web of his right hand and was pushing him backward toward the building, moving like he was a young man again. Nazario's oversize head rammed into the wall hard enough to make him grunt with the sudden agony. Nazario jerked and tried to get free. Big Slim tightened his grip again and shoved Nazario right back into that wall.

That gave me time to get my wind and get to my feet.

"You b-b-better get off me." Nazario tried to yell, but it came out in a garbled, frustrated whisper. That solitary eye was open so wide he looked like a grotesque figure from Greek mythology. "I'm gonna kick y-y—"

Nazario's eye widened with surprise. He gagged and ran out of air. He was taller than Big Slim, but it didn't show. I expected Nazario to get away, but the grasp around his throat was still tight. He couldn't break free from that steel trap. Nazario kicked at Big Slim's groin, but all he managed to do was make his shorts flap like a flag in surrender.

Big Slim's face contorted, a straining noise roared from him, like he was using all his energy, and that old man never took his mangled hand away from Nazario's throat.

Nazario twisted and jerked his body down the brick wall. Where he went, Big Slim followed, almost as if he was scared to let go. Nazario swung wild punches like a boxer that was in the last round and behind on all the judges' scorecards. He put his fists deep into Big Slim's flabby face three or four good times. Big Slim's jowls fluttered with each blow.

Big Slim growled, "I knows chirren that hit harder than that, boy."

Nazario closed his eye and kept on punching. Big Slim didn't give him any slack.

Nazario's whacks got lighter and lighter, downgraded from solid punches to love taps. Nazario's face tensed and he looked toward me with that one wide, frightened eye.

I could become his savior.

After all he had done to me—destroyed my front door, pissed on my world, had me attacked in Boyle Heights, and killed Oscar—after all of that pain and destruction he was begging me to forget that he'd rained on my life, expecting me to help him out.

I gritted my teeth and shook my head.

Big Slim yelled in Nazario's ear, "I'm gonna teach you how to respect your elders."

Nazario started slapping Big Slim's arm the way a wrestler beat the canvas when he was giving up. Three weak slaps, rest, try to breathe, then three more slaps. The slaps got weaker, the rests longer.

In a dark alley, underneath dull streetlights, Nazario was about to earn a tombstone.

Now I wasn't so sure about not helping Nazario.

Then Big Slim started wheezing. Age and illness were catching up with him. Big Slim tightened the handshake on Nazario's neck until he went limp. Big Slim let him go; Nazario collapsed on the ground. That ox had been downed by an aging buffalo.

I stood there with my mouth open in disbelief.

Seconds dragged by like hours.

Nazario moved his fingers, his hand opened and closed, then his legs moved in slow motion like he was trying to run to his car. He opened that eye, showed fear like I'd never seen before, stared up at the moon and wheezed his way back to the living.

Big Slim was leaning against the wall, holding himself up with one hand.

He said, "He . . . he . . . he betta be glad I ain't as mean as I used to be."

I took a deep breath. My arm was numbed with pain from where I had crash-landed. Wasn't a damn thing I could do if Nazario rose to his feet. Sweat ran down my head into my face.

Big Slim yelled down at Nazario, "You want some mo' of this, boy?"

That took away most of that aging buffalo's energy. He staggered two steps.

Nazario gagged like he was about to throw up, then put his hand on his throat and panted. His hairy chest was drenched and his face was dripping with sweat.

Big Slim flexed his hand to get his circulation going. He spat down on Nazario.

"Don't you never . . . don't you never come back in my place . . . in my place of biddness." Big Slim barely got his words out. He sounded dizzy. "You ain't . . . ain't gonna be so lucky next go round."

Big Slim hobbled away from the crowd, moved like a drunk man for a few steps, then straightened up his stride. One of the women who had been inside was at the back door. She was holding it open, looking out at the scene with her mouth wide open. Big Slim went by that woman and hobbled back inside. She stepped outside and I caught the back door before it closed, limped in on Big Slim's heels, then made sure that metal barrier was locked behind me. Somebody tapped on the door, but I didn't turn around. If the people out in the alley wanted to come back in, they'd have to walk all the way around and enter from Ventura Boulevard.

So would Nazario.

Big Slim asked, "Where my . . . where my gun at?"

Big Slim's twelve-gauge was resting on the counter at the circular booth. The music was jamming, a few people were dancing, and none of them had any idea what was going on fifty feet away.

I told Big Slim where his peacemaker was resting, asked him if he wanted me to go get it. He didn't answer. His breathing was too choppy to talk. Big Slim put his hand out against the wall to hold himself up. I tried to help him, but the way my arm was throbbing, he was on his own.

He said, "Needs . . . needs . . ."

"Your medicine."

He nodded. "Get me . . . my room . . . open do' fo' me."

I took his keys and opened his door, tried to get him in before anybody saw him like this. The hallway wasn't as bright as the rest of the place. And the music was loud; Nina Simone singing "Mississippi Goddam" covered us wounded warriors coming down the narrow corridor.

Pam was drinking with the grifters, working on getting her degree in back-stabbing and dirty deals. Something out there had her attention. Something had everybody's attention.

Jackson had come back. Robin was there too, frazzled and upset. Jackson was confronting Scamz. That was why they hadn't run out back. A powder keg was in here along with the sparks and they didn't want to miss the explosion.

I hustled Big Slim inside his room, pushed the door up behind me.

He made a jittery motion toward the television. His medicine was resting between Annie Mae's picture and her obituary. I rushed to get his pills. Opened one of each. He couldn't get his hand up this time. I had to put them in his mouth. His lips were damp with slobber and held the stench of liquor.

I said, "Let me call 9-1-1."

He did a faint side-to-side motion with his head. He'd die before he let people see him look weak.

Big Slim said, "Annie Mae. Brang her to me."

I didn't know what he meant at first, thought that old man was delirious. He did a hand motion and I understood. He wanted that picture of his woman. I got it for him and he held it to the heart side of his chest. A closer look at his face showed me that those blows Nazario had laid on him had damaged him real bad. Again I was scared.

Then Jackson's voice rang out over the song that was playing.

I was stuck in nightmare after nightmare.

I left Big Slim where he was and headed toward the new commotion.

Jackson and Scamz were having words. Scamz could snap his fingers and at least five people in the room would rush to protect their king, but they all stayed where they were. Scamz must've told them all to stand down. This was Scamz's world. The thieves, beggars, robbers, con people, everyone between these four walls were his people. If Jackson had double-crossed one of us, he'd become Judas to us all. There was an honor among us.

Pam moved over by Sierra and Arizona. People were getting out of trouble's way.

Scamz said something and walked away from Jackson like he was nothing.

Whatever he said froze Jackson where he was.

Sounded like something broke in Big Slim's room, like maybe he'd tried to get up, then collapsed. I was about to hurry and check on him, but as soon as I turned my back there was a crack that echoed like an explosion. Jackson had whacked Scamz upside the head with a pool cue hard enough for the wood to break. That wood flew across the room.

Scamz staggered, regrouped, and went after Jackson, caught him in the gut with a front kick. Jackson was hurt too bad to fight Scamz off and all he could do was drop to the concrete floor. Scamz grabbed a pool cue and returned the favor, whacked Jackson across the face, then dropped his knee down on Jackson's chest and pulled his fist back, ready to strike.

I shouted, "Scamz—"

He hit Jackson more times than I could count, each blow sounding like bones and flesh being molded into a new face. Jackson yelled out a warrior's cry and swung back, got in a good blow, but Scamz got in three solid ones. That slowed Jackson down.

Robin ran over and tried to save her man. Her emotions were on high. She hit Scamz, called him a motherfucker, a son of a bitch, other things. Scamz shoved her back, she stumbled into me.

My chest was rising and falling, overwhelmed by the desire to fix this. This wasn't my fire. Those jailhouse screams came back and filled the inside of my head with noise and memories.

Scamz's temper had been set free, his rage made him sound crazed. "You help set me up, then walk back up in here like it was no big deal."

Jackson struggled, tussled, refused to give up. "Dante is just a kid. Let him go."

He was sweating, his face swelling, blood seeping from a cut on the side of his face.

My heartbeat was wild. I'd moved deeper into a nightmare that wouldn't go away. I couldn't decide if I should help and create another moment of regret. It was like watching two brothers fight.

Scamz hit Jackson a few more times. The crowd stood there and watched. Each blow sounded harder than the one before. Each time it hurt my heart. I was having too many thoughts and feelings to control at one time. Too many to set free without going over the top, without exploding like I did when I attacked my father.

I snapped, "Back off the man, Scamz."

Scamz didn't slow down. He was panting, sweating, but still wreaking havoc on Jackson.

There was an explosion. It was a flash, like a thousand Polaroids had gone off inside my head. I was blinded. It startled me back to when I was fifteen and a half. I saw my father's face, saw that look of surprise when he saw me holding his service revolver in my hand. Saw his fear when he saw me moving toward him. Heard his voice calling my name. Saw his lips moving in apology for the way things had turned out between him and my momma. In my memory, I raised his gun. Heard that blast. Felt that power surge through my body. Inhaled that cordite fragrance.

I tried to yell that memory out of me. Tried to make it go away.

Just as fast as my mind had yanked me away from this world, it sent me back. Blues rang out loud and I was on the floor, on my knees, shivering, reaching for a pool table, a wall, anything to get me back on my feet. Waves of energy had rolled though me, had done the same with everyone in the room. Most of the customers were cowering, some had hit the floor just like me, others were crouched or down on their haunches, a couple positioned like soldiers in a foxhole.

It wasn't my imagination. Everyone had seen that explosion, had felt that thunder because it made everyone in the room jump or scream, had deafened every ear at the same time.

I had no idea what had happened until I looked around at the destruction.

Big Slim's twelve-gauge had erupted and silenced the room. But Big Slim didn't pull the trigger.

Robin was a few feet away from me, dazed and on her ass, that smoking twelve-gauge right next to her. She had fallen and bumped her head, had hit the concrete floor hard enough for her to grab her head with both hands and tighten up in fetal position, as if getting back into the womb would kill her pain.

While all the commotion had everybody's focus, Robin had taken Big Slim's shotgun from the top of the circular counter. In the movies people shot up in the air, blew a hole in the ceiling to get the room to quiet down, or to stop a fight. She didn't do that. She had shot Scamz in the upper body, had blown him away from Jackson. The shotgun had bucked like a mule and had laid her on her ass, all the wind knocked out of her.

Scamz's lips were moving out of sync with the Bobby "Blue" Bland song that was on the jukebox. I expected him to get up and dust his suit down. He didn't. His dark suit had become wet with the fluids of life, and that dampness was seeping to the floor. Words tried to come out of his mouth, but there was only sputtering. The look on his face didn't resemble fear; it was more like an irritated sneer than anything else, one that said you couldn't kill what wouldn't die.

Then a mask of pain eased across his face.

He gasped out a breath and the sputtering stopped. That put a ton of ice in my belly. All around the room people stood with pool sticks in hand, openmouthed.

Scamz tilted to the side like a rag doll.

There was a scream. I thought it came from Arizona, maybe Sierra, but that came from Pam. She turned her back to the scene, did that like death had visited her one time too many.

It had to be an illusion. All of this had to be an illusion. The world went numb. Time stopped, ceased to exist. Everything shifted. That surge of newness eased through me.

All around me was this sense of incredible shock.

Pam turned back around and stood there with her hands clamped over her mouth, muffling her own shrieks, breasts moving with her hard breathing, fear in her body and tears in her eyes.

Jackson was lying next to Scamz, unable to move, frozen in his own fear and pain.

Robin sat up and saw what she had done, then started shaking her head like she was trying to undo a nightmare.

"*No, no, no!* What y'all done done in my place of biddness?" Big Slim was barking his way into the room. He had struggled and made his way out of his bed and down the narrow corridor, had pushed people out of his way so he could see what had happened. His breathing was labored, but not as thick as before. He stopped next to me, let out a long, twisted, agony-filled whining sound when he saw what had gone down. His bruised face was slackened because he didn't have his teeth back in his mouth. Big Slim's long moan, that blues howl filled with agony, faded, his expression said that what he was seeing was impossible.

People started back to breathing, began looking at each other, then at Scamz, then at each other. They kept doing that like they were waiting for confirmation that their savior was dead.

I stepped over Jackson and went to Scamz. I touched him.

He was gone.

I backed away and looked at Robin. Somebody grabbed my arm. They thought I was about to go after her. Wherever I was, there was no pain. It didn't feel real. I looked back at Scamz. Somebody so powerful couldn't go out like that, not that easily, not in an accident.

The sense of everybody's lives shifted and we all fell into a vacuum of time. I saw it in their faces. Their hopes vanished with Scamz's last breath. Shock was followed by a surprising realization of the actual loss. Some had lost their jobs. Others had lost their god.

Women cried rivers. Men cursed.

I don't know how long I stood there, seconds or minutes, but that surreal feeling started to fade and the air became heavy with the seriousness of things. Sirens were in the background, waking us up. People remembered that they had parole officers, then grabbed their coats and headed out the door, moving with quickness. No one wanted to be in this den if rainbows surrounded this room.

Jackson was on his feet. His eye was puffed out, his face wasn't recognizable. Robin made it up too. They were leaning against a pool table, holding each other. They put their backs to this scene.

Robin's cries made her back hump up and down in a nonstop motion.

"Lawd have mercy on his soul." That was Big Slim shaking his head, sounding distraught. Then his rage shook the room. "Why you go and hurt that boy like that? Not in my place of biddness. Not with my peacemaker."

I went over to Pam. I said a few things to her, held her shoulders and shook her, but she wasn't blinking. She couldn't hear me. Her world had gone mute.

Sierra and Arizona were both near the bar, underneath that disco ball, holding each other like they were all they had left in this world. Sierra tried to pull away. Arizona held her sister back for a moment, until the struggle got too dramatic, then she let her go.

Big Slim raised his voice at Robin, yelled at her over and over.

Robin's cries escalated.

Sierra pulled her hair away from her face and kneeled down next to Scamz. Her eyes were wide, but the rest of her childlike face showed silent sobbing and hysterical movements of her lips. She shook him like she thought he was a sleeping child. Her bottom lip trembled.

Arizona took her sister by the arm and led her away in a hurry. She rushed Sierra out the door and came back, stood over Scamz. She shivered and tears fell from her eyes, dampened her face. She inched closer and kicked his arm with her foot. He didn't move.

She said, "I love you."

She spat on him, then turned and hurried out the door.

30

Big Slim stood and stared up at that picture of Annie Mae. He mumbled a few soft words to her, then lowered his head and sat behind the circular counter, his face in his hands, those mutilated fingers massaging his razor bumps.

Time was slipping away, so I took over.

After the room was almost clear, I went out on Ventura Boulevard. The shops across the street at Jinky's Café were closed, so was Westwood Insurance. A thousand cars passed by, none had stopped.

I went back inside, went to Pam. She looked like a different woman now. The reality of this world didn't seem so glamorous and promising.

I told her, "I need you to do some serious acting right now."

She wiped her eyes and wobbled where she stood. "Okay, okay."

"Put on your happy cap and walk out the door. Go to your car and drive home."

"Don't know if I can drive—"

"Then start walking home."

"What about when the police come—"

"Did you understand what I just told you?"

"I want to be a witness—"

"We don't need any witnesses."

"—let them know that Jackson was being beat up and that girl didn't—"

"Don't worry about that. We have our own law down here."

Pam didn't comprehend what I was saying, and that didn't matter.

I led her to the door, pretty much pushed her out to the curb. She folded her arms across her breasts and headed down Ventura. Her heels clacked a disturbed beat. She took a few steps before she looked back at me.

I told her, "You ain't been here. You don't know anybody down here. We've never met."

She gave me a long look, then took off jogging. That jog turned into a run.

Pam vanished into the night. I went back inside and made sure the front doors were locked. Then I took off my leather jacket, threw it across a pool table, and got ready to work.

I asked Big Slim, "Plastic?"

He motioned toward the bar and said, "Grab one a' dem table covers."

I grabbed one of the brown plastic covers used to keep the dust off the pool tables.

I told Robin, "Help me."

She didn't move. "Are the police—"

I snapped, "Get up off your ass and get over here, dammit."

She did what I said, helped me put that dusty plastic over Scamz. With the pain in my arm that was a struggle.

She said, "I didn't mean to—"

"Too late for that," I said, then hurried over to Big Slim. "How attached are you to that carpet in the Money Room?"

"I ain't no mo'."

He reached under the counter and pulled out a box cutter. He said, "My hands can't handle this the way I need to."

"I got it."

It took a while with my arm banged up, but I managed to cut a large square of that Berber out of the floor. I put the carpet down in the pool room. I had to get the car keys out of Scamz's pocket.

I tossed the cellular phone to Big Slim. He dropped it

on the floor and crunched it to pieces with his steel-toe shoes. I took all the bogus ID in Scamz's pocket and handed that to Big Slim as well. There was a wad of cash. I tossed that to Big Slim. He looked at that money like it was the root of all evil.

Jackson wanted to help, his heart wanted to help get Robin out of trouble, but he was too banged up. We left him leaning against a pool table, his long hair loose and wild. His mouth was bloody. He was silent and sweating from the pain.

Big Slim and Robin helped me move Scamz to the edge of the carpet. We gazed down on him, mourners at a funeral. Then we rolled him up like a joint and wrapped it around with duct tape.

Robin sobbed the whole time, telling us how she was scared, kept saying how she didn't mean to pull the trigger, that the way Big Slim always carried that thing around she didn't think it was loaded.

Big Slim barked at her, "Shut up, gal. Too late for that now."

We carried Scamz down the hallway to the back door.

Robin asked, "What are you going to do?"

"Don't worry about it," I said. "Less you know, the better."

They waited until I pulled Scamz's Benz around to the back and knocked. I popped the trunk and then we bumbled him inside. I was hurting, Big Slim wasn't one hundred percent, and Robin didn't have any real upper-body strength, but we got him in.

I had Robin bring her car around and we got Jackson inside.

I told Jackson, "Leave your truck. Send somebody to get it."

He didn't argue, just looked at me. He said, "I was trying to set things right, that's all."

"I know."

"Didn't want you . . . This was my fault. I had to try to—"

I said, "Let it go. We gotta keep our heads clear and move forward."

Jackson was hurt pretty bad. We all were.

Then I told Robin to get him to an emergency room. I added, "Take him to one a long way from here. Drive to one in the hood."

She asked, "What can I tell them?"

"Anything but the truth," I responded. "You ain't been down here. Neither one of you."

She nodded. Cranked up her engine. EYE FLY 4 U took to the alley with the lights turned off. She made a left toward Moorpark, her lights came on, and then they were gone.

You'd think that I'd rush away, or that Big Slim would rush to get back inside, but we stood in the cold air like two pallbearers at a fresh gravesite. I think we both wanted to hear Scamz wake up. This wasn't a Hollywood movie. Not a play. Anybody who was killed was gonna stay dead.

There was sadness. There was disbelief. But there were no tears.

I asked, "Your shotgun registered?"

"Naw."

"I'm gonna need you to give it to me."

"I don't thank you can trace a shotgun."

"Don't take a chance on it. New technology out there, you never know."

He went inside and came back with that twelve-gauge. I wiped it down, then opened the trunk long enough to toss it inside. It rolled over the carpet and landed near the backseat.

He said, "That boy's girlfriend shot that man down."

"I know."

"Jackson turned his back on you and you still helping him."

"I know."

"You helping everybody and you ain't gotta do nothing but walk away."

"I know."

"Scamz always said that you try to save people."

"That's just who I am. I can't fight that, so I won't try."

"He said that nobody ever saves you."

"You did."

Big Slim made a negative motion with his right hand. "I did that for myself."

"And you saved me at the same time."

I took a rag and started wiping down the Benz. Had to buff my fingerprints off anything that had been touched. Would be easier to do most of that now than later.

Big Slim asked, "What you gonna do?"

"You don't need to know. I need my coat. Left it inside."

He stuck a prop in the back door and went inside.

I finished cleaning up and stood near the car door. Big Slim came back with my jacket. He threw it inside the car. Both of us had our eyes on the trunk.

Big Slim said, "That's the most expensive coffin that I done ever seen."

"Same here."

"At least he gon' ride in style."

"At least."

He looked at me with paternal eyes. "Dante, you all right?"

That was the first time Big Slim had ever said my name.

"I'm cool." I wiped my face. My shoulder was throbbing. Scratches were on the side of my face. I'd heal in a few days. I told him, "Everything's a'ight. You?"

"Everythang'll pass one way or another."

"I'm gonna handle this, then I'll be right back at first light to help you clean up. You have to open up like nothing ever happened."

He shook his head and frowned. "Keep on movin' when you leave."

We stood eye to eye for a moment.

That aging buffalo shook his head and said, "If you stay in a room with somebody who has the flu long enough, eventually you'll get the flu too."

"What you saying?"

"It's somethin' my daddy use t' say."

"A proverb."

"You ain't got no biddness down here. You ain't never had no biddness down here."

I nodded and I understood.

He added, "The best thing to do is not t' hang round sick people. That way you won't get infected in the body or the head."

"Somebody needs to check on you."

"Annie Mae got her eye on me. She waiting for me to come home, but I won't go see her before it's my time."

We shook hands, held on to each other for a long while, the way people do when they're saying their good-byes. I wished that he was my granddaddy, my uncle, something.

He said, "Be careful out there, Dante."

"You do the same in there."

I gassed up that chariot at a Mobil down on Woodman. I took the 405 north until it ended at the Golden State, then kept driving north. Had to go right now because daylight and too many CHP would be out in a few hours. I set the cruise control at a few miles above the speed limit, enough to not look suspicious, stayed in the right-hand lane as much as I could, and drove through the night.

The inside of the car smelled like sweet cloves.

Four hours, six Tylenol, and a large cup of truck-stop coffee later I made it to the 580 interchange. The sun was rising and I was in the flow of traffic heading into the Bay. An hour after that I was on the edge of Oakland. I'd made one stop on the way up. Outside of coffee and Tylenol I'd bought gas, shades, gloves, and a sweat suit at that truck stop, changed my gear, put Neosporin and Band-Aids on my wounds, stuffed all of my battered rags into a big green trash bin, then moved on.

The Bay had a decent wind. The skies were as gray as my mood.

I rode into East Oakland. With all the clouds overhead, rain was on the way. That worked for me. I needed

a day with rain. I stopped at a hand car wash and rinsed
that ride down. The hawk was nipping at my ears and it
was cold enough to numb my head. I coughed. Nose was
running a little bit. I was the only person at the car wash
on an overcast day. That worked for me.

Not long after that the rain did come. A steady rain
that was creating a lot of snow in the mountains. I drove
around until I found a good spot where I could walk
away unnoticed, then parked right under a sign for a
low-level con that read EARN UP TO $1000.00 A WEEK
STUFFING ENVELOPES IN THE PRIVACY OF YOUR OWN
HOME. SEND $10.00 TO FIND OUT HOW.

My gloves were still on, but I wiped the inside of the
car down again. Wiped down the glove compartment,
door handles, dome lights, ashtray, and undersides. My
father was a cop. I remembered hearing him talk about
how people got busted for not being meticulous after a
crime. I wanted to thank him for that right now. That
was why some of my roommates were with me back in
juvenile hall, for not knowing how to scrub a crime
scene. Another skill that I couldn't put on my résumé.

I wanted to look in the trunk and make sure Scamz
wasn't trying to claw his way out, like in an Edgar Allan
Poe story, but I didn't.

I ditched the plates along with everything else that
was inside the glove compartment, then parked that
high-end chariot on a side street. I turned on the CD
player, left it on some of Scamz's favorite classical
music. I closed my eyes and took a deep breath, inhaled
that sweet clove scent before I locked all the doors. My
stride had a sadness, had to walk away with my shoulders hunched and I couldn't look back, that classical
music sounding like a funeral procession that was fading with my every step.

It wasn't until then I put my leather coat back on.
Something thick was in the right pocket. Felt like a ball.
I reached in and pulled out a wad of money. The same
wad that had been on Scamz. Big Slim had put it in my
pocket before he brought me my jacket. The cash felt

dirty and covered with death. I was tempted to put that
money in that car, but I didn't.

I used an old newspaper as my umbrella and walked
until I saw a bus, then rode that until I got to a subway
entrance, and took that underground transportation
down to Thirteenth Street and Broadway, a mile
above Jack London Square. A Gap was right across
the street when I came out into that crowd of African
Americans. This was downtown, and there was a mixture of both homeless and business people, so no matter what condition I was in I didn't stand out here. I
went in and bought some baggy jeans, underwear, a
sweater, a cap, and a coat. A Walgreen's was across the
street from the Gap. I went in and bought a toothbrush, face towel, hand towel, soap, deodorant. I was
hurting too bad to carry all of that, so I bought a
cheap luggage-on-wheels thing at a shop next door. I
rolled my luggage-on-wheels a couple of blocks down
to the Hilton and washed up in a bathroom. Left all of
my old and used stuff inside that luggage and abandoned it in the lobby.

I caught a taxi to the airport and bought a ticket for
the next flight heading back to Burbank.

Then I thought about what was waiting for me at the
place I called home.

Nazario and that cycle of foolishness could continue,
or I could let this be. Part of me refused to let him
punk me. That part of me would never change. But I
remembered what Big Slim had said, that a man
should never pay a man no more than what he owed
him. I had the pawnshop receipt for Nazario's wife's
wedding ring in my pocket. His address was engraved
in my mind. I could mail it back to him, let him pay the
five hundred to recover his loss, and let that be the end
of that.

I'd think on that a few days. Other people were more
important in my mind.

I had gone to Ed Debevic's and watched Pam from a
distance for a while, and it seemed like she'd been a part

of my life forever, but I'd only known her for three days. Three of the longest days in my life. I'd touched her, loved her, wanted her in a way that she didn't want me. Her scent was still on me. Her heat still in my skin. Not like we had the same history and undying devotion that Robin and Jackson had. But I did lust after her. And if it already hadn't, I did want that lust to change into love. She was the first woman I'd ever felt that way about.

I'd chastised Pam for wanting to work for Hollywood, a place that showed her no love.

I could say the same about myself and the widget factories I'd been chasing.

Trying to get a job. That's all I was trying to do. Just trying to survive.

I was twenty-five.

Just yesterday I was a teenager standing next to my momma. Wearing a dark suit coat. She was pretty and we were getting ready to go to church. Could smell her rosy perfume, could see her milky white usher dress, the saintly whiteness that hid bruises on her back and hips.

Exhaustion covered me.

I went to the bathroom to wash my face again and caught my reflection in the mirror. Stared at myself. My mother's eyes. My father's brief forehead. My mother's small nose. My old man's shallow eyebrows. My mother's grade of hair growing from my shaved head. Her complexion was my complexion. My old man's height and his build belonged to me. I reached out and touched us.

We'd always be here.

My life had been mean and violent, so all of that colored my perception. I saw the dark side of a wonderful city even when the sun was shining. Hard to find peace in a storm.

I'd been waiting for the storm to leave me.

Sometimes you had to leave the storm.

I took my ticket for Burbank back to the counter and got ready to trade it in. I stood in that long line and

looked to see when the next flight to either Atlanta or
New Orleans was.

Morehouse was in Atlanta.

Grambling was in Louisiana.

Whatever flight was next was fine with me. Both had
Alphas, Kappas, Qs, Sigmas, and sorority women in
search of a decent life. Down there I'd find a woman
who wanted to be my coffee in the morning and my tea
at night. She might be my age. I wanted her to be older
and wiser, but she might be a few years younger. Maybe
I'd get lucky and find my Annie Mae.

That whole time that I was flying, thought about
Scamz and the places he had been: New York, South
Beach, Montreal, New Orleans, Playa del Carmen,
Ecuador. Nice cars. Pretty women. A classical man
who spoke several languages and loved Greek mythol-
ogy. And he ended up dying on the floor of a pool hall
and being left in the trunk of a car in gang territory in
Oakland.

I imagined that a lot of those swindlers, the pool hall
down on Ventura Boulevard would have an emptiness,
would echo like an empty cave, like living in a world
that had no God. That was how they saw Scamz.

I didn't see him that way.

He was my friend. He was an ordinary man. He never
betrayed me.

His death would weaken some; others it would make
stronger.

It was like that R. Kelly song where he was eulogizing
his brother, thinking back on all the thug shit that they
had done together. Those days were over. I'd collected
another sunset.

I turned my head toward the window and cried a little.

I had a pocket filled with cash.

I still had the ATM card that was worth three hundred a day for the next month. I had more than enough
to get Pam her operation. Enough to get Jackson out of
the hole.

But I was gonna save myself this time.

I could look for Pam on television and the big screen.
I could send Big Slim a card at Christmastime.
I could call and check on Jackson once in a while.
But I couldn't go back. I had to save myself.

Epilogue

Ten seasons went by before I called back west. I hadn't missed L.A., not the land, but I did have thoughts about the people I had left behind. I was sitting at my desk in DuBois Hall, studying for a midterm, when I picked up my phone and dialed Jackson's number. A lot of time had passed. I didn't know if the number had changed, or if he had moved. He answered on the second ring.

He sounded happy to hear from me.

Jackson told me that he was working a couple of jobs. He had a part-time gig at the Target near his house. The other was a full-time gig out at FedEx. Sabrina had helped him get on at the LAX facility. Boeing was hiring some people down in Anaheim on the defense side of the plant, and he was at the top of the list for getting hired down there. War was generating revenue in the defense field, just like it did in the early eighties, and he was going to try to hop on that while he could.

I asked him, "How've you been holding up?"

That sentence carried a lot of questions and he understood all. He told me that he was doing fine. We didn't talk about Scamz or the pool hall or Boyle Heights. Not directly. He told me that he walked with a subtle limp, but it wasn't enough to slow him down from playing with his two little girls. From the way the words flowed, you'd think anything bad that we had done had never happened.

I asked, "How did that court thing turn out?"

Sounded like he shifted with his thoughts. I imagined

that Jackson smiled a little, ran his hands over his pony-tail, then said, "The DNA test came back not long after I got out of the hospital."

He told me that his youngest daughter, the one he had doubts about, that test came back at damn near one hundred percent. That released the doubt that had been anchored to his mind.

I said, "That should make you feel better about the situation."

His voice wasn't happy. "It did."

"You never thought she was yours, now you know the truth."

"Glad she is. Would've loved her just the same either way."

I asked, "What else happened?"

It took him a minute to say the rest of what was on his mind. I waited until he was ready. He told me that the oldest kid had flunked the DNA test.

I said, "You gotta be joking. She looks like you."

He told me that the test percentage that gave the probability of the kid being his came back lower than his shoe size. He took the test twice. Same result.

I said, "You're joking."

Silence settled between us.

Then he made a chuckling sound, a nervous laugh of disbelief, the kind of noise a person gave up when they'd gone through so much bullshit for no reason at all. I gave up the same kinda chuckle.

He said, "If I had known the first baby wasn't mine, there never would've been a second one."

I paused and didn't know what to say. "Guess that made it easier on your pocket."

"It dropped to about four grand. Then Sabrina withdrew the case."

I didn't ask him any more about that.

We said a few more things. Then the conversation became awkward.

I asked, "What happened to Big Slim? Sent him a card and it came back."

"Heard he passed about six months back. Said he went in his sleep. Pool hall closed down."

I imagined him being reunited with Annie Mae. "You ever see Pam around anywhere?"

"I don't get out much. Kids keep me busy."

I smiled a bit, sounded a little proud when I said, "I saw her on a soap opera for a minute."

"Robin told me the same thing. Ever hear from her?"

"Nah. Where is Robin?"

He told me that Robin wasn't flying anymore. She wanted a job that could keep her feet on the ground. She was working real estate. Their baby was due in about four months.

I asked, "Boy or girl?"

"Finally gonna have a boy."

He sounded happier than I'd ever heard him sound. I smiled.

That was all he said about Robin and the new baby. That was all I wanted to know.

He said, "You sound different."

"Do I?"

"You sound a lot younger."

"Guess college does that to you."

He said, "So you're in college?"

"Yeah."

"Good. That's real good."

"Kicking it at . . . I'm chilling, getting edjumacated at a HBCU."

"Nobody knew what happened to you."

I said, "I wanna keep it that way."

"What's your major?"

"Criminal justice and psychology."

"Popping a double major. You're gonna be there a minute."

"I ain't in no hurry to get out into the real world."

"Must be nice to be out of L.A."

I said, "If you need a break and you get some free time, come down south for a while."

"Wish I had free time. My kids need me on a daily

basis. Sometimes they get sick and I wanna be the one
to take 'em to the doctor and give 'em their medicine."

"Of course."

"That makes it easier on their momma."

"Right, right."

"And they like to go to movies most every Saturday
afternoon."

"I understand."

"Jobs keep me busy. And have to be with Robin. We
have Lamaze classes every Thursday."

"Right, right."

"Can't leave my wife here all swollen up and wobbling
like a Weeble."

We laughed.

Then came awkwardness.

Jackson said, "It was really nice hearing from you
but—"

"Didn't mean to disturb you."

"Gotta get the girls."

"Yeah. I understand. I gotta get to a fraternity meeting anyway."

There was a heavy pause. The air between us became
emotional.

He said, "Thanks, Dante."

"Take care."

"Keep them grades up. Stay outta trouble."

"A'ight. You do the same."

"Once again, thanks."

We hung up.

Acknowledgments

This is a work of fiction. These people don't exist.

God, I've always wanted to say that.

I was looking over my notes for TP, the book you're holding, checking out the evolution of Dante's story. I had started working on this concept while I was in the writer's program at UCLA. Think I was taking a class on how to write a good old mystery. Back then I was working on this novel (one that got out of control, plot and character-wise) about a guy named Raheem, his fiancée Rochelle, his shady buddy Scamz, and a cast of colorful characters. People who were short on money and living lives that had lots of action and plenty of crime. And of course some romance, but not the Harlequin kind. The kind that was true to that kinda world.

While hanging out and taking classes via the extension program at UCLA, I met this great guy, Anthony Lyons. We sat side by side for a couple of classes. Anthony is a great writer, a poet who was one of the founders of Leimert Park's World Stage, a father, and a damn good critic. He's been a wonderful friend and supporter since we first shook hands. That was around eight, maybe nine years back, and whenever I talked to him, he always asked me about the "Scamz story."

I wish I could remember the teacher's name, the one who pushed us to a new level in that mystery class. If it sucked, he said it, but he told you why it didn't work. That, my friend, is priceless. He was from New York and co-taught with another writer. At the time, he was loving the edginess and grittiness of the tale. That was our story. A thousand apologies for that memory lapse, but taking your class was wonderful.

The story started off being called "Trapped." (Gotta start somewhere.) And that idea came from an exercise in a writing book called "What If?" where I had to create an opening line, a catchy one, to start a story. That line wasn't used (not yet, and don't ask) but that exercise got my juices flowing. Gave me a man down on his luck and had to get to the pool hall to make his ends meet. A lot of that story changed somewhere down the line. It was originally set in Leimert Park, same apartments that both Leonard (F&L) and Vince (LG) lived in, but it moved to Sherman Oaks. Raheem's name changed a zillion times and ended at Dante, no doubt having to do with Dante's *Inferno* being on my mind at some point. Rochelle became Dana became Pam. (I was chatting with a friend from Carver High School, Pamela Morman and . . . always liked her name, so dat was dat.) I was listening to a blues record, then reading the names of a few blues singers, and Big Slim was born. I had a conversation with Maria (one of my favorite aerobics instructors at 24 Hour Fitness in L.A.) and we talked about her homeland, Ecuador. Something clicked, and a character called Emil became Nazario. So on and so on. You get the point.

I'm always doing something a li'l different, have to in order to keep from going stale, and my agent, Sara Camilli (thanks!) has been behind me all the way. I've done things that peeps (da purists) say a writer shouldn't do in every book. I ain't never been big on walking in somebody else's footsteps, not even my own.

Believe it or not, I cut out quite a few characters, got rid of a subplot or two, and actually toned down the action a hella-lot in this one. And I made a few of the characters (if not all that got callbacks from their initial audition) a tad bit softer. There was a lot more story I wanted to tell, but that deadline was calling, and calling, and calling, and. . . .

One day I might get back to the rest of what I wanted to do, but knowing me I'll just come up with a new cast in a story with a similar tone. Maybe. Right now I'm not big on sequels. Reading 'em, yep. Writing 'em, nah. But you never know. (Pam said something in this one that got me to thinking. She told Dante that, since everybody else in the grift world had lied about their names, she didn't think his real name was Dante. Hmmm. That got me to thinking. What if she was right?) Right now I'm working on something else, but Dante and his (new and improved) crew might start talking to me one night while I'm sitting in front of my laptop, and BAM!, it'll be on and poppin'.

I don't always read the same type of books, which is no doubt why I don't always write the same book, and I'm more interested in fresh characters and new motivations and what those characters have to say than that good old genre trapping. To me it has always been about the characters, not the writer. If I do a decent job, the writer vanishes by the end of page one and the characters appear for the rest of the journey. That's the way I flow. If you ever had a chance to look at my notes you'd find stories about characters ranging from serial killers in mental wards, to old couples in a story about unrequited love, to a sci-fi short about people trapped on a planet with three moons to . . . hell, I can't remember most of it. But I would love to make 'em all into something bigger.

That's why I have to give thanks to the peeps who have hung in there with me for the books and the anthologies and short stories. And I have to thank the people who love and understand me as a writer-in-training, who encourage me to do my thang, no matter what (insert name of critic or playa-hater) has to say.

Thanks to all the peeps who support me year after year, rain or shine.

To the people at Dutton/NAL, thanks for all the hard work. Thanks to Audrey LaFehr, Lisa Johnson, Kathleen Schmidt, Betsy DeJesus, Jennifer Jahner, and all the peeps behind the curtain.

Thanks to Anthony Lyons. When I started working on this, you were the first person I called. Hope I did a decent job with the "Scamz story." We be going way back. (Remember the instructor who kept falling asleep? LOL.) I wish that I could've incorporated one-half of all the shit we talked about, but you know how it goes.

Tiffany Pace, thanks for dogging me out and never letting me forget the error count in *Between Lovers*. ROFL, now, but not a year ago. You know how that imperfection gives me angst. Thanks for your help in that department. And brainstorming with you and playing "What if?" for those long hours got me over dat ol' writer's block. Hope the choices I made were the best. Now, finish your book!

Emil "Jake" Johnson, my dawg for life, your input was invaluable. Thanks for the brotherly love and unconditional friendship through all of my careers. I got yo' back.

Stacey Turnage, thanks (again) for reading this as it came off the printer. This ain't Nic and whatshisface, but it's just as good.

Brenda Stinson, Dana Wimberly, thanks for handling my biz when things got too hectic for me. (Hide the razors and break out the Prozac, this has been a hellified year.) If it weren't for your assistance, I'd be in a rubber room singing whatever people in rubber rooms sing.

Natalie Godwin, thanks for the tour of the valley, Jinky's Café, info on Fashion Square, and that North Cakalaki thang. Thanks for introducing me to Nanda (Benz expert), Julie (stair master), Thelma Mae (queen of the pool table). Wha wha wha? Don't get it twisted. (heh, heh)

To my man in ATL, Jihad Uhuru. You are off the chains. Thanks for giving me the lowdown on the grift world. You helped me take the initial concept to another level.

Thanks to Lolita Files, Victoria Christopher Murray, and Yvette Hayward.

Can't leave out the boyz: Audrey O. Cooper (L.A.),

Travis Hunter (ATL), Ron Hightower (L.A.) and Courtney G. (L.A.)

Tseday Aberra, thanks for the dialogue. Took me seven years to use it, huh?

To my people at the University of Memphis: Veronica (Ronnie, the DST) Oxford, Richard (Poppa, the Q) Jones, Angela Grigsley (B&N), LaTanya Lane, Harold Byrd (Bank of Bartlett), Judge Carolyn Blackett, U of M President Dr. Shirley Raines, and the men of Alpha Phi Alpha, Kappa Eta chapter. Much love to all of you. Thanks for that down-home support and for launching and sponsoring the Eric Jerome Dickey Library and Literary Enrichment Fund, which will benefit U of M's Ned R. McWherter Library. Thanks for allowing future authors to have access to the tools they need. I am truly honored.

If I left anybody out, my apologies. It wasn't intentional. Just rushing to get to the next book.

I'm out.

Peace and blessings to you and all you touch.

ejd 2/23/02 9:50 p.m.
'06
www.ericjeromedickey.com

I shouldn't have been surprised when I met my husband's lover, but I was.

This is the face of the woman in the mirror, the wholesome face of a woman who has been married for four years: I have brown skin and cinnamon freckles that come alive in the sun, delicate freckles that all of my former lovers loved to play connect the dots with, or pretend that my face was the sky and the freckles were the stars and find as many constellations as they could. I'm in my early thirties, but on a good day, with the right makeup and the right clothes, I can pass for early twenties. Men in their twenties are the ones who ignore the ring and flirt with me the most. I think it's the locks. Ever since I lost the perm, people say I look younger.

This is the life of the woman in the mirror, the life of a woman balancing her marriage and career as a news producer: I drive an hour and fifteen minutes in traffic every day—and that's in one direction—to the 10 westbound so I can drive La Brea into the edges of Hollywood, trying to get to a job that stresses me out to the nth degree. Some days the Freeway God shines down on me and I only have to deal with road rage for an hour, but if it's a rainy day, it could take two and a half. If somebody has lost it and killed somebody on the freeway, make it closer to four. Pretty irritating, spending that much time in traffic, either alone or looking for somebody to call on the cell phone and talk with to help take the edge off.

Before I bounce to work, I rush to cook dinner and

leave it in the microwave or oven, ready for my husband. If not a full dinner, then at least sandwiches. Just like my mother always did for us, there is always food in the house. When I get home at night, after working on stories on all the freeway chases, and the murder coverage, and the child abuse segments, and earthquake reports, I leave the pessimism at the door—refuse to bring negative energy into my household. I stop being a news producer and focus on being a wife. That's the Pisces in me. The emotional and sexual part of me that believes in love and is ruled by spirit.

Charles is from Slidell, Louisiana, a small country community east of New Orleans. He's a Libra, well-balanced, has a high sex drive, is emotional at times, and hates drama. He has eight brothers and sisters back home, all by the same parents, all with the same black curly hair, the kind that looks wavy when it's brushed, but Charles and his mother are the only ones with hazel eyes. Very family oriented. Alligator meat, crawfish, and gumbo, that's what he was raised eating, and he can make some hellified beignets and can throw down some thigh-fattening bread pudding with enough whiskey sauce to make you feel like you're DUI. And don't let him get his hands on some catfish. He'll fry the hell out of that bottom feeder.

My husband has a solid build, broad shoulders, and a great smile. He has a few scars here and there from being in so many fights as a boy, and from boxing as a teenager and young adult, the kind of marks that make him look more rugged than pretty. His soft hair makes me wanna run my fingers through it all night. And I love his Southern accent; it's mild, not with too much twang. The kind of accent that tells you he'll treat you like a lady, open doors, and defend your honor. When he smiles with one side of his face, I know he's thinking of the position he wants to get me in. Sex is communication. Sex is food. I believe in feeding my man. And I believe in being fed. Feed him or he'll eat somewhere else. That wisdom came from Momma. She told us that a woman has to be a woman to her man, or some other woman will be.

Charles goes to bed by ten, nine if there's not a game on and he can manage to be done grading papers. He has to get up by six so he can drive thirty miles east on the 60 freeway to get to West Covina and teach social studies to middle-school rugrats. My postshow meeting runs over some nights because we have to go over what was good about the late-night broadcast, what sucked, what could've been better, and if something was hot, we have to have it ready for the next day. That can have me at the station until midnight, sometimes damn near one in the morning.

By the time I make the drive home, Charles is dead to the world. I come in through the garage and drag myself upstairs to a dark bedroom and silence. Sometimes I just stay downstairs, massage my temples, undress, then tiptoe up to the guest bedroom and just have some "me" time. Give myself a facial and take a long bath by candlelight. With his early schedule, Charles hates to have his sleep interrupted. But I'm wired and up until two, maybe three in the morning, trying not to make too much noise. Those are lonely hours, when the world is asleep and I'm wide awake, no one to talk to, feeling like Tom Hanks in that movie *Castaway*. All they have on Showtime are erotic movies—some pretty bad fucking, but fucking all the same.

Watching them make love turns me on. When the moon is high and my hormones are on fire, voyeurism is nothing but damn torture. In those bewitching hours, I creep into the bedroom, touch Charles, try to get his penis to rise, and he pats my hand, asking me to let him sleep.

Then it's me, loving a cappella. Or me, myself, and my little rabbit; ménage à trois.

Sometimes Charles drinks a little too much ginseng mixed with noni juice and wakes up at the crack of dawn with the energy of a sixteen-year-old, rubbing against me with a raging boner, kissing that sensitive spot on my neck, his morning breath uneven and wanting.

After three hours of sleep, I'm a rag doll. My nipples don't rise, but I don't push his hand away, never have, not since we stood before God and made promises. He rubs against me and my hand drifts down, takes his girth and hardness and guides it toward my hollow. He moves inside with gentleness, but the dryness stings. Seldom do I come like that, being half awake and barely aware, because by the time my back starts to arch and moans begin crawling from my mouth, he's holding my ass with a firm grip, his strokes strong, deep, and steady, shuddering because he's trying to keep from letting his orgasm get the best of him, and letting out that preorgasmic groan that sounds like an apology for being premature.

He jerks inside me, fills me with pain and pleasure, with hot, liquid heat that excites me into consciousness, and I hold him, move up against him as he slows down, contract the muscles of my vagina around his softening penis, and try to orgasm as he catches his breath.

He rubs his hands over my locks, swallows, then whispers, "You okay?"

I sing, "Good morning."

I rub his back, feel his solidness and strength over me, run my fingers through his soft hair, kiss his face. Then I tell him how good that felt, how wonderful he is, how much I love the way his dick feels inside me, and ask him to chill out with me for a moment.

"Freeway time, baby. Can't be late."

I put on a schoolgirl pout. "Thirty seconds?"

I feel him, unfocused and on edge, glancing at the red numbers on the digital clock. In less time than I've asked for, he pulls himself out of my vagina, breaks our Siameseness, leaves my emptiness tingling to be filled, legs ready to open wide for another ride.

His feet hit the carpet and he's a silhouette moving away from me.

I say, "Maybe we can finish tonight."

No answer.

I hate it when he hops right up and runs to the shower. But he can't be late for work, has to beat traffic so he can get across the freeway at least thirty minutes before the bell rings for first period, even earlier on Tuesday because of the teachers' staff meeting.

Sometimes I sit up, fight the sandman, and watch Charles shower. He knows I'm watching, enjoying the way the water runs over his body, but he's rushing, doesn't look my way. I think he's ashamed when he comes that fast, or takes me like that, invading my dryness with his hardness, all without warning. I like to think that he finds me so irresistible that he can't help himself, that he has no control when it comes to wanting me. That makes me feel as if I am the master, that he is the slave to his desires for me, and only me.

That's what I pretend.

He throws on his jeans and a nice polo shirt, grabs a jacket if it's cool, then kisses my lips.

He says, "The remote is right here."

"Have a good day. Love you. Call me."

He leaves me, some mornings his honey drying between my legs, the smell of our sex on my skin, the remote at my side. He always leaves the remote within arm's reach because he knows that I go to sleep with the news and I wake up in search of Katie Couric.

My morning is pretty much the same day after day: get up, start a load of laundry, take a four-mile run around CSUDH, come back and lift some light weights to tone my upper body, then do a few hundred sit-ups. I'm no Janet Jackson, but I do want my body and tummy as tight as possible before I get pregnant and have our two-point-five kids; only God and Miss Cleo know what will happen to my figure afterward. Then I'm throwing clothes in the dryer, rushing to make myself a low- to non-fat breakfast while I figure out what I'm going to make for dinner, pulling my locks into a ponytail and taking a quick shower, then throwing on some jeans and tennis shoes and heading back to do battle with the congestion on the 10 westbound, blowing my horn at people who cut me off or refuse to let me merge, losing my religion and becoming one of the heathens, changing lanes like a maniac, listening to the "all news and traffic" station KFWB.

"What year is that Mustang?" A man in an overpriced sports car rolls down his window, breaks his neck trying to get my attention when I get caught at a light at La Brea and Washington, the edges of the urban and Hispanic area that leads into Hollyweird.

I answer, "Sixty-four and a half."

"And a half? That's the one they introduced at the World's Fair."

"Sure is." That chunk of knowledge about my Baby Blue makes me smile. My car is very rare. Before Shelby, before fastbacks, this was the ultimate pony car. The grandfather of all muscle cars. "Fully restored from the ground up. Every nut and bolt and clip replaced."

"How much you put into it?"

"Close to ten thousand."

"Wow."

"New paint, brakes, belts, radiator—it's all new."

"Baby blue with white interior. Awesome."

"Thanks."

"You look good topless." With the double meaning comes the devilish smile. "Wanna gimme your number?"

I wave my wedding ring.

He waves his own wedding band, then shrugs as if that symbol has no value.

I adjust my shades, the light changes, and I speed away, top down, laughing the way a woman laughs at an idiot, the cool wind blowing over the top of my locks. He tries to race with me, tries to keep up, but I move in and out of three lanes of traffic like butter and lose him at Olympic when he gets caught by the light. I wave good-bye with my middle finger.